About the author

Stephen Leather was a journalist for more than ten years on newspapers such as *The Times*, the *Daily Mail* and the *South China Morning Post* in Hong Kong. Before that, he was employed as a biochemist for ICI, shovelled limestone in a quarry, worked as a baker, a petrol pump attendant, a barman, and worked for the Inland Revenue. He began writing full time in 1992. His bestsellers have been translated into more than ten languages. You can find out more from his website, www.stephenleather.com.

STEPHEN LEATHER

Live Fire

HODDER

First published in Great Britain in 2009 by Hodder & Stoughton
An Hachette UK company

First published in paperback in 2009

1

A CIP catalogue record for this title is available from the British Library

ISBN 978 1 444 71290 2

Typeset in Plantin Light by Palimpsest Book Production Limited,
Grangemouth, Stirlingshire

Printed and bound by
Clays Ltd, St Ives plc

Hodder & Stoughton policy is to use papers that are natural, renewable and
recyclable products and made from wood grown in sustainable forests.
The logging and manufacturing processes are expected to conform to the
environmental regulations of the country of origin.

Hodder & Stoughton Ltd
338 Euston Road
London NW1 3BH

www.hodder.co.uk

Nicola James tottered out of the nightclub and turned to kiss the man who had bought her two bottles of champagne and three brandy-and-Cokes and who, unless he did something terribly wrong in the next thirty minutes, was the man she would probably wake up with. His name was Philip and he owned two factories in China that made cheap toys, which, he said, were sold by every department store in London. He also said he had a Ferrari parked nearby. Nicola hadn't seen the factories or the Ferrari but she had seen the wad of fifty-pound notes in his wallet and the black American Express card he'd used to pay his bill, and that was all the incentive she needed to accept his invitation to have a nightcap back at his place. 'All right, darling?' he asked, in a gravelly Essex accent, as he slipped his hands around her waist.

She kissed his cheek, then bit his earlobe playfully. 'I'm going to lick you all over,' she promised.

'Let's get a cab,' said Philip. 'I'm too drunk to drive.'

She pouted. 'I want to see your Ferrari,' she said. Her pout was one of her best features, she knew. It almost always got her what she wanted. It had done ever since she was eight years old. She hadn't met a man yet that she couldn't twist around her little finger.

'Too much bubbly,' said Philip, and burped to prove his point.

Nicola slipped her arm through his and rubbed her breast against him. 'Come on, I've never given a blow-job in a Ferrari before.'

'You're terrible,' laughed Philip.

'No, I'm not, I'm pretty bloody amazing, actually.' She licked her upper lip suggestively.

Philip shook his head, still laughing. 'Okay, you've talked me into it,' he said.

He kissed her, and then they walked along the pavement. It was Friday night and Soho was buzzing, the pavements filled with the overspill from the area's pubs and bars. Five Elvis impersonators walked towards them, arms linked, their plastic wigs glistening in the street-lights, the jewels on their white stage suits winking like stars as they hummed 'Return To Sender'. Nicola was feeling light-headed and it wasn't just from all the alcohol she'd drunk. She really liked Philip. He was good-looking, he had a fit body, a great sense of humour, and he was rich. If there really was a Ferrari she might well decide that he was the one. 'You're not married, are you?' she asked.

'No, darling, young, free and single,' he said, patting her backside.

Nicola's left heel gave way and she lurched to the side. Philip grabbed her around the waist as she cursed. She took off her broken shoe and glared at it. 'Bloody Gucci,' she said.

Philip took it from her. 'Looks like a knock-off,' he said.

'Cost me two hundred quid, they did,' said Nicola. She threw the shoe into the gutter. Two men kissing in a doorway broke off to stare at her and she blew them a kiss.

'You can get it repaired,' said Philip.

'Bollocks to that,' said Nicola. She took the other shoe off and tossed it down the road. 'Come on, give me a ride.' She kissed him, and ran her hand between his legs, laughing when she felt him grow hard. 'Turn around. Tonight you're my trusty steed.' Philip did as he was told and Nicola jumped onto his back and wrapped her arms around his neck. 'Giddy-up,' she said, and gripped him with her thighs.

Philip staggered unsteadily down the road. A small saloon drove by slowly and five young men wearing baseball caps sneered at them. 'Come with us, darling,' shouted the driver. 'We'll give you a real lift.'

'He's got a Ferrari!' shouted Nicola.

'Yeah, and I've got a dick like King Kong.' The driver stamped on the accelerator and the car shot down the street.

'Arsehole!' screamed Nicola.

'Leave it, babe,' said Philip. He was panting with the effort of carrying her.

Nicola snuggled against his neck and sighed. 'I am so horny,' she said. Actually she felt a bit queasy. She'd been drinking tequila shots with her friend Becky before they'd gone to the nightclub. She frowned. She hadn't seen Becky for at least an hour, not since her friend had been stumbling towards the toilets, a hand cupped over her mouth. 'Did you see Becky?' she asked.

'Who?' asked Philip. Ahead a grey Mercedes was parked in front of a print shop. The air inside the car was shimmering as if it was filled with steam. 'Look at that, will you?' he said, stopping.

'Giddy-up!' shouted Nicola.

'Look at the car,' said Philip. 'There's something wrong.'

Nicola tried to focus. 'What?' she said.

'Inside,' he said. 'It's all blurry.'

Nicola laughed. 'It's what?'

'Blurry,' said Philip. 'Inside. Look.' He lowered her to the pavement. He peered at the car and stepped forward. Through the rear window he spotted something red. As he got closer he saw plastic petrol containers.

'I can smell petrol,' said Nicola. 'Can you?'

Philip took another step towards the Mercedes. There were three blue propane gas cylinders in the back, wedged between the petrol containers and the front seats. Philip sniffed. Nicola was right: there was a strong smell of petrol.

'Philip, don't go near it,' said Nicola. 'Let's go. Come on.'

A mobile phone was stuck between two of the containers. As Philip started to back away the phone's display glowed. A fraction of a second later the car exploded in a ball of flame.

The blast hit him full on and blew him backwards. Nicola had turned to run and was knocked off her feet. Philip lay on his back, gasping. His face was burned, his ears were ringing and he could smell scorched hair. He patted his chest gingerly, sure that he was bleeding, but there was no blood. He sat up. He worked his jaw, trying to clear his ears, but they continued to ring. Slowly he got to his feet. He was shaking with shock, but he was alive.

Nicola was lying face down a few feet away and he hurried over to her. 'Are you okay, babe?' he asked.

'What happened?' she said. She rolled over. Her face was grazed where she'd hit the pavement but other than that she didn't appear to be injured. Philip helped her to her feet and hugged her. 'I can't believe it,' he panted. His whole body was trembling.

Nicola giggled, close to hysteria. 'This is going to be one hell of a story to tell our grandchildren.'

In the distance they could hear the sirens of the emergency services, heading their way. 'We were that close to a car bomb,' he said. 'I was sure we were dead. The flash, did you see it?'

'I felt it,' she said. She put her hand to her cheek, touched it gingerly, then looked at the blood on her fingertips. 'We were lucky.'

The two men who had been kissing each other were running full pelt down the road, their trainers slapping on the Tarmac.

'We should get away from here,' said Philip. He put his arm around her and they started walking down the road, following the crowds. Two uniformed policemen were shouting and pointing towards Oxford Street, telling people to move away from the still-burning wreckage. High overhead a police helicopter hovered, scanning the area with its searchlight.

'Who do you think did it?' she asked.

'The bloody Muslims of course,' said Philip. 'Bastards.'

Three young men with shaved heads wearing England football shirts hurried past them, cursing and swearing. One was holding a can of lager and drank from it as he jogged down the road. He stopped next to Philip and Nicola. 'Are you guys okay?' he asked, in a near-impenetrable Newcastle accent.

'Just winded,' said Philip.

'We were right next to it when it went off,' said Nicola.

'You're sure you're okay?' said the guy. 'We've got a car down the road. We can take you to the hospital if you want.'

'We're fine,' said Philip. 'Really.'

The man nodded, then hurried after his friends.

'You think it was al-Qaeda?' Nicola asked Philip.

'Who else would it be?' he replied. 'Come on, let's get a taxi.'

'What about your Ferrari?'

Philip grimaced. 'Darling, I'm pissed and I've just survived a car bomb. I ain't driving anywhere. We're getting a taxi.' He reached for her hand. As his fingers touched her, the car they were standing next to exploded. Shards of metal and glass ripped through Philip and Nicola, killing them instantly. The deadly shrapnel injured another twelve people. Shop and office windows along the road were shattered and broken glass showered the pavements with the sound of wind chimes. Dozens of car alarms went off and those pedestrians who hadn't been knocked unconscious by the explosion were running down the street, crying and screaming.

Owen Crompton wanted a cigarette but smoking wasn't allowed in the bank and he knew that the two men sitting on the other side of his desk wouldn't allow him to go outside for one. 'I don't think I can go through with this,' he said.

'You'll be fine,' said the younger of the two men. 'It'll soon be over.'

Crompton's mouth was so dry that swallowing was painful. There was a bottle of Evian water on his desk. It was reserved for customers but he poured himself a glass and gulped it. He twisted around to the bank of CCTV monitors behind him. There were four, each showing a different view of the banking hall on the floor below.

The older of the two men looked at the clock on the wall. 'It's time,' he said.

Crompton pressed the intercom on his desk. 'Jean, can you send Sandra in, please?'

'Will do, Mr Crompton,' said his assistant.

Crompton settled back in his chair and tapped his fingers on the desk, avoiding the eyes of the two men sitting opposite. He had another drink of water and glanced at the wall clock. Time seemed to have slowed to a crawl. Sandra Ford knocked on the door and came in before he had the chance to say anything. His door was usually open but the men with him had insisted it stay closed. She was wearing a short grey skirt, showing off her shapely legs, and a pale blue blouse. Her bank ID was hanging around her neck, the chain nestling between her breasts. Ford was one of the prettier employees at the bank, but she had been promoted to deputy manager on the back of her first-class degree in economics and her knack of managing people rather than her looks. Crompton had no doubt that within a couple of years she would be in charge of her own branch.

'Sandra, these two gentlemen are with the Metropolitan Police's Robbery Squad,' he said.

'The Sweeney?' asked Ford, brightly. 'How exciting.'

The younger of the two men grinned as he flashed his warrant card. 'We try not to call ourselves that, these days,' he said. 'People get the wrong idea. We're still the Flying Squad but we've lost the sheepskin jackets and the shoot-outs.'

'More's the pity,' said his companion. He showed her his warrant card. 'I'm Inspector Michael Franklin. My colleague is Detective Sergeant David Brewerton.'

'They're here about a robbery, Sandra,' said Crompton.

'I hadn't heard about any robbery,' said Ford, frowning.

'It hasn't happened yet,' said Franklin, putting away his warrant card. 'That's why we're here. A gang have been casing this bank for the past two weeks and the intelligence we have is that they're going to move in today.'

Ford's jaw dropped. 'Wow,' she said. She looked at Crompton. 'But if they've checked the branch they must know we have the full range of security measures, bullet-proof glass, hidden alarms . . .'

Franklin held up a hand to silence her and smiled apologetically. 'This is a highly professional team, Miss Ford,' he said. 'They have assault rifles with armour-piercing ammunition and they have explosives.'

'My God, they sound like an army!'

'Ex-army,' said Brewerton. 'They all served in Iraq. A couple of years ago they were being shot at in Basra. Now they're the ones doing the shooting.'

'They robbed a bank in Glasgow last month and we believe they intend to hit your branch this morning,' said Franklin.

'Head Office has asked that we co-operate fully with the police and that we do everything they say,' said Crompton.

'Absolutely,' said Ford. 'But obviously the safety of our customers and staff is paramount.'

'That goes without saying,' said Crompton.

'The best way of ensuring that nobody is hurt is to do exactly what the robbers ask,' said Franklin. He leaned forward conspiratorially. 'Between you and me, Miss Ford, we have a man under cover in the gang. That's how we know they're planning to hit this branch today. He's a very experienced officer and he'll be doing everything he can to make sure that no one gets hurt.'

'So you'll catch them in the act – is that the plan?' asked Ford.

Franklin chuckled. 'As my colleague said, we try to avoid shoot-outs these days. No, we know where they'll be heading and we'll have them under surveillance every step of the way. When we can scoop them up without anyone getting hurt, we'll move in.'

'What about dye packs and such?' asked Ford.

'Nothing like that, Sandra,' said Crompton. 'Nothing that will slow them down or get them annoyed.'

'All you have to do is to follow the instructions they give,' said Franklin. 'Try not to anticipate anything because that will tip them off that something's wrong. Just do exactly as they say. Give them what they ask for and let them get out as quickly as possible. Our men will do the rest.'

Ford's eyes were wide. 'This is so exciting,' she said. 'Like a movie.'

'Sandra, this is a very serious business,' stressed Crompton. 'There must be no panic, nothing to alarm the robbers.'

'Actually, that's not strictly speaking true, Mr Crompton,' said Franklin. 'If everyone's too calm they might well get suspicious. They will be expecting the people in the bank to be scared. That's why we're not telling everybody, just the key personnel.'

'That's you, of course,' said Crompton. 'And I'll be

calling in Max and Peter. But everyone else has to stay in the dark. I'll put Max and Peter on the window, and I want you to be close by. When the robbers come in, the three of you can handle the money. Just tell everyone else to stay calm and keep their heads down. From what we've learned from our inside man they'll be wanting access to the safe-deposit boxes.'

Ford frowned. 'We don't have a master key for the boxes. The customers have their own keys.'

'They'll have drills,' said Brewerton.

'So, how long will they be in the bank?'

'Fifteen minutes at most,' said Brewerton. 'So far as we know.'

'Where will you be, Owen?' asked Ford.

'Mr Crompton will be here upstairs with us,' said Franklin. 'It's important that everything appears exactly as usual. In the mornings Mr Crompton is usually in his office, so that's where he has to be. Do you think you can handle things downstairs? As deputy manager we'd prefer it if you were holding the fort but if you think you might not be able to cope we can get one of the male assistant managers to step in.'

'I'll be fine,' said Ford, brusquely.

'You're sure?' asked Franklin. 'There's nothing to be ashamed of in admitting you'd rather take a back seat.' He looked at his colleague. 'We've got fifteen years in the Flying Squad between us and I still get the chills when I see a guy with a sawn-off heading my way.'

'That's the truth,' said Brewerton.

'It won't be a problem,' said Ford. 'Do we have any idea what time they'll be here?'

'All we know is that it'll be this morning,' said Franklin.

He smiled. 'You'll do just fine, Sandra, I'm sure. Now, what's really important is that immediately they leave you calm everyone down, explain that the police are on the case and that the men will be apprehended within the hour. I don't want anyone phoning the *Evening Standard* or the TV.'

'They're going to be pretty stressed out,' said Ford.

'Which is why we'll be relying on you to keep everyone calm,' said Franklin. 'Now, can you send up Simon so that we can brief him? And don't forget, other than the three of you, mum's the word.'

'You can rely on me,' said Ford.

Franklin and Brewerton watched her close the door. 'Nice tits,' said Brewerton.

'I can't do this,' said Crompton. He put his head in his hands. 'My heart's thumping like it's going to burst.'

'Deep breaths,' said Franklin. 'Take deep breaths and think happy thoughts. It'll soon be over.'

Brewerton stood up. His jacket swung open, revealing a semi-automatic in a nylon holster under his left arm. 'Don't worry, Owen,' he said. 'This isn't our first time, we know what we're doing. Just make sure you tell Max and Peter what to do. If anyone trips the silent alarm this could all turn to shit. And you know what that'll mean.'

The white Transit van bore the scars of a thousand or so days of battling the London traffic, with dented wings and scrapes on both sides. It was mechanically sound, though, and the engine had been carefully tuned. The vehicle was the clone of one used by an electrician in Brixton with identical registration plates and tax disc. The driver was in his late forties. Two decades earlier he had been a London taxi driver, one of the breed who knew virtually every street and landmark in the city by name. Don Parkinson had long since given up his taxi badge and now plied his trade as one of the most respected getaway drivers in the country. During the course of his criminal career he had acquired the nickname 'DP', which had nothing to do with his initials and everything to do with his habit of muttering, 'Don't panic,' to himself whenever things got serious. He looked at his watch. There was a small digital clock in the dashboard but he didn't trust electrical timepieces. The Rolex on his left wrist was half a century old and it had never failed him or his father before him. 'It's time,' he said. A man was sitting next to him in the passenger seat and three more in the back. All were wearing long coats.

'Rock and roll!' said the man in the passenger seat. His name was Robbie Edwards and he was a veteran of more than two dozen armed robberies. He was thick-set with well-muscled forearms and a rock-hard abdomen, but in the blue pinstripe suit and cashmere overcoat he looked like any other well-heeled businessman in the city. He was well tanned, and though his black hair was flecked with grey he still seemed younger than his forty-five years. He took a pair of dark glasses from his coat pocket and put them on.

The three in the back of the van were in their thirties. They were all thinner than Edwards but had the look of men who spent a lot of time in the gym. Ricky Knight was the tallest, with dark brown hair and Ray-Ban sunglasses. Geoff Marker was also wearing shades, his hair had been shaved to disguise his receding hairline and he had a small diamond in his left earlobe. Billy McMullen was blond with a neatly trimmed goatee beard. The one thing they had in common, other than the long coats and the scarves around their necks, was that they were all cradling loaded Kalashnikov assault rifles.

'Glasses,' Knight said to McMullen.

'I know.' McMullen scowled, taking a pair of Oakley shades from his coat pocket and putting them on. 'You're as bad as my bloody mother. Wear your scarf, button your coat, don't forget your dinner money.'

Knight grinned. 'Rough childhood?'

'It was okay. She was just a bit of nag. Dad left when he couldn't stand it any more so we kids took the brunt. She was a bit on the over-protective side.'

'She still alive?'

McMullen shook his head. 'Dead. Cancer. Ten years back. She was nagging the doctors and nurses right until the end.' He took the magazine out of the Kalashnikov, then re-inserted it. 'Wonder what she'd make of my chosen career. She'd probably tell me I was using the wrong gun and wearing the wrong sort of shades.'

'Mothers, huh?'

'Can we stop all this touchy-feely heart-to-heart crap?' snapped Marker. 'I'm trying to get into character here.'

Knight winked at McMullen but they fell silent. They knew what Marker meant. In a minute or so they would be inside a bank wielding automatic weapons, but the guns weren't enough: the people in the bank had to believe that the men were serious about using them. It was an act because they had no intention of shooting anyone – that would mean a life sentence where life meant life, and they had no intention of spending decades behind bars.

'Here we go,' said Edwards. He opened the passenger

door. He was carrying a black Adidas sports bag.
McMullen pushed open the van's side door and stepped
into the street, his Kalashnikov under his coat. Knight and
Marker followed him and headed straight for the entrance
to the bank. Like McMullen, they had their weapons under
their long coats. McMullen glanced left and right – no
one was paying them any attention – and hurried after
Knight and Marker.

McMullen, Knight and Marker pulled the bank's doors
closed and spread out across the floor, keeping the weapons
under their coats and pulling the scarves up over their
faces. Edwards stood by the doors. He took a printed sign
out of the sports bag, pulled off the adhesive backing and
pressed it against the glass. The sign read, 'POWER CUT –
CLOSED UNTIL FURTHER NOTICE. PLEASE USE OUR BRANCH
IN REGENT STREET.'

Edwards looked at McMullen and nodded. As
McMullen swung his Kalashnikov out from under his
coat, Edwards flicked the locks on the doors.

'Everyone against the wall!' McMullen bellowed. 'This
is a robbery and if anyone so much as looks at me wrong
I'll blow their fucking head off!'

Knight and Marker pulled out their assault rifles and
levelled them at the customers gathered at the counter.
'You heard him!' shouted Knight. 'Against the wall – now!'
Keeping the customers in one place made them easier to
control, and against the far wall they couldn't be seen
from the doors.

Edwards pulled a large handgun from his sports bag
and flicked off the safety.

A young man in a grey suit fumbled with his mobile
phone. Marker rushed over to him and slammed the butt

of the Kalashnikov into his stomach. He fell to the ground, gasping for breath, and Markham stamped on the phone. 'Any other heroes?' he shouted, and kicked the man in the ribs. 'Anyone else want some of this?'

The rest of the customers huddled together by the wall. There were two elderly women in cloth coats clutching handbags, a young girl with a baby in a push-chair, three middle-aged businessmen in suits and a teenager in a black leather motorcycle jacket and torn jeans.

Knight and Edwards walked over to the counter and aimed their weapons at the tellers behind the bulletproof screen. Knight gestured with his Kalashnikov. 'The bullets in this will go right through that glass without breaking sweat,' he said. He nodded at the door to the left of the counter. 'Now, open the door or I'll pull the trigger.'

The girl with the baby began to cry. Marker walked over to her and pointed a gloved finger at her face. 'Stop blubbering, you bitch!' he hissed.

'Leave her alone, she's only a girl,' said one of the businessmen. He was black with greying hair and he was clutching his briefcase to his chest.

Marker left her and confronted the businessman. 'Another bloody, hero, huh?' he said. He gestured at the man in the grey suit who was crawling towards the rest of the customers. 'You want what he got, do you?'

He glared at Marker defiantly. 'You don't have to threaten girls to get what you want.'

Marker thrust his face close to the man's. 'You want some, do you?'

'I just want you to take what you want and go. It's the bank's money you're after, not ours. No one here is going to stop you, so just get on with it and leave us alone.'

Marker could see that the man wasn't intimidated by the rhetoric or the gun. He stepped back and slammed the butt into the man's face, splintering his teeth. Blood gushed from his mouth and he dropped the briefcase. Marker hit him again, this time on the side of the head. He slumped to the ground without a sound. 'Anyone else?' he shouted, turning back to the rest of the customers. 'Anyone else want to give me any grief? Because I'll kill the next person who steps out of line. Do you morons understand?' They pressed together, too scared to look at him. One of the elderly women had her eyes closed and was muttering a prayer. Marker pointed the gun at them, waiting for any signs of defiance or resistance.

Knight aimed his Kalashnikov at a blonde woman in a pale blue blouse. 'Open the door, darling, before anyone else gets hurt. And don't even think about hitting the silent alarm.'

She moved towards the door. Edwards covered the other tellers with his revolver. 'You two get back against the wall and keep your hands where I can see them.'

Knight walked towards the blonde, keeping the Kalashnikov pointed at her chest, his finger on the trigger. 'Don't get any ideas,' he warned her. 'Like my friends said, the bullets in this will go straight through that glass.'

She opened the door with trembling hands and Knight stepped through, Edwards behind him. 'Everyone on the floor!' Edwards shouted. 'Face down with your hands on the back of your head.' He pointed to the stairs that led up to the offices. 'Anyone comes down, you take care of them,' he said to Knight.

McMullen and Edwards went through to the safe-deposit

room. Edwards dropped his sports bag on the metal table in the middle of the room and took out two electric drills. He handed one to McMullen, then pulled a folded sheet of paper from the inside pocket of his coat. He scanned the list. 'You do two-five-eight and two-five-nine to start,' he said.

McMullen ran his gloved hand down the bank of boxes until he found two-five-eight. He pulled the trigger on the drill and pressed the whirring bit against the lock. As he drilled out the lock mechanism, Edwards started on another box.

Brewerton and Franklin watched the robbers leave the bank on one of the monitors on the wall behind the manager's desk. On another Sandra Ford was comforting the customers. One of the pensioners was crying and she put an arm around her.

'See, Owen, that wasn't too hard, was it?' said Brewerton.

'What happens now?' asked Crompton, looking anxiously at the gun in Brewerton's shoulder holster.

'Now we'll be on our merry way,' said Franklin, standing up.

'What about my wife and son?'

'They'll be fine, Owen,' said Franklin. 'You did everything we asked – you did us proud. Your wife and son will be released in one hour. All you have to do is wait one hour and she'll call you. As soon as she does you can call the cops.'

'My career's over, you know that?' said Crompton. 'They'll think I helped you. They'll think I was your inside man.'

'What do you want, Owen?' asked Brewerton. 'Do you want I put a bullet in your leg or we beat the crap out of you?'

'I'm just saying, the police always think there's an inside man.'

'We kidnapped your wife and your boy. They'll understand you had to co-operate.'

Crompton folded his arms and shook his head emphatically. 'You don't get it, do you? Even if the cops don't blame me, my bosses will never trust me again. My career's over.'

'Owen, if you keep whining like this we will shoot you,' said Brewerton. He pointed at the bank manager. 'Count your bloody blessings. Your family are okay, nobody died, we got our money.'

'All's well that end's well,' said Franklin. 'And much as we'd love to keep on chatting, we've got to go. Remember, you wait here until your wife calls, then you phone the police.' Crompton nodded. Franklin grinned. 'Be lucky,' he said, as he and Brewerton headed for the door.

Don Parkinson pulled hard on the steering-wheel and drove through the narrow alley, the dented wings of the Transit only inches away from the weathered bricks on either side. At the end he swung the wheel to the right and accelerated under a railway arch, then made a hard left turn down a road that led to a disused factory. It had once made fireproof safes but had closed in the face of cut-throat competition from China and South Korea. A sign at the entrance to the yard announced that a property-development firm had acquired the premises and would soon be turning them into upmarket apartments. The chain that had kept the gates locked had been cut and they were pulled opened by a man in a blue tracksuit and gleaming white trainers. Parkinson drove through. The man flashed Edwards a thumbs-up and began to close the gates as Parkinson drove to the delivery area at the side of the main building.

The metal roll-shutter door was already opening but Parkinson revved the engine impatiently. 'Easy, DP,' said Edwards.

'They should've had it open,' said Parkinson. 'Bloody amateurs.'

As soon as the shutter was high enough, he stamped on the accelerator and drove inside. The factory was half the size of a football field with lines of square concrete pillars running up to a metal framework supporting the roof. Fluorescent lights festooned with cobwebs hung from the beams. The machinery that had once been manned by hundreds of workers had been stripped out and the only sign that it had been a thriving business was a line of offices at the far end. Rats scurried in the corners and pigeons cooed from the safety of the nests they had built in the joints of the beams high in the ceiling.

Another man, wearing a tracksuit and training shoes, was standing between two black BMW saloons, the boot lids open. He was the father of the man who had opened the gates for them. Dean and Roger Barrett had worked together even before Dean had been old enough for a driving licence and they were two of the best drivers in London. Knight, McMullen and Marker piled out of the rear of the van with the nylon bags.

'Right, get the money in the motors and torch the van,'

shouted Edwards. He looked at his watch. 'I want us out of here in three minutes flat.'

Roger Barrett climbed into one of the BMWs and started the engine. His face was professionally impassive. 'Guns in that motor,' shouted Edwards, pointing at Barrett's BMW. 'Two bags in each.'

Knight, McMullen and Marker threw the bags into the boots and put their weapons into the boot of Barrett's car. They slammed the doors, then ran back to the van and stripped off their gloves and coats. Parkinson was sloshing petrol from a red can over the bonnet.

Edwards tossed his gloves and coat into the back. Knight, McMullen and Marker did the same. Edwards gave the inside a final check, then nodded at Parkinson, who threw petrol into the back, then tossed the can inside. He took out a box of matches, lit one and flicked it at the can. There was a whoosh of flame and the van was ablaze.

Dean Barrett ran into the factory, climbed into the second BMW and fired the engine. He looked at his father and nodded. Roger Barrett nodded back, his hands caressing the steering-wheel as he gunned the engine.

Edwards looked at his watch again. 'Come on, guys, in the cars and let's roll.' He hurried over to the BMWs and climbed in next to Roger Barrett. Knight got into the back. 'You okay, Ricky?' he asked.

'No worries,' said Knight. 'Your jobs always as sweet as this?'

'Always,' said Edwards. 'Once you've got the manager on side, the rest is easy.'

McMullen and Marker walked quickly to the second BMW, Parkinson following. The van was now engulfed

in flames and thick black smoke was billowing up to the
rafters.

The two BMWs drove out of the factory and Roger
Barrett slammed on the brakes. Knight leaped out of the
car, ran to the gates and pulled them open. He froze, then
swore and slammed them shut again. 'Cops!' he yelled.
'There's cops everywhere!'

He raced back to the cars. A split second later the
gates burst open and a police Land Rover with a re-
inforced wire cage over its bonnet roared through, then
two Range Rovers and two armed-response vehicles. The
Range Rovers and ARVs fanned out across the yard, tyres
squealing.

Roger Barrett cursed as the Land Rover pulled up just
inches from the front bumper. He glanced into his rear-
view mirror. His son's car was jammed up behind him.
'I'm sorry, boss,' he said, his professionalism dented. He
slowly took his hands off the steering-wheel and turned
off the engine.

Men in bullet-proof vests piled out of the ARVs and
Range Rovers, their MP5 assault rifles at the ready. 'Armed
police, drop your weapons!' one screamed.

Edwards smiled thinly. They didn't have any weapons.
All the guns were in the boot of the BMW. But even if
they hadn't been, his team wouldn't be looking for a shoot-
out against professionals. There were a dozen armed police
and every one of them had been trained to kill.

'Not your fault, Roger,' he said. In the wing mirror he
glimpsed Knight's fast-retreating figure. 'Where the hell
does that dopey bastard think he's going?' He raised his
hands. 'Oh, well, some you win, some you lose.'

*   *   *

Knight's feet pounded on the cement and his arms powered back and forth like pistons. He glanced over his shoulder. Only one man was giving chase, an officer in his forties, MP5 cradled in his arms. The rest of the CO19 unit were standing around the BMWs, their weapons pointed at Edwards and his team.

Knight's chest was burning but he ignored the pain and ran faster. He hurtled into the factory, eyes watering from the smoke billowing around the burning van. He gave it a wide berth, bent double to keep his head low and ran towards the offices. 'Armed police, stay where you are!' shouted the officer behind him.

Knight ran to the nearest office and hit the door with his shoulder. The wood around the lock splintered and he barrelled into the room. There was a window overlooking a rear yard but there were bars on it. There was a connecting door to the left and he grabbed the handle and pulled. It opened and he ran through into what had probably been a meeting room. There was a large whiteboard on one wall and a worn carpet with the impressions made by a table and a dozen or so chairs, but no window, just a glass door leading to a corridor. He heard the armed cop run into the office behind him and pulled open the door. He looked up and down the corridor. To the left was the factory floor, to the right were more offices, and at the end, a fire exit, some thirty paces from where he was standing. He headed for it but had only taken a few steps before the police officer was behind him. 'Armed police! Stay where you are and keep your hands where I can see them!'

Knight stopped and leaned against the wall, his chest on fire, panting like a horse that had been raced too hard. 'You got me,' he said.

The officer grinned. 'Thought you were a runner,' he said.

'I'm a runner, not a sprinter,' Knight gasped. 'There's a difference.'

'You okay?' The officer's concern was genuine.

Knight put his hands on his hips and took deep breaths. 'I'm all right,' he said.

'Let's get this over with, then,' said the officer. He raised his MP5 and fired a short burst over Knight's head. Three bullets thudded into the ceiling and bits of polystyrene fluttered to the ground. 'Oops,' he said. He spoke into his radio mic. 'Everything secure?'

'All accounted for, sir,' replied a tinny voice. 'You okay in there?'

'Mine got away. I'm on my way back,' he said. 'That's it then,' he added, to Knight. 'Job well done.'

Knight went to the emergency exit, kicked it open and gave the CO19 officer a thumbs-up. No alarm sounded: it had been disconnected by a SOCA technician the previous evening. 'Thanks,' he said.

'All part of the service, Spider. You take care now.'

Dan 'Spider' Shepherd, undercover agent with the Serious Organised Crime Agency, took his Ray-Ban sunglasses from his pocket, put them on and walked out into the sunshine.

Three men were sitting on the bench, the morning's newspapers spread out on the floor in front of them. Two were in their twenties, the third in his early thirties, and they all had dark brown skin, jet black hair and were casually dressed in sweatshirts, jeans and brand-name white trainers. The bench was in the Rose Garden, a quiet area of the Paddington Recreation Ground in Maida Vale, north-west London. The park had once been a place where elderly ladies walked their dogs and mothers watched their toddlers take unsteady steps, but now it was a meeting place for the various immigrant groups crammed into the damp flats of nearby Kilburn. On any one day there would be clusters of young men from Kosovo, from Bosnia, from Iraq, from Afghanistan, from West Africa, a veritable United Nations of refugees who had fled to Britain for a better life. They had quickly discovered they were not welcomed by the majority of the population. They were hated because they were a different colour, because they spoke a different language and wore different clothes, but mostly they were hated because they refused to integrate. They stayed in their tight groups and spoke English only when it was absolutely necessary. Several times a day the council security guards who prowled the park made a half-hearted attempt to move them on, but they simply returned a few minutes later. There was nowhere else for them to go.

The three men on the bench weren't refugees, or asylum-seekers, and they spoke with northern English accents. They were all British-born, they supported English football teams and they were studying at British colleges or universities. If they had been asked for their nationality they would have said unhesitatingly that they were British, because that was what it said on their passports. But the three men didn't feel British. They felt as alien as the recently arrived refugees dotted around the park. They had no love for the country that had educated them, no empathy with its people. In fact, when there was no one to hear what they were saying, they would proclaim their hatred for the British and everything they stood for.

A fourth man joined them. He had unkempt blond hair and blue eyes, and was wearing brown cargoes and a Levi's T-shirt. 'Greetings, brothers,' he said. His name was Paul Bradshaw. It was two days after his twenty-fifth birthday, two years and three months since he had converted to Islam.

'We did it,' said the youngest of the group, punching the air with a clenched fist. Rafee Talwar had been born in Leeds but his parents were from Pakistani Kashmir. He wore a sweatshirt with the logo of the South Bank University, where he was studying economics. But it had been more than six months since Talwar had read anything other than the Koran. He was short-sighted and wore large, black-framed spectacles that gave him the look of an Asian Buddy Holly.

'We did nothing,' said Bradshaw, sitting next to him. He looked at his watch, a cheap plastic Casio. 'Where is Kafele?'

'He is coming,' said Talwar, and gestured to the entrance to the Rose Garden. A young man wearing a Gap sweat-shirt was approaching the gate.

'He's always late,' said Bradshaw. 'It shows disrespect to us all.'

No one spoke until Kafele al-Sayed had walked over and sat down on the bench. Like Bradshaw, he wasn't of Pakistani descent. His father was an Egyptian engineer, his mother a Scottish primary-school teacher. He had inherited his mother's pale skin and curly brown hair, his father's hooked nose and dark eyes.

'I said ten o'clock,' said Bradshaw.

'The Tube was delayed,' said al-Sayed. 'Someone threw themselves under a train at Queen's Park. We had to wait until the line was clear.' He scratched a patch of red-raw skin on his neck, just above his collar.

Bradshaw's jaw clenched. Al-Sayed always had an excuse for his tardiness. It was a character flaw. It showed a lack of commitment, it showed a lack of planning, but above all it showed a lack of respect. Bradshaw's three years in the army had taught him the value of self-discipline, but he knew there was nothing to be gained from criticising al-Sayed in front of the others, so he bit his tongue. The rash on the man's neck was a sign of his nerves, and Bradshaw had no wish to stress the man even more than he already was.

Talwar rubbed his hands together and grinned. 'What next?' he asked.

'We wait,' said Bradshaw. 'We wait and we plan.'

'We showed them what we can do,' said the man on Bradshaw's right. Jamal Kundi was the smallest of the group, though at thirty-three he was the oldest. He worked as a car mechanic. 'We have to keep the momentum going,' he said, and lit a cigarette.

'We killed two people,' said Bradshaw. 'That's all we did. Nine or ten people die every day in road accidents. So, what did we achieve?'

'We struck terror into their hearts,' said the fifth member of the group, popping a stick of chewing-gum into his mouth. Samil Chaudhry's father ran a fast-food franchise in Leeds, and years of eating burgers, kebabs and fried fish had given him the build of a sumo wrestler by the time he was a teenager. He'd had a miserable child-hood and had hated school, where he had been teased mercilessly over his weight and the spots that plagued his complexion.

Everything had changed when Chaudhry turned twenty. He had met two older men in his local mosque and they had offered to help him with his Koran studies, but before long they were teaching him about politics and his responsibilities towards his Muslim brothers and sisters. They never once teased him about his weight but explained it was his duty to keep fit to be better able to carry out the wishes of Allah, that obesity was a sign of Western laziness and that no true Islamic warrior should allow himself to be anything other than in perfect condition. They encouraged him to run, and to join a local gym that they went to, and for the first time in his life he felt he had real friends, friends who cared about him. It was his new-found friends who encouraged him to revisit his roots in Pakistan, and from there it had taken only a little encouragement for him to enrol at an al-Qaeda training camp, where he spent six months being groomed in warfare and fundamentalist politics.

He had returned to Leeds a changed man, and shortly afterwards he had moved to London, signing up for a hotel-management course he never attended. The running and the training meant that the pounds had dropped off, and now that he had turned twenty-five he was lean and fit, with the stamina to run ten miles without breaking sweat. He was, Bradshaw knew, the most volatile of the group and the one who needed the most careful handling. Bradshaw needed Chaudhry's abilities, honed in the al-Qaeda training camp, but he was constantly having to rein in Chaudhry's enthusiasm. He would have made the perfect *shahid*, but Bradshaw had no intention of throwing away such a valuable resource on a suicide mission.

'We should keep up the pressure. Plant more bombs. Kill more of the infidels. Strike while the iron is hot.' Chaudhry chewed his gum noisily as he waited for Bradshaw to reply.

Bradshaw smiled. 'We scared them, brother,' he said. 'We made their hearts beat a little faster, but that is all. Do you think the brothers who died on July the seventh achieved anything other than their own glorious deaths? Do the dogs stay off the Tube? No. It's as if it never happened.'

Kundi blew a plume of smoke, taking care to keep it away from the others. 'So, what do you want to do, brother?' he asked. 'Do we join the ranks of the *shahid*? Do we give our lives for *jihad* and take our places in Heaven?'

Bradshaw snorted. 'We're in this world to fight for Islam, not to die for it,' he said. 'A suicide-bomber makes his point just once, like a comet burning up in the night sky. A true fighter burns for years. That's what we are, brothers. We're true fighters for Islam.'

'So I ask you again, brother, what is it you want us to do?' said al-Sayed.

Bradshaw stretched out his long legs and looked up at the cloudless blue sky. In the sky to the north three airliners were making their approach to Heathrow airport in the west. A fourth plane was just visible as a small dot. They were two miles apart, descending on the flight path to the airport, one of the world's busiest. The nearest were close enough for Bradshaw to see the markings on their tails. The second was a Boeing 747, with the red, white and blue stripes of British Airways, the country's flag-carrier. Bradshaw pointed up at the plane and his four companions followed his gaze. 'That is what we do, my brothers. That is how we strike terror into their hearts.'

Dan Shepherd caught a westbound Circle Line train at Paddington, got off at Bayswater, crossed to the eastbound platform and waited ten minutes before boarding another back to Paddington. He had no reason to think he was being followed but checking for tails had become second nature, especially when he was on his way to visit Charlotte Button. She was the head of SOCA's undercover unit and had been his boss for two years.

He bought a Starbucks coffee at the station and a cup of English Breakfast tea. The road leading to the station concourse was packed with commuters having a last cigarette before their journey home, and he threaded his way through them, trying not to breathe in their smoke. The address she had given him was a flat above a travel agent in Praed Street, not far away. There were eight buttons on a panel by the entrance and he pressed number five. He grinned up at the CCTV camera covering the door and the lock clicked open. There was a small hallway, a stack of junk mail and a notice stuck to the wall saying that Rentokil would be around to deal with a rodent infestation next week. As Shepherd climbed the stairs, he heard a door open above him. Button was on the landing, wearing a dark blue blazer over faded jeans. 'You are a sweetie,' she said, taking the cup from him and sniffing it.

'Anything but Earl Grey. I know,' he said.

She led him into a small flat. There was a black vinyl

sofa under the window, which overlooked the street, a circular table with three chairs, a small kitchen area, with a sink, a microwave and a fridge, and a door that led to a small bedroom. Shepherd saw a single bed with the duvet turned down as he went to the table. 'This is a new one on me,' he said, handing her the tea.

'It's a hop, skip and jump from Paddington Green, and I've got a briefing there later with Special Branch,' she said. Paddington Green was the high-security police station on Edgware Road, possibly the most secure police station in the UK outside Northern Ireland. It was where most terrorist suspects were questioned before they were transferred to Belmarsh Prison.

'Anything interesting?'

Button sipped her tea. 'It's always interesting with Special Branch,' she said. 'They want to talk about penetrating some Muslim cells in the Midlands.'

'Using SOCA? I didn't think we had any Muslim agents.'

'We've a couple,' said Button, 'but, frankly, I think they're a bit delicate for what's involved. My old colleagues tend to scoop up the best qualified for intelligence analysis and translating, and what's left aren't that interested in doing drugs and crime, which are our bread and butter, pretty much.' Before joining SOCA, Button had been a high-flyer with MI5. 'Anyway, congratulations are very much in order. We rounded them up and not a shot was fired.' She smiled. 'Other than the CO19 officer making a mess of the ceiling. Nice touch that. Edwards is telling everybody that it was you shooting at the cops and that you blasted your way out.'

'Wasn't quite like that,' said Shepherd. 'I didn't have a gun for a start.'

'It's expanding with the telling,' said Button, 'which is no bad thing. It all adds to the legend.'

'Crompton's wife and son are okay?'

'They were released an hour after you left the bank, just as they promised.'

'I know we had to let it run its course, but I feel sorry for the boy and his mother.'

'We couldn't have warned them, Spider,' said Button. 'They weren't in any danger – Edwards never hurts the family. He threatens to, but in the five robberies where he's kidnapped family members they've never been hurt.'

'Yeah, well, there's a first time for everything.' He drank some coffee. 'You've told the cops that Crompton had nothing to do with it? I know the way they think, and the first thing they'll do is put him in the frame. Edwards knew exactly which boxes to go for so he definitely had someone on the inside.'

Button grinned. 'Good news on that front,' she said. 'We've been listening in on his phones, and he made two calls to Sandra Ford, deputy manager at the branch. She's being questioned as we speak.'

'Excellent,' he said. 'At least that puts Crompton in the clear. And you nailed Randall and Simpson?' They were the two gang members who had pretended to be detectives at the branch.

'All present and accounted for,' said Button.

Shepherd stretched out his arms. 'Excellent,' he said. 'So, I'm due for some R and R, aren't I?'

'Yes, I need to talk to you about that,' said Button. 'How comfortable are you with the Ricky Knight legend?'

'He's not my favourite but, yeah, I'm comfortable

with him.' Shepherd narrowed his eyes. 'Have you got something in mind?'

Button reached under the table and pulled out a Louis Vuitton briefcase. She clicked open the locks and slid a manila file across the table. Shepherd opened it. Inside he found a dozen surveillance photographs of five men, mostly taken with a long lens. They were sitting around a swimming-pool with several topless Asian girls.

'Mickey Moore, East End boy made bad, and his crew.' She tapped a photograph of a big-chested man with receding hair, a cigar in one hand and a bottle of beer in the other. 'Old-school villain, loves his mother, loyal to his friends, never grasses, pays his debts. He's been behind at least half a dozen robberies over the past five years, none of which has netted less than a million pounds.'

She tapped another photograph, of a man lying on a sun-lounger while a girl with waist-length hair appeared to be giving him a manicure. 'This is Mark Moore, Mickey's younger brother. He just turned thirty – Mickey's thirty-eight. Mark followed his brother into the family business but he's a bit of a loose cannon. Having said that, the Moore brothers have yet to fire their guns in anger.'

'Armed robbery is all about front,' said Shepherd. 'You go in hard but the idea is not to shoot unless you really have to. For no other reason than that a fired gun leaves forensics.'

One by one, Button identified the three other members of the gang – Barry Wilson, Davie Black and Andy Yates. 'They're a tight group. They've known each other since they were at school. And between them they've not spent a day behind bars.'

'That's unusual for armed robbers,' said Shepherd.

'They're an unusual bunch,' said Button. 'The Flying Squad breathed a collective sigh of relief when they left our shores and set up shop in Thailand. But their relief turned out to be a bit premature. They're funding their life in the sun with regular visits back to the UK. Like I said, six robberies in five years with a total take of almost fifteen million. And that's just the ones we're sure they're behind. There's bound to be others.'

'And never caught?'

'They haven't even come close,' said Button. 'Everything's always planned to the last detail.'

'And how do they manage that if they're based in Thailand?'

'Good question,' said Button. She handed him a head-and-shoulders shot of a man in his sixties, totally bald, squinting at the camera through thick-lensed spectacles. 'This is the brains behind the outfit. Stuart Townsend. They call him the Professor, though he left school at fifteen to work with his father who, back then, was one of London's top safe-blowers.'

'Safe-blower rather than cracker?'

Button nodded. 'Townsend senior's skill was in explosives and he taught his son everything he knew. He must have forgotten something, though, because in the late eighties Townsend Junior miscalculated the amount of explosive he was using on a safe in a Hatton Garden jeweller's and ended up with two blown eardrums. He's been deaf ever since. He did seven years for the botched jewellery job and his disability put paid to his safe-blowing career. That was when he moved into planning jobs for other criminals, and the Moore brothers are his best customers. They leave the planning to him, and when the ducks are in a row they fly over and do the job.'

'Presumably you've got Townsend under surveillance?'

'On and off,' said Button. 'The problem is his deafness. Eavesdropping and bugging don't work because he never uses the phone. All communication is face to face or via email. And he's a difficult guy to follow because he tends to be more aware of what's going on around him than a hearing person.'

Shepherd sipped his coffee. He knew what was coming next.

'Have you ever been to Thailand?' asked Button.

'I had a spell in the Malaysian jungle with the SAS but I never made it to Thailand,' said Shepherd. 'That's the plan, is it, to send me to Thailand to infiltrate the gang?'

'Ricky Knight has a track record, and he's on the run. Pattaya is the new Costa del Crime – it's full of old familiar faces. There's every reason he'd go there.'

'But they're a tight group, you said.'

'We'll let them make the approach,' said Button. 'They've got a police general on their payroll and a couple of police colonels, so we'll send out a Europol warning on you. The cops will tip off the brothers so they'll be looking out for you.'

'But why would they be interested in me, seeing as how they're doing so well?' asked Shepherd.

Button tapped one of the pictures. A black man in his twenties was standing on a diving-board. 'They're shorthanded,' she said. 'This is Terry Norris, the youngster of the crew. Ex-army, weapons expert, he was their technical man.'

'Was?'

'Well, still is, but he's broken his back so he won't be

travelling. He smashed up his motorcycle and severed his spinal cord. He's in hospital now, but when he gets out he'll be in a wheelchair. So that leaves the Moore brothers a man short. It's been five months since their last job so they're due.'

'If you know they did these jobs, why haven't you pulled them in?'

'Knowing and proving, as you're aware, are two different things. They're pros, Spider. No forensics, no useful witnesses, and they're experts at laundering and hiding their money. They've stolen bearer bonds, jewellery, art, bullion and cash. Every job is different. There's nothing predictable about them so we've no idea where they'll strike next.'

'What about red-flagging them at the airports and following them when they come back?'

'The Flying Squad tried that two years ago but they keep coming in under the radar. You know yourself how porous our borders are. Last time they flew from Bangkok to Paris, Paris to Dublin, and then we lost them. Presumably they either drove over on the ferry or went up to Belfast and flew from there.'

'Because Belfast is in the UK so no passport control?'

'Exactly. Hindsight is a wonderful thing. After a big job has gone down, we can find out what flights they were on. But the fact that they left Thailand when the robberies were committed isn't evidence that they carried them out.'

Shepherd knew there was nothing to be gained from trying to second-guess Button, but the questions helped to put his thoughts in order. 'Will the Thais know I'm there under cover?'

'We can't take the risk of making it official. If the wrong cop finds out, you'll be dead.'

'That's reassuring,' said Shepherd.

'There won't be any arrests made on Thai soil,' said Button. 'We'll wait until they're back in the UK and hopefully we'll catch them in the act.'

'And what were you planning in the way of back-up?'

'Ricky Knight's on the run from the cops, so legend-wise you'll be on your own,' said Button.

'You won't be there?'

Button smiled thinly. 'A Western woman in Pattaya isn't exactly going to blend in, though I'm told there are quite a few Russian hookers plying their trade there now.'

'Charlie, with the best will in the world you can't send me to another country without some sort of back-up. If the shit hits the fan I'll need to be able to call on someone local to pull my nuts out of the fire.'

'Leaving aside the mixed metaphors, I take your point,' said Button. 'Who would you suggest?'

Shepherd gestured at the surveillance photographs. 'Who took those?'

'Bob Oswald, but he's surveillance. He wouldn't be any good as back-up and anyway we need him for a job in London. He can brief you when you get to Pattaya but then I'll need him back here.'

'Jimmy Sharpe, then,' said Shepherd. 'He could go over as a tourist and keep away from the bad guys, but be around if I need him.'

'Agreed,' said Button.

Shepherd studied the photographs. The Moore brothers looked like a couple of easy-going working-class blokes, the type who, if they'd made different choices, might have ended up in the army or the police. They were both well muscled, with thick gold chains hanging around their necks and chunky Rolex watches on their wrists. He'd seen their type in nightclubs and gyms all over the country. He could guess the sort of cars they drove and the houses they lived in and the girls they slept with. Over the course of his undercover career, first with the police and then with SOCA, Shepherd had befriended dozens of men like them. Befriended them and ultimately betrayed them. That was his job, and he was good at it.

'I realise it's on the other side of the world, Spider, and I know you don't like being away from your son. But with Terry Norris out of commission, we've got a window of opportunity that I'd hate to miss.'

'I'll do it,' said Shepherd. 'I'm guessing the sooner the better, right?'

'Saturday will be soon enough,' said Button. 'I've booked you on a flight from Heathrow at nine thirty in the evening. That'll give you a couple of days with your boy at least.'

'I'm already booked on?'

'I figured you'd want the assignment, Spider. It's right up your street.' She reached into her briefcase and took out a bulky padded envelope. 'Here's a passport with your picture in the name of John Westlake and a ticket to go with it. There's no legend so you can wing it, whatever you feel comfortable with. The brothers will know you're Knight and that you're using fake ID. Keep the Knight credit cards and use them in Pattaya.' She hefted the envelope. 'There's cash as well. Five thousand pounds. I'll arrange to send you more by Western Union if you need it and I'll see about setting up a bank account for you.'

Shepherd smiled. 'So I'm Dan Shepherd pretending to

be Ricky Knight pretending to be John Westlake? It's a
wonder I'm not schizophrenic.'

Button pointed at the steel Cartier watch he was
wearing. 'I'll need that back,' she said.

Shepherd held out his arm. 'It's a perfectly okay watch
for a villain.'

Button reached into her briefcase again and took out
a gold one. 'The Moores are watch fanatics,' she said.
'This'll give you something to talk about.'

Shepherd took off the Cartier and put it on the table,
then slipped on the other and clicked the strap shut.

'It's a Breitling Emergency,' said Button. 'It cost ten
thousand pounds, so do, please, take care of it.'

It had a rotating bezel marked in degrees, analogue
hands and two small digital screens, one in the top half
of the face and the other lower down. Below the face there
was a cylinder almost an inch long with a screw at the
end. 'I've heard about these,' said Shepherd. 'It's got a
transmitter inside, right, and if I unscrew it, it broadcasts
on the aircraft emergency frequency?'

'Exactly,' said Button. 'In theory every aircraft within
a hundred miles will triangulate your position and the
coastguard will send a helicopter to pick you up.'

'Nice bit of kit.'

'And we'll be wanting it back when the job's over,' said
Button, putting the Cartier into her briefcase. She took
out an envelope and poured the contents into his hand –
a sovereign ring, a gold money clip and a thick gold chain
bracelet. 'The Moores are a bit flash with their jewellery,
so this will help you blend,' she said. 'You can stick with
the Ricky Knight clothing and personal effects you've
already got.'

'I don't need anything for the Westlake legend?'

'Just the passport. We want the Moores to see through it straight away.' She glanced at her own watch, a slim gold Chopard. 'I've booked you a briefing with an intelligence officer at Scotland Yard,' she said. 'You should take Razor with you. You'll be told who you might run into while you're in Pattaya. Do you want to give Razor the good news or shall I?'

Shepherd grinned. 'Let me.'

Jimmy Sharpe cursed and sounded his horn at the bus that had just pulled out without indicating. 'Thailand?' he said. They were in Sharpe's own car, a year-old Lexus he'd bought at a bargain price from a Customs and Excise auction. It had been used to bring forty kilos of cocaine on the ferry from Calais and, other than a bit of damage to the rear seats, it was in near-new condition.

Shepherd checked that his seatbelt was fastened. 'She wanted me to go solo but I said I needed back-up.'

'Business class?'

'Hell, Razor, I don't know.'

'I can't sit for twelve hours in economy. What's the job?' He jammed on his brakes as the traffic-lights ahead turned red.

'A team of blaggers holing up there. They pop back now and again to replenish their coffers.'

'Land of Smiles,' said Sharpe. 'That's what they call Thailand. Maybe it'll put a smile on your face. When was the last time you got laid?'

'None of your bloody business,' said Shepherd. Actually, he knew pretty much to the day when he'd last had sex. It had been with a woman in Belfast whom he'd suspected was a serial killer, and the relationship had been doomed from the start. Before that, his last experience had been with a South African contractor in Baghdad and it had been very much a one-night stand. Carol Bosch had made no attempt to contact him after he'd returned to the UK and he'd decided that as she was working in Iraq there was no point in pursuing a relationship. All in all, Shepherd's sex life had been unsatisfying to say the least, but it wasn't a subject he was prepared to discuss with Sharpe.

'I'm just saying, from what I hear, anyone can get laid in Thailand,' Sharpe continued, not perturbed in the slightest by Shepherd's unease.

'Razor, the last thing I want at the moment is another job that takes me away from Liam.' He saw his eleven-year-old son infrequently at the best of times, but at least when he was in the country he could always drive back to Hereford if there was a problem. If he was under cover in Thailand, getting on a plane to the UK to see his son wouldn't be an option. 'Plus the team I'll be infiltrating are hard bastards. It won't be a holiday – not for me, anyway.'

'And all I have to do is watch your back?'

'That's the plan.'

'Excellent,' said Sharpe. He tapped his steering-wheel impatiently as the traffic-lights remained stuck on red. 'I might have to pull a flanker on the wife,' he said. 'Tell her I'm off to Spain or something. Not sure she'll be happy about me going to Thailand.' A cycle courier in a black Lycra jacket and tight black trousers rested his arm on the roof of their car. His blond hair was tied back in a ponytail. Sharpe glared at him and he moved away. 'Bloody traffic,' said Sharpe. 'You know what it is? It's those bloody bombs near Soho Square. Forensic teams are still there so the traffic's being diverted. I don't know what those Paki bastards are thinking. How do bombs outside night-clubs help their cause?'

'Razor, please.' Shepherd groaned.

'What?'

'You know what,' said Shepherd. 'The racial-awareness course – remember?'

'What? You don't think they're mad Paki bastards?'

'No one knows who they were, and the chances are they'll be British-born, same as the Tube bombers.'

'Two words, Spider. Dog. Stable.'

'What the hell are you talking about now?'

'What I'm saying is that just because a dog's born in a stable it doesn't make it a horse. Those guys who went down the Tube with bombs in their backpacks might have had British passports but they sure as hell weren't the same as you and me. We haven't been through al-Qaeda training camps on the Pakistani border for a start.'

Shepherd was bewildered by Sharpe's flawed logic. 'Blaming the Asian community for what's happening is like blaming all the Irish for what the IRA did,' he said. 'There's three million Asians in the UK, and a few hundred at most are terrorists or potential terrorists.'

'A few thousand, according to the spooks.' Sharpe grinned. 'And by spooks I mean MI5 before you accuse me of being racist again.'

'It's a small percentage of bad apples in a very large barrel,' said Shepherd.

'Let's say it's three thousand potential terrorists,' said Sharpe. 'You don't think that's something that should concern us? Three thousand Muslims planning mayhem and destruction?'

'I'm not saying it shouldn't concern us, I'm saying we can't go around slagging off the whole Muslim community.'

'Not all Muslims are terrorists, fair enough, but it's a plain fact that, the way things are at the moment, all the terrorists operating in the UK are Muslims. And most of the really bad ones are Pakis.'

'I give up,' said Shepherd. 'Sometimes there's no arguing with you.'

'Because you know I'm right.'

'Just drive, Razor. Drive and let me get some rest.'

'Sometimes you're no fun,' said Sharpe. He turned on the radio and tapped on the steering-wheel in time to the music.

They parked the Lexus in a multi-storey car park close to New Scotland Yard but took a circuitous route to the building. They walked into the reception area under the watchful eye of two police officers in bullet-proof vests cradling MP5 carbines. They showed their ID cards to the bored sergeant on duty. 'Home Office,' said Sharpe. 'Here to see Kenneth Mansfield. Intelligence.'

The sergeant tapped on his computer keyboard, then handed over two visitor badges. While Sharpe and Shepherd clipped them to their jackets he made a phone call. 'He'll be right down,' said the sergeant. 'If you're carrying firearms you'll have to check them in here.'

Sharpe patted his jacket. 'Do we look like we're armed?'

'We get all sorts of Home Office types in here,' said the sergeant. 'We have to ask everybody. If you are, best to say now before the metal detector starts buzzing.'

'It's just a social call,' said Sharpe. 'We're not planning to shoot anyone – we leave that up to you guys.'

The lift doors opened and a man in his late twenties stepped out, tall and thin with a slight stoop and wrists that projected several inches beyond the sleeves of his cheap chain-store suit. 'You the SOCA guys?' he asked.

'We're supposed to say Home Office,' said Sharpe. 'Low profile.'

'I'm Kenny,' said the man. He smiled, showing uneven yellowed teeth, and shook hands with them. His finger-nails were bitten to the quick. In his left hand he had a pack of Rothmans and a disposable lighter. 'Don't suppose you guys are smokers?' he asked.

Shepherd and Sharpe shook their heads.

'I'm gasping,' said Mansfield. 'Do you mind if we start the briefing outside while I have a cigarette?'

Shepherd could hardly believe what he'd heard. 'Yeah, we do mind,' he said. 'It might have escaped your attention but we're SOCA undercover agents. The only reason we've agreed to come here for a briefing is because your boss insists that the information you have is too classified to leave the building. What we're not prepared to do is stand on the pavement in central London being briefed while God-knows-who walks by.'

'Right,' said Mansfield, his face reddening. 'Sorry.'

'Patches,' said Sharpe.

'What?' said Mansfield.

'Nicotine patches,' said Sharpe. 'Slap a couple on your arse. You'll be fine.'

'Right,' said Mansfield, slipping his cigarettes and lighter into his pocket. 'Look, I'm sorry. I'm a sixty-a-day man and they won't let us smoke anywhere in the building.

I work twelve hours a day, I get phoned at home in the middle of the night and my wife says if I don't get a job with regular hours she'll divorce me. I'm trying to sell my house because we've a kid on the way and I've been gazumped twice. I'm a bit stressed out and this briefing was dumped on me at short notice. I just wanted a cigarette, that's all.' He shrugged apologetically.

'Bloody hell, Razor, I thought we had stressful lives.' Shepherd patted Mansfield's shoulder. 'Okay, Razor and I can have a coffee in the canteen while you go and suck on a coffin nail.'

'Are you sure?' asked Mansfield.

'They're your lungs,' said Shepherd. He gestured at Sharpe. 'And if he doesn't get his caffeine he won't be able to concentrate. We'll see you up there. The canteen's still on the fourth floor, right?'

'I'll have to come with you,' said Mansfield. 'Visitors have to be escorted at all times.'

Shepherd and Sharpe put their mobile phones, keys and coins into a grey plastic tray and Mansfield walked them through the metal detector. He took them to a lift and up to the fourth floor. It had been three years since Shepherd had last been in the Met canteen and it still had the same drab orange walls and chipped plates. He and Sharpe sat at a table by the blast-proof windows that looked over Victoria station. Mansfield got mugs of coffee for them, then hurried out for his smoke.

'The new face of policing,' said Sharpe.

'He's okay,' said Shepherd, sipping his coffee and pulling a face. It hadn't improved since his last visit.

'A puff of wind and he'd blow away,' said Sharpe, dismissively. 'Can you imagine him at an Old Firm game, trying to keep Rangers fans and Celtic fans from killing each other?'

'He's intelligence, Razor. He doesn't need muscle.'

'A cop is a cop,' said Sharpe. 'And cops used to be cops. Big guys you could depend on. Guys that could run a couple of hundred yards without gasping for breath. Guys you could depend on if punches started to fly. Now they've dropped pretty much all the physical requirements. They've got short cops, overweight cops, short-sighted cops. I bet before long they'll have cops in wheelchairs. The world's gone mad.'

Shepherd grinned at him. 'Have you looked in a mirror lately?'

'I've put on a few pounds, I'm not denying that,' said Sharpe, 'but I'm middle-aged and I've been doing the job for almost twenty years. Back in the day, I was a fit bastard and you had to be, walking the beat in Possilpark. These days, most of the bobbies on the beat couldn't chase after a villain, never mind wrestle them to the ground.'

'Just be glad you're in SOCA,' said Shepherd.

'SOCA's worse, and you know it,' said Sharpe. 'SOCA's full of civil servants and pencil-pushers. Guys like you and me, we're the exceptions. You think Charlotte Button could go up against a guy with a knife?'

Shepherd ran his finger around the rim of his coffee mug. 'Actually, Razor, I do. And she runs marathons. She's fit.' He glanced around the canteen and had to admit that none of the men and women there seemed to be tucking into salads and most were overweight. A uniformed sergeant walked in who was barely five and a half feet tall. Shepherd knew that height alone was no guide to fitness, but when it came to controlling unruly crowds or subduing violent criminals, every inch helped.

Sharpe sat back in his chair and stretched out his legs. 'You know what I don't understand about SOCA?'

Shepherd sighed. 'No, but I'm sure you're going to tell me,' he said.

'Where's the other A? There should be another A in there.'

'What the hell are you talking about, Razor?'

'We work for SOCA, right? The Serious Organised Crime Agency. Shouldn't it be the Serious And Organised Crime Agency? So it should be SAOCA.'

Shepherd frowned, not understanding what Sharpe was talking about. 'It's SOCA,' he said. 'The agency was created by the Serious Organised Crime and Police Act 2005. Went through the House of Commons in November 2004 and given Royal Assent in April the following year.'

'I wish I had your trick memory,' said Razor.

'It's not a trick. I just remember pretty much everything I see and hear.'

'I can't even remember my wedding anniversary,' said Sharpe. 'But here's my point. There's no "and" in there, right? It really is the Serious Organised Crime Agency.'

'I already said that. You really do have a problem with your memory, don't you?'

Sharpe ignored the question and continued his train of thought. 'Organised crime by definition has to be serious, doesn't it? Or do they mean that there's serious organised crime and pretend organised crime? The way I see it, crime can be serious and it can be organised so it should be the Serious And Organised Crime Agency. SAOCA.'

Shepherd closed his eyes. He was getting a headache. 'Whatever you say, Razor.'

'So, here's my point. Did someone screw up? Do you think someone just forgot to put the "and" in there? Some idiot civil servant made a mistake, and by the time they realised it was too late?'

'I don't know, Razor. And, truth be told, I don't care.'

'We should raise it with Charlie next time she gives us a case that doesn't involve a serious organised crime. Say a crime that's serious but not organised. Or organised but not very serious. See if she thinks the missing "and" is important.'

'I can pretty much guarantee that she won't,' said Shepherd, 'but you can mention it if you want.'

Kenny Mansfield reappeared, cutting short any further discussion. He took them upstairs to his office, a window-less box piled high with papers and files. 'Sorry about the mess,' he said, clearing a stack of magazines off a chair.

There was another chair by the door and Shepherd pulled it over to Mansfield's untidy desk. He and Sharpe sat down while Mansfield turned his computer's flat-screen monitor so that they could all see it. 'Do you know anything about Pattaya?' he asked.

They shook their heads. Mansfield dropped down into his high-backed chair and clicked on his computer mouse to start a PowerPoint presentation. A series of photographs flashed up on the screen, views of a beach resort. 'Pattaya is a town about two hours' drive from Bangkok on the eastern seaboard. It's probably the biggest single prosti-tution centre in the world with estimates of the number of working girls varying from ten thousand to fifty thousand, depending on whether or not the American fleet is in. They get upwards of five million visitors a year and they're not there for the sun or the sand.'

In most of the photographs, overweight Western tourists were walking with scantily dressed Asian girls or sitting on bar stools in sweat-stained T-shirts.

A map filled the screen, showing the location of the town. 'In the last ten years or so, criminal elements from all over the world have moved in,' said Mansfield. 'We've got your run-of-the-mill Brit crims rubbing shoulders with the Russian Mafia. The Nigerians are there, you've got Serbian conmen, Albanian Mafia, motorcycle gangs, Burmese drug-dealers – pretty much any criminal gang you can think of is represented. If you want drugs, fake passports, guns, counterfeit money, someone in Pattaya will sell them to you. There are murders nearly every week.'

'Nice,' said Sharpe.

Photographs of apartment blocks and luxury villas flashed up. 'Brits are moving in big-time,' said Mansfield, 'buying up villas and apartments, investing in bars and nightclubs. There's a lot of dirty money washing around and generally no questions are asked. We reckon there are now more faces in Pattaya than there are in Spain.'

'What about extradition?' asked Shepherd.

'It happens, but it takes time and, frankly, Pattaya is so far from the UK that, providing they stay there, we're taking the view that out of sight is out of mind. It's not like Spain where they're only a couple of hours away. Thailand's on the other side of the world. We'd probably pursue a paedophile or a murderer, but with a small-time drug-dealer we'd probably just say good riddance.'

'Do you have undercover guys over there?' asked Sharpe.

'Not that I know of,' Mansfield said. 'Could be that they'd fly guys over on specific investigations but there's no watching brief. We do send people over every few weeks to take photographs, run them through facial-recognition programs so we have a good idea who's there.'

'And the Thais aren't doing anything?'

'Providing they don't break any Thai laws, the Thais don't care,' he said. 'We can access their immigration databases so we know which British citizens are in the country, but that doesn't tell us where in Thailand they are. Long-term residents are supposed to register with the local police every ninety days but most don't. Plus the serious crims are all on fake passports anyway.' He clicked to end the PowerPoint presentation. 'What they don't tell you in the glossy brochures is that more Brits die in Thailand than anywhere else outside the UK.' He grinned. 'They're not all murdered,' he added, 'but every year more than two hundred and fifty Brits die there. To put that into perspective, that's about ten times as many Brits as died in Iraq. Most are accidents or straightforward deaths, or old guys taking too much Viagra and over-exerting themselves. But there are half a dozen murders and a couple of dozen suicides every year. And a fair number of the suicides are disguised murders – a fall from a balcony or a plastic bag over the head or an overdose of drugs.'

'Sounds like a regular Glasgow weekend,' said Sharpe.

'Pattaya's a tough town,' said Mansfield. 'It's an easy place to get a gun, but it's even easier to hire someone to pull the trigger. You can get a hitman for less than a thousand pounds, sometimes much less.'

'What about Brits doing the killing?' asked Shepherd.

'You only hear about the ones who get caught, and they're usually guys who throttle their girlfriends,' said Mansfield. 'If you're a bad guy and want to get rid of the competition, you'd probably pay someone else to do the dirty deed. Who exactly are you interested in?'

'Can't tell you that, I'm afraid,' said Shepherd.

'Well, we can,' said Sharpe. 'But then we'd have to kill you.'

'Ignore my colleague's attempt at humour,' said Shepherd. 'It's an undercover operation so everything is classified. What we need is a briefing on every villain you know who is either in Pattaya or is a regular visitor.'

'That would be well over a thousand faces,' said Mansfield.

'That's okay,' said Shepherd. 'We just need to know if anyone there might be in a position to identify us.'

'Got you,' said Mansfield. He tapped on his computer keyboard. 'Alphabetical order work for you?'

'That's fine,' said Shepherd.

Mansfield tapped on the keyboard again. A face flashed up on the screen: a grey-haired man in his fifties, with worry lines etched around his eyes and the haunted expression that comes from years spent behind bars. 'Eric Anderson,' said Mansfield. The man's details had appeared down the right-hand side of the screen – date of birth, last known address, and a comprehensive list of the criminal offences he'd committed, which varied from being drunk and disorderly as a teenager to three counts of grievous bodily harm.

Shepherd peered at the screen. 'Where is he in Pattaya?' he said.

'We don't get that sort of info unless he's been targeted,' said Mansfield. 'You just get the basic CRO data and that he's known to be in Pattaya.'

Mansfield clicked on his mouse. Another face popped up. Derek Armitage. Younger, with only two convictions, both drug-related. 'And so on, and so on,' said Mansfield.

'Can't you dump the files on a thumb-drive for us?' asked Sharpe.

Mansfield shook his head. 'A couple of years ago that wouldn't have been a problem but the Government's lost so much data recently there's been a clampdown. You can only access the files on an online terminal.'

'It's not a problem,' said Shepherd. 'I've got a pretty good memory. How long do you think it'll take to go through them all?'

'If you just want to look at names and faces, then five to ten seconds a file. You should be done in about three hours.'

'We've got the time,' said Shepherd. 'Are you okay if Razor and I do it here?'

'Whatever you want,' said Mansfield. 'I've got a briefing with Vice and Clubs in half an hour. I'll go grab a ciggie first. You need anything?'

'We're fine,' said Shepherd.

Sharpe loosened his tie and kicked off his shoes as Mansfield headed out of his office. He grinned at Shepherd's expression. 'My shoes are killing me,' he said. 'Now, do you want to click the rat thing, or shall I?'

'It's a mouse, Razor, and you'd better do it because you're a slow reader.'

Sharpe clicked onto the next file and Shepherd settled back in his chair to watch the monitor. He had no idea how his trick memory worked, but all he had to do was to see a picture, read or hear something and he remembered it for ever. He recognised some of the faces, high-profile villains who had appeared in the tabloids, and there were several major drug-dealers he'd heard discussed in Europol intelligence briefings. The vast majority, though, were strictly small-time. Wife-beaters, car thieves, petty criminals. The faces clicked by, the pictures and details filed away for future reference.

'Shit,' said Sharpe, staring at a photograph of a middle-aged man with a shaved head and a wicked scar across his left cheek that had probably been done with a pint glass. 'I know him.'

'Yeah, but does he know you?' asked Shepherd.

'He thinks I'm an alarms specialist from Bishopbriggs and reckons it was my incompetence that led to him doing a seven stretch in Barlinnie,' said Sharpe. 'He doesn't know I'm a cop, but he'll still take a swing at me if he sees me.'

'Neither of us are cops any more, Razor, remember?' said Shepherd. 'We're civil servants now that we work for SOCA.'

'Roses by any other name,' said Sharpe. He peered at the screen. 'He's only been out for six months. Must have headed straight out to Thailand. Can't say I blame him – if I'd been banged up for seven years I'd want some sea, sand and sex.'

Jason Reece was a burglar who had graduated from breaking into homes to banks, though he was more inclined to go in through the roof at night rather than the front door with guns during business hours. He had three convictions for violence – a stabbing during a burglary and two punch-ups in pubs.

'Does he think you went down?' Shepherd asked.

'The story was that I got probation after helping the police with their enquiries.'

'So he thinks you're a grass?'

'It'll be okay. I can take care of myself.'

'I'm more worried about Ricky Knight being seen in the company of a police informer,' said Shepherd.

'So we won't drink together,' said Sharpe. 'It'll be fine.' He leaned down and pulled open the bottom drawer of the desk.

Shepherd frowned at his colleague. 'What the hell are you doing?'

'He's bound to have a bottle of Scotch somewhere. Smokers drink – that's a rule.'

'Stop pissing about,' said Shepherd, and he wasn't joking. 'It's been a decade at least since they allowed alcohol in New Scotland Yard. Just keep clicking that mouse and we can get the hell out of here.'

'Then we can have a drink?'

'Yes, Razor,' said Shepherd, patiently. 'Then we can have a drink.'

Bradshaw walked through the prayer room, careful not to touch any of the prostrate men. It was large enough to hold five thousand worshippers, but it was still crowded. His bare feet whispered along the red carpet into which were woven the patterns of hundreds of individual prayer mats. High above his head, a painted dome was decorated with brightly coloured mosaics, a massive crystal chandelier hung from the middle. Inscriptions from the Koran, the most holy of books, had been painted around the edge. Several faces turned to look at him, registering surprise to see a Caucasian in their midst, but Bradshaw simply smiled blandly. He was used to being stared at in mosques and knew that he was watched out of curiosity, not hostility. He found a space close to the front and began to pray, eyes closed, the better to appreciate the power of the words he chanted.

When he finished he opened his eyes. He felt cleansed, as he always did after prayer. Some of the men standing and kneeling around him were wearing traditional Muslim dress, long flowing shirts that almost reached the ankles and skullcaps, and several were carrying well-worn copies of the Koran. Bradshaw was dressed casually but smartly in a linen jacket and trousers, and a shirt he had ironed that morning. Clothing was important, he knew. It was camouflage. Many of the men had long beards but he was always clean-shaven. That was also part of his camouflage, as was the slight smile that always played on his lips. He had taught himself to smile even when he was unhappy or worried. People trusted smiling, clean-shaven men in smart clothes. They didn't trust angry-looking men with beards, wearing long shirts.

The man he had come to see was over to his right. Bradshaw knew he was a regular worshipper at the Regent's Park Mosque. He was almost fifty years old and had a ragged beard that almost reached his chest. He was barrel-chested and wore baggy cotton trousers that flapped above his ankles, a long-sleeved pinstripe shirt buttoned up to the neck, and a beaded skullcap. In his right hand he held a string of amber beads and ran them through his fingers as he prayed. His name was Hakeem and he was Palestinian. As Hakeem stood up and adjusted his shirt-sleeves, Bradshaw walked over to him.

'Brother Hakeem,' he said quietly. 'It is an honour to meet you.'

Hakeem eyed him coldly. 'You have not met me yet, brother,' he said, his voice a guttural rasp.

Bradshaw did not avert his eyes. He stared back at Hakeem, even though his stomach was churning. There was no human warmth in Hakeem's eyes: it was as if they had been carved from black marble. They bored into Bradshaw as if they could see into his very soul. 'I was told you would be expecting me,' said Bradshaw, fighting to keep his voice steady.

'You are Bradshaw?' The question was almost certainly rhetorical because Bradshaw doubted that Hakeem was regularly approached by Caucasians in the mosque.

'I am,' he said.

'You are younger than I expected.' He continued to finger the amber beads as he studied Bradshaw's face. 'I shall see you outside in the park,' he said. 'Wait for me there.'

Bradshaw finished and turned away hurriedly to hide his embarrassment. He was not used to being treated like a fool and his first instinct had been to curse the man and his rudeness, but Hakeem had what he wanted so he forced himself to conceal his anger and walked away, still smiling. He retrieved his shoes from the racks outside the prayer hall and left the mosque.

He walked across the grass, watching a group of middle-aged women exercise their dogs as they gossiped in upper-class voices about house prices and the difficulty of getting decent cleaners. Two Goths, dressed from head to foot in black, sauntered hand in hand towards Baker Street. They wore tight black jeans, black boots, leather jackets, and white makeup with black mascara. It was only the swelling breasts that marked them out as female. A businessman in a pinstripe suit with a brief-case in one hand and a mobile phone clamped to his ear walked purposefully across the grass, barking at his assist-ant on the other end of the line. Bradshaw hated them all – hated them so much he could almost taste it.

He turned to look at the mosque, its gleaming gold dome glinting in the sunlight. Hakeem was coming towards him, still holding his string of beads. He did not break his stride when he reached Bradshaw. 'Walk with me,' he said.

He kept up a brisk pace and Bradshaw, who was several inches shorter, struggled to match it. 'I was told you can help us with funding,' he said, but Hakeem silenced him with a curt wave.

'I shall be deciding the flow of this conversation,' he said.

'I'm sorry,' said Bradshaw. 'I didn't mean—'

'And I don't need your apologies,' said Hakeem.

Bradshaw opened his mouth to apologise again but just as quickly closed it. He waited for Hakeem to continue. His legs were burning and he could feel a stitch growing in his side.

'Which mosque do you use, brother?' asked Hakeem.

'I used to go to Finsbury Park, but not any more,' said Bradshaw. 'There are too many spies there now. The Government has spies in all the mosques.' He was panting, and his forehead was bathed in sweat.

Hakeem nodded. 'So where do you pray?'

'At home. With my brothers. Don't worry, I pray five times a day. I am a good Muslim.'

'I didn't doubt that, brother,' said Hakeem.

'I have proved myself,' said Bradshaw.

'How, exactly?'

Bradshaw lowered his voice to a whisper. 'The car bombs in Soho.'

Hakeem turned to look at him for the first time since they had started walking. He raised his eyebrows. 'That was you?'

'That was me and my brothers,' said Bradshaw.

Hakeem stopped suddenly and faced him. 'Others have claimed responsibility.'

'They wanted the glory. They are welcome to it. I am not doing this for the glory. I am doing this for *jihad*, for Allah. I am carrying out His will.' There were those among the Muslim community, men that Bradshaw hated almost as much as he hated the unbelievers, who argued that *jihad* meant 'struggle' and not 'holy war'. But Bradshaw had no doubt what the Prophet Muhammad had meant. *Jihad* was the duty of every good Muslim. *Jihad* was the reason that every Muslim drew breath. *Jihad* was what every Muslim lived and died for.

'And where were you trained, brother?'

'I was a soldier.'

'You served in Iraq?'

'Yes.'

'And the army taught you to make bombs?'

Bradshaw shook his head. 'I was an engineer more than a soldier,' he said.

'But the bombs were professional, according to the newspapers.'

'Everything you need is on the Internet, these days. And two brothers with me have been trained. We knew to use that model of Mercedes for the second bomb because the petrol tank is exposed. We learned how to turn light-bulbs into detonators and how to use a mobile phone to set it off.'

Without any warning, Hakeem started to walk again. 'And funding – where did you get the money from?' he asked.

'It was not expensive, brother,' said Bradshaw. 'I have some money and there are brothers prepared to support me.'

'Where did you get the cars from?'

'One of the brothers worked for a body shop in Kilburn. We waited until he had a customer with the type of Mercedes we needed and he got a spare set of keys. The other car we stole from the street.'

'Is there not a danger that the Mercedes will be traced to the body shop?'

'We waited a long time,' said Bradshaw. 'We let six months pass after we got the keys. Two months ago he left and got another job. I'm certain that the car will not be traced to him. The other we stole in south London.'

Hakeem stopped again. He steepled his fingers under his chin as he studied Bradshaw. 'And who guides you?' he asked.

'Allah,' said Bradshaw, quickly. 'I am doing his work.'

'But who on the mortal plane gives you instructions?'

'No one,' said Bradshaw.

'No one?' repeated Hakeem. 'You are a totally self-contained cell?'

'That is what gives us our strength,' said Bradshaw. 'We can betray no one, and no one can betray us.'

'Then what is it you need from me?' asked Hakeem.

'Funding,' said Bradshaw. 'I am told you have access to finance.'

'And who told you that?'

Bradshaw shrugged. 'A brother who knows of my need for money.'

Hakeem was walking again, and Bradshaw hurried after him. 'How much do you need?' asked Hakeem.

'Half a million pounds,' said Bradshaw.

Hakeem exhaled through clenched teeth. 'That is a lot of money.'

'It's one per cent of one per cent of one per cent of one per cent of a day's oil revenue in Saudi Arabia. And I'm told that money flows from the Kingdom into your bank accounts.'

'You have been told a lot, my friend.'

'Information is power,' said Bradshaw. 'Information and money.'

'And what do you know about me?'

'Enough to know that you are a man to be trusted. A good Muslim who is doing the work of Allah.'

'Specifics?' said Hakeem.

'You are from Palestine, though you now hold British citizenship. Your family were murdered by the Israelis. They fired rockets at your house and killed your parents, your brother and your three sisters. You became a bomb-maker and you sent more than a dozen suicide-bombers into Tel Aviv before you moved to France and then to London. The authorities know nothing of your background, of course.'

'Of course,' said Hakeem. 'It seems you have me at something of a disadvantage, as I know nothing about you.'

'Who I am is of little importance,' said Bradshaw.

'What matters is what I have done and what I have yet to do.'

'The people who entrust me with their money will need proof that you are indeed working for *jihad*.'

Bradshaw reached into his jacket pocket and took out a small white thumb-drive. He gave it to Hakeem. 'Photographs of the car bombs being constructed. The drive is password-protected. You must enter your family name as the password. Failure to do that will erase everything on the drive.'

Hakeem pocketed it. 'And they will need to know what you plan to do with the money.'

Bradshaw leaned forward and in a whisper he told Hakeem what he planned to do.

As he listened, Hakeem smiled.

Shepherd climbed out of his car and sighed. It had been two months since he had last mown the lawn in the front garden and even longer since he had done any weeding. It showed. The door opened and his son hurtled down the path towards him. 'Dad!' shouted Liam. Shepherd picked him up and hugged him. 'Dad, I'm twelve, I'm not a kid!' he protested.

'You're *almost* twelve and, anyway, I figure that until you're actually a teenager I can pick you up and hug you whenever I want to.'

'Did you get me anything?'

Shepherd lowered his son to the ground. 'Is it me you're happy to see or your present?'

'Tough call,' said Liam. 'But that means you did get me a present, right?'

Shepherd grinned and pulled a Virgin bag from his

pocket. 'Two games for your Xbox,' he said. 'Shoot-'em-ups, lots of blood and gore, just the way you like them.' Shepherd had given up trying to stop his son playing violent video games. When Liam had been younger Shepherd had banned them from the house but his son simply went to his friends' homes and played there. Eventually Shepherd had capitulated. At least if Liam played at home he'd be able to keep an eye on him, though he'd never understood why anyone, least of all a child, would take pleasure from murder and mayhem.

'Thanks, Dad!'

'Don't blame me if you end up as a psychopathic killer,' said Shepherd.

'If I do, it won't be the video games.'

'What do you mean by that?'

'Joke,' said Liam.

Shepherd took his suitcase from the back of the car. 'Have you been a good boy while I was away?' he asked.

Liam looked up from the computer games. 'What have you heard?' he asked.

'Nothing,' said Shepherd.

Liam grinned. 'Then I've been good,' he said.

'When's the next parent-teacher meeting?'

'Next year maybe. Katra's cooking dinner.'

Shepherd noted the change in subject but didn't comment on it. 'What's she making?' he asked, heading for the front door.

'Pigs' testicles,' said Liam. 'It's a Slovenian speciality.'

Shepherd stopped walking, horror on his face.

Liam laughed. 'Got you,' he said. 'Joke. It's shepherd's pie.'

'Yeah, right.'

'I'm serious, Dad.'

'With real shepherds, no doubt.' He carried the suit-case into the house and left it by the hall table. There was a stack of unopened mail on the table. Katra was sitting in the kitchen reading *Hello!*, a mug of tea in front of her. She looked up in surprise when he walked into the kitchen. 'Dan!' she said. 'You're back!'

'It is my house,' he said.

'I just meant I wasn't expecting you, I thought you were coming tomorrow.' She got up from the kitchen table and moved towards him as if she was about to hug him, then appeared to change her mind and headed for the kettle instead. 'Coffee?' she asked. She was wearing a short denim skirt that was frayed at the bottom and a pink Diesel T-shirt. She had her hair tied back in a ponytail, her usual style when she was in the kitchen or cleaning. Shepherd had hired Katra as an au pair almost three years earlier, shortly after she had arrived in the country from Slovenia, and now he didn't know how he'd manage without her. She took care of the house and she was great with Liam. He'd given her a cheque book and access to one of his bank accounts, and she paid all the household bills and even her own salary. Shepherd trusted her totally, with Liam and with his finances. 'Are you hungry?' There was hardly a trace of her old accent. She practised her English accent by listening to BBC newsreaders and endeavouring to copy them.

'Famished,' said Shepherd, sitting down at the kitchen table. He picked up the magazine. It was full of photo-graphs of people he had never heard of.

'I'm doing shepherd's pie,' said Katra.

'See? I told you,' said Liam, sitting down at the table. He grinned at Katra. 'He didn't believe me,' he told her.

The kettle boiled and Katra poured the water into a cafetière and put it in front of Shepherd with a carton of milk and a mug.

'Can we change our cars, Dad?' asked Liam.

'What?'

'The Honda CRV and the BMW X3. Have you any idea what their carbon footprints are?'

'I'm more concerned with fingerprints than footprints,' said Shepherd.

'It'd be better for the environment if we had a hybrid.'

'Says who?'

'Mr Walker at school. We drew up a list of all the cars our families have and looked at the mileage and the pollution and everything.'

'So Mr Walker was asking you what sort of car I drove?'

Liam sighed. 'It was for environmental studies, Dad,' he said.

'I'd rather you didn't give him personal information like that.' He pushed down the cafetière's plunger and poured coffee into his mug.

'What was I supposed to say? "No comment"? Come on, Dad, you're being paranoid. He was just proving a point. Most of the kids in my class have gas-guzzling SUVs. And we've got two.'

Shepherd splashed some milk into his coffee. 'Gas-guzzling? The CRV does twenty-four to the gallon. You should ask Mr Walker about the batteries.'

'What batteries?'

'The batteries in hybrids. Ask him what happens to them. Car engines can be recyled pretty much, and the metal can be melted down and used again. But the batteries in hybrids are full of toxic compounds. And ask him how much energy is used in making those batteries. I'm not saying electric cars aren't the way to go, but right now the old-fashioned combustion engine is a hell of a lot more efficient than people give it credit for. And I like my BMW. It's safer than the average hybrid, and so is the CRV. If, God-forbid, you're ever in an accident I want you strapped into an SUV, not sitting in some battery-operated death trap.'

'Dad—'

'Don't "Dad" me on this,' said Shepherd. 'I'm serious. You look at the cars that members of our government drive. Gas-guzzlers one and all. When the prime minister and his wife start driving around in hybrids maybe I'll trade in the BMW and the CRV, but until then we're keeping them.'

'What about biofuels?' asked Liam. 'Can't we use biofuels? At least they're organic.'

'Half the world is short of food, Liam. People are starving in Africa and Asia. Do you think it's fair to grow crops just to put fuel in cars here in the West?'

'But Mr Walker said biofuels are the fuels of the future.'

'They are,' said Shepherd. 'And when we've got enough food to feed all the people, we can grow crops for fuel. But that's not going to be for a long time. It's the same with battery cars. They're for the future too. But the way things stand at the moment, we're stuck with oil, we're stuck with cars, and you're stuck with me as your father.' He ruffled his son's hair. 'But just so we can start saving the world you can walk to school from now on.'

'Dad—'

'Didn't do me any harm,' said Shepherd. 'And my house

was three miles from school. You can walk to yours in twenty minutes.'

'What about when it rains?'

'You'll get wet.'

'It's not safe for kids to walk to school.'

'We live in Hereford, the home of the SAS. Kids can walk the streets safely, trust me.'

Liam folded his arms sulkily. 'There's no point in talking to you sometimes.'

'Liam, I like my car. I like driving it. I even like cleaning it when I get the chance. It cost me a lot of money and I don't see why I shouldn't get some pleasure from it now and to again. I certainly don't see why some idiot in a corduroy jacket with patches on the elbows should tell me how to live my life.'

Liam frowned. 'How do you know Mr Walker wears a corduroy jacket?'

'I guessed.' Shepherd laughed. 'Okay, we're due to change the CRV soon anyway so why don't we agree on this? You can decide on what we replace it with. But bear in mind that you're the one who's going to be driven to school in it every day. I'm sure your friends think the CRV is a pretty cool car, but if you'd rather turn up at school in a three-wheeler with a solar panel on the roof, that's fine with me. Just make sure it's got a boot big enough to hold the shopping for Katra.'

'Are you serious?'

'About the solar panel?'

'About letting me choose the car.'

'So long as you stop moaning about my X3, and providing it doesn't cost more than the CRV, the world's your lobster.'

'Oyster,' corrected Liam.

'Joke,' said Shepherd. He took his coffee through to the sitting room and dropped into one of the sofas. He picked up the remote and switched on the television. Liam sat on one of the armchairs. He was still holding his Xbox games. 'I've got a football match on Saturday,' he said.

'That's great,' said Shepherd. 'How's it going?'

'Mr Graham says I've got a great right foot but I need to work on my heading,' said Liam, enthusiastically. 'He says I mustn't be afraid – you have to head it like you mean it.'

'He's right,' said Shepherd. 'Tell you what, after dinner we'll go out and have a practice in the garden.'

'Cool. And can you come to the match on Saturday?'

'What time is it?'

'One o'clock. It's at the school so it's not far.'

Shepherd groaned. 'I'm sorry, Liam, I've got a job. I've got to be at Heathrow by six.'

'No worries.' Liam took one of the video games out of the bag and began reading the cover.

'Liam, really, I'm sorry. It's a big job and I have to go.'

Liam didn't look up. 'It's okay,' he said. 'Really. Katra's been coming to my games and all my friends think she's hot.'

'But we can practise tonight. And tomorrow.'

'Sure, if you want,' said Liam, his voice a dull monotone.

'So your friends think Katra's hot, do they?'

Liam looked up, smiling. 'They think she's my step-mum, which is crazy because she's only twenty-five.' The smile vanished. 'Did she tell you she wants to go back to Slovenia?'

'What?'

'Her dad's not well so she wants to take care of him.'

Shepherd's heart sank. When he'd hired her, Katra had told him her mother had died and that she was one of six children, the only girl. She went back twice a year to visit her family but every time Shepherd had been left in no doubt as to how much he had come to rely on her. He dreaded having to replace her. 'I'll talk to her,' he said.

'What's the job?' asked Liam.

'Thailand,' said Shepherd. 'Bank robbers.'

'They're robbing banks in Thailand?'

'It's complicated,' said Shepherd.

'How long will you be away?'

'They never tell me. Until the job's done, I guess. I promise you, after this job we'll spend some time together. I'll take some leave and we can have a holiday.'

'You said that last time, Dad.'

'This time I mean it.'

'You said that last time, too.' He went back to his computer game.

'Plug it in, I'll give you a game,' said Shepherd.

'You're terrible at video games,' said Liam.

'I've been letting you win,' said Shepherd. 'But that changes as of today.'

Liam went to bed just before nine o'clock. Shepherd tucked him in, then went down to the kitchen where Katra was loading the dishwasher.

'The shepherd's pie was great,' he said.

'It was on television,' she said. 'Jamie Oliver.'

Shepherd sat at the kitchen table. 'Liam said your father wasn't well.'

Katra closed the dishwasher and switched it on, then

joined Shepherd at the table. 'He's very sick,' she said. She tapped her chest. 'His lungs. Cancer. He has smoked his whole life. My mother nagged him all the time and when she died I nagged him, but he wouldn't listen to anybody.'

'I'm sorry, Katra. That's terrible.'

'He'll be starting chemo next week so I want to be with him. I'm sorry it's such short notice.'

Shepherd groaned inwardly but didn't say anything. Katra was the man's only daughter – of course she had to be with him. But it couldn't have happened at a worse time.

'I'm sorry, Dan,' she said.

'Hey, he's your dad, you have to go,' he said.

'Are you here for a while?' she asked.

'I'm leaving on Saturday.' Her brow furrowed and she bit her lower lip, as if she was about to cry. 'Katra, it's not a problem, I'll talk to Liam's grandparents. They'll be able to look after him, I'm sure. And it's not as if he's a handful, is it?'

'He's a good boy,' said Katra. 'I'll miss him.'

Shepherd leaned forward. 'You are coming back, right?'

'I think so,' she said.

'You think so?'

'He's very sick but he pretends everything is okay. I won't know how sick he is until I've talked to the doctors.'

'If there's anything I can do, you just have to ask,' said Shepherd.

She nodded earnestly. 'I know.'

'Your brothers, how old are they now?'

'The oldest is twenty-two, the youngest sixteen. But they are men and in Slovenia . . .' She shrugged. 'He needs me. He needs his daughter.'

'I know,' he said. 'That's not what I meant. I meant that at least they're old enough to take care of themselves.'

She smiled. 'They've had to since I left,' she said. 'All the time I was in the house they never cooked a single meal or ironed a shirt.' The smile faded. 'I will miss you, Dan.'

'I'll miss you too,' he said. 'You do a great job looking after us.'

Her lower lip was trembling and Shepherd could see she was close to tears. 'I mean I'll really miss you,' she said. She put her head down so that her cheek was resting on her hands. 'I don't want to go. I want to stay here with you and Liam, but he's my father so I have to go.'

Shepherd felt suddenly awkward. 'I'll make you some cocoa,' he said.

'I'll do it,' she said. She got up, rushed to the fridge, took out a carton of milk and poured some into a pan. She stood with her back to him and wiped her eyes with a tea-towel. Shepherd didn't know what to say. He empathised, but couldn't think of any words that would make her feel better. Katra sniffed. 'Are your parents alive, Dan?' she asked, still with her back to him.

'My father is. My mother died a long time ago,' he said.

'You never talk about your father.'

'We don't get on. Haven't for a long time.'

She busied herself stirring the milk with a wooden spoon even though it was nowhere near boiling. 'What happened between you?' she asked.

'It's complicated,' he said.

'Liam says you always say that when it's something you don't want to talk about.'

Shepherd chuckled. 'He's probably right,' he said.

'You only have one father, Dan,' she said. 'One day he won't be around.'

'You're right,' said Shepherd. 'But, like I said, it's complicated.'

Shepherd dropped Liam at school on Friday morning, making a point to use the BMW X3. He grinned when he saw some of Liam's friends gazing admiringly at it and decided his son wouldn't be asking for an electric car again anytime soon. He drove to the house of his in-laws, just ten minutes from the school. He parked in the empty driveway of the neat semi, the lovingly tended garden putting his own to shame.

Moira had the front door open for him as soon as he was walking towards the house. 'Daniel, so lovely to see you,' she said. 'Until you phoned I didn't even know you were back.'

Only his mother-in-law could pay him a compliment and make him feel guilty at the same time. And only his mother-in-law called him by his full name. 'Is Tom at work?' he asked.

'He makes it a point always to be first in at the bank,' said Moira. 'He has done for the past twenty-three years and I don't see him changing now. Tea?' She air-kissed both his cheeks and he caught the scent of the perfume she had worn ever since the first time he'd met her, sixteen years ago. Tom and Moira were creatures of habit. 'Go through to the sitting room, Daniel,' she said, closing the front door.

Shepherd went in and sat down on one of the over-stuffed sofas. In the days when their daughter had been alive, there had been dozens of photographs of Sue on the mantelpiece and on the bookcase next to it. Now there were just two, at opposite ends of the mantelpiece, one of her aged twelve in her school uniform, and another of her holding Liam, a few hours after she'd given birth. There were no photographs of Shepherd, but he wasn't offended that the wedding photographs had been moved. Sue was their child, Liam was their grandchild, and Shepherd wasn't a blood relation. And now that she was dead, there was no point in making the room a mausoleum to her. They were the two best pictures they had of her – it was just the luck of the draw that Shepherd wasn't in either. He smiled at the photograph of Sue and Liam. Tom was a keen amateur photographer and he'd fussed like an old lady as he'd taken the pictures, but his pickiness had paid off. Sue's maternal pride poured out of the image, and he'd managed to catch the newborn with his eyes open, an expression of wonder on his face as he stared up at his mother. Shepherd felt tears well in his eyes and he blinked them away. It was almost five years since Sue had died in a senseless car accident but there hadn't been a day when he hadn't missed her.

He heard Moira walking down the hallway and brushed his eyes with the back of his hand. He was wearing a broad smile when she appeared at the door with a tray of tea. She placed it on the ornate coffee-table, and he poured a little milk into the delicate china cups. Moira always insisted on the milk going in first as she'd once read that that was the way the Royal Family took theirs.

'You said Katra was going back to Slovenia?' she said.

'She only told me yesterday,' said Shepherd. 'Her father's sick so she's flying back as soon as she can get a ticket and I'm off to Thailand tomorrow. I'm sorry to spring this on you, Moira, but can Liam stay with you and Tom until I get back?'

'Of course he can,' said Moira. 'You don't have to ask, you know that. We'd love to have him. We haven't changed his room since he was last here. In fact, there's still some of his PlayStation games up there.'

'It's Xbox now,' said Shepherd. 'He's moved on.'

'How long will you be away?' she asked. She sipped her tea, her little finger crooked.

'It's open-ended,' said Shepherd. 'A few weeks. Maybe more.'

'You're spending too much time away from the boy,' admonished Moira. 'It was bad enough when Sue was here but, if anything, you're spending even less time with Liam than you were before . . .' She couldn't bring herself to finish the sentence and covered her discomfort by taking another sip of tea.

'I'll make more time for him,' said Shepherd. 'It's been a busy few months.'

'I hate sounding like a broken record, Daniel, I really do. I thought things would improve once you moved back to Hereford but you're hardly ever here.'

'I'm not sure that's true,' protested Shepherd.

'Daniel, you've just been away for three weeks, and from what Liam said, you hardly ever phoned him.'

'I was under cover, Moira. And when I did get the chance to call it was usually late at night and I didn't want to wake him. He isn't allowed to use his mobile at school . . .' He tailed off. He was just making excuses. She was right, and so was Liam. Shepherd had been away for three weeks and had probably spoken to his son fewer than half a dozen times.

'Last year you were in Belfast for weeks. You were out in the Middle East before that. You missed Christmas last year and since then you've been away – what? Three times? Four? To be honest, half the time we don't know where you are.' She put her cup down. 'I know it's not my place to nag you but as Liam's grandmother I do think I have the right to speak up on his behalf. He misses you, Daniel. Justifiably so.'

'I know, Moira, but it's my job.'

'Then maybe you should think about changing it, taking something that allows you to see more of your son. It's not just for his sake. You only get one chance to watch them grow, then they're gone for good. These years you're missing, you'll regret them one day.'

Again, Shepherd knew she was right. But he also knew how much his work meant to him, and that he would never be satisfied with a nine-to-five desk job. It was Sue who had persuaded him to leave the SAS, once she had fallen pregnant. She, too, had insisted that he took a less dangerous job, one that would allow him to spend more time with his family. He'd agreed and opted for the police, but within months of applying he'd been plucked from basic training and put into an elite undercover unit where the work had proven to be every bit as dangerous as his time with Special Forces. Recently he'd moved to the SOCA undercover unit, and because it investigated criminals right across the UK he was away from home for even longer periods than he had been when he was in the army.

'Why on earth are they sending you to Thailand?' asked Moira.

'Bank robbers,' he said. 'They live there but come to the UK to carry out robberies.'

Moira tutted. 'With all that's going wrong in this country, haven't they got better things to do than send you to Thailand?'

'What do you mean?'

'The car bombs. The bombings on the Tube. These Islamic terrorists. Why aren't you tracking them down? I really don't know what the world's coming to.'

'They rob banks, Moira. They terrorise people.'

'They steal money, that's what they do. And it seems to me that as a society we worry more about our financial institutions than we do about the people who live here. I heard on the radio last week that MI5 is watching more than a thousand potential terrorists in this country, and that they're almost all British-born. Is that true?'

'I'm afraid so.'

'And they said that all they can do is watch them, but they can't even do that properly because they don't have enough manpower.'

'That's probably true, too,' admitted Shepherd.

'They should just put them in prison and have done with it.'

'Moira, you can't put people in prison until the case against them has been proved in court. And that's easier said than done.'

'It'd be a lot easier if you weren't wasting your time in Thailand, that's for sure.' Moira added some tea to her cup. 'Weren't you going to ask the Regiment if you could rejoin as a member of the training staff?'

'The directing staff, they call it,' said Shepherd. 'I could,

I suppose, but it wouldn't be as challenging as what I'm doing now.'

'There are times, Daniel,' she said frostily, 'when you have to put your family above yourself, and that's all there is to it.' She forced a smile. 'I sound like a nagging old woman, but I do know what I'm talking about,' she said, her eyes on the photographs. 'Tom and I have lost Sue, but nothing can ever take away the memories we have. And, Daniel, I have a lifetime of memories.' She turned to Shepherd again. 'Tom and I were with her for every important event in her life when she was a child. I saw her take her first steps, heard her say her first words. I saw Tom teach her to ride her bike. I was there the first time she took her horse over a jump.'

'I get it, Moira.'

'Do you, Daniel? Are you sure? Because I want you to think about the memories you have of your son. It seems to me that at the moment most of them consist of you saying goodbye to Liam or apologising for being away.'

Shepherd didn't say anything. There wasn't anything he could say because, for the third time, he knew that his mother-in-law was right.

Paul Bradshaw was not a fan of sports but he enjoyed squash. It required fitness, but playing well depended as much on intellect as it did on the ability to run around the court. It was all about angles and strategy, about putting the ball in a place where your opponent couldn't reach it. It was like chess, and the really great players were the ones who could look several strokes ahead. Bradshaw wasn't a great player but he was the best at his university where he was captain of the team. Thursday night was practice night and as usual he played for a full three hours and never lost a game.

Bradshaw showered and changed, then went with his team to the student bar and drank pints of orange juice with lemonade as they downed lager. Bradshaw was a good Muslim and he never touched alcohol. It hadn't always been like that. As a teenager he had spent his evenings in the pubs of Bradford, drinking with his friends, talking about football, girls and television. As a soldier he'd been part of an even harder drinking culture, where a night on the town meant half a dozen pints of lager at least. But as a Muslim he allowed no alcohol to touch his lips.

He felt no great affection for his teammates but it was important to be seen as sociable. Loners attracted attention. So he laughed at their inane jokes and listened to their boring stories, and at just before ten o'clock he headed home. His bedsit was a short walk from the student bar but he used several routes and varied them at random. As he walked he checked reflections in windows and car mirrors and memorised the number-plates of vehicles that passed him. He used counter-surveillance as a matter of course, even though he had no reason to expect that anyone was following him. From the moment he had decided to embrace *jihad*, Bradshaw had acted as if he was on the Government's most-wanted list. He assumed he was under surveillance and that his every move was being watched, his every phone conversation listened to.

He saw the white Transit van heading down the road towards him and his eyes flicked to the numberplate.

He heard a rapid footfall behind him and glanced over his shoulder. It was a jogger in a university sweatshirt, an iPod clipped to the waistband of his shorts. Bradshaw turned back. The van had stopped and a man was getting out of the passenger side, a baseball cap pulled low over his face. Bradshaw frowned. There were no shops in the street, no reason for the van to be unloading. The man pulled open its side door then something hit Bradshaw hard on the back of his head. He stumbled forward and the man grabbed his arm. The jogger pushed him in the small of the back, a canvas bag was forced over his head and he was dragged into the van. The last thing he heard was the door being slammed and someone shouting, 'Drive, drive, drive!' He was punched on the chin and slid into unconsciousness.

When he came to, the vehicle had stopped and he was being pulled upright. His shoulder hit the side of the van. He tried to steady himself but his hands had been bound behind his back. The door rattled open and Bradshaw was dragged out and over a concrete floor, then forced down onto a hard chair. He heard a tearing sound and felt his legs being taped to the chair. His heart raced and he fought to stay calm. If they'd wanted to kill him, there was no point in binding him to a chair. They wanted to talk to him, which meant they had an agenda.

He heard the click-clack of a round being chambered. 'Your name is Paul Bradshaw,' said a voice. It was a question, not a statement.

'So you know my name.'

'We know a lot about you, Paul. More than you can imagine.'

Bradshaw couldn't place the accent. It was from the

north of England, but not Yorkshire. Not Manchester, either, but possibly from the Lancashire side of the Pennines. 'I'm an engineering student,' he said.

'We know who you are,' said the man. 'And we know what you are planning to do.'

'I am nobody,' said Bradshaw. 'You have me confused with someone else.'

'You're no Brazilian electrician,' said the man. 'You're a terrorist and no one's going to shed a tear if we put a bullet in your head. Now, who are you working with?'

'I'm an engineering student,' said Bradshaw, fighting to keep his voice steady. 'Is this because I'm a Muslim? Is that it? Who are you? The BNP?'

'It doesn't matter who we are. What matters is that you're a traitor to your own people. You're British but you're helping the bloody Arabs destroy our way of life.'

'You don't know what you're talking about,' said Bradshaw. 'I'm a Muslim, sure, but that doesn't mean I'm a suicide-bomber. I read the Koran, I pray to Allah, I try to live like a good Muslim.'

The man pushed the barrel of his gun to Bradshaw's forehead. 'We know it was you behind the Soho car bombs,' he hissed.

'So put me on trial,' said Bradshaw.

'We're not in the business of making martyrs,' said the man. 'You either co-operate or we end this now.'

'Then end it now,' said Bradshaw.

'Tell us who helped you with the car bomb.'

Bradshaw said nothing.

'Tell us who got you the Mercedes.'

'You have the wrong man. I'm an engineering student.'

'You met recently with a man called Hakeem.'

'I don't know anyone called Hakeem.'

'He's an al-Qaeda paymaster. He's funding you.'

'I don't know anyone called Hakeem,' Bradshaw repeated.

'You asked him for half a million pounds,' said the man. 'We know what you're planning to do. We know everything. All we need now are the names of your co-conspirators. Give us their names and we will give you a new identity, a new life. Tell us what you know and you will live. Stay silent and you will die. The choice is yours.'

'There is no choice,' said Bradshaw. 'Do what you have to do.'

Bradshaw felt a thump on the top of his head and the hood was ripped off. He blinked. Four figures were standing in front of him, all wearing ski masks, gloves and dark clothing. Only one was carrying a gun. The other three stood with their arms folded.

The man with the gun pointed it at Bradshaw's face. 'Last chance,' he said quietly.

Bradshaw glared at him defiantly. 'If it is the will of Allah that I die, then so be it,' he said.

The man's finger tightened on the trigger. 'After you're dead, we're going to cover you with pig's blood and bury you in the grounds of a synagogue,' he said. 'There'll be no place in Heaven for you.'

'I'm ready to die,' said Bradshaw. 'And no matter what you do to my body, my place in Heaven is secure. I die for *jihad* and there's no better way for a Muslim to die.'

'Tell us who you're working with,' said the man.

'*Allahu akbar*,' said Bradshaw. 'God is great.'

'I will shoot you.'

'*Allahu akbar*,' said Bradshaw, louder this time.

'I mean it.'

'*Allahu akbar!*'

'You're a dead man – a dead man!' shouted the gunman.

'*Allahu akbar!*' screamed Bradshaw, at the top of his voice.

The man pulled the trigger and the gun jerked in his hand. But there was no explosion, just a metallic click.

Bradshaw stared at the gun, gasping for breath, unable to believe what had happened. Had it misfired? '*Allahu akbar*,' he whispered. 'Allah has saved me.'

'Not Allah, my friend,' said the man on the gunman's right. He pulled off his ski mask and scratched his straggly beard. It was Hakeem. 'You saved yourself. By your words and your actions.'

Bradshaw sagged in the chair. 'You bastard.'

Hakeem nodded at the man with the gun. 'Untie him,' Hakeem said. The man tucked the weapon into his belt and knelt beside the chair. 'We had to test you, my friend,' Hakeem said, to Bradshaw.

'What did you think? That I wanted to steal your money?'

'You could have been MI5 or MI6, or an undercover policeman,' said Hakeem. 'They are sending agents to infiltrate us all the time.'

The third man went behind Bradshaw and used a penknife to cut the plastic tie around his wrists.

'And how do you know that I'm not an agent, that I just saw through your ruse?'

'You looked into the barrel of the gun as the trigger was pulled,' said Hakeem. 'You faced death and you praised Allah. No agent, not even a Muslim agent, could do that. A Muslim who works for MI6 is not a true Muslim. He would not be prepared to die for his salary.'

'And do you test everyone this way?' asked Bradshaw, massaging his wrists.

'Only the ones who ask me for half a million pounds,' said Hakeem. He patted Bradshaw's shoulder. 'I shall arrange for the finance that you need and I shall need a number to contact you.'

'I rarely use mobile phones,' said Bradshaw, 'and when I do, I change Sim cards every few days.'

The three men with Hakeem took off their masks. All were Asian. Bradshaw wondered which of them spoke with the Lancashire accent.

'So how do I reach you, other than by picking you up off the streets at night?' asked Hakeem.

'I'll give you a Yahoo email address and the password to access the account.'

'Sending emails is risky,' said Hakeem. 'The authorities screen them.'

'I don't send emails,' said Bradshaw, scornfully. 'If you want to contact me, you compose a message and leave it in the drafts folder. I'll log on to the account, read it and reply. The message is never sent so it can never be intercepted.'

Hakeem arched one eyebrow. 'You have undergone no formal training,' he said, 'yet your tradecraft is almost perfect.'

'Most of it is common sense,' said Bradshaw. 'The rest I learned from the Internet.' He dabbed at his bleeding lip.

'I am sorry for what happened tonight,' said Hakeem. Bradshaw held up the blood-spotted handkerchief.

'This?' he said. He sneered. 'This is nothing compared with the blood I'm about to shed.'

Shepherd arrived at Heathrow just as the sun was going down. It had been a tiring drive from Hereford and he stretched as he climbed out of his BMW in the long-term car park. He had kicked a football around with Liam before leaving Hereford, but the boy was obviously unhappy that he was going away again. Shepherd had made the usual promises about gifts on his return and spending time with him when he got back, but Liam had said it didn't matter. The apparent lack of concern was more hurtful than the times when Liam had cried and begged him not go. Shepherd couldn't tell whether his son was hiding his emotions or if he really didn't care that his father was going away again.

Liam would move in with Moira and Tom tomorrow and Katra was flying to Slovenia the following day. She had wanted to buy a one-way ticket because she didn't know when she'd be coming back, but Shepherd had insisted on paying and had bought her a business-class open return.

Button had booked him on a flight with EVA Air, a Taiwanese airline that went from Heathrow to Bangkok before flying on to Taipei. Jimmy Sharpe had gone with Thai Airways the previous day. Shepherd checked in, handing over a Samsonite suitcase, then spent forty-five minutes going through Security. He was carrying his tooth-paste and shaving foam in a clear plastic bag and removed his shoes and belt before going through the metal detector, but the machine still beeped. A surly Asian man patted him down roughly as if Shepherd was an inmate in a

Category A prison. 'Your watch – take it off,' said the man, pointing at the Breitling.

'No problem,' said Shepherd, removing it. He thought of telling the man that he could kill him in a dozen ways that wouldn't involve the watch but there was nothing to be gained by scoring points. The men and women who manned the security checks held all the power, and they knew it. His only option was to smile and comply. He went back to the X-ray machine, put his watch in a plastic tray and returned to the metal detector.

An old man was being helped from his wheelchair by an airline employee so that he could go through the arch. He was clearly frail and his hands were shaking, but the security personnel stood watching impassively. The man staggered through and his wheelchair followed. That was ridiculous, thought Shepherd. In no way could the old man be a threat to anyone. Nor could ninety-nine point nine per cent of the passengers queuing to go through the metal detector. But everyone was subjected to the same demeaning treatment by men and women who clearly enjoyed the power they wielded. Shepherd heard no 'please' or 'thank you' from the security staff, saw no smiles. There were just blank faces and barked instructions. If the aim of the terrorists who had laid siege to London was to undermine the basic rights and freedoms of the country's citizens, then at Heathrow airport they had already succeeded.

The second time he went through the metal detector it made no sound and Shepherd retrieved his carry-on bag, then headed for the lounge. He didn't like flying and he never had done. It wasn't that he was scared, more that he hated being packed into an aluminium tube with several hundred strangers for hours on end. He knew that all the experts said it was a bad idea to drink alcohol when flying but Shepherd had a double Jameson's and soda before he boarded and slept most of the way to Bangkok.

The airport terminal was clean and modern, all steel and glass, and its efficiency put Heathrow to shame. Shepherd was through Immigration in ten minutes with a thirty-day visa stamp in his John Westlake passport. His suitcase arrived in the cavernous baggage hall just fifteen minutes later. As he walked into the arrivals area, two young Thai men in dark suits holding clipboards asked him if he wanted a car. He saw that they had photographs of modern saloons, including a Mercedes and a BMW. Behind them a line of backpackers was waiting for public taxis and he decided to go for the luxury option. He was Ricky Knight, bank robber on the run, and he was entitled to do things with a little style. They asked him where he was going and Shepherd showed them an email confirming his booking at the Sandy Spring hotel in Pattaya. The two men had a rapid conversation in Thai, then one spoke into a two-way radio, and five minutes later Shepherd was in a Mercedes heading away from the airport on a six-lane motorway.

'First time to Thailand?' asked the driver, a man in his fifties with slicked-back hair. A Buddhist amulet and a garland of red and white flowers were dangling from the rear-view mirror.

'Sure is,' said Shepherd. He closed his eyes, not wanting to continue the conversation, and the driver took the hint.

After half an hour they left the motorway and powered along a four-lane concrete road flanked by rice fields and coconut-palm plantations. The farmland was dotted with factories, smoking chimney stacks, industrial units and container-storage yards. Most buildings flew the Thai flag, a red stripe top and bottom, with a blue one on a white background in the middle. There were huge billboards on scaffolding in some of the fields, advertising hospitals, condominium developments and cars. It wasn't pretty countryside. The ubiquitous palm trees were easy enough on the eye but it was clear that the land was a commodity to be built on and exploited. There was litter everywhere – plastic bags, chunks of blown tyres, discarded packaging materials.

Pattaya was a low-rise sprawl of shops, markets and billboards, the skyline strewn with sagging electricity wires strung between rough concrete pylons. The most modern buildings were banks, petrol stations and car showrooms. For the first time since he'd left the airport he saw Westerners, usually bare-chested, driving small motorcycles, sometimes with Thai girls riding pillion.

The biggest building was a white concrete tower topped with a cross in red, white and blue, and a large sign identifying it as Bangkok Hospital, Pattaya. They pulled up at red traffic-lights. In the central reservation there was a large circular photograph of the King of Thailand, a kindly-looking man with spectacles and an SLR camera with a long lens around his neck. The light turned green and the Mercedes made a right turn down a road lined with furniture shops, open-air restaurants and low-rise hotels and spas. There were more Westerners, shopping, eating and strolling around in swim suits and T-shirts. The city was starting to look more like a holiday resort, with gift shops, art shops and

Indian-tailor shops promising made-to-measure suits in twenty-four hours for less than a hundred dollars.

They drove past the Dusit Thani Resort and ahead was the sea. They reached the beach road and turned left. It was a one-way street, a narrow strip of sand covered with deck-chairs and umbrellas on the right, and on the left, bars, restaurants and shops with swimming rings and inflatable dolphins blowing in the breeze. Most of the signs were in English and Thai, but Shepherd saw plenty of Russian and Arabic, too. Strung across the street, Thai flags were interspersed with yellow pennants. The driver pointed down a street to their left. 'Hotel there but cannot go,' he said. 'One way.'

Shepherd saw a no-entry sign and the driver continued along the beach road and turned into the next side road. It was lined with bars, with names like Club Nevada, Lion Bar, Kittens Bar, and Hot and Cold A-go-go. In the middle, the Pattaya post office was decorated in the colours of the national flag. At the end of the street they turned left again, then made another left so that they were heading the right way down the one-way street. It was just after six o'clock when the car pulled up in front of the hotel and the sky was darkening. Night seemed to come quickly, as if a dimmer switch was being turned down.

The hotel was an uninspiring cube with a line of small trees in pots at the front. A uniformed bellboy took Shepherd's suitcase from the boot of the car and followed him inside. The lobby was functional but the four young women at the reception desk beamed at him. He gave them his John Westlake American Express card and signed for a week's stay. The bellboy took him up to the seventh floor and showed him into a suite with a sea view, and

Shepherd tipped him with a red hundred-baht note. He put his hands together as if in prayer and bowed, so Shepherd knew he'd over-tipped. The man left, closing the door behind him.

Shepherd stood at the window. There were dozens of boats in the water, and to the left of the bay two huge floating restaurants bedecked with white lights. The sky was grey now and the sea almost black. He walked around the suite. It was two separate rooms, one with a sofa, a dining-table, a television and a small kitchen area, with a full-size fridge; a door led to a shower room. The bedroom was the same size as the sitting room with another television, a wardrobe with a built-in safe and a bathroom. It was bigger than the first flat he and Sue had lived in, the year before they had married.

Shepherd's bedside phone rang and he answered it. 'Welcome to Pattaya,' said a gruff Geordie accent. 'Are you free for a wee chat?'

It was Bob Oswald. Button had said he was a surveillance expert and she was right. Shepherd had been in the hotel for less than ten minutes so he must have been outside watching for his arrival. 'Sure. Come on up.'

A few minutes later there was a soft knock on the door. Shepherd opened it to find a lanky man with sandy hair and a shock of freckles across his nose and cheeks. They shook hands. Oswald was holding a carrier-bag and he took out two cans of Heineken lager. 'Thought you might need some refreshment,' he said. 'It's a hell of a long flight.' He tossed one to Shepherd and opened the other as he sat down on the bed. 'Charlie's got me on a flight back to the UK tomorrow. I'd offer to take you for a run around the town but I guess we shouldn't be seen together.'

He reached into the bag and pulled out a bulky manila envelope. 'She wasn't sure how much cash you'd bring so she sent me five thousand pounds by Western Union. Three hundred thousand baht, give or take. Should tide you over for a while. She's getting the SOCA finance people to set you up an account with Bangkok Bank – they've got branches everywhere. She said she'll courier it to you at the hotel as soon as it's ready.' He opened his wallet and took out a small green Sim card. 'Thought you might need this,' he said. 'It's a pay-as-you-go and I've put a couple of thousand baht in it for you. You can get top-ups at any 7-Eleven.'

Shepherd thanked him. 'How long have you been here, Bob?' he asked.

'This trip, two weeks,' said Oswald, 'but I've been here four times in the past six months.'

'Always checking on the Moore brothers?'

'Mainly them, but Charlie's asked me to take a look at a few other faces as well.'

'Can't be easy,' said Shepherd. 'I reckon a lot of the guys out here wouldn't want cameras pointed in their direction.' He opened his suitcase and took out one of his spare mobile phones, then sat on the bed and inserted the new Sim card.

Oswald grinned. 'It's not been the easiest job I've had,' he said. 'The surveillance is simple enough, though, because it's not the sort of city where you stay home at night. And there's a fair amount of drugs and drink consumed. But those shots of them at the pool took me the best part of twenty-four hours. I had to crawl to some scrubland overlooking it at night and dig myself in, then lie there all morning. I got them in the afternoon but had to wait until dark before I could crawl back out. You don't want to hear about my toilet arrangements.'

'You're right, I don't,' said Shepherd. He switched on his phone and watched as it searched for a signal. It showed TH GSM on the display. 'Was it your idea to book me in here?'

'It's convenient,' said Oswald, 'and no one gives anyone a second look. It's known as being "guest friendly" and a lot of Bangkok-based expats stay here.'

'Guest friendly?'

Oswald chuckled. 'It means they don't care who the guests bring back at night,' he said. 'Some of the hotels charge a fee for girls who stay overnight and make them leave their ID cards at Reception.'

'I'm not here to fraternise with the locals,' said Shepherd. He sipped his lager, more to be sociable than because he wanted a drink.

'Didn't mean to imply that you were,' said Oswald. 'But Charlie said I should find you a place that fitted with the legend of a guy on the run who was in Pattaya for the first time, and this is the place. It was a toss-up between the Sandy Spring and the Dynasty next door but I'm in there so I said you'd be better here.' He reached into the carrier-bag again and this time brought out a glossy brochure and a business card, which he gave to Shepherd. 'This is an estate agency run by a guy who's a friend of the Moores, Dominic Windsor. He's totally legit but he has a few dodgy friends and acquaintances. I thought you could pay him a visit and get him to show you a few villas for rent. Find yourself a decent place, and he'll be sure to mention you to the Moores.'

'Thanks,' said Shepherd. 'Did he sell the Moores theirs?'

'Nah, they bought the land through a Thai lawyer and had their villas built for them. I'm told there are secret rooms and basements and an escape tunnel, but a lot of what you hear is total bullshit.'

'Charlie says they live in a compound, right?'

'There are half a dozen villas surrounded by a high wall. There's a hill that overlooks the compound, which is where I took the snaps. There are two gates in the wall and both are manned twenty-four hours a day by off-duty cops with guns.'

Shepherd's jaw dropped. 'What?'

'That's how it works out here. Jewellery shops and VIPs pay cops to act as guards.'

'Even though the Moores are armed robbers?'

'Money talks,' said Oswald. 'There's a lot of blind eyes turned in Pattaya. Counterfeit goods, hookers, drugs, child porn, it's all out there, and they don't even bother covering it up. It's a dangerous place, believe me.'

'Yeah, I've been told.'

'I'm serious,' said Oswald. 'I've been in some pretty rough neighbourhoods over the years but nothing compares with Pattaya. If something went wrong in that compound, they could do whatever they want with you and there'd be no repercussions. None at all. The cops would probably help them get rid of the body.'

'What goes on there?' asked Shepherd.

'Sex, drugs and rock and roll,' said Oswald. 'I've spoken to girls who've been to some wild parties and apparently anything goes. Cocaine, heroin, amphetamines, cannabis. Mark's a bit of an animal, from what I hear. Likes to slap the girls around. Mickey's more level-headed, but Mark's his little brother so he gives him a lot of leeway. Mark's got into a few fights and there's a few locals gunning for him.'

'What about around town?' asked Shepherd. 'Where do they hang out?'

'They're regulars around the strip,' said Oswald. 'It's called Walking Street, down by the beach. At night they block it off to traffic and it's the main bar area. There's a go-go bar called Angelwitch that they like, and another called Living Dolls. Restaurant-wise, there's a steak place on Second Road they go to several times a week.'

'They're a tight group, right?'

'They go out as a posse, pretty much, but they're fairly sociable. They're well known around town.'

'As criminals?'

'It's like the Costa here,' said Oswald. 'The bad guys get treated like rock stars. The bigger the crime, the more the glory. Every wannabe face you meet claims to be tied to one London criminal or another. If you believe half of what you hear then every man and his dog down here has done favours for Terry Adams or Frankie Fraser or got a piece of the Brink's Mat gold.'

Shepherd sipped his lager. He could never understand the adulation that high-profile criminals prompted in supposedly intelligent people. It was a phenomenon he'd experienced countless times while working under cover. If he was playing the part of a villain he'd be patted on the back by nightclub bouncers, club managers would send over bottles of champagne, and girls would throw themselves at him as if he was a Hollywood movie star. But Shepherd had seen first hand the damage criminals did. They killed, they maimed, they ruined lives, and they did it for money.

'What can you tell me about the other three guys in the crew? Barry Wilson, Davie Black and Andy Yates?'

'There's four,' said Oswald. 'Terry Norris.'

'Norris is in hospital, isn't he?' asked Shepherd.

Oswald raised his can in salute. 'You, sir, are on the ball. He got knocked off his bike last week. No helmet, slammed into a truck, lucky to be alive but he's never going to walk again. He was out with Chopper at the time.'

'Chopper?'

'Andy Yates. Chopper's his nickname. They both have a thing for Harleys. They used to race them around town all the time, drunk or sober. Barry Wilson is a whole different ball-game. Teetotal, and the only time you see him in the bars is when he's with the Moore brothers. Stays in most nights playing computer games. Davie Black is gay, so when he's not with the Moores he can usually be found in Boyztown. He does ride a motorbike, though.'

'Boyztown?'

'It's the gay-bar area, not far from Walking Street,' said Oswald. 'Gay go-go bars, mainly, and a few gay-friendly hotels.'

'You've followed them around town?'

'Not too closely, but almost everyone bar-hops so it wasn't too hard to keep track of them when they were out. I couldn't get pictures – they don't allow cameras inside the bars.' He drained his can and tossed it into the waste bin. 'What's your game plan to get in close?' he asked.

'I'll play it by ear,' said Shepherd. 'Flash a bit of cash, put myself about, and see how it goes.'

'Rather you than me,' said Oswald, taking another can

from the bag and popping the tab. 'You might think about Tony's Gym. They hang out there lifting weights and eyeing up the local talent three or four times a week. Afternoons usually. And there's a kickboxing camp they go to. It's called the Fairtex. Mark's a bit handy with his feet.'

'Charlie said you specialised in surveillance?'

Oswald grinned. 'She did, did she? Did she tell you I used to be paparazzi?'

'No, she didn't.'

'I was one of the best. Spent a year following Madonna, for my sins, before she settled down with that director chappie.'

'So how does a paparazzo end up working for SOCA?'

'Drugs,' he said. 'Not me, I hasten to add. I was spending so much time on the road that my daughter went off the rails. I was in Miami and she took an over-dose. Heroin.' He shook his head. 'Strictly speaking, it wasn't an overdose. The bastards who sold it to her cut it with something toxic and she nearly died. I flew back and got her to tell me who sold her the gear and then I went to the cops. They didn't give a shit. Told me they didn't have the resources to go after small-time dealers.'

'Drugs Squad?'

'Yeah, up in Leeds.' Oswald nodded. 'I spoke to some little prick who thought policing meant writing reports and giving presentations. Didn't want to get his hands dirty. So I spent three months staking out the bastard who'd sold heroin to my daughter, then went up the food chain, photographing them all. Photographed their customers, too, including quite a few showbiz people and football stars. Photographed the dealers going into the banks and building societies they used, the flats they owned and the cars they drove.'

'Then the cops took you seriously?'

'Fuck the cops,' said Oswald. 'I went to the *News of the World*. They ran it as the splash and three pages inside. Embarrassed the hell out of the chief constable. Local MPs asked questions in Parliament, and within a month the cops had done what they should have done in the first place – they arrested the lot of them, including the scumbag who sold the gear to my daughter. He got three years, which meant he only did eighteen months, but at least he's in the system now. And they went after his assets and took the lot.' He gulped some lager. 'It wasn't as satisfying as smashing his kneecaps with a baseball bat, but at least I did something.'

'And your daughter's okay?'

'Funnily enough, it worked out well. Scared the shit out of her. She hasn't touched drugs since. She's at university now, media studies. Wants to be a journalist. Anyway, after the pictures were in the paper I got a call from Charlie, and a month after that I was working for SOCA.'

'Not for the money, I presume,' said Shepherd.

'The pay's okay,' said Oswald, 'there's plenty of overtime, but you're right. There's no chance of making a killing like there is in showbiz. Get a picture of Britney's nipples and you're talking six figures.' He wiped his mouth on the back of his hand and tossed the can into the bin. 'While I think of it, don't be surprised if over the next few days people chuck water over you and wipe talcum powder across your face.'

'What?' said Shepherd, thrown by the change of subject.

'It's Thai New Year,' Oswald explained. 'It used to be

a sign of respect for people to pour water over the hands of their elders but it's become a free-for-all. All you can do is grin and bear it. In theory it should stop when the sun goes down but you can't bank on that. Keep your phone and wallet in a plastic bag and dress to be drenched.'

'Thanks for the heads-up,' said Shepherd.

'Anything else you need to know?'

'I think I'm good,' said Shepherd. 'How do I get around? I didn't see any taxis as I came in but there were pick-up trucks with seats in the back. What's the story with them?'

'They're called baht buses,' said Oswald. 'You'll see them everywhere. They charge ten baht but you have to go where they want to go. You pay the driver when you get off. Best bet, though, is to hire yourself a car. You can do it on a street, all cash, no questions asked.' Oswald stood up. 'Good to have met you, Spider,' he said. 'You could answer me one question before I go.'

'Go for it,' said Shepherd.

'Your nickname,' said Oswald. 'Why do they call you Spider?'

'I ate one once.'

'By mistake?'

'It was a bet. Well, a competition, really. In the jungle. To see who could eat the most repulsive thing. I ate a tarantula.'

Oswald pulled a face. 'Ugh. And you won?'

'Came second.'

'The guy who won, what did he eat?'

Shepherd laughed. 'You don't want to know.'

After Oswald had left, Shepherd showered. As he was towelling himself dry his UK mobile rang. It was Jimmy

Sharpe, on a Thai mobile. Shepherd said he'd call him back, picked up the phone with the Thai Sim card and dialled Sharpe's number. 'Settled in?' asked Sharpe.

'Just met with Oswald. He's heading back to the UK. Pity, because he'd be useful to have around.'

'How was your flight?' asked Sharpe.

'It was okay.'

'Did you fly business class?'

'Why?' asked Shepherd, warily.

'Because Button had me booked in economy and it was a bloody nightmare. I was stuck between a fat Thai woman and a human blob from Bolton who farted the whole way. I kid you not. The movies were shown on a TV screen on the ceiling. And the food was crap.'

'Sorry to hear that, Razor.'

'She hates me, you know.'

'She doesn't hate you.'

'She called me a dinosaur.'

'That was a year ago and it was in context. My flight wasn't brilliant, if you must know.'

'Really?'

'Yeah, Pinot Grigio wasn't chilled enough.' Shepherd grinned. 'We're here now, let's just get on with the job in hand.'

'Yeah, about that. Some tosser threw a bucket of water over me this morning – what the hell was that about?'

'It's Thai New Year.'

'Yeah, well, this tosser wasn't Thai. He was a Yank.'

'So what happened?'

'Like I said, he dumped a bucket of water over me while I was on my way to the supermarket to buy some beer.'

'I got that, Razor. I'm assuming there were re-percussions.'

'Damn right there were repercussions. I decked the twat.'

'Razor . . .'

'He provoked me. My phone died, Spider. Which meant I had to buy a new one and they're not cheap here. I don't see Button letting me have it on expenses, do you?'

'You hit him?'

'Flat on his back,' said Sharpe. 'He folded like a deck-chair.'

'You're supposed to be under cover – the last thing we need is for you to be hauled in by the local cops,' said Shepherd.

'Yes, Grandmother, and I suck eggs from the pointy end, right?'

'I give up,' said Shepherd. 'What hotel are you in?'

'It's called the Penthouse.'

'Sounds salubrious.'

'Well, it's not. It's right next to Boyztown, the gay area. There's all sorts of comings and goings. I think Button's put me in here as some sort of sick joke.'

'I don't think she'll have done the bookings herself, Razor.'

'Yeah, well, I wouldn't put it past her. Shall I pop around for a drink?'

'Best not show your face at the hotel,' said Shepherd. 'I'm supposed to be here on my own. I'll drop by tomorrow.'

'Not too early, I'm planning to hit a few bars.'

'Razor . . .'

'It's work,' said Sharpe. 'Ear-to-the-ground sort of stuff.

Testing the water. Seeing how the land lies. I can come up with clichés until the cows come home.'

Shepherd cut the connection. He switched on the TV and lay down on the bed. Virtually all of the cable shows were in Thai. There was a sports channel, and a movie channel seemed to be showing a pirate copy of *Rambo 2*. Despite the blurry picture and fuzzy sound he watched it but fell asleep long before Sylvester Stallone had saved the day.

The house was an unassuming two-up, two-down terrace in a side-street in Southall. Bradshaw took the Tube, then spent half an hour window-shopping to make sure he wasn't being followed before he took a circuitous route to his destination. He didn't see anyone who wasn't Asian. There were two youths with baseball caps pulled low over their faces leaning against a wall at the end of the road, and as he walked by one took out a mobile phone. A man was sitting in an old Mini parked several houses down from the one Bradshaw was visiting: he spoke into a hands-free microphone, his face turned away.

A waist-high wrought-iron gate, propped open with half a brick, led into a small garden, which had been paved over. Straggling weeds pushed their way up through the gaps between the slabs. Grubby lace curtains hung at the windows and the black paint was peeling off the front door. There was a plastic bell push to the right of the door, and Bradshaw pressed it with the knuckle of his right middle finger so as not to leave a print. From deep within the house he heard the rasp of a buzzer, then shuffling footsteps. An old woman, her skin the texture of chamois leather that had been left too long in the sun, opened the door and blinked at him from under a black headscarf. She did not seem surprised to see a Caucasian standing on her step. 'I'm expected,' he said.

She held the door open for him. She was as wide as she was tall and Bradshaw had to scrape against the wall to avoid touching her. To the left, stairs led up to the bedrooms, and doors to the right into cramped reception rooms. The woman closed the front door so hard that the walls shook. Bradshaw went into a kitchen where two men were sitting at a Formica table with cans of orange Fanta and two handguns in front of them. Like the watchers outside, they were wearing gloves and baseball caps with the peaks pulled down. They nodded at Bradshaw and he nodded back. He waited for the woman to tell him where to go. She pointed upstairs and grunted, then waddled off into the front room. Bradshaw could hear Arabic voices, a man and a woman arguing, and it took him a few seconds to realise it was soap opera. He went up the bare wooden stairs, his hand hovering over the banister.

There were three bedroom doors and only one was open. He walked slowly into the room. A man was sitting on a chair behind a circular glass table on chrome legs. A glass of water, an ashtray and a well-thumbed copy of the Koran lay on the surface. He was in his late fifties with a long grey and white beard and a brown skullcap perched on thinning hair. He was wearing a padded sleeve-less jacket over a heavy wool sweater and baggy cotton trousers that ended several inches above his ankles. He was holding a packet of tobacco and sprinkling some into a cigarette paper. 'Do you smoke?' he asked, as he rolled it into a cigarette.

'No,' said Bradshaw.

'Because you are scared of dying?' said the man. He chuckled, the sound of dead leaves rustling. He licked the edge of the paper with the tip of his tongue.

'If I was scared of dying, I wouldn't be here,' said Bradshaw.

The man waved his homemade cigarette at a chair by the window. 'Please, sit while we talk,' he said. 'I assume you are not scared of sitting.' He put a match to his cigarette while Bradshaw pulled the chair to the table and sat down.

'What is your name?' asked Bradshaw.

'My name is not important,' said the man. 'And I am not here to answer your questions.' He blew smoke at the ceiling.

'Why are you here, then?'

The man smiled, without warmth. 'That is a question, and I already told you that you are not my inquisitor. You have asked for funds. I am here to determine if you are worthy of such. Does it not say in the Koran that you cannot enter Heaven without being tested?'

'What it says is "Did ye think that ye would enter Heaven without Allah testing those of you who fought hard in His Cause and remained steadfast?" Being tested by God is one thing, being quizzed by a man is another.'

'You are a scholar of the Koran?'

'How can one call oneself a Muslim if one has not studied the Book of God?'

'So you would know the ninety-nine names of Allah and their meanings?'

Bradshaw sneered at the man. 'So, this is a quiz?'

'You do not wish to answer?' The man took a long drag on his cigarette, held the smoke deep in his lungs, then blew a cloud towards Bradshaw.

He folded his arms and fought the urge to cough. 'What do you think? That if I was a traitor I wouldn't know my Koran? Or that a white man can't be familiar with the teachings of Allah?'

The man said nothing but continued to stare at Bradshaw through the smoke with coal-black eyes.

Bradshaw sighed. 'Fine,' he said. One by one he went through the ninety-names of God, from Ar-Rahman, the All Beneficent, the Most Merciful in Essence, to Ar-Sabur, the Patient, the Timeless.

When he had finished, the man stabbed out the remains of his cigarette in the ashtray.

'Did I pass?' asked Bradshaw, scornfully.

The man dismissed the question with a languid wave. 'When did you begin studying the Koran?'

'I read it for the first time in Iraq. A friend gave it to me.'

'Reading and studying are not the same thing.'

'I read it, and my friend answered my questions. He set me on the path. When I came back to England I was tutored by an imam in Bradford, but I study the Koran every day as every good Muslim should.'

'Which mosque do you attend in London?'

'I pray at home and with close friends,' said Bradshaw. 'The mosques in London are no longer safe for the followers of *jihad*. They're filled with spies.' He leaned forward and stared intently at the man. 'These questions are a waste of my time and yours. I have proved myself already. You know what I've done and you know what I'm capable of doing.'

'You killed two people,' said the man, flatly.

'I set off car bombs in central London.'

'And where did you learn the technique of multiple explosions?' asked the man.

'That was common sense.'

'It is a tried and trusted technique.'

'Multiple bombs cause more casualties. You initiate an explosion to cause panic, to drive people towards a second, bigger, explosion. Or you delay the second to hit the emergency services once they have responded to the first.'

'But multiple bombs require substantial manpower. How many men do you have with you?'

They heard the squeak of footsteps on the stairs and both men stiffened. The man's hand disappeared inside his jacket and Bradshaw glimpsed the butt of a gun. Then they heard the woman saying she had tea for them. The man relaxed and his hand reappeared from inside his jacket.

The woman waddled into the room holding a brass tray on which was a glass jug of tea, two tall glasses and a bowl containing sugar lumps. They thanked her and waited until she had wheezed back down the stairs before continuing their conversation.

'For the car bombs I had four,' said Bradshaw.

'What were their roles?'

Bradshaw didn't understand the question. 'We worked together,' he said.

'But you were the leader?'

'Of course. I assigned two to drive and each had a companion to assist. I triggered the bombs.'

'Who designed them?'

'I did.'

'And you put together the components?'

Bradshaw nodded.

The man poured tea into the glasses, then pushed one towards Bradshaw. 'You learned these skills in the army?'

'I was a soldier and I've had some demolitions training,' he said. 'But I've been careful to disguise it. The car bombs were based on designs available on the Internet.'

The man dropped three cubes of sugar into his glass. 'When did you leave the army?'

'Three years ago.'

'Was anyone in your cell trained abroad?' asked the man.

'Two,' said Bradshaw. 'But they went prior to the July-seventh attacks and have not left the country since. Trips to Pakistan by British nationals are a red flag to the security services now.'

'Their names?'

'Jamal Kundi and Samil Chaudhry.'

'Before the car bombs, they did nothing else?' The man stirred his tea methodically.

'Their handler was killed by the police two years ago. I had met them and persuaded them to wait. To become sleepers.'

'They trusted you?' He dropped a fourth sugar cube into his tea as he watched Bradshaw's face closely.

'Obviously.'

'Even though they are older and more experienced than you?'

Bradshaw smiled. 'Before they met me their dream was to blow themselves to oblivion. I explained that a true fighter for Islam wants to fight, not die.'

'You are smarter than them? So they listen to you?'

'I am able to guide them, as Allah guides me.'

The man's eyes sparkled. 'So Allah guides you, does He?'

'We are all following the will of Allah, nothing else,' said Bradshaw, choosing his words carefully. 'Everything I do is at His behest. I'm thankful that He allows me to guide Jamal and Samil to serve Him better.'

'The fact that you are Caucasian, has that been a problem?'

'I am a Muslim, and that is all that matters. My brothers do not care about the colour of my skin, only that I am a good Muslim and a true follower of *jihad*.'

'And when did you first decide that you wanted to follow *jihad* and lead men like Jamal and Samil?'

'It was a slow process. A gradual realisation.'

'You were in Iraq, with the British Army?'

Bradshaw nodded.

'But you were not then a Muslim?'

'I was nothing. My parents were not religious and I had no idea of what Islam was. I just thought we were in Iraq to fight for democracy.'

'You knew about Islam, though?'

'I'm from Bradford, which is full of Asians, so I had grown up with Muslims and went to school with them, but I had no interest in their religion.'

'So what changed this?'

'I had an interpreter in Baghdad. He used to be an English teacher in an international school but after the Americans moved in there was no money to pay his wages so he began working as a translator.'

'His name?'

'Yusuf. He was a good man. He just wanted to be a teacher. But his country was turned upside down and he had to work for us to feed his family.'

'And what happened to him?'

Bradshaw narrowed his eyes. 'How do you know something happened to him?'

'I can tell from your voice. And because you said he *was* a good man. You didn't say he *is* a good man.'

Bradshaw smiled ruefully. 'Of course,' he said. 'Yusuf is dead.'

'And how did that happen?'

'You want to know why I am a Muslim?'

'I want to understand you,' said the man, 'because from understanding grows trust.'

'And you think Yusuf is the key?'

The man said nothing. He sat quietly and waited for Bradshaw to continue.

'Yusuf was killed by the Americans,' said Bradshaw, eventually. 'His wife was pregnant and the baby came early. There were no ambulances so he borrowed his uncle's car and they drove her. There was a roadblock about a mile from the hospital. American soldiers told him to stop and he slowed the car and shouted that his wife was giving birth but they kept yelling at him to stop the car and get out. Then they started shooting. They killed him. His wife took a bullet in the belly and the baby died.'

'You were there?'

Bradshaw shook his head. 'I heard about it afterwards. There was an inquiry but the Americans lied. They said that Yusuf was shouting at them in Arabic and refusing to obey instructions. But Yusuf spoke almost perfect English. There's no way he would have used Arabic with American soldiers. They killed him, they killed his kid and his wife's in a wheelchair but no one was even reprimanded.'

'And that made you angry?'

'You have no idea,' said Bradshaw. 'It opened my eyes to what was going on out there. Do you know what the rules of engagement were for the contractors – not the army, but the contractors? If an Iraqi car got too close to their convoy, they would fire a warning burst in front of it. If the car didn't back off, it was okay to shoot at it. Can you believe that? They could shoot to kill with no ramifications. And, believe me, they did. It was as if the Americans stopped treating the Iraqis as human beings. The contractors were getting rich while the Iraqi people were starving, yet they wouldn't even afford them basic human rights.'

'And because of that you became a Muslim?'

'Because of that I started to hate Americans,' said Bradshaw. 'I hated them for what they did to Iraq and for what they're trying to do to the rest of the world. But it was afterwards, after Yusuf was killed, that I began to read the Koran. To really read it, and then to understand. Islam is the true religion, the only religion, and Allah is the only God. And what is happening in Iraq and Afghanistan is about the West's determination to crush Islam and its followers.'

'So why the car bombs in London?' said the man. 'Why not turn your anger against the Americans? Why not bomb New York or Los Angeles?'

'Because it's not just about the Americans, is it? The British are as much to blame. It's not about countries fighting each other, it's about one system of belief trying to crush another. And if we don't fight back now, we won't get another chance.'

'We?' said the man, with an amused smile.

'I am a Muslim now,' said Bradshaw. 'I have chosen which side I'm standing with. And I will stand with the Muslims so long as Allah permits me to live.'

'But why attack your own country? That is what I find difficult to understand.'

'I'm not attacking the country. I'm attacking the system. I love my country but I hate what it has become and I want to do what is necessary to change it. When I got back to England, I started to see Muslims here for what they are, and to see the trials they now face. I started to see how the British hated Muslims and hated Islam. They put brothers and sisters in prison just for visiting Islamic websites. They banned the headscarf – they treated Muslims like they were the enemy. They broke in the doors of good Muslim homes, dragged fathers and sons away from their families and kept them in prison for weeks, then released them without so much as an apology. Mosques were desecrated, girls were spat at in the street because they dressed modestly. I saw the hatred that was directed towards Muslims and I knew I had to do something about it.'

'So what did you do?' asked the man.

'I read,' said Bradshaw. 'I read books, and then I went onto the Internet. I'd enrolled on an engineering course in London and I never used my own computer or computers at the university. I went to Internet cafés so I could not be tracked. And I studied the Koran in a way I had never looked at it before. Then I came across Sheik Abdullah Azzam's *Join the Caravan*. It opened my eyes to *jihad*.'

The man smiled. '*Ilhaq bi l-q filah*. It is a work that every Muslim should know by heart. You know the main reasons that Sheik Abdullah gave for *jihad*? There are eight.'

'I do,' said Bradshaw, coldly. 'Am I now to be tested on *Join the Caravan*? I didn't realise I was coming here to be tested on my memory.'

The man ignored Bradshaw's sarcasm. 'Of the eight reasons, which is the one that you most identified with?'

'There are two that inspired me,' said Bradshaw. 'That the disbelievers do not dominate, and establishing a solid foundation as a base for Islam. Both seem to me to be reason enough for *jihad*.'

'And when was your eureka moment? The moment when you saw that reading was not enough, that you had to take action.'

Bradshaw smiled, but his eyes remained flint-hard. 'It was Prince Harry, going to Afghanistan.'

'Ah,' said the man. 'That started the fire, did it?'

'It fanned the flames,' said Bradshaw. 'I couldn't believe that the British Government would allow a member of the Royal Family to prance and preen in the desert, as if Afghanistan was his personal sandpit. Do you remember the pictures? Prince Harry firing a machine-gun, playing around with a motorcycle, kicking a football with his soldier friends? As if he was on holiday, while all around him our brothers and sisters were suffering. And do you know what task he was given while he was in Afghanistan? Do you know what his duties were?'

'He was a forward air controller,' said the man.

'Exactly,' said Bradshaw. 'The controllers call in bombers and planes to attack, to bring death and destruction raining down on innocent civilians, on women and children, our brothers and sisters. That was my eureka moment, as you call it, the realisation that the Government and the Royal Family didn't care about our religion or our people. That was when I decided it was time to do something. That the time for reading and talking were over.'

'You know that his first choice was Iraq? He wanted to join the army of occupation.'

Bradshaw nodded enthusiastically. 'It was a slap in the face to all Muslims in the UK. But it showed us once and for all where the Establishment stood. Before that the public was happy to blame the invasion on Bush and Blair, but when they sent the prince to fight we saw the true face of the great British public. They supported him, which meant they supported the war, which meant they approved of the fight against Islam. That is why I decided I had to fight back.'

'Do you know why the casualties were not higher,' the man asked thoughtfully, 'when your two bombs exploded?'

Bradshaw had been expecting the question but the sudden change of subject took him by surprise. It was a tactic to wrong-foot him, but he knew he had no alternative other than to be truthful. He took a deep breath. 'It was the design of the bomb,' he said. 'I did not have access to high explosives. It was designed to start as a simple petrol fire, which would then cause the gas cylinders to explode. They would add to the shrapnel.'

'Because it is the shrapnel that does the damage?'

'Exactly. But in both cases only the petrol ignited. The cylinders remained intact.'

'So the design was flawed?' The man studied Bradshaw's face to see how he would react to the implied criticism.

Bradshaw didn't answer and returned the man's baleful stare.

'It is nothing to be ashamed of, brother,' said the man. 'You are on a learning curve. And you have achieved on your own far more than many of your brothers have, even those who have been through the training camps in Pakistan.'

'I want to do more.' His eyes burned with a fierce intensity. 'That is why I need the funding. With the money I can strike fear into their hearts like never before.'

'And when you were in the army, you were trained in the use of the equipment you are seeking to purchase?'

'No.'

The man frowned. 'Then who is going to operate it?'

'The two men who were in Pakistan have been fully trained.'

'Live fire?'

'Live fire,' repeated Bradshaw. 'They were trained in Pakistan but spent three months in Afghanistan. They were with a team that brought down an American helicopter.'

'And where do you plan to buy the equipment?'

'It is available in the former Yugoslavia, for a price.'

'You have a connection?'

'A man has promised me a connection. A former soldier I served with has a friend in the arms trade.'

'And you will travel there to make the purchase?'

'That is my intention,' said Bradshaw.

'You understand that if you lose the money we give you, there will be consequences?' said the man.

'I understand,' said Bradshaw. 'So when will I get the funds I seek?'

'When you have proved yourself.'

Bradshaw felt a flare of anger deep inside, but he quelled it and smiled good-naturedly. 'Have I not done that already?'

The man stood up and took off his jacket. 'You think what you have done is proof?' he said. 'It proves nothing.' He pulled off his sweater to reveal a chest pockmarked with irregular scars. 'This was a fragmentation grenade in Afghanistan,' he said. 'It killed two brothers, blinded a third, and it was only Allah's mercy that saved my life that day.' He removed the shirt and turned around. He raised his left arm. A chunk of muscle was missing just above the elbow, as if a dog had taken a bite, and the skin was puckered and wrinkled, like plastic that had come into contact with a naked flame. 'This was an American bullet from a machine-gun in Baghdad,' he said. 'Again, it was only Allah's mercy that kept me alive. That, and the three brothers who bound my arm and took me to a doctor.' The wound had healed but the scarring was horrific. The medical care he had received had been basic, to say the least. 'It is not pretty, is it?' said the man.

'No,' said Bradshaw.

'I am proud of this arm,' he said. 'It shows that I faced the enemy and I survived. What about you? Do you have any scars to show me?' He slipped on his shirt.

'No, I don't,' said Bradshaw. 'I was in the army but Allah in His benevolence kept me from harm.'

'Scars are proof, and you have no scars,' said the man. 'And it is proof that we need. Proof of who you are and proof of what you say you have done. Yes, two bombs exploded in London and, yes, you provided us with photographs of the bombs being constructed. But what do we really know about them? Do we really know that two people died?' He finished buttoning his shirt.

'It was on the television,' said Bradshaw.

'And do you believe everything you see on the television, brother?' asked the man, sitting down again. 'Do you think that the security services do not feed false information to the media? Did you believe it when the BBC told you Saddam had weapons of mass destruction?'

'The car bombs were real,' said Bradshaw.

'I am sure they were,' said the man. He sat down, picked up another cigarette paper and sprinkled tobacco onto it. 'But the bombs alone are not proof that you are a true soldier of Islam. It shows only that you had access to the bombs while they were being constructed.'

'You think I'm a spy?' said Bradshaw.

'Not a spy,' said the man. 'But a trap, perhaps. Bait, to lure in the true soldiers of Islam.'

'I'm an engineering student,' said Bradshaw. 'I used to be a soldier.'

'Yes, you said.'

'And now I am fighting for *jihad*,' said Bradshaw. '*Jihad* is my life.'

'That you must prove,' said the man. He lit the cigarette and took a deep pull on it.

'You think that MI5 set off two bombs in central London so that I could claim credit for it and get close to you? Is that what you really think?'

'You would be surprised what MI5 has tried,' said the man, flicking ash into the ashtray.

'Why would MI5 send someone white? Someone who has been in the army? On paper I'm the last person they'd send to infiltrate the Muslim fundamentalist movement.'

'It is not easy to persuade a true Muslim to spy on his own people,' said the man. He smiled. 'Perhaps you are a double bluff. Perhaps they think you are the last person we would trust, and therefore we would trust you. Who knows how they think?'

Bradshaw took a deep breath and interlinked his fingers. There was logic to the man's argument, and it was not of the sort that could be overruled by a raised voice or a display of anger. It was up to Bradshaw to prove himself worthy of the man's trust. He bowed his head. 'Tell me what you want done and, *inshallah*, I shall do it.' *Inshallah*. God willing. The phrase that all Muslims used to show that everything a mere human did was only accomplished because the all-powerful God permitted it.

The man put down his cigarette. He rested a hand on Bradshaw's shoulder and, in a low, hushed voice, spelled out slowly what he wanted him to do.

Shepherd woke, and for a few seconds he was disoriented. Hotel rooms were always the same, no matter where in the world they were. A bed, a dressing-table, a cupboard with a television on it and a fridge. The television was still on and this time it was Bruce Willis preparing to save the day. Pattaya. He was in Pattaya. He blinked the sleep from his eyes and squinted at the Breitling. It was three o'clock and beams of sunlight were lancing through the gaps in the curtains so Shepherd figured it was three o'clock in the afternoon, but then he realised he hadn't reset his watch to Thai time so he had to add six, which meant it was nine o'clock in the morning.

He rolled out of bed and padded to the bathroom to

shower and shave. Then he he pulled on a polo shirt and a pair of jeans. He opened the curtains. The sky was an unrelenting azure blue and the sun was blinding. Jet-skis with plumes of water spurting from the back sped across the bay. The floating restaurants he'd seen the previous night were still there, bobbing in the water amid dozens of smaller craft, motor-cruisers and sailing-boats. Half a dozen speedboats were zipping to and fro, towing parachutes behind them. On the hill overlooking the bay giant orange letters spelled out 'PATTAYA' and, in smaller white letters, 'CITY'. The view to his left was less inspiring, a patchwork of roofs and terraces with rusting metalwork and peeling paint, forests of television aerials and mobilephone masts, and clothes strung from lines, flapping in the wind blowing towards the sea.

His room looked down on the hotel's swimming-pool where already a dozen men were lying on loungers, their skin glistening with suntan lotion. They were all overweight and flabby, with almost no muscle tone. One was face down while a young Thai girl in a dark blue bikini gave him a massage. She had a large scorpion tattooed across her left shoulder. Her face was a blank mask as she stared into the middle distance, her fingers working on the man's back.

The hotel served breakfast in the lobby but Shepherd decided to go out for a walk to get the lie of the land. The bellboy who had carried his suitcase upstairs was on duty. He pulled the main door open for Shepherd and wished him a good morning. Shepherd headed down the road towards the beach. A group of Thai men in green vests were sitting on motorcycles, smoking hand-rolled cigarettes. Their skin was uniformly mahogany brown and leathery from years in the burning sun. 'Where you go?' asked one.

'For a walk,' said Shepherd.

'Too hot to walk,' said the man. His hair was jet black and spiky and he had a spider's-web tattoo on his neck that might have been done with a needle and a bottle of ink.

'I'm okay,' said Shepherd.

'We take you,' said the man, after a drag on his roll-up. 'Where you go?'

'What do you mean?' asked Shepherd.

The group laughed. 'We motorcycle taxi,' said a younger man. He had a thick gold chain around his neck from which hung three circular amulets. 'You pay us, we take you.'

Finally Shepherd understood. They were waiting for customers. A teenage girl with waist-length hair in a pale blue knee-length suit spoke to one of them in Thai and he kick-started his bike. She climbed on and sat side-saddle, her handbag in her lap, smiling sweetly at Shepherd as she sped off down the road. 'Later,' he said, and headed down the beach road. The side furthest from the sea was lined with stalls selling cheap clothing, counterfeit DVDs and tacky souvenirs. Two Thai toddlers giggled and squirted his legs with water pistols. Their mother spoke to him in Thai and she was smiling, so Shepherd smiled back. 'Happy new year,' she said.

Shepherd said, 'Happy new year,' back to her. It was a strange way to celebrate the new year but it was so hot that the water had been welcome.

As he crossed a side road, he saw three Jeeps parked by the kerb with 'FOR RENT' signs on the windscreens.

He walked up and looked at them. They were open-topped with wide wheels. One was black, another vivid red and the third metallic blue with 'Born To Rock' in silver across the bonnet. An old man with a huge mole on his nose was sitting at what appeared to be an old school desk. 'You want car?' he grunted.

'How much to rent the black one?'

A fat woman, her hair tied back with a metal bulldog clip, waddled over. 'One thousand baht, one day,' she said.

'What if I wanted it for a week?' asked Shepherd.

'One thousand baht one day. One week seven days, seven thousand baht.'

Shepherd smiled. 'What if I wanted it for a month?'

'Which month?'

'This month.'

'This month thirty days, one day one thousand baht, thirty days—'

Shepherd held up his hand to silence her. 'I get it,' he said. 'Thirty thousand baht.'

'You smart *farang*,' she said, then muttered to the old man at the desk. He chuckled, cleared his throat and spat greenish phlegm into the road.

'I'll come back with the money,' said Shepherd. 'Keep the black one for me, yeah?'

'You not want the blue one? Bigger engine.'

'I wasn't born to rock,' said Shepherd.

'I need your driving licence,' she said.

'I'll bring it with me,' promised Shepherd. He headed back to the Sandy Spring.

Next door to the hotel a bar called the Sportsman, with a blackboard outside, was touting its Mega-breakfast. Shepherd's stomach rumbled, reminding him that he hadn't eaten since he'd been on the plane, and he pushed open the door. Four waitresses sprang to attention. True to its name, the bar had three televisions, all showing different sports – rugby, cycling and tennis. Shepherd sat down at a circular table and ordered coffee and the special Mega-breakfast – double egg, double sausage, double bacon, bubble and squeak, baked beans, mushroom, tomato, black pudding, fried bread, toast and marmalade. Cholesterol on a plate, but it was exactly what he felt like eating.

The bar was dotted with horse brasses, and a rack of English newspapers stood by the door. There were only two other customers – a man in his sixties, who seemed to have fallen asleep over a copy of the *Sun*, and a middle-aged man in a running vest, who didn't look as if he'd done much running in the past decade or so. He had a beer belly as full as a late pregnancy hanging over his shorts as he played pool with a girl half his age at the far end of the room.

Shepherd sipped his coffee and half-heartedly watched the tennis. His food arrived on a huge rectangular plate. 'Enjoy your breakfast,' said the waitress, with a beaming smile. Already on the table there were bottles of Heinz tomato ketchup, HP brown sauce and malt vinegar. He tucked in with relish.

After he had finished, he paid his bill and went back to his hotel room. He was bathed in sweat so he showered again and changed into a shirt and a pair of shorts. He checked himself in the mirror and smiled at his reflection. It wasn't his style, but it was the sort of outfit that an armed robber on the run might wear. He put on his Ray-Bans. 'Perfect,' he said.

He took his John Westlake driving licence and a wad
of banknotes from the safe, put the estate agent's business card into the pocket of his shirt and went back
downstairs. The bellboy opened the door for him again
and gave him another bow. Shepherd headed back to the
beach road and along to the line of Jeeps. The fat woman
took his driving licence, slid it into the pack on her belt,
then counted the banknotes he'd given her. Shepherd
pointed at her pack. 'I'll need my licence back,' he said.

'No need,' she said, smiling broadly. 'I keep for when
you bring car back.'

'But if the police stop me, they'll want to see it.'

The woman's smile widened. 'Police no want to see
licence,' she said. She held up one of the banknotes. 'Police
want to see money,' she said, and cackled. 'One hundred
baht okay, maybe two hundred baht.' Two hundred baht
was less than three pounds, so Shepherd decided his
licence wasn't vital. The woman finished counting the
money, then recounted it, slipped it into her pack and
zipped it up. She said something to the man at the wooden
desk. He opened a drawer and took out a key on a chain
with a small plastic football. He gave it to Shepherd and
mumbled something in Thai.

'Sorry, I don't speak Thai,' Shepherd said.

The woman cackled again. 'He said if you lose, you
pay. If you crash, you pay.'

Shepherd shrugged. 'I'll be careful,' he said.

'Careful or not careful, you still pay,' said the woman.
The smile vanished, she turned her back on him and
began talking to the man in Thai.

Shepherd climbed into the Jeep and fired the engine.
He reversed back slowly, then joined the flow of traffic.

The baht buses that Oswald had told him about crawled along the kerb, looking for customers. Motorcycles buzzed around him, weaving in and out of the traffic. The Thais were on small Hondas or Yamahas, while the Westerners preferred bigger bikes, 1000cc Suzuki street bikes or throbbing Harley Davidsons. Most of the motorcyclists wore cheap plastic helmets and little in the way of protective clothing. Almost all the Thais had on flip-flops – Shepherd dreaded to think what would happen if they had an accident.

He kept his speed low and the Jeep in third gear. The side roads to his left were identified by numbers on blue circles; his hotel was in the one numbered thirteen. The office of the estate agent was in number seventeen. When he reached the turn, he indicated left and took a quick look over his left shoulder. The motorcyclists behind him seemed oblivious to the Jeep's flashing amber light and continued to overtake him on the inside. Shepherd slowed to a crawl as he made the turn. The street was lined with bars, and motorcycles were parked on the left all the was along, front wheels against the kerb. Shepherd drove slowly. Every third or fourth business was a bar and young girls sat in front of them, wearing short skirts and revealing tops. Many waved at him. 'Where you go, handsome man?' shouted one, and giggled.

'I want go with you!' shouted another.

Despite himself. Shepherd smiled. He could see how easily a man might come to believe his own publicity in a place like Pattaya.

The estate agent's office was between two bars, one flying the flag of Sweden, with banners offering free pool and free Wi-Fi connection, the other with the cross of

St George offering a full English breakfast and a pint of Chang beer for the bargain price of two hundred baht. It was a little after eleven but both bars had customers, middle-aged Westerners in T-shirts, shorts and flip-flops, nursing bottles of local beer and gazing blearily at the street.

Shepherd parked the Jeep behind a pick-up truck delivering plastic sacks of ice. He walked back to the estate agent's office, stepping off the pavement to allow an old man to pass: he was carrying a pole over his shoulder with two baskets hanging off it, one containing eggs, the other a metal stove filled with smoking charcoal. He smiled, showing blackened teeth. 'Eggs?' he asked hopefully.

Shepherd shook his head and turned to peer into the estate agent's window. Two dozen photographs of apartments and villas, each with a brief description of a property, were Blu-tacked to the glass. There were three desks in the office, occupied by petite Thai girls in pale blue suits. They were watching a television set in the corner, which seemed to be showing a Thai soap opera. One was munching a chocolate bar, another was using chopsticks to attack a bowl of noodles and the third was eating crisps. None looked up as Shepherd walked in. Leading off the office there was a smaller room in which a middle-aged Westerner in a yellow polo shirt and long khaki shorts was tapping away on a Hello Kitty calculator.

'Are you the boss?' Shepherd asked him.

The man stood up. 'For my sins,' he said. He had long hair slicked back, pale blue eyes, and the weathered skin of a man who spent a lot of time on boats. 'Dominic Windsor,' he said. 'My friends call me Dom.'

'John Westlake,' said Shepherd. They shook hands. Windsor had a gold chain on his left wrist, the thickness of a pencil, and another around his neck from which hung a small Buddhist figure.

'Can't place your accent,' said Windsor. 'Midlands, I'd guess.'

Shepherd smiled amiably. 'I've been moving around a lot,' he said.

'I'm from Norfolk,' said Windsor. 'A long way from home.' He waved Shepherd to the seat on the other side of his desk. 'Take a pew and tell me how I can help.'

Shepherd sat down and crossed his legs. 'I'm thinking of buying a place here,' he said.

'It gets in your blood, Thailand,' said Windsor. 'Every day I get a dozen guys from England wanting to sell up and settle here. The way England's going, who can blame them, huh?' He picked up a cheap ballpoint pen. 'What sort of budget do you have, Mr Westlake?'

'I want somewhere decent,' Shepherd said. 'Three or four bedrooms, pool, view of the sea, maybe. Watch the sun going down with a bottle of bubbly, know what I mean? And call me John. Whenever I hear "Mr Westlake" I think I'm back in court.'

Windsor raised his eyebrows. 'Are you a lawyer?'

Shepherd laughed. 'No, Dom, I'm definitely not a lawyer,' he said. 'Didn't get the A levels. So, here's the thing. I've got a place in Spain that cost me eight hundred thousand euros. Probably worth a million and a half now. I'd spend about the same here.'

Windsor's eyes sparkled. 'A million and a half euros?' he said. 'That's about seventy-five million baht. You could get a palace for that.'

'A villa will be just fine,' said Shepherd. 'I'd want secure parking for three cars, maybe four. And a decent security system would be a bonus, though I can always fit one myself.'

'Is privacy an issue?' asked Windsor, making a note on his pad.

'I don't want to be overlooked, but I've no problem with neighbours,' said Shepherd. 'So long as the place is secure. High walls for sure, and a decent electronic gate to keep out the riff-raff.'

Windsor continued to scribble. 'Do you have family, John?' he asked.

'Not here,' said Shepherd. 'I've an ex-wife back home but she won't be joining me.'

Windsor chuckled. 'Coals to Newcastle,' he said, 'bringing a girl out here. Why would you when there's so much on offer?' He gestured at the three in the office, who were still eating, their eyes glued to the television. 'See those little angels? All look like good little university girls, don't they? Wouldn't say boo to a goose.' He grinned. 'Wrong,' he said. 'They all used to work in a soapy massage place on Second Road. I hired them as eye-candy but they've taken to property like the proverbial ducks.' His grin widened. 'I'll let you into a little secret, John. We have a bonus scheme here. Every guy who buys a property from me gets a free blow-job from one of the girls. How about that? Is that a deal or what?'

Shepherd wasn't sure if he was joking.

'Mind you, if you buy a seventy-five-million-baht villa from me I'll let you have all three,' added Windsor, and Shepherd realised he was serious.

Windsor stood up and went over to a filing cabinet.

'I have to say, John, that right at the moment I don't have anything over forty million, but the ones I have are as luxurious as you'll get in Pattaya.' He flicked through the cabinet and pulled out several brochures. 'Why don't you have a look at what I've got on my books and I'll make a few phone calls, see what else I can drum up?'

'Sounds good to me,' said Shepherd. 'Can you show me a few rental places as well? I'm not happy staying in hotels – I like my privacy.'

'Don't we all?' said Windsor. He winked and carried on sifting through the files.

Sweat dripped down Shepherd's face and he wiped his brow on his shirt sleeve. They were standing at either end of a swimming-pool to the rear of a three-bedroom villa. 'Is it always this hot?' he asked Windsor. The estate agent was at the far end of the pool, looking towards the sea.

'I'm afraid so, but it's cooler in the evenings and the mornings. If you wanted to get some swimming in, that's when you'd do it.'

'I'm more of a runner than a swimmer,' said Shepherd.

'I wouldn't want to run in this climate,' said Windsor. 'A few guys jog along the beach road in the mornings and evenings but you should see the state of them. Take it from the Thais – you never see them running if they can avoid it.' He pointed to the sea. 'The great thing about this place is the view, plus you're up the hill so you get a breeze.'

'But too far to walk into town,' said Shepherd.

'You've got your privacy, though. And no noisy neighbours with pool parties in the early hours.'

'What about the seller?' asked Shepherd.

'Guy in his late sixties. Used to be a teacher in Birmingham, cashed in part of his pension to build this place and lived off the rest. Had more sex in the five years he was here than he'd had his whole life.'

'So why's he selling?'

'He got sick,' said Windsor. He tapped his chest. 'Dicky ticker. Insurance wouldn't cover his treatment because they said it was a pre-existing condition so he's back in Blighty, being treated on the NHS.'

'And how much does he want for this?'

'Oh, it's well below your price range. Four million baht is all he wants. You're right, the location's against it, but if you wanted to rent for a few months, I'm sure we could get you a deal. Thirty thousand baht a month, maybe?'

Shepherd went back inside the villa. It was small and not particularly well built. The furniture was cheap, there were cracks in the plasterwork and the tiled floor was uneven. Windsor followed him. 'I've got to be honest, Dom. I want better than this.'

The estate agent nodded. 'Not a problem,' he said. 'It's just I know I can get a good deal for you on it because the guy's desperate to sell.'

'I don't want a good deal. I want bigger and I want better,' said Shepherd. 'I want a big pool, and I want a bit of land. Trees, coconuts, bananas – you know what I mean. And I want to be closer to the action than this place is.'

'Heard and understood, John,' said Windsor. 'On the rental side, how much could you run to?'

'Five grand a month. Six. To be honest, cash isn't a problem.'

'The reason I ask is that I do have something a little

special. The owner lives in Singapore and he only comes out a few times a year. I know he doesn't have a trip planned for a few months and he rents it out from time to time. I think if you could run to half a million baht a month I could probably swing it.'

'That's about eight grand?'

'Give or take,' said Windsor.

'Let's have a butcher's, then,' said Shepherd.

They went out through the front door and climbed into Windsor's Toyota. Like the limousine that had driven Shepherd from the airport, a Buddhist amulet swung from the rear-view mirror. As Windsor started the engine, Shepherd asked him about the amulet.

'It's the wife,' said Windsor. 'The monks came to bless the car and said we should have this fellow to look after us.' He gestured at white fingermarks on the roof above his head, dotted with gold leaf. 'They did that too. Seems to have done the trick because we haven't had a scratch in three years.'

Windsor drove back to the city. He was careful, rarely getting into fourth gear, and his eyes were constantly flicking between his rear-view and wing mirrors. Shepherd guessed it was the way he drove rather than divine intervention that had kept his car in such pristine condition. Every time they went over a bump or a pothole Windsor reached up with his left hand to steady the amulet.

The second villa was a thirty-minute drive from the first, on an estate surrounded by a high wall. A uniformed guard saluted them as they drove in. There were just ten homes on the estate, around a large man-made pool surrounded by palm trees. Each was encircled by its own wall with its own gated entrance, and trees had been planted around the perimeter of each plot giving it complete privacy.

'This is more like it,' said Shepherd. CCTV cameras covered the entrances to the villas and several bore signs in Thai and English, announcing that they were protected by private security firms.

'The security is first class,' said Windsor. 'The guys at the main entrance screen all visitors, and if there's someone you don't want to see, they'll turn them away. If you want, you can arrange your own security for the villa. A guard at the gate will cost you about five hundred baht a day for a twelve-hour shift. The one I'm showing you has full electronic security. Flip the glove-box, will you, and press the bleeper thing to open the gates?'

Shepherd found the remote control and clicked it. A large metal gate rolled back to reveal a well-tended garden with dozens of mature palms. The driveway curved in front of a large single-storey villa with a Thai-style pitched roof trimmed with teak and a garage with three doors. Windsor pulled up in front of it. Behind them, the metal gate rattled shut.

Shepherd climbed out of the car. The villa was quite secluded, the walls were high and, from where he was standing, he couldn't see any of the others on the estate. 'Who looks after the place?' he asked.

'There's a gardener who comes in every day. He does the pool, too. His wife works as a full-time maid when the owner's here, but when he isn't she comes in every few days to air the place. If you wanted her services, a couple of hundred baht a day would do it. She cooks, too.'

'I'm happier on my own,' said Shepherd.

The estate agent took a set of keys from his pocket. 'Let me show you around. This is something special, I can assure you.' He opened the door and a burglar alarm beeped. There was a console halfway down the hallway and he walked over to it, then tapped out four digits. The beeping stopped. They were standing in a hallway with high ceilings and a marble floor. There was an ornate mirror opposite the alarm console and under it a waist-high marble table. 'The owner likes Italian things and he imported a lot,' said Windsor. 'It's not to everyone's taste, but it's all amazingly expensive.'

The hallway ran left to right and there were ornate teaks doors at either end that looked as if they were more than a hundred years old. Windsor opened one. 'The design is quite clever,' he said. 'This way leads to the bedrooms. The master is huge but the other three are almost as big. And there's a smaller one, if you ever want a live-in member of staff. Each has its own bathroom, and french windows leading to the pool area.' He pointed to the other door. 'That takes you to the sitting room, the study and the games room.'

Windsor ushered Shepherd down the corridor to the last bedroom. It was three times the size of his hotel suite, with a massive bed and glass doors looking on to a magnificent pool. On the far side he could see into the main sitting room. Next to it was a room with a pool table and a big plasma screen. The villa was effectively a huge horseshoe shape built around the swimming-pool. For the next fifteen minutes Windsor took Shepherd around the villa, showing off all its features as if it were his own home.

The owner clearly had more money than taste. The

furniture was all modern Italian with sleek lines and stainless-steel legs but not at all comfortable. There was a dining-table big enough for sixteen but the chairs were straight-backed and so narrow that sitting on them for more than a few minutes would be painful in the extreme. The lighting system was computer-controlled, with automatic settings depending on the owner's mood, which apparently varied from daytime reading to watching television to what Windsor referred to coyly as 'a romantic evening with the ladies'. The villa appeared to have been designed for a photo spread in a lifestyle magazine rather than for living in, but Shepherd knew it was perfect for a villain like Ricky Knight, a man with little taste but money to burn.

'I'll take it,' he said.

'I knew you'd like it,' said Windsor. 'It's got your name written all over it.'

'I'll rent it for now, but I want you to find me something as good to buy. Or we can talk about getting one built.'

'I'll need two months' deposit and a month in advance, so that's a million and a half baht.'

Shepherd pulled out his wallet. 'It might take me a day or two to get it here,' he said, and counted out twenty one-thousand-baht notes. 'Have this on account.'

The estate agent pocketed it. 'I'll draw up the contract tonight, and as soon as you send me the money, you can move in.'

Shepherd smiled to himself as, at the far end of the pool, water trickled down a rock wall into which had been set small pots of orchids. There was a stone statue of a crouching tiger at the top, its head up in a snarl. Shepherd could imagine the same look on Charlotte Button's face when he told her what his new accommodation was going to cost.

Bradshaw was the last to arrive. He had worked a clock-wise circuit of the park, then stopped for a drink at the outdoor café by the children's play area to satisfy himself that he wasn't being followed. From his table he had seen al-Sayed arrive at the Rose Garden, five minutes after Bradshaw had said he should be there. Al-Sayed was a good Muslim and cool under pressure, but his time-keeping was a constant source of annoyance. Bradshaw had spoken to al-Sayed twice about it, and the other man had been apologetic, but nothing had changed. It was not a trivial issue: being five minutes late for a meeting mattered little, but for what Bradshaw was planning timing would be crucial and the difference between success and failure might be just seconds.

As he approached the bench, the four men looked up expectantly. 'Did he say yes?' asked al-Sayed. He moved to the side to make room for Bradshaw.

'The money's coming, but we've been given a task,' he said.

'What sort of task?' asked al-Sayed, eagerly.

'If you listen, I'll tell you,' said Bradshaw.

'It is *jihad*?' asked Talwar. He was shaking with antici-pation and pushed his glasses higher up his nose with the middle finger of his right hand.

'Oh, yes,' said Bradshaw. 'It's *jihad*.'

'*Allahu akbar*,' said Talwar.

'*Allahu akbar*,' echoed the others.

'God is great,' said Bradshaw. 'God is great and we

are His servants. Now, listen as I tell you what we have
to do.'

As soon as he got back to the Sandy Spring, Shepherd
phoned Button and told her about the villa. 'That's more
than we budgeted for,' she said archly.

'It fits with the legend,' said Shepherd.

'How many bedrooms?'

'Four or five.'

'Why on earth would you need that many?'

'It's not about the number, it's about style. It's about
showing that I've got money and that I'm prepared to throw
it about. I could get a one-bedroom flat in a tower block but
if I did that the brothers aren't going to take me seriously.'

Button sighed. 'You're right, of course. So, how much
will you need?'

'It's five hundred thousand baht a month and I've
agreed to a six-month lease. One month's rent in advance
plus two months as a deposit so the agent wants one and
a half million up front. That's a shade under thirty thousand pounds in real money.'

'This had better be worth it,' said Button. 'I think
SOCA's got more accountants than investigators and
they're all keen to justify their salaries.'

'Can you transfer the money today?'

'I'll do it now,' she said. 'We've already FedExed the bank
paperwork to you. You should get it tomorrow. All you have
to do is go into the main Pattaya branch with your Westlake
passport, give them your signature and you're sorted. We've
fixed up a cash-machine card and a Bangkok Bank credit
card. Any other expenses I should know about?'

'I'm going to fix up a gym membership. There's a deal

at the moment, lifetime membership for just under twenty thousand baht.'

'Lifetime membership? If all goes to plan you'll be back within the month.'

'I've got to look like I'm serious about staying here.'

'Anything else?'

'I've rented a Jeep. I'll probably rent a Harley, too.'

'Just make sure you keep receipts for all this,' said Button.

'I'm not on holiday,' said Shepherd. 'Trust me, if I was, Pattaya would be the last place I'd choose.'

'Is it grim?'

'Let's just say I've seen more beer guts, ponytails and tattoos in the last twenty-four hours than ever before.' He ended the call and showered. It was only just getting dark outside but the jet-lag was kicking in and he felt exhausted. He switched on the television and lay on his bed. It was Stallone, again, grunting and killing. Shepherd couldn't tell if it was the same *Rambo* movie he'd watched the previous night, but even if it wasn't he was still asleep within minutes.

Mark Moore looked around the crowded discothèque. It was just after midnight and it was already almost full to capacity. He grinned at his brother. 'No point in us all fighting our way to the bar,' he said. 'You guys stay here, I'll get the beers in.' Mickey patted him on the back and went to talk to Wilson and Yates, who had managed to find a space by the wall. They were in a glorified pick-up joint on Walking Street. Half the women were bargirls who had already been with a customer or were on their day off, or freelancers hoping to strike it lucky with a tourist.

Most of the men were Westerners looking to pick up a girl without having to pay for sex – but they all expected payment in one form or another

Mark eased his way through the crowd to the bar and ordered four Singha beers from the obviously gay barman. He had to shout to make himself heard above the thumping beat from the sound system. Two young girls were standing to his right and smiled at him.

'How are you doing?' asked Mark.

'Fine,' said the prettier of the two. 'Where are you from?'

'England.'

The girl spoke to her companion in Thai and they giggled. The barman returned with Mark's beers and placed the bottles on the bar. As Mark reached into his pocket for his wallet, a large man in a tight T-shirt and baggy shorts pushed between him and the girls and began talking to them.

Mark paid the barman, and as he waited for his change, he leaned around the man and winked at the pretty girl. The man shifted to block her, banging into Mark's shoulder as two others moved in behind the girls, circling them like wolves. The barman gave Mark his change and a smile. Mark picked up one of the beers, took a swig and leaned back to catch the girl's eye again. The man sensed what he was doing and stepped back, knocking Mark's hand. The bottle fizzed and beer dribbled over his fingers. Mark tapped on the man's shoulder but he ignored him. Mark tapped again, harder, and the man turned. 'What do you want?' he snarled. He was Australian, square-faced, with a nose that had been broken and badly reset.

'Just be careful, pal,' said Mark. 'You've banged into

me twice already.' He held up his bottle of Singha. 'And you spilled my beer.'

The Australian was a good four inches taller than Mark and bent down to glare at him. 'Listen, mate, just get on with whatever you're doing and leave me alone,' he snapped.

Mark smiled amiably. 'Excuse me?' he said.

'Yeah, fucking excuse you,' said the Australian. He prodded Mark in the chest. 'Mate, I'm your worst fucking nightmare. You give me an excuse and I'll kick the living shit out of you.' He turned back to his two friends. They were just as tall and muscular. All three men were wearing tight T-shirts to show off their biceps and chests. They laughed and clinked their bottles together. They had the thick necks and overdeveloped muscles that came from long-term steroid use, not exercise. Mark had muscles but they were in proportion and the result of long, hard training sessions. He wasn't in the least bit fazed by the size of the men. He knew that, when it came to a fight, technique and stamina counted, not bulk. Mark looked at his brother to check that he'd seen what was going on. Mickey winked and gave him a thumbs-up. Mark put his beer bottle on the bar and tapped on the Australian's shoulder again.

'I bloody well warned you—'

Mark drove his right elbow up in an arc, catching the Australian under the chin. As he staggered back, Mark grabbed his shoulders and slammed his knee into the man's stomach. The Australian bent forward, gasping for breath, and Mark punched the side of his head, twisting his fist so that it ground into the skin. Then he stepped back, hands up, ready to move, but there was no fight left in the Australian. He dropped to his knees and looked up at Mark quizzically. Mark kicked him in the side of the head and he toppled over, unconscious.

One of the Australian's friends stepped forward, grabbed the neck of his Singha bottle and swung. Mark blocked the blow with his left hand, then punched the man in the neck. The bottle tumbled from his hand and he staggered against the bar, clutching his throat.

The third man threw a punch at Mark's head but he was slow and Mark had all the time in the world to tilt his body to the side and watch the fist go by. He punched him in the sternum three times, left, right, left, and put all his weight behind the last blow so the man moved a full two feet backwards before slumping to the floor at the feet of the pretty girl who had smiled at Mark earlier. Now she was staring at him with horror.

Three Thai men in black T-shirts with 'SECURITY' on the front and back raced across the dance-floor, pushing customers out of the way. They were all off-duty policemen so Mark raised his hands to show that he wasn't a threat. 'They started it,' he said laconically.

The tallest man put a hand on his shoulder. 'Khun Mark, you are always getting into trouble,' he said. His name was Sombat and he was a traffic cop, usually based near the airport. He also trained at the kickboxing gym where Mark spent much of his spare time.

Mark lowered his hands. 'Really, Sombat, I was just minding my own business.'

'I've told you, Khun Mark, if you want to fight, take them outside. My boss hates it when there are fights inside. It's bad for business.'

'I'll remember, Sombat.'

Mickey appeared at Mark's shoulder and nodded at the security men. 'How's it going, guys?' he said.

'It would be good if you went now and didn't come back for a day or two,' said Sombat, smiling.

'Understood,' said Mickey. He shook hands with Sombat, and slipped him a thousand-baht note. The money disappeared into the back pocket of the Thai's jeans.

Mark put his arm around his brother and they walked outside. 'The thing I don't get is why big guys get verbal,' said Mark. 'If I'm not intimidated by his size, why does he think lines from a bad movie are gonna make me shit my pants?'

'Beats me,' said Mickey.

'Did you see the way I used the elbow?'

'Classy.'

'I think I broke his jaw.' Mark licked his grazed knuckles. 'He'll be on liquids for months.' He butted his head gently against his brother's. 'Come on, where to next?'

Mark pointed at a sign for the Angelwitch go-go bar. 'I want to see some naked women.'

The brothers walked down a narrow alley, past food stalls and tables covered with cheap plastic cloths, threading their way though sweating waitresses hurrying around with trays of food. Wilson and Yates followed. They passed tanks filled with live fish, prawns and crabs, and woks flaring over flames. Several touts tried to persuade them to go inside their bars but the brothers brushed by and continued down the alley to Angelwitch.

A big Thai man pulled back a red curtain and they walked inside. The bar had a double-height ceiling with chrome poles stretching from an oval dance-floor to the roof. Heavy-metal music was pounding from large speakers, and on the stage more than a dozen young girls were gyrating, all in black outfits, draped with chrome chains, boots and fishnet stockings. Around the stage, tiers of red vinyl seats were filled with mainly middle-aged Westerners. The *mama-san*, a woman in her fifties with her hair tied back in a bun, showed the Moores to a row of empty seats, and two pretty young waitresses in black scurried over to take their order.

One of the dancers waved at Mark and blew him a kiss with a lace-gloved hand. He waved back. 'What's her name?' he asked Wilson.

'Nit or Noy, something like that.'

'Great tits,' said Mark. 'I've been with her, right?'

Mickey slapped him on the back. 'You've been with them all, mate.'

A customer in front of Mickey handed a waitress a five-hundred-baht note in exchange for a bucket of ping-pong balls. The girls on the dance-floor screamed as he started throwing them – each ball they retrieved was worth twenty baht. One girl gathered up half a dozen and held them in the air triumphantly.

A man appeared at the end of their row, holding a bottle of Heineken. He raised it in salute. It was Dominic Windsor. 'Hi, lads,' he said. He saw Mark licking his knuckles. 'Been winning friends and influencing people?'

'Just one of those nights, Dom,' said Mark. He shuffled along to make space next to him. 'Come on, sit down and get an eyeful of the talent.'

The estate agent dropped onto the seat and sipped his beer.

'How's business?' asked Mickey.

'Swings and roundabouts,' said Windsor. 'The strong baht isn't helping. And there's so much new stuff coming on stream that the second-hand market's dead.'

'You should try London, mate,' said Mickey. 'Russian and Arab money's pouring in. Most of it in bloody suit-cases.'

'Yeah, but he wouldn't get laid in London, would he?' laughed Mark. He put an arm around Windsor, pulled him close and kissed his cheek.

'Had one guy with money to burn,' said Windsor. 'Have you come across him? John Westlake. Wants to spend a mill or so on a villa. I'm renting him that place I showed you when you first came out here, the one on the estate.'

'What's he paying?' asked Mark.

'I got half a million baht a month.' He raised his bottle. 'Who's a clever boy, then?'

'You were only asking four hundred thousand when you showed it to us,' said Mickey.

'Yeah, he's only just off the plane, seemed a shame not to take advantage.'

'You're a bastard, Dom.' Mickey laughed.

'He's an estate agent,' said Mark. 'All estate agents are bastards.'

'Leave it out, guys,' said Windsor. 'I'm just trying to make a living. He seems okay. He made some crack about court that made me think he might have done time.'

'Oh, a guy's been to prison and you think we'd know him?' said Mark. 'What are you getting at?'

'I was just saying, he'll be here for a while so your paths might cross, that's all,' said Windsor.

'What's he do for a living?' asked Mickey.

'He didn't tell me,' said Windsor. 'But one thing's for sure, the guy's loaded.'

The lights in the bar dimmed and two girls with long, dyed-blonde hair, in black leather domination gear, appeared on a gantry near the ceiling. Spotlights picked them out and they slid gracefully down the poles to the dance-floor.

'You've got to see this, Dom. It's the new show,' said Mark. 'Bloody brilliant.' He leaned forward as one of the girls knelt on all fours and the other girl raised her whip. 'Go for it, girls.'

Shepherd woke to the sound of his bedside phone ringing. He groped for the receiver as he squinted at his wristwatch. It was ten o'clock in the morning. A girl at reception told him that a FedEx courier was downstairs with a package for him. Shepherd told her to send him up and grabbed his trousers. A few minutes later his doorbell rang and a middle-aged man in a FedEx polo shirt and baseball cap handed him a large envelope. Shepherd signed for it and tipped him a hundred baht. He closed the door, sat on his bed and opened it. Inside, a computerised bank statement showed that John Westlake had an account with the Bangkok Bank containing three million baht. There was also a letter of introduction to the manager of the Pattaya branch.

Shepherd showered and changed into a clean shirt and shorts, then phoned Jimmy Sharpe.

He answered with a groan. 'This better be important, I've got one hell of a hangover.'

'I've got to visit the bank, then I thought I'd pop around for a chat,' said Shepherd. 'Where's your hotel?'

'I'm three roads up from yours, heading towards

Walking Street. Come down the beach road with the sea on your right, you can't miss it. Just look for a street full of go-go bars, massage parlours and poofter prostitutes. I'm in room five two six.'

Before Shepherd could say anything, the line was dead. He picked up the FedEx envelope and went downstairs. He asked the motorcycle taxi drivers at the end of his road if they knew where the Bangkok Bank was and they said they'd take him for fifty baht. He climbed on the back of a Honda and the driver roared off. They wove through the traffic on the beach road, and as they made a left turn a small girl threw a bucket of water at them, screeching with laughter. The driver almost lost control of the bike and braked unsteadily. The child jumped up and down and shouted something at them.

Shepherd wiped the water from his eyes. 'What did she say?' he asked.

'Happy new year,' said the driver, and chuckled. '*Sawasdee pee mai.*'

Shepherd was soaking. He held the FedEx envelope to the side and shook it. The driver accelerated and drove in the middle of the road, moving to the side only when oncoming traffic was heading straight for them. At almost every street corner Thai families were standing next to huge blue plastic barrels of water, which they used to replenish their buckets and water pistols. They were all wet and many had white powder streaked across their faces and chests. Most of the men doing the water-throwing seemed drunk, even though it wasn't yet midday. Tourists were joining in the festivities, and several times they passed groups of Westerners in T-shirts and shorts firing huge water pistols at anything that moved.

The motorcyclist dropped Shepherd in front of a large concrete building. As soon as he went inside, the air-conditioning chilled his wet clothes and he shivered as he waited to be served. A pretty girl in a grey suit, her hair tied back with a pink and white ribbon, read his letter, then disappeared into an inner office with it and his passport. She reappeared a few minutes later with a file and handed him an ATM card with 'John Westlake' on it, a Bangkok Bank Visa card, a cheque book, and a statement showing how much he had in his account. Three million baht. She asked him if there was anything else he needed and he smiled and said just dry clothes. She laughed and told him that the worst of the celebrations were yet to come: the holiday only started in earnest later in the week when the banks and most of the country's businesses were shut.

It was the first he'd heard of a bank holiday so Shepherd decided he'd go straight to Dominic Windsor's office and pay for the villa. A group of motorcycle taxis was sitting outside the bank. He tried to explain where he wanted to go but none of the riders spoke English. They kept shrugging good-naturedly but it was clear they didn't understand a word he was saying. Then he remembered he had Windsor's business card in his wallet. He fished it out and turned it over. On the reverse side the name and address were printed in Thai. He handed it to one of the men, who squinted at it. 'I know,' he said.

'Great,' said Shepherd. He climbed onto the back of the motorcycle. During the five-minute drive to Windsor's office, he was drenched half a dozen times. When Shepherd pulled up in front of his shop Windsor was at the window and waved, then laughed when he saw how wet he was. He held open the door and asked one of his girls to fetch a towel. 'Thai new year,' said Windsor. 'Didn't anyone warn you?'

'I have to say they didn't tell me how bad it was.' Windsor's air-conditioning was as bracing as the bank's had been and he was shivering again. He held up the wet FedEx envelope. 'I've brought my cheque book. I thought I'd get everything sorted today before the banks close.'

'Excellent,' said Windsor. 'Tea? Coffee?'

'Coffee would be great,' said Shepherd.

Windsor told one of his girls to fetch it while he did the paperwork for the villa. Shepherd wrote a cheque. 'I'd like your passport, too, if you don't mind,' said the estate agent, holding out his hand. 'It's one of the things they do out here, I'm afraid, photocopy your passport.'

'Not a problem,' said Shepherd. He took it from the back pocket of his shorts. Luckily it had escaped the worst of the drenching and was only slightly damp. Windsor photocopied it, gave it back to him, then asked him to sign the copy. 'Don't ask me why, but that's a thing they do out here as well,' he said apologetically. 'Every bit of paper that's photocopied has to be signed.' Shepherd signed 'John Westlake' with a flourish.

Windsor compared the signature with the one in the passport and the one on the cheque, then smiled, satisfied. 'Right,' he said. 'I'll get it to the bank this morning and we'll have it rushed through. Assuming all's well I can let you have the keys this afternoon.'

'Tomorrow will be fine,' said Shepherd. 'I've still got to check out of the hotel, and there's no rush.'

Windsor sat down at his desk, opened a drawer and pulled out a Ziploc plastic bag. He gave it to Shepherd. 'For your phone and wallet,' he said. 'Old hand's trick. It's going to get wetter over the next few days. If I were you, I'd stay locked up in your villa until new year's over.'

Shepherd thanked him and put his phone, passport and wallet into the plastic bag. 'What's the story about building out here?' he asked. 'Suppose I wanted to buy a bit of land and design my own place?'

'It can be done,' said Windsor. 'Strictly speaking, foreigners can't own land but everything's flexible. You'd have to do it through a Thai company but I've got Thai lawyer friends who can handle it. Once you've got the land, construction costs are quite low. Do you want me to look around for you?'

'You know guys who've done it, yeah?'

'Absolutely,' said Windsor. 'I helped put together quite a big development for some English guys a year or two back. They've got a great place, six villas in a compound, huge pool, communal games area, staff accommodation. Big bucks, though.'

Shepherd waved his cheque book. 'I've got big bucks, Dom,' he said. 'Any chance of a viewing some time?'

Windsor looked pained. 'I'm not sure about that, John,' he said. 'Like you, they value their privacy.'

'No problem, but if you could swing a tour, that would be great. Give me something to go on, you know.' He stood up. 'Thanks again for all your help. I'll pop around tomorrow for the keys.'

'Pleasure,' said Windsor. He grinned lecherously at the two girls sitting at their desks. 'And don't forget our special bonus offer.' He winked suggestively.

'Rain check,' said Shepherd. He thanked Windsor again and went outside. He saw a group of bare-chested Thai men with buckets of water heading his way and jogged down the road towards the sea. He realised his mistake as soon as he got to the end of the street – the beach road was mayhem with hundreds of people throwing water. Pick-up trucks were parked along it with barrels in the back from which revellers were throwing water over everybody they could reach. Music blared from roadside speakers and everybody was soaked. Tourists with high-powered water pistols were squirting jets of water into the air and girls with bowls of talcum powder were rubbing it into the cheeks of anyone who would let them. Shepherd turned back the way he'd come but a bucket of water drenched him from head to foot. His Thai assailant grinned and said, '*Sawasdee pee mai.*'

Shepherd forced a smile. 'Happy new year.' The man offered him the bottle of Thai whisky he'd been drinking. Shepherd shook his head. 'I'm not that thirsty right now,' he said. He turned back to the beach road – he was as wet now as he was ever going to get – slipped through the trucks, then threaded his way between the deck-chairs and umbrellas towards the sea. The sun was blinding and even though he knew he was risking sunstroke it was the quickest way to dry out.

He walked along the water's edge in the direction of Sharpe's hotel. A motorboat sped by, pulling a banana-shaped inflatable through the waves. Four Asian tourists were hanging on as if their lives depended on it. Diving boats were returning from the morning's outings and jet-skis roared by. There were few swimmers and those who had gone into the water stayed close to the shore. An old Thai lady held out armfuls of silk and grinned at him, showing blackened teeth. He wondered if anyone walking along the beach had ever bought anything from her. Ice cream he could understand, or cold drinks, but silk seemed a strange choice for a beach vendor. A hundred feet further on a slightly younger but still ancient woman offered him laminated maps of Thailand and posters of the country's wildlife.

Sweat was pouring from his face and his legs were burning. The sky was cloudless and the sun fierce. He looked to his left, trying to judge how close he was to Sharpe's hotel, saw a Starbucks sign and headed for it. As he reached the lines of umbrellas a Thai man wearing a Singha beer vest offered him a deck-chair but Shepherd pointed at the road and walked on. A pedestrian pathway dotted with palm trees ran between the beach and the road and he followed it, ducking behind tree-trunks when anyone threatened to throw water over him. Eventually he spotted a gap in the traffic and darted across. Two small boys with water pistols as big as themselves appeared from nowhere and squirted ice-cold water into his face, giggling with glee. Their mother looked on proudly.

Shepherd had just opened his mouth to wish them a happy new year when a torrent of freezing water slapped into his back. He spun round. A black pick-up truck was behind him, with an obese Westerner standing in the back next to four scantily clad girls. He was holding an empty bucket and smirking drunkenly. The vehicle moved ahead and the man almost fell over the tailgate. The girls screamed with laughter and held him upright.

Shepherd watched the truck lurch along the road as water dribbled down his face. A group of motorcycle-taxi drivers were laughing at him. Shepherd noticed that they were dry. No one had so much as squirted them with a water pistol. They were a tough-looking bunch with hard faces and skin blackened from years in the sun, and most wore large Buddhist medallions on thick gold chains around their necks.

He flicked his hair to the side and jogged down the street to Sharpe's hotel. The go-go bars were shut, a dismal sight in daylight with flaking paint and slipshod electrical wiring hanging around the doorways. He walked past a street vendor selling fried insects from a wheeled stall bolted to a motorcycle. A pretty girl in her twenties was watching the vendor shovel into a paper bag what appeared to be a dozen or so fried cockroaches.

The further he got from the beach road the fewer people were throwing water, and when he finally reached the Penthouse he was no longer dripping but still far from dry. As he went into Reception, a good-looking Westerner with slicked-back black hair walked out hand in hand with a teenage Thai boy. The Westerner smiled at Shepherd but the boy looked away, embarrassed.

Shepherd went up to Sharpe's room. He knocked on the door and Sharpe opened it. Sharpe was wearing a threadbare bathrobe and blinked sleepily at him. 'The early worm . . .' he grunted. 'You're sweating like a pig,' he observed.

'It's not sweat,' said Shepherd. 'And you're one to talk – you smell like a brewery.'

'I've been working,' said Sharpe, walking into the room, his robe flapping around his ankles.

'Yeah, it looks like it.' Shepherd scowled, shutting the door. He sat on a chair by the window. 'And it's the afternoon, Razor.'

'Screw you,' said Sharpe, flopping down on the bed. 'I was out until five o'clock this morning, following the Brothers Grim around town. And you can't stand in the bars drinking water and not attract attention so, yes, I had the odd beer or two.'

'And?'

'And you'll have no problem bumping into them. They were in three discothèques and half a dozen go-go bars and they're treated like royalty everywhere they go. Mark got into a fight and beat the shit out of three bodybuilders. Watch him, Spider. He's a tough bastard.'

'You gotta be careful, tailing these guys on your own,' said Shepherd.

'Nah, it's not a problem,' said Sharpe. 'The town's full of middle-aged white men wandering around aimlessly. It'd be impossible to show out.' He groaned and rubbed his temples. 'Can you get me a hair of the dog out of the fridge?'

Shepherd leaned over, opened it, and tossed him a can of beer. He popped the tab and drank greedily. 'What do you think about the Moores?' asked Shepherd.

Sharpe sat up and rested his head against the wall. 'They're what my old dad used to call ODCs. Ordinary Decent Criminals. Old school. Don't go out of their way to hurt civilians, don't touch hard drugs, never hurt women or kids.'

'Good to their mothers? Like the Krays?'

'You can mock, but the world was a better place when ODCs were committing crimes. These days, it's all drugs, drive-by shootings and bombs on Tube trains. Remember that case in Tottenham? The ten guys who raped that girl, then poured caustic soda over her to destroy the DNA evidence? That's the sort of scumbags we're dealing with now. ODCs wouldn't go near hard drugs, like crack and heroin, and if they ever used violence it tended to be against other criminals.'

'I guess they're a dying breed, all right.' Shepherd grinned. 'A bit like your good self.'

'I'm only ten years older than you,' protested Sharpe. There were banging sounds from the room next door, followed by loud grunting. Sharpe gestured at the wall. 'That goes on all night,' he said.

'Is that a girl?' The grunting had turned into loud squealing.

'I don't think so,' said Sharpe. 'Your hotel's more upmarket, right?'

'I'm moving out tomorrow,' said Shepherd. 'I've got a villa.'

'Great,' said Sharpe. 'I'll get packed.'

'You can't stay with me, Razor. I'm in Pattaya alone, remember? On the run from the cops.'

'It's a big place, right?'

'Huge. With a pool.'

'So put me in a spare bedroom and I'll stay out of the way.'

'You know it's not going to happen.'

Sharpe sighed. The screaming next door reached a crescendo, and stopped suddenly. 'I'm not staying here,' said Sharpe.

'Fine, check into somewhere else – the place is full of hotels.'

'Do you think Charlie will run to a villa for me?'

'Why don't you ask her?' he said. 'Let me know what she says.'

'Why don't I just make the Moores my new best friends and move in with them?'

'Sounds like a plan,' said Shepherd.

'Screw you.'

'Not an option,' said Shepherd. 'But if you're on the turn, you're in the right part of town.'

'Seriously, Spider, this place is getting on my tits. I don't see why I can't be in a four-star place. It's not as if hotel prices are steep. This place is only twenty quid a night.'

Shepherd held up his hands. 'It's nothing to do with me. Like I said, you'll have to talk to Charlie.'

Sharpe finished his beer and tossed the can into a plastic bucket beside the toilet door.

'How approachable were the Moores?' asked Shepherd.

'They put themselves about a bit, but it was more other guys coming up to pay homage, shaking hands, a pat on the back, but they stayed pretty tight as a team. You worried about an in?'

'I'm not sure it's gonna work if I hang around and bump into them. If they're criminal royalty, everyone's going to want to bask in the reflected glory, right?'

'Don't see you've much choice. There's no one here can give you an introduction. You tried the estate agent, right?'

'He might mention me to them, but he's not going to get me into the compound.' Shepherd smiled encouragingly. 'I thought we might try a bit of theatre. Get me noticed.'

Sharpe groaned. 'Last time we did that I ended up with a broken nose.'

'It was only a fracture. And a small one at that.'

Sharpe gestured at the fridge. 'Get me another beer and let me think about it.'

The girl had said she was twenty-three but she looked as if she was barely out of her teens. She'd told Shepherd she had been working in the bar for three weeks and before that she had been assembling televisions in a Japanese factory in Udon Thani, in the north-east of the country. Her name was Nong, she had never been married and she didn't like Thai men because they were lazy and beat their wives. Shepherd had the feeling that it was a story she'd told a hundred times and that she had been a bargirl for a lot longer than three weeks. She'd asked him if he'd buy her a drink and he'd said yes. When she'd tottered to the bar on her high heels he'd seen that her stomach was pitted with stretch marks.

When she came back with her drink she'd told him how she had to send money to her mother every month because her family was so poor, but Shepherd could see that her heart wasn't in it. Lying to people was a skill, a craft that had to be honed, and reciting a list of untruths didn't make you a good liar. You had to believe in the story you were selling. Shepherd knew all about lying. It was what he did for a living. He decided that most of the guys Nong spoke to were so drunk or stupid they never questioned what she told them so she'd given up making an effort.

It was a little after eleven o'clock and he was in a go-go bar in an alley off Walking Street. The Moore brothers were at a table close to a dancing podium at the far end with Yates and Wilson. Shepherd had visited a dozen such bars before he'd found the brothers, then phoned Jimmy Sharpe to let him know where they were. He had sat with his back to the brothers and watched the dancers until Nong had come up behind him, put her hands over his eyes and whispered, 'Surprise!' It was her opening gambit, pretending she'd mistaken him for somebody else. Then she'd slid on to the stool next to him, rubbed his thigh and told him her tale of woe.

The curtain at the entrance to the bar drew back and Jimmy Sharpe came in. He was wearing baggy shorts, a sweat-stained T-shirt advertising Singha, and flip-flops, the uniform of the sex tourist on the prowl. He went to the bar, ordered a beer to match the logo on his shirt and leered at the dancing bargirls. Then he pretended to see Shepherd for the first time and walked unsteadily to his table. He banged down his bottle and grinned at Nong. 'Hello, darling,' he said. 'What's your name, then?'

Her face tightened and she moved closer to Shepherd.

Sharpe reached out and ran his fingers down her arm. 'Lovely little thing, aren't you? Come here and give me a kiss.'

'She's with me, mate,' said Shepherd.

'She's with whoever pays her bill, pal,' he said, 'and my money's as good as yours.' He shouted the last sentence and heads turned to see what the commotion was about. Sharpe took out his wallet and waved a thousand-baht note in front of her. 'Come on, darling, let's get out of here.'

Shepherd slid off his stool. 'I already told you, pal. She's with me.'

Sharpe pushed Shepherd in the chest, hard enough to

move him back. 'Get out of my face!' he yelled, his Glaswegian accent heavier than usual. He grabbed his beer bottle and smacked it against the side of the table. It shattered, leaving him holding the neck and a wickedly sharp shard, which he thrust at Shepherd's face. Shepherd swayed back, grasped Sharpe's wrist with his right hand, and twisted savagely. Sharpe yelped in genuine pain and the remains of the bottle fell to the floor.

Shepherd stepped forward, increased the pressure on Sharpe's twisted arm, then swung him to the side and threw him against the wall. Sharpe hit it hard, but immediately came back at Shepherd, swinging his fists and cursing. He managed to clip Shepherd on the side of the chin, jolting his jaw, but then Shepherd grabbed his T-shirt and pulled it halfway over his head. Shepherd kept the momentum going, pulling Sharpe towards him, then stepped to the side, like a matador avoiding an angry bull, and pushed him head-first into the wall. This time Sharpe went down on his hands and knees, swearing loudly.

Two Thai waiters were heading purposefully for Shepherd. The curtain at the entrance to the bar was pulled aside and another two looked in. Shepherd knew that he had only seconds to end the fight before they piled in. He grabbed the back of Sharpe's shirt, dragged him to his feet and frogmarched him to the door. Blood was dripping from his nose and Shepherd hoped he hadn't broken it. The Thai doormen moved aside to let Shepherd through. 'Get the hell out, and stay out!' Shepherd roared, kicking Sharpe's backside. He followed him into the alley. 'And if I see you in here again I'll kill you!' he yelled, and kicked him again.

Sharpe ran off down the alley, heading away from

Walking Street. There were cheers as Shepherd walked back into the bar and a round of spontaneous applause from three skinheads standing at the main dancing podium. Shepherd gave them a mock-bow, then went back to his table. Nong threw her arms around his neck and kissed his cheek. 'You very brave man,' she said.

'Not really,' said Shepherd. Mark Moore and Andy Yates were looking in his direction. Mickey was standing with his back to him, holding a banknote up to a bare-breasted dancer. Yates was saying something to Mark, who was nodding. Shepherd was sure they'd seen the fight so he'd achieved his objective. He finished his drink and called for his bill.

'I come with you?' asked Nong hopefully.

'Sorry, love, I promised myself an early night,' said Shepherd. He paid, waved goodbye to his skinhead fan club and left the bar. He walked slowly down the alley to make sure no one was following him, then increased the pace as he headed for the Penthouse Hotel.

Jimmy Sharpe opened the door to his room, clutching an icepack to his forehead. He grunted at Shepherd, then lay down on his bed. 'You're a bastard,' he muttered.

'I didn't think you'd hit the wall as hard as you did,' said Shepherd. He dropped onto the chair by the window and swung his feet onto the end of the bed.

'You pulled my shirt over my bloody head so I couldn't see where the hell I was. That wasn't what we'd planned. Bottle, grab my arm, against the wall, I throw a punch, you grab me and throw me out. That was what you said, right?'

'I improvised and I'm sorry,' said Shepherd. 'But it

looked bloody good, I can tell you. I'm pretty sure they bought it.'

'I think it's broken,' muttered Sharpe.

'I'm sure it's not. How can I make it up to you?'

Sharpe lifted the icepack and squinted across at him. 'You can talk to Charlie and get me into a decent hotel,' he said slyly.

It had been a long day and Simon Montgomery was looking forward to a beer and a curry in front of the television. Thursday was his wife's bridge night, the one night of the week when she allowed him a curry in the house. Eileen hated the smell of Indian food, let alone the taste, and the first curry she had eaten with him had been her last. They had gone to one of Montgomery's favourite restaurants in the East End of London. They were both in their early twenties, he was an up-and-coming barrister, she a copywriter with a top London advertising agency. Despite his suggestion that she should keep clear of seafood, she had had king prawn dhansak, and three hours later she had been throwing up like there was no tomorrow. That had been thirty-four years, three children and five grandchildren ago, but Eileen had refused ever again to be even in the same room as a curry.

Simon pressed the remote control to open his garage gates and drove the Jaguar in slowly. The house was almost two hundred years old and the two-car garage was a relatively recent addition. There had been just enough space to fit it in between the house and the garden wall and there was only just enough room for the Jaguar and his wife's Mini Cooper. Montgomery knew that a fair amount of sherry was consumed at the weekly bridge session and that his wife's parking abilities were dubious even when she was completely sober so he parked as close as he could to the wall. He closed the garage and unlocked the internal door that led into the kitchen, tapping the code into the burglar alarm before hanging his coat over the back of a chair and taking his briefcase to his study. He kept his takeaway menus in his desk because his wife tended to throw away the ones he left on the refrigerator door. He sat at his desk and took them out of the top drawer. There were three Indian restaurants within a mile of Montgomery's house, but his favourite by far was Tandoori Nights. He knew the menu by heart but he still made the effort to look through it. Then he picked up the phone and ordered exactly what he'd decided on during the drive home – chicken jalfrezi, lamb rogan josh on the bone, sag paneer, a garlic naan and boiled rice.

He went upstairs to shower, then changed into a polo shirt and chinos. He had just taken a bottle of Kingfisher beer from the fridge when the doorbell rang. A console in the hallway allowed him to view the images from the CCTV cameras that covered the front and rear of the property. The delivery boy was at the gates, a baseball cap pulled low over his eyes and, behind him, the 50cc moped with a red back carrier that had the name of the restaurant on it. Montgomery buzzed him in and went to open the front door.

He was a teenage Bangladeshi, the nephew of the owner. He was a nice enough lad but Montgomery knew from experience that he was careless so he checked the order carefully, then gave him thirty pounds and told him to keep the change. The boy hurried back to the gate and

Montgomery closed the door. He pressed the button on the console to open the gate again, then went through to the kitchen, humming quietly to himself. He switched on the extractor fan above the oven and laid out the foil cartons on the kitchen table. 'Lovely,' he whispered, and sipped his Kingfisher. His wife hated the beer almost as much as she hated the food. Generally he followed her lead and drank either wine or sherry, but beer was the only possible accompaniment to Indian food, and ideally it had to be Kingfisher or Cobra. He poured it into a pint glass. His mouth was watering and he thought, for the thousandth time, that a good Indian meal was, more often than not, more satisfying than sex – certainly the sort of sex he'd been getting in recent years. The doorbell rang again and he frowned. He went to the console in the hallway. The delivery boy was back. He opened the front door. The boy was standing on the doorstep, the baseball cap low on his face. 'What's wrong?' asked Montgomery. 'Didn't I give you enough?'

The boy looked up and Montgomery frowned. It wasn't the Bangladeshi. This boy was dark-skinned but he was older than the delivery boy and his eyes were hidden behind sunglasses. Montgomery wondered why he was wearing them at night, then looked over the boy's shoulder and saw that the motorcycle had gone. He opened his mouth to speak but the boy punched him in the sternum, knocking the wind from his lungs. He staggered back, gasping for breath, his chest on fire. The glass of beer dropped to the floor and shattered into a dozen shards, beer splashing over his legs. Two more men appeared, in hooded sweatshirts and dark glasses. They grabbed Montgomery by each arm and pulled him down the hallway. His bare feet scrabbled for balance.

Sportster motorcycle for the past half an hour. The Moores and their crew were regulars at the gym and Andy Yates and Davie Black usually turned up on motorbikes. Shepherd had rented his from a shop close to Jimmy Sharpe's hotel, paying cash for three months. He wasn't a fan of motorcycles and generally preferred four wheels to two, but the bike would give him a reason to talk to Yates or Black.

Shepherd had spent the morning moving into the villa and stocking up with provisions from a local supermarket. Now it was just after three o'clock. He planned to give it another fifteen minutes and if the crew hadn't turned up he'd go into the gym on his own. He hadn't exercised since he'd arrived in Thailand and he could feel his body tightening up. He'd considered swimming in the villa's pool but the sun was too fierce during the day for him to be in the water for an hour or two. As he wiped his forehead again, he heard the sound of two powerful motorcycles in the distance. He started his engine.

As he put the bike in gear he saw Yates and Black pull into the car park. Yates was on a customised Harley Fat Boy chopper with handlebars that curved high into the air and a low-slung seat, while Black had a 1500cc V-twin Suzuki Intruder. Neither men was wearing a helmet. Shepherd headed after them and parked next to Black's Suzuki. He took off his helmet. 'Nice bikes,' said Shepherd. He pointed at the customised Harley. 'Haven't seen many of those in Pattaya.'

'Had it hand-built in California and shipped over,' said Yates. 'Davie here bought his in from Japan.' He nodded at Shepherd's bike. 'Rental?'

'Yeah, I left mine in England. Not sure whether to bring it over or buy here.' He stuck out his hand. 'John Westlake.'

'Davie,' said Black, shaking his hand. 'Davie Black.'

'Andy,' said Yates, also shaking his hand. 'Most guys here call me Chopper.'

'Because of your bike or because of your . . .' Shepherd gestured at the man's groin.

Yates laughed. 'Bit of both,' he said. He looked at Shepherd. 'Didn't I see you kicking the hell out of some guy last night?'

'Might have done,' said Shepherd. 'Some Scottish geezer was getting lippy with the bird I was with. Next thing I know he's trying to bottle me.'

'You sorted him out, though, gave him a right good hiding.'

'Nothing he didn't deserve,' said Shepherd.

Yates nodded at the gym. 'Are you going inside?'

'Yeah, I used to run to keep fit but it's too bloody hot here so I thought I'd give the gym a try.' The three men walked in together. Yates and Black went to the changing rooms while Shepherd filled in an application form. By the time Shepherd had changed, Yates and Black were in the weights area. Black was lying on his back lifting and Yates was watching him. Shepherd nodded at them and went over to a row of treadmills. He set one to a five per cent incline, jogged for five minutes as a warm-up, then ran at full pelt for half an hour. He preferred to run outside, ideally with a rucksack full of bricks on his back to build stamina. Treadmills always reminded him of hamsters on exercise wheels, a lot of effort to go nowhere.

Two young girls in skin-tight leotards and Lycra shorts

were jogging on adjacent machines, watching a Thai soap opera on an overhead TV screen. They smiled at him as he walked by and he smiled back. The Thailand Tourist Authority liked to describe the country as 'The Land of Smiles' and it was an accurate description. The Thais did smile a lot, but he had no way of telling if they meant it or not.

Yates and Black were still in the weights area, sitting on benches and working on their biceps. Shepherd went to them and draped his towel over a bench. 'All right, lads?' he said.

They nodded and carried on with their reps. Shepherd rarely trained with free weights. He had no interest in building muscle mass and found weight training boring, but it was the sort of activity that men like Ricky Knight thrived on, especially when they had spent time inside. He went over to a rack and picked up a five-kilo bar, sat down on a bench opposite them and began working on his right arm. 'How easy was it to bring your bikes over?' he asked Yates.

'Cost you a couple of grand to ship it over, and there's an import tax, plus you'll probably have to grease a few palms at the port but it's no big deal,' said Yates. 'Are you gonna be here for a while, then?'

'Foreseeable future,' said Shepherd. 'What about you guys? How long have you been in Pattaya?'

'Couple of years,' said Black. He switched his weights from the right arm to the left.

'Did you buy a place?' asked Shepherd.

'Yeah,' said Yates. 'What about you?'

'Just rented a villa but I think I'll probably buy. It's my first time here so I'm still feeling my way.'

'You've got to be careful because *farangs* can't own land, but there's ways around it,' Black told him.

'*Farangs*?'

'That's what they call foreigners. We're all *farangs*. Apartments are okay, but not land.'

'Yeah, I was talking to the estate agent that got me my place. Dominic Windsor. He said as much.'

'You know Dom, do you?' said Yates. He stood up, clenched and unclenched his hands, then flexed his shoulders.

'Just given him one and a half million baht in rent,' said Shepherd. 'Three months. Nice place, owned by some guy in Singapore.'

Yates laughed. 'Oh, you're the newbie he was talking about.'

'What?'

'You were robbed,' said Black.

Shepherd stopped lifting his weight. 'What do you mean?'

'Half a million a month, you're paying? He's been pushing it at four hundred thousand for the last six months. He showed it to a friend of ours a few years ago, couldn't shift it then and it was a lot cheaper than half a million.'

'Bastard,' said Shepherd, with venom.

'Nah, he's just making a living,' said Yates. '*Caveat emptor*, right? It's not his fault you're a newbie.'

'I'll break his sodding legs,' said Shepherd. He transferred the weight to his other arm and began pumping.

'He's all right, is Dom,' said Black. 'How long have you been in Thailand?'

'A few days,' said Shepherd.

'This is your first time and you're thinking of settling down? Bit sudden, that.'

'I needed a change. The wife caught me screwing a neighbour and set her lawyer on me. I figured she'd have a hard job finding me out here.' It was a weak story, but that was what Shepherd needed. If the John Westlake legend was full of holes it wouldn't take them long to see through it.

'You'll do plenty of shagging out here,' laughed Yates. 'You tried out the local talent yet?'

'Not really,' said Shepherd. 'Truth be told, I'm still a bit jet-lagged.'

'Come out with the guys tonight,' said Yates.

'The guys?'

'Me and a few mates. We'll be out on the town having a few beers. You'll normally find us in Angelwitch or Living Dolls down on Walking Street.'

'Yeah, I'll swing by. I could do with some tips on the way it works out here.' Shepherd stood up and took the weight to the rack.

Yates grinned. 'There's one golden rule out here,' he said. 'Cash is king. If you've got the money, you can do pretty much what the hell you want.'

'Sounds like my kind of town,' said Shepherd.

Simon Montgomery blinked as the hood was ripped from his head. 'What the hell is going on?' he asked, trying to inject some authority into his voice.

Bradshaw ignored the question. He was standing between al-Sayed and Chaudhry and all three men were wearing camouflage fatigues and black leather boots, with red and white checked scarves tied around their necks.

The only furniture in the room was the chair that Montgomery was sitting on. His arms were still tied behind his back. Bradshaw nodded at al-Sayed, who went behind Montgomery and used a pair of scissors to cut the tape from around his wrists.

As Montgomery massaged his tingling fingers, Bradshaw tossed him an orange jumpsuit. 'Put that on,' he said.

'I'll do no such thing,' said Montgomery, standing up.

Al-Sayed punched his head and Montgomery staggered sideways. Chaudhry rushed forward and slapped him across the face. Bradshaw held up his hand. 'Enough!' he said.

Montgomery put a hand to the wall to steady himself. There was blood on his lips. Bradshaw pulled a handkerchief from the pocket of his fatigues and gave it to him. 'You're bleeding,' Bradshaw said.

Montgomery dabbed at his lip. 'Thank you,' he said.

Bradshaw took the handkerchief back. 'Please put the overalls on, Mr Montgomery. If you refuse, we will dress you forcibly.' He picked up the jumpsuit and put it on the back of the chair. 'That would be embarrassing for you and probably painful.'

'What is it you want?' asked Montgomery.

'I want you to put on that jumpsuit. I shall count to ten, and if you're not wearing it by the time I've finished . . .'

Montgomery stared at the jumpsuit. 'What sort of people are you?' he said.

'One,' said Bradshaw. 'Two. Three.'

Montgomery took off his chinos and polo shirt and slowly pulled on the jumpsuit. 'I don't know what you expect to achieve by doing this,' he said.

'That's not your problem,' said Bradshaw. Al-Sayed tossed Montgomery's clothes into the corner of the room.

'I'm a High Court judge. The police will hunt you down no matter where you go.'

'Let me worry about that,' said Bradshaw. 'Now, please zip up the jumpsuit.' Montgomery did as he was told, then al-Sayed retied the judge's hands behind his back.

'Is it a ransom you want?' asked Montgomery. 'Is this about money? I have money, in the bank. If your demands are reasonable there'll be no problem getting it to you.'

'This isn't about money,' said Bradshaw.

'What, then?' asked Montgomery. 'What is it you want?'

'I want you to be quiet,' said Bradshaw. 'Are you a religious man?'

The question seemed to take Montgomery by surprise. 'Am I what?'

'Do you follow any religion?'

'As much as anyone,' said Montgomery. 'I'm Church of England.'

Bradshaw sneered at him. 'You're a *kafir* and you'll burn in Hell, but if it gives you any comfort I suggest you commune with your God. Now kneel down.'

'What?' said Montgomery, confused.

Bradshaw gestured at al-Sayed who pressed the sole of his foot behind Montgomery's left knee. Montgomery stumbled forward and went down on his left knee. 'Kneel down,' repeated Bradshaw. 'And be quiet. If you are not quiet, we will gag you.'

The door opened and Talwar walked in. Like the others he was wearing camouflage fatigues and a checked scarf. He had his glasses on over the scarf and was holding a small digital video camera. 'Are we ready?' he asked.

'Yes,' said Bradshaw.

'Ready for what?' asked Montgomery.

Bradshaw ignored him and kept looking at Talwar. 'Are you sure that thing's working?' he asked. 'We'll only get one chance.'

'Once chance for what?' asked Montgomery, apprehensively.

'I've tested it half a dozen times and the battery's fully charged,' said Talwar.

'Where is Jamal?' asked Bradshaw.

'In the car, outside,' said Talwar. 'He'll call if he sees anything.'

'Then let's do it,' said Bradshaw. He took a pair of impenetrable sunglasses from the top pocket of his fatigues and put them on, then wound the scarf around the bottom of his face. Chaudhry and al-Sayed did the same.

Montgomery swallowed nervously. 'Look, can we talk about this?' he said.

The men ignored him. Talwar was looking at the screen of the video camera. He flashed a thumbs-up at Bradshaw.

Bradshaw held up his knife and stared at the camera. 'We do this in the name of Allah, in the name of Islam,' he said.

'Islam?' said Montgomery. 'You're not a Muslim,' he said accusingly. 'What do you mean, you're doing this in the name of Islam?'

'Why do you think I'm not a Muslim? Because I'm not brown-skinned? Because I'm not a wog? Is that what you mean?'

'No . . .' said Montgomery. 'That's not what I meant.'

'I know what you meant, you racist bastard. Christians are white, Muslims are brown and black. That's what you meant.' He turned back to the camera and addressed the lens. 'We want freedom for our brothers who have been unjustly incarcerated. The four brothers who attempted to kill themselves on the Tube on the twenty-first of July 2005 were carrying out the will of Allah, and mortal man has no right to judge them for what they did. The British police are corrupt, the British judiciary are corrupt, and the British Government, from the prime minister down, are corrupt. Now is the time to stem the tide of corruption that has made Britain the yapping lapdog of the United States.'

Al-Sayed and Chaudhry went to stand behind Montgomery. He twisted around to look up at the faces but Al-Sayed grabbed his hair and forced him to confront the camera.

'We want our four brothers released and taken to Stansted airport where there will be a fully fuelled jet waiting for them. These are our demands, and we insist that our demands are taken seriously.'

He turned to Montgomery. The blood had drained from his face and he was biting his lower lip. 'Simon Montgomery is a member of the corrupt British judiciary responsible for unjustly convicting our brothers and as such we will make an example of him.'

'Please don't do this,' Montgomery mumbled.

'He will be the first, and there will be others. We will continue to exact our revenge until our brothers are freed.' He waved the knife above his head. '*Allahu akbar!*' he shouted. '*Allahu akbar!*'

Al-Sayed and Chaudhry punched the air and joined in the shouting.

A damp patch spread at the groin of Montgomery's

jumpsuit and urine pooled around his knees. He began to sob and rocked from side to side.

Talwar moved in closer, holding the camera steady with both hands. Al-Sayed pulled back Montgomery's head, exposing his throat. Tears were streaming down his face and he was groaning like an animal in pain.

'*Allahu akbar!*' shouted Bradshaw. His hand was shaking but it was from the adrenalin rush, not because he was concerned about what he was going to do. The life of Simon Montgomery was worth less than that of a dog, or even an insect that crawled on the ground. Unlike animals and insects, Montgomery had had the opportunity to embrace Islam and declare Allah as the one true God, Muhammad His only messenger, but he had worshipped a false god so he deserved to die and burn for ever in the fires of Jahannam.

Bradshaw placed the blade against Montgomery's neck. Montgomery tried to pull away but al-Sayed kept a tight grip on his hair. Montgomery's breath was coming in short, sharp gasps and his eyes were wide and staring. There were flecks of white froth at the corners of his mouth and a vein pulsed erratically in his temple. Bradshaw pushed the knife, and blood blossomed around the steel blade. He pushed harder and felt resistance as the blade bit into the cartilage so he pulled it hard across the throat. Blood gushed over his hand. '*Allahu akbar!*' he shouted. Montgomery was thrashing around but al-Sayed kept a tight grip on his hair, pushing his neck against the knife. Bradshaw hacked again at the windpipe and felt the blade bite deep into the cartilage and slice through the neck muscles.

Montgomery gurgled as his windpipe filled with blood,

which was sucked down into his chest. His eyes were staring and he was still conscious.

'*Allahu akbar!*' screamed al-Sayed. His eyes were as panic-stricken as the victim's and his legs were shaking. '*Allahu akbar!* Kill him! Go on – do it!'

Talwar stepped to the side so that he could see the knife. He was muttering, '*Allahu akbar*', to himself like a mantra.

Bradshaw pulled out the knife and blood spurted from a sliced artery, a thin dark red stream that splattered against the wall, then gradually petered out as if a tap had been turned off. Montgomery's shoulders shuddered but his eyes were still open. Bradshaw locked eyes with the dying man. '*Allahu akbar!*' Bradshaw growled, and the words sounded like a curse rather than the prayer they were meant to be.

Al-Sayed released his grip on Montgomery's hair and the man pitched forward. Talwar stepped back, his nose just inches from the video camera's screen, still muttering to himself.

Now Bradshaw squatted over Montgomery. He could see the ridges of the man's spine against the orange jumpsuit. Montgomery was still alive despite the gaping wound in his neck and the blood that was pooling around his shoulders. His feet were drumming against the floor and his chest was still heaving.

Bradshaw slid the knife under Montgomery's neck and, with his left hand, grabbed the man's hair. He yanked the head back and began to saw with the knife, chanting, '*Allahu akbar*,' as he worked the blade back and forth. He angled the blade up and severed the vertebra's connection with the skull, then all that was left was muscle and skin, which cut as easily as tender steak. Suddenly there was no resistance and the head came away from the body. The chest made wet slushy sounds as the lungs continued to suck in air.

Bradshaw stood up and waved it in triumph as Talwar moved in for a close-up.

'*Allahu akbar!*' screamed Bradshaw, in triumph. 'Death to all those who refuse to accept Allah as their saviour!' Montgomery's blood dripped onto the floor, pitter-pattering like rain.

Shepherd left his Jeep and bike at the villa and caught a baht bus on the nearby road. A middle-aged woman in a black Armani T-shirt was sitting next to the driver and asked Shepherd where he wanted to go. He told her Walking Street and she said it would cost a hundred baht. Shepherd climbed into the back. The baht bus drove to the beach road. The sun had gone down and most of the water-throwing had stopped, but the occasional drunken tourist managed to shoot him with a stream of water from a high-powered water pistol as the bus went by. The path on the beach side of the road was busy with tourist couples walking hand in hand, Thai children playing tag and old Western men ambling along in shorts and flip-flops. A lot of Thai women in their twenties and thirties were sitting on concrete benches trying to make eye contact with any Western man who passed them. They had the tired smiles of working girls who knew they were past their prime, and their cheap clothing and worn footwear suggested they were living from hand to mouth.

The bus dropped him at the pedestrianised road that was Walking Street. It was parallel to the shore, with shops and bars running its full length. A white van was parked at the entrance and behind it was a line of tables at which were sitting several uniformed Thai policemen and Westerners in black polo shirts with TOURIST POLICE VOLUNTEER across the back.

The street was packed – bargirls in tight jeans and low-cut tops, overweight middle-aged Westerners with glazed eyes, groups of young men drinking bottled beer, Asian tour groups walking in formation with video cameras at the ready. Outside the go-go bars, girls in short skirts and high heels, and male touts in white shirts and thin black ties, tried to coax the passers-by inside. Shepherd threaded his way through the crowds. On his right were seafood restaurants, with glass tanks of live crabs, lobsters and fish of every description. Diners were choosing their fish and walking onto piers over the sea, where waiters hurried around with trays of beer and buckets of ice. Shepherd took out his mobile phone and sent a text to Jimmy Sharpe, asking him where the Moores were. Thirty seconds later the phone vibrated. 'Angelwitch. Mickey, Mark, Yates.'

Shepherd scanned the signs advertising bars and restaurants and saw a red 'Angelwitch' pointing into a side alley. He headed down it, ignoring the touts. As he approached Angelwitch, a large Thai man bowed and pulled back a curtain. He walked in and immediately his ears were assailed by pounding rock music. A dozen girls in black G-strings and boots were dancing around chrome poles while customers sipped their drinks and stared at the naked flesh on display.

Shepherd saw Yates and the Moore brothers at the far side of the bar, sitting with bottles of beer in front of them. He moved to a seat where he knew Yates would have no problem seeing him and ordered a Singha. It arrived with a paper chit in a beaker, which the waitress put in front of him. A young girl with a tattoo of a crouching panther on her shoulder did a little shimmy down her chrome pole for his benefit and he raised his bottle to her.

Every few minutes he glanced to where Yates was sitting and eventually the other man waved him over. 'Hey, John, good to see you,' said Yates. He slapped Shepherd's back and gestured at the Moores. 'This is Mickey and this is Mark. Mickey and Mark Moore. The M&Ms they call them.'

'Not to our faces they don't,' said Mickey. 'How are you doing, John?'

'Great,' said Shepherd. 'John Westlake.' He shook hands with Mark, then Mickey, and sat down next to Yates.

'Saw you kicking the arse of that obnoxious Jock,' said Mark. 'Gave him a good seeing-to, you did. If he'd come at me with a bottle, I'd have pushed it back in his face.'

The Aerosmith track ended and the dancing girls lined up to leave the stage. A new group slid down the poles from the gantry near the ceiling to take their places. A thin girl with shoulder-length hair and surgically enhanced breasts skipped over to where Mark was sitting and plonked herself on his lap. She put her arms around his neck and began kissing him on the mouth.

'You drive a Harley too?' Shepherd asked Mickey.

'Bloody deathtraps,' said Mickey. 'Did Chopper tell you one of our mates is in hospital because of a bike? Got hit by a truck. He's going to spend the rest of his life in a wheelchair.'

'Tel was unlucky,' said Yates.

'Yeah, well, if he'd been in a Range Rover and not sitting on a bike he'd have been a hell of a lot luckier,' said Mickey.

'What's the story?' asked Shepherd.

'A truck ran him off the road. He almost died. Like Mickey says, he's not going to walk again. Bloody nightmare. Doctors don't think he'll be able to shag, either. That's the real pisser. Surrounded by sexy girls and he can't touch them.'

A waitress came over carrying the beaker and chit that Shepherd had left behind. She smiled and placed it in front of him.

'Do you use Tony's Gym?' Shepherd asked Mickey.

'Yeah, but not as much as I used to,' said Mickey. 'Most of the time we go to a kick-boxing place. It's a better workout.'

Mark broke off from kissing the dancer. 'Get him to come to Fairtex,' he said to his brother. 'He can wear the red-man suit.'

'What's that?' asked Shepherd.

'They use it for training,' said Mickey. 'You get someone to wear the padded suit and then you kick the shit out of them.'

'You do a lot of kick-boxing, yeah?' asked Shepherd.

Mickey jerked a thumb at his brother. 'Mark's the expert. I just do it to keep fit.' He noticed the watch on Shepherd's wrist. 'That's a Breitling Emergency, yeah?'

Shepherd held it out so that Mickey could get a better look. 'You pull out this knob here and it transmits on the emergency frequency that planes use and in theory they send a helicopter to pick you up.'

'Gold?'

'Yeah.'

'Nice. Not sure if I believe the hype about the helicopter rescue, though.'

'Hopefully I'll never have to put it to the test.' He indicated the Rolex on Mickey's wrist. 'You like the Daytona, yeah?'

'It's a nice watch. My favourite is an old Patek Philippe but that's too good to wear out here. I've a couple of dozen old Rolexes back at my villa and a really nice Cartier that Mark got me one Christmas.'

Mark untangled himself him from the bargirl. 'Chopper said you've rented a place through Dom Windsor,' he said.

'From the sound of it I got ripped off. You've built your own, right?'

'Yeah, you should come out and see it some time.' Mickey finished his drink and banged the glass on the table in front of him. 'We're off to go *katoey*-watching, do you want to come?'

'What's that?' asked Shepherd.

'Come with us and you'll find out.' Mark laughed.

They paid their bills, left the bar and started back to Walking Street. Mark and Mickey walked ahead, deep in conversation. Shepherd fell into step with Yates. '*Katoey*?' he asked.

'*Katoey*s are ladyboys,' said Yates.

'Terrific,' said Shepherd. 'When you promised me a boys' night out, I didn't think that was what you meant.'

Yates laughed. 'We're just watching, mate,' he said. 'It's a laugh.'

Mickey and Mark turned into a bar with wicker seats and tables. They sat down and ordered a round of beers as Yates and Shepherd joined them. A Thai girl in a tight red dress that barely concealed her backside squealed when she saw Mark and practically threw herself at him. Most of the Westerners drinking in the bar looked as if they had just walked off the remand wing of a prison – they were all wearing Nike tracksuit bottoms, T-shirts and gleaming trainers, and sported a selection of West Ham and British bulldog tattoos.

Across the street Shepherd noticed a large outdoor bar with a boxing ring. Two heavy-set Thais were kicking each other so hard that he could hear the dull thuds from almost fifty yards away. To the right escalators led to go-go bars on the upper floor. Standing close to the bottom were half a dozen of the prettiest girls Shepherd had seen since he'd arrived in Thailand – like leggy supermodels, they walked with an exaggerated swing to their hips, preening themselves and tossing their hair. They were wearing short dresses, with impossibly high stilettos, and carried small designer bags. They were constantly taking out mirrors to check their makeup. They were all taller than the average Thai girl and had breasts so perfect that they could only have been the result of a surgeon's skill. They weren't women, Shepherd realised. They were transsexuals.

Yates was grinning at him. 'They're something, aren't they?'

'They're all guys?'

Yates pointed at the bar to the right of the escalators. A sign read JENNY STAR BAR. Under it, another dozen or so stunning ladyboys were mingling with male customers. 'Every one,' said Yates. 'It's a ladyboy bar. There aren't any girls.'

Mickey leaned over. 'What do you think, John?'

'They're lovely, mate, but have they all had their tackle removed?'

Mickey slapped his leg. 'Never been close enough to find out,' he said.

'None of them have had the operation,' said Mark. 'They're sick bastards. But not as sick as the bastards that go with them.'

'Gays, you mean?' said Shepherd.

'Gays won't touch them,' said Mickey. He lit a cigar and blew smoke towards the road. 'Our mate Davie's a pillow-biter and he reckons they're an abomination. If you're a gay guy you like men, is the way he tells it. Straight guys like women.'

'Obviously,' said Shepherd.

'But if a gay guy fancied a *katoey*, he might as well go with a woman,' said Mickey.

Shepherd nodded. 'So that brings me back to the question, who goes with the *katoeys*?'

'Sad bastards,' said Mickey, flicking ash onto the floor.

Mark stroked the girl's backside and asked her to fetch another round of beers. 'Guys who've been inside, for one,' said Mark. He grinned at Shepherd.

Shepherd stared at him. He didn't want a confrontation with the man but he was Ricky Knight, and Ricky Knight wouldn't let a remark like that pass, even when he was pretending to be someone else. 'You mean something by that?' he asked.

Mark's face hardened. 'You got a problem, John?'

'If you're giving me grief, yeah.'

'I'm just making conversation,' said Mark. 'Just saying that guys who've been inside aren't averse to chasing the chocolate chutney, that's all.'

Mickey patted Shepherd's leg. 'John, he didn't mean anything personal.'

Mark put down his beer. 'Shit, have you been inside? Sorry, mate, I didn't know.'

'Yeah, well, it's not something I boast about.'

'You don't look the type, mate,' said Mark.

'I'll take that as a compliment,' said Shepherd. 'But I can tell you one thing, there was never any question of chasing the chocolate chutney.'

'No offence, mate.'

'All right, mate. None taken.'

The men drank their beer and watched the comings and goings at the Jenny Star Bar. Every few minutes a ladyboy would leave hand in hand with a Western man. They walked down an alley to the left of the bar they were sitting in, the ladyboys tossing their hair like thoroughbreds ready for the off, the men avoiding eye contact with anyone who looked their way.

'Where are they going?' asked Shepherd.

'Short-time hotel for a bit of how's-your-father,' said Mickey. He puffed contentedly at his cigar.

'The guys know, right? They know they're not real girls?'

'I would think so,' said Mickey.

'Funny old world, innit?' said Shepherd. He picked up his beer bottle and took a swig.

'So, you'll be here for a while?' said Mark.

'Foreseeable future,' said Shepherd. 'What about you guys? Why did you choose Thailand?'

'Other than the sun, sea and sex?' laughed Mark. 'Give me a break! Where else would you want to go?'

'The Costa?'

'Spain's a shit-hole, these days,' said Mickey. 'And they've got the same EU crap that they have in the UK. They can put you in prison now for smoking, or putting the wrong rubbish in your wheelie-bin. In Thailand you can do what you want and no one will give you any grief.'

'We love it here,' said Mark. 'Wouldn't live anywhere else.'

'And what do you do to earn a crust?'

'Banking,' said Mark, and laughed. Mickey flashed him a warning look and Mark flushed. 'Joke,' he said.

'We're in property,' said Mickey. 'We've done a few projects in Spain and we've got a few things going here.'

'You're not builders, though?' said Shepherd, playing the innocent.

'We put the deals together,' said Mickey. 'Arrange to buy the land, get an architect, hire the builders and then an agent to sell the properties.'

'Pays well, obviously.'

'Pays bloody well,' said Mark.

'What about you, John?' asked Yates. 'What's your game?'

'Bit of this, bit of that,' said Shepherd. 'Cars, mostly. Buy cheap, sell high, pocket the difference. Thought I might try it out here, bring in some luxury motors. They drive on the left, same as in England, so I figured maybe I could import a few Aston Martins and the like. Lots of rich Thais here, right?'

'Bloody rich,' said Mickey. 'But you've got to reckon with the import duty on expensive cars. Doubles the price, and some.'

Shepherd grinned. 'Yeah, I know. The trick is to get them really cheap.'

'You mean nick 'em,' said Mark, jabbing a finger at him.

'You might say that, Mark, but I couldn't possibly comment,' said Shepherd. He raised his bottle in salute.

'You're a tea leaf?' said Yates. 'Bloody hell, you can't trust anyone these days.'

'Guys, leave it out,' said Shepherd. 'I'm just here for a bit of sun, that's all.'

'Seriously – you deal in hot cars?' said Mickey. 'We might be interested.'

Shepherd lowered his voice conspiratorially. 'Look, I don't go hot-wiring motors or anything like that. I'm a middle man. I know some people who have a knack of acquiring luxury motors and I find markets for them. We ship a lot out to the Caribbean, places like Jamaica and Barbados because they drive on the left there so you don't have to start messing around with steering-wheels. Just shove them into a container and Robert's your mother's brother.'

'You should look at other countries while you're out here,' said Mickey. 'Japan, Malaysia, Macau, Singapore, they all drive on the left.'

A group of young men walked by in England football shirts. They all had shaved heads and tattooed arms and were carrying bottles of Chang beer. 'Pattaya seems to be pretty popular with Brits,' said Shepherd.

'You're not wrong,' said Mark. He took a swig of Singha. 'At the last count there were more than fifty thousand living in Thailand and a good chunk of them are here.'

'For the sun, sea and sex?' Shepherd laughed.

'It's not just that,' said Mickey. 'Sure, it's easy to get laid but Mark and me never had problems getting laid back in London. And most of the girls here are hookers, don't forget. You might get a great shag but she's probably done a thousand or so guys over the years.'

'Sloppy seconds,' said Mark, grimacing.

'Sloppy thousands, more like,' said Mickey.

'But they do love us, the Thais,' said Mark, slipping his arm around the girl in the red dress. She giggled and rested her cheek against his shoulder while she massaged his thigh. 'Don't you, darling?' asked Mark. The girl was smoking a cigarette. He took it from her and had a drag.

'I love you too much,' she said, and giggled. 'I love you long time.'

'See?' said Mark, as if he'd just proved a complicated theorem.

The girl took the cigarette back from Mark and kissed his cheek. 'Long time, five thousand baht.'

Shepherd paid the driver of the baht bus and pressed the remote control to open the gates. He walked unsteadily along the path to the front door. He was drunk – drunker than he'd been in a long time. When he was under cover he favoured spirits and mixers so that he could dilute his alcohol but the Moores and their team were beer drinkers and he wanted to fit in. He let himself into the villa and for a moment couldn't remember the code to silence the beeping burglar alarm, but then his memory kicked in and he tapped in the four digits.

He went into the kitchen, took out a bottle of Evian water and drank most of it. Then he walked outside to the swimming-pool, sat on one of the wooden sun-loungers and called Charlotte Button. He filled her in on what had happened.

'Well done, you,' she said. 'So, you're in?'

'I'm a drinking buddy and, yeah, we're getting on okay. They've seen me at the gym and in the bars and Mickey's invited me around to their compound.'

'But so far they think you're John Westlake?'

'Yeah. I've been dropping hints that I've spent time inside and I've told them I deal in dodgy cars. It's just a matter of time now, and the Europol info getting through to them.'

'Are you okay? You sound a bit blurry?'

'I'm drunk as a skunk, actually,' he said.

'Oh dear,' she said. 'Well, drink lots of water and try to sleep on your front.'

'Is that the voice of experience?' he said.

'I was a student once,' she said. 'A long, long time ago. I had my moments.'

She said goodbye and cut the connection. Shepherd lay back and gazed up at the stars. They began to whirl around and he felt his stomach lurch. He tasted bile at the back of his throat, his chest heaved and he threw up over the terracotta tiles. He groaned and got to his feet. 'I'm getting too old for this,' he muttered, and went back to the kitchen for a fresh bottle of water.

'You did well, brother,' said the man. He lit his hand-rolled cigarette, then took a deep drag and held the smoke in his lungs as he watched Bradshaw. They were sitting in the bedroom of the safe-house in Southall. The man's minders were again in the kitchen downstairs but this time the woman had not brought them tea.

'Are you satisfied now?' asked Bradshaw. 'Or do you have more tests for me?'

The man smiled without warmth. 'You would not expect us to take you at your word, would you? The day might come when you are in my position and someone you do not know asks you to trust them. I hope if that day comes you remember what happened between us.' He scratched his beard.

Bradshaw interlinked his fingers and bowed his head slightly. 'I'm sorry if I appear impatient,' he said.

'You are showing your passion, and passion for Allah can only be a good thing,' said the man. 'Many Muslims are Muslims in name only. You are a true Muslim, a true warrior for Islam. So the answer to your question is, yes, I am satisfied.' He swung the briefcase onto his lap and clicked open the locks. Bradshaw's face fell when he saw that it contained only a large manila envelope. 'You expected it to be full of money?' the man asked.

'Of course not,' said Bradshaw.

The man handed him the envelope and closed the briefcase. Bradshaw put the envelope into his jacket pocket. 'Inside there are five ATM cards, each of which can be used to withdraw two hundred pounds a day,' said the man. 'That gives you one thousand pounds a day for expenses. Remember that ATM machines have cameras.'

'How much is in each account?' Bradshaw asked.

'Twenty thousand pounds,' said the man. 'The PIN numbers are in the envelope, which is all the information you need to make withdrawals. Also in the envelope are the details of a safety-deposit box in Kensington. There are six hundred thousand euros in five-hundred-euro notes inside it.'

Bradshaw had asked for sterling but appreciated that the high-denomination notes would be easier to transport.

'You must understand that you will be held accountable for the money,' said the man.

'It won't be wasted.'

'I know that is your intention,' said the man, 'and I have no doubts about your integrity. But there are many conmen and charlatans out there who will happily take the money from you and give nothing in return. If that were to happen . . .' He left the sentence unfinished and stood up. He stubbed out the remainder of his cigarette in the ashtray.

'It will not,' said Bradshaw. *'Inshallah.'*

'Brother, if you squander that money, it will not be Allah who shoulders the blame,' said the man. 'Have no doubt about that.' He held out his right hand. 'I wish you luck.'

Bradshaw stood up and shook it. 'I will not fail you, and I will not fail Allah,' he said.

Mickey Moore beeped the horn of his Range Rover and the uniformed security guard jerked awake. He grinned shamefacedly as he stood up and hurried over to raise the red and white pole. Mickey pointed a finger at him. 'Don't you go bloody sleeping on my time, mate,' he warned. The man was a police sergeant who had a taste for Thai whisky but he was the brother of a senior police officer in Pattaya so Mickey couldn't get rid of him without losing one of his best contacts.

'No problem,' said the man, smiling so widely that he revealed two gold teeth at the back of his mouth.

'I'll give you no problem,' muttered Mickey. He couldn't remove the man from the payroll but he'd make sure in future that he wasn't on the main gate. He gunned the engine and drove into the compound. Around the edge were six villas, and in the middle a main building with a large landscaped pool and a terrace protected by a pagoda-type roof. Mickey lit a cigar as he jogged up the stairs into the central hallway and walked along to the bar area.

When he went in, Mark and Yates were sitting on one of the sofas with their feet up on the coffee-table watching the sixty-inch LCD television. Three Thai girls wearing only T-shirts were curled up on another sofa like napping kittens. Yates was flicking through the channels while Mark was tossing salted peanuts into the air and trying to catch them in his mouth. Wilson was standing by one of three amusement-arcade video shooting games, blasting away at Zombies and Aliens with a plastic gun in each hand. 'Who do they belong to?' asked Mickey, jerking a thumb at the girls.

'Chopper brought them back,' said Mark.

Yates frowned. 'I thought you did.'

'Not mine, mate,' said Mark. 'Kicked mine out first thing this morning.'

'Leave them alone. They're with me,' said Wilson. 'I'm done with them, Mickey, if you want to take them for a spin.'

'I'll get my own sluts, thanks,' said Mickey. He dropped two dozen DVDs onto one of the coffee-tables. 'Got the latest Tom Cruise movie, and it's a perfect copy,' he said. 'And the new series of *CSI*.'

Mark waved a large white envelope in the air. 'Your mate Wanlop was around with the latest Europol watch list,' he said. 'Gave him fifty thousand baht and he went on his merry way.'

Mickey took the envelope from him and went to the bar. He pulled open the double-doored fridge and took out a Singha. 'Anyone else want one?' he asked.

Three voices chorused 'Yeah' in unison. Mickey pulled three beers from the fridge and tossed them to Yates, Wilson and Mark, then flopped on to one of the sofas. 'Where's Davie?' he asked.

'He went for a massage,' said Yates. 'Said he'd be back in time for the West Ham game.'

'What time's it start?'

'Another hour yet,' said Yates.

Mickey slit the envelope with his thumbnail and took out a sheaf of computer printouts. He swigged his beer and flicked through them.

'Anything interesting?' asked his brother.

Mickey grimaced. 'Paedophile. Paedophile. Drug-dealer. Paedophile.'

'Same old, same old,' said Mark. 'Sling over the paedophiles – be handy to know who we can beat the crap out of, if we get the chance.'

Mickey passed over a handful. 'Knock yourself out,' he said. He turned a page and his eyes widened. 'Bloody hell,' he said, under his breath, and his teeth clamped on his cigar.

'What's up?' asked Yates, craning his neck to see what Mickey was looking at.

Mickey's brow furrowed as he read the printout in his hand. Blue smoke streamed from between his clenched teeth. 'You will not believe this,' he said. 'You will not bloody well believe this.'

* * *

Shepherd spent two hours in the gym, an hour running on a treadmill, thirty minutes on a rowing machine, and the rest doing sit-ups and press-ups. There was no sign of the Moore brothers or their team. He showered and changed, then went outside to where he'd parked his Jeep. He tossed his gym bag into the back and stretched. Yates had given him his mobile number but Shepherd didn't want to call him yet. He smiled to himself. It was a bit like calling a girl for a second date – too soon and you appeared too keen, leave it too long and they lost interest. He drove out of the gym's car park and headed for Second Road, so called because it ran parallel to the beach road. He parked a couple of hundred yards from the Penthouse. As he climbed out of the Jeep a pickup truck drove by and three pretty girls standing in the back threw buckets of icy water over him. He yelped and jumped back but the damage was done. He was soaked. The girls whooped and waved, and Shepherd forced a smile and waved back as the truck drove off. He retrieved a towel from his gym bag and draped it over his shoulders. He managed to avoid further drenching on the way to Sharpe's hotel. The girls at Reception giggled when they saw how wet he was, and pools of water collected around his feet as he rode up in the lift.

Sharpe opened the door. 'Been for a swim?' he asked brightly.

'Happy new year,' said Shepherd, sourly, walking into the room.

'The trick is to stay inside during the day and only go out at night,' said Sharpe, closing the door.

'I'm under cover trying to penetrate a criminal gang, Razor, not infiltrating a pack of vampires.' He sat in the chair by the window. He was already shivering from the room's aircon. 'How's the nose?'

'It hurts, but I'll live. How are you getting on with the Brothers Grim?'

'Like a house on fire.'

Sharpe gestured at the fridge. 'Do you want a beer?'

'I'm floating in the stuff from last night,' said Shepherd. 'I'll take a water if you've got one.'

Sharpe opened the fridge. 'Why would I have water?'

'Soft drink?'

He held the fridge door open so that Shepherd could see it was stocked with nothing but beer. Shepherd shook his head in disgust and used his towel to dry his hair. Sharpe took out a bottle of Heineken and flipped off the cap with an opener fixed to the fridge door. 'Do you think they'll bite?' he asked.

'I'm not picking up any vibes that they're going to sign me up,' said Shepherd. 'They might just think I'm one of the guys, someone to have a few pints and a laugh with.'

'They know you're a villain, right?'

'They know I'm a car thief and they know I've been inside, but so far as I know they just think I'm John Westlake.'

'I thought the plan was for Button to get Europol to tip off the local cops and that they'd tip off the Moores?'

'Yeah, well, maybe the message didn't get passed along. Has Charlie been in touch?'

Sharpe rolled his eyes. 'Did you ask her about me switching hotels?'

'I didn't get the chance. I will, though.'

Sharpe looked at his watch, then stretched his arms. 'I'm stiff as a board, sitting in all day,' he said. 'Thought I might go out for a massage tonight.'

'Razor . . .' said Shepherd.

'Therapeutic,' said Sharpe. 'Purely therapeutic. Unless you need me to tail you?'

'I'll be okay,' said Shepherd. 'They tend to stick to the same bars, and if they were going to do something, they're hardly likely to try in Walking Street.' His phone rang and he took it out of its Ziploc plastic bag. He looked at the screen and motioned for Sharpe to be quiet. It was Andy Yates.

'Hi, John, what are you doing?' asked Yates.

'Just been to the gym. How are things?'

'The guys are planning to do some Muay Thai training, do you wanna swing by?'

'Muay Thai? What's that?'

'Thai kickboxing. Great way of keeping fit.'

'Yeah, okay. I don't see why not. Where do I go?'

'It's the Fairtex Sport and Racquet Club. You can't miss it. It's a huge building on the North Pattaya Road, with Chinese dragons and shit outside. See you there in about an hour.'

Shepherd put the phone back into its plastic bag. 'They want me to go kickboxing,' he said.

'Lovely,' said Sharpe. 'Give me a chance to get a massage.'

'Just make sure it's a real girl doing the massaging,' said Shepherd.

'What do you mean?'

'The guys took me ladyboy-spotting and, trust me, it's difficult to know for sure.'

'I thought you just look for an Adam's apple.'

Shepherd smiled. 'Apparently not,' he said. 'According to the guys, a lot of the ladyboys start taking female hormones before puberty so their voiceboxes don't develop.'

'Bullshit,' growled Sharpe.

'I kid you not. I saw some that you'd never know were guys, not in a million years. So, you be careful.' He stripped off his wet shirt. 'Have you got a dry shirt I can borrow? I won't have time to get back to the villa.'

Sharpe went to a pile of clean, ironed laundry and tossed Shepherd a garish Hawaiian shirt covered with parrots and palm trees. 'Are you sure you don't need me to ride shotgun?' he asked.

'You enjoy your massage.'

Shepherd parked behind the complex and walked into the reception area. A receptionist with waist-length hair showed him where the Muay Thai training facilities were. There were four boxing rings, a training area with punch-bags, and a weights area. Half a dozen Thais were training, each with a tracksuited coach close by. Mark was in one of the rings, lashing out at two plastic pads being manipulated by a thickset Thai in a pale blue tracksuit. Mark was wearing red gloves and gold shorts but was barefoot. He kept on his toes and ducked from side to side as he hit out at the pads, alternating fists and breathing out through clenched teeth with each blow.

Mickey and Yates were standing at the side of the ring, leaning on the ropes. They waved when they saw Shepherd. Davie Black and Barry Wilson were in the weights area. Wilson was lying on his back doing bench presses while Black stood over him, urging him on.

Mark's trainer barked at him in Thai and lowered the pads. Mark stood panting in the middle of the ring, his gloved hands on his hips. His face and chest were bathed in sweat and his shorts were soaking. 'Hi, John,' he said, between breaths. 'How's your luck?'

The trainer climbed out of the ring and went to the main area where half a dozen Thai fighters were taking it in turns to attack the punchbags.

'Holding up,' said Shepherd. 'What's the story here?'

'This place has produced some of the world's best Muay Thai fighters,' said Mark. The current featherweight champion's in their stable and I've had a few bouts against a guy by the name of Atachai. He's been voted Thailand's fighter of the year.'

'How did that go?' asked Shepherd.

Mark grinned. 'He beat the crap out of me but I managed to hurt him with a couple of kicks.' He banged his gloves together.

'So Muay Thai's – what? Like karate?' asked Shepherd.

'Karate's Japanese,' said Mark. 'Karate is kicking and punching but you can't grab and, more often than not, there's only token contact. Muay Thai is full on.' He banged his gloved hands together. 'Fists, feet and knees are the main forms of attack. You can grab with your hands and put the knee in the stomach. But nothing below the belt. So, do you wanna put the red-man suit on, then?'

'So you can kick me senseless?'

'That's what the suit's for,' said Mark. 'Protects everything. I wouldn't be able to do you any damage.'

'Except to my self-respect, of course.'

'Are you chicken, John?'

'Not exactly.'

Mark flapped his arms and made clucking noises. Shepherd shook his head.

Mickey and Yates joined in. The Thais who were training stopped what they were doing and looked over to see what the noise was about.

'Guys, leave it out,' said Shepherd. He knew there was no way he could avoid getting into the ring with Mark, but it was important to play his role to the hilt. 'I'm a lover, not a fighter.' The three men were still making chicken noises. 'You're mad,' he said. 'All of you. Bloody crazy.'

'Go on, John, put on the suit and get into the ring,' said Mickey.

It was a test, Shepherd knew, like dogs scrapping to assert their place in the pack. Mickey and Mark were top dogs so it was important to prove that, and the only way to do so was to give Shepherd a public kicking. Mark had been right: the padded suit would protect him from serious injury, but it would slow him down and hinder his movements. He held up his hands in surrender. 'Okay, okay,' he said. 'I'll do it. But I'm not wearing the sissy padding. You want to fight me, let's do it properly.'

Mark stopped waggling his arms. 'Have you done kickboxing before, John?'

'I've boxed a bit,' said Shepherd.

'Boxing and Muay Thai are way different,' said Mark. 'I could hurt you.'

'Yeah, or you could bore me to death,' said Shepherd. 'If you want a scrap, I'll give you a scrap.'

Mickey raised an eyebrow and nodded approvingly. 'Ballsy,' he said.

'Bloody idiot,' said Yates. 'John, Mark's been doing Muay Thai for almost ten years. He was south of England champion before we moved to Thailand.'

'Hey, if John wants to try his luck, let him,' said Mark.

'I'd wear the suit if I were you, mate,' said Mickey.

'I'm okay,' said Shepherd. 'Where do I get changed?'

Mickey showed him where the changing rooms were. Shepherd went inside and put on the sweat-stained T-shirt and shorts that he'd been wearing in the gym. There was a full-length mirror on one wall and he watched his reflection as he loosened up. He had never done any kickboxing but he had no qualms about getting into the ring with Mark. Shepherd knew that on the street most martial arts were worse than useless for self-defence because they each had their own set of rules, and anyone who followed the rules could be beaten. A boxer wouldn't use his feet, a karate expert wouldn't grab or gouge, a judo expert was unable to punch. Once you knew what the rules were, you knew the fighter's weaknesses. Shepherd had no rules when he fought. He fought to win and would do whatever it took to achieve that objective. The problem was that when he got into the ring with Mark, he would have to follow the rules of the sport. He could punch and he could kick and he could use his knees and elbows, and he couldn't kick him when he was down. Shepherd smiled at his reflection. His SAS training had stressed from the start that in combat there were no rules. Kicking a man between the legs was a valid technique, as was gouging out his eye or smashing his trachea. In a fight to the death you did what you had to do to survive.

Shepherd went up onto the balls of his feet, clenching and unclenching his hands. Killing Mark Moore would be easy. What was going to be more difficult was fighting with him, following the rules of Muay Thai, and letting him win. If Shepherd got into the ring and beat him, his infiltration of the Moore crew would be over. Mark and Mickey were the dominant alpha-males, the leaders of the pack, and they would not allow anyone in their gang who threatened the status quo. So, Shepherd had to fight, and fight well, but ultimately he had to let Mark win. He took a deep breath and went back into the training area.

Mickey had a pair of boxing gloves ready for him and he fitted them while Mark did some stretching exercises in the ring. 'You sure about this, mate?' said Mickey. 'The padded suit will take the sting out of the punches and kicks.'

'Yeah, and make me look a right twat,' said Shepherd. 'I'll be okay.'

Mickey fastened the glove on Shepherd's left hand. 'Your call,' he said. 'Look, watch out for his roundhouse kick with his left leg. You won't be expecting it because he normally kicks with the right. He'll punch to the face, then fake a straight kick with his right leg, but then he drops the right and kicks with the left. He doesn't do it a lot, but when he does, nine times out of ten it's a knockout.'

Yates came over with a gum shield. 'You'll need this,' he said. Shepherd opened his mouth and Yates slipped it in.

Mickey did a final check of Shepherd's gloves, then helped him into the ring. 'No rounds, just a bit of sparring,' said Mickey. 'Anytime you want to stop, just say.'

There was a bell on a table at one side of the ring and Yates rang it. Mark and Shepherd faced each other and gently touched gloves. They stepped back, both falling into defensive positions. Mark had his left leg back and both hands high, almost at the level of his forehead, palms down, chin pushed against his chest. He stared fixedly at Shepherd, breathing through his nose.

Shepherd was more relaxed and had his hands just above waist level, confident that he could move fast enough to block any attack from Mark. He faked a punch with his right hand to see how Mark reacted. His hands dropped to block the blow. Shepherd began to kick out with his right leg but as he did Mark stepped forward and launched a flurry of blows at Shepherd's face. A glove clipped Shepherd's nose and he jumped back, blinking. Mark continued his attack with an upper-cut that just missed Shepherd's chin and three short jabs to his chest.

Shepherd fell against the ropes and Mark rushed forward, putting his gloves on Shepherd's shoulders and driving his knee into Shepherd's stomach. The breath exploded from his lungs and he twisted to the side, elbowing Mark in the chest. As Mark turned to follow him, Shepherd turned and hit him three times in the chest, left, right, left, then kicked him in the stomach. Mark staggered back, and Shepherd moved to the centre of the ring, fighting to get his breath back. Mark grinned at him and winked. 'You had enough?' he asked. Shepherd shook his head.

Mark shuffled forward, then kicked with his right foot. Shepherd stepped to the side but as he did Mark hit him with a punch to the chin that jerked his head back. Mark regained his balance as Shepherd put up his hands to protect his face. Seeing that Shepherd's chest was unprotected, Mark jabbed him three times above the solar plexus with his right hand, grunting with each punch.

'Go on, Mark!' shouted Yates. 'Give him some!'

Shepherd moved closer to Mark, not wanting to give him the chance to use his feet. He kept his head down to protect his chin and throat, and bobbed from side to side looking for a gap. Mark moved with him, keeping his hands high. Shepherd faked a punch to the chest, then swept Mark's legs from under him with a sweeping kick. Mark hit the ground hard and rolled over before getting up. As he straightened, Shepherd kicked him in the chest, putting all his weight behind the blow. Mark fell back against the ropes but used them to bounce back into the ring, arms pumping like pistons. Shepherd blocked the blows and then got in two hard punches to Mark's face. Mark shook his head as he ducked and wove, then lashed out with his right fist, narrowly missing Shepherd's chin.

Shepherd shuffled backwards, feigning a punch to Mark's face, then faked a kick.

'Get him, Mark!' shouted Wilson.

'Go on, my son!' screamed Yates.

It was time to finish the fight, Shepherd knew. And he had to make it look convincing. He stepped back and raised his arms, opening up his stomach. He started breathing heavily, making it look as if he was more tired than he actually was.

Mark grunted and threw a half-hearted punch at Shepherd's head, which Shepherd blocked easily. Then Mark lashed out with his right leg. Shepherd lowered his arms to block the kick, knowing what was coming next. Mark dropped his right leg, transferred his weight to it, and twisted his hip to start the roundhouse kick. Shepherd saw it coming but kept his hands low. As the foot connected with the side of his head he moved to the right, trying to absorb as much of the blow as possible, but it was a powerful kick and hit him hard. His mouthguard spun across the ring. He heard a yell of triumph from Yates, then felt his legs buckle and slumped to the ground. He rolled onto his back and the room spun. He tasted bile at the back of his throat and swallowed, not wanting to throw up. He saw Mark grinning down at him triumphantly and closed his eyes to concentrate on his breathing.

Something slapped his cheeks gently. 'Hey, come on, mate, you're okay.' It was Mickey.

Shepherd blinked. The room was still spinning and he closed his eyes again. Water splashed over his face and found its way between his lips. He coughed. Through half-closed eyes, he saw Mickey peering down at him, holding a plastic bottle of water. 'Are you okay, mate?' asked Mickey.

Shepherd opened his mouth to speak but winced at the pain in his jaw. He swallowed and tasted blood. 'Did I win?' he croaked.

Mickey laughed. 'No, mate, you didn't. I warned you about his roundhouse kick, didn't I?'

Shepherd groaned. 'Yes, Mickey, you warned me. Next time I'll wear the bloody suit, okay?'

Bradshaw put on his sunglasses and pulled the peak of his baseball cap low. He was wearing gloves in case the ATM swallowed the card. There were two machines in the wall of Lloyds TSB in Edgware Road and neither was being used. He walked up to the one on the right and slotted in the card. He tapped in the four-digit code, then held his breath. In his mind he heard alarm bells ringing and boots pounding on pavements, and pictured himself surrounded by armed policemen shouting at him to get on the ground, then guns firing and bullets ripping through his body. The machine whirred, returned his card and a few seconds later ejected a wad of ten-and twenty-pound notes. Bradshaw pocketed the money and walked away from the machine, keeping his head down. He smiled to himself. He hadn't checked the safety-deposit box yet, but he was certain that the money would be there.

Mickey waved at a waitress to bring over more drinks and slapped Shepherd on the back. 'You all right, John?' he asked.

'My head's still ringing but that could be the booze,' said Shepherd. They were in the Angelwitch go-go bar. On stage more than a dozen lithe girls in black leather bondage gear and high-heeled black boots gyrated around the chrome poles. One of the girls, with dyed blonde hair and pneumatic breasts, kept trying to make eye contact with him, and every time his eyes met her she blew him a kiss.

Mickey, Mark and Shepherd were standing close to the stage while Yates and Wilson were sitting at a table with two bargirls.

'She wants you, mate.' Mickey laughed.

'She wants my money,' said Shepherd.

'If you're hoping for a love job, you're in the wrong place,' said Mickey.

'Where's Davie?' asked Shepherd. Black had left them as soon as they'd arrived at Walking Street.

'He's off to Boyztown,' said Mark.

'Boyztown?'

'It's the gay area,' said Yates. 'Gay go-go bars, gay short-time hotels, gay saunas. It's a poofter's paradise.'

'You'd never know he was gay by looking at him, would you?' said Shepherd.

'He's gay, not camp,' said Mickey. 'We've known him since he was a kid and it was obvious before he was a teenager that he wasn't interested in girls. Doesn't matter a toss. Davie's Davie and that's the end of it.'

A tall girl with shampoo-commercial hair came up behind Mark and caressed his backside. She had on a black dress tight enough to show that she wasn't wearing underwear. Mark twisted and kissed her. 'What about you, John?' he said.

'I don't want to get the clap,' said Shepherd.

'These girls are fine,' said Mark, waving at the dancers. 'They're tested every month.' He stroked the hair of the girl by his side. 'They check you, right?'

'Check?'

Mark spoke to her slowly, as if he was addressing a retarded child. 'Doctor check you for Aids and everything?'

The girl nodded vigorously. 'I fine,' she said. 'Doctor check every month.'

'And how many guys do you think they go through in four weeks?' said Shepherd. He indicated a small brown girl with a tattoo of a red and green dragon on her back. 'She left with a guy an hour ago and is already back up there dancing and waiting for another customer. That's not for me, mate.'

An obese Westerner in a Chelsea shirt, his shaven head bathed in sweat, tried unsuccessfully to climb onto the podium and fell back into a waitress, almost crushing her against the wall. He grinned at her drunkenly and slumped to the floor.

Two pretty girls appeared at Mickey's shoulder. They were wearing tight jeans and low-cut black T-shirts and could have been twins. 'Right, I'm taking Bee and Boo back to the villa for a seeing-to,' he said.

'Which one's Bee and which one's Boo?' asked Shepherd.

Mickey put his arms around them. 'Who cares?' he asked. 'What are you going to do?'

'I'll head home,' said Shepherd.

Yates and Wilson paid their bill, then joined Mickey. 'We're going to Lucifer's, pick up a few freelancers,' said Yates.

The clammy night air washed over them as they walked through the curtain into the alley. Mickey lit a cigar and tossed the match into the gutter. The tables around the food vendors were busy, with bargirls and their customers perched on stools eating rice and noodles on plastic plates. Yates and Wilson waved goodbye and headed through the Walking Street crowds to Lucifer's disco.

Mickey and Shepherd had parked their vehicles not far from Sharpe's hotel and they walked together towards the beach road. Young Thai girls dressed in skin-tight shorts and low-cut tops smiled hopefully at Shepherd, and touts tried to tempt them inside the establishments that paid their wages. They walked by the police volunteers' van and past a series of outdoor bars where hundreds of Thai girls flashed teeth and thighs at any foreigner.

'Handsome man!'

'Where you go?'

'I go with you!'

The beach road was packed with baht buses and cars,

all preparing to turn left at the pedestrianised Walking Street. Mickey and Mark guided their girls to the path that ran alongside the beach and Shepherd followed them. More girls stood at the side of the path or sat on concrete benches, handbags clutched in their laps. They were older than the girls Shepherd had seen in the bars, and most had bad skin, unkempt hair, cheap clothes and worn shoes. They were at the bottom of the city's sex industry, women whose last hope was a tourist too drunk to see clearly. Shepherd doubted they had regular medical checks – they were clearly more concerned about where their next meal was coming from than their health. One stick-thin woman must have been in her fifties, her mouth a slash of scarlet lipstick across a wrinkled face, bloodshot eyes blank as she scratched a bleeding scab on her knee. Shepherd had an urge to give her some money, do something to improve her hellish life, but he could see from the telltale marks on her arms that any cash she had would go straight into her drug-dealer's pockets.

Some of the girls at the roadside were barely out of their teens. Shepherd couldn't tell if they were working or not but at one o'clock in the morning it was a fair assumption that they were.

'Hey, Mickey, that's one of the paedos,' hissed Mark.

'Where?'

'Over there, talking to those two Thai kids.'

Shepherd saw a middle-aged man in horn-rimmed glasses, wearing a sweat-stained vest and shorts, sitting on a concrete bench under a palm tree, with a Thai boy on either side of him, one aged about ten, the other closer to Liam's age. The man had his hand on the younger boy's knee.

'You sure?' said Mickey.

'Yeah – his name's Slater or something.'

'How do you know he's a paedophile?' asked Shepherd. The older boy was talking to the man but he seemed more interested in the younger one. He pointed to a hotel on the other side of the beach road and said something. The younger boy nodded and smiled.

'I saw his picture on the—' began Mark.

'Doesn't matter how we know,' Mickey interrupted, 'but we know. He's from Bristol, got caught fiddling with a young boy and did a runner.'

'What do you wanna do, Mickey?' asked Mark.

Mickey blew a plume of smoke towards his feet. 'Do you want to see what we do to nonces out here, John?' he asked.

'Same as we do in England, I hope,' said Shepherd, playing his role but worrying about where this was headed. 'Bastard.'

'On the beach?' asked Mark.

'Short and sweet,' said Mickey. 'Come on.' He patted the girls' backsides. 'Bee, walk on down there and wait for us,' he said.

'I'm Boo,' said the girl, pouting.

'Bee, Boo, whatever your name is, go down the road and wait for us.' He held up his right hand, fingers splayed. 'Five minutes.' He handed her his cigar. 'Keep that warm for me, darling.'

The girls tottered down the road on their precariously high heels. Mark's girl followed them, glaring reproachfully at Mickey.

Mickey and Mark headed purposefully towards Slater, who looked up as they approached but had no time to react. 'Come here, nonce,' said Mark, grabbing him by the vest and pulling him to his feet.

Slater opened his mouth to scream but Mark seized his throat and pushed him towards the beach.

A Thai woman in her thirties who had been watching Slater hurried to the two boys and ushered them away. Shepherd wondered if she was their mother or their pimp. The younger boy said something to her and she clipped him around the ear.

Mickey came up behind Slater, grabbed him in a bear-hug and carried him onto the sand. Mark had released his grip on the man's throat and now seized his legs. Slater kicked out but Mark thumped him in the solar plexus and he went into spasm. Slater was struggling but Mickey and Mark held him tight.

Shepherd followed them onto the sand. 'What are you going to do to him?' he asked Mark.

'Kick the shit out of him,' said Mark. 'He's a nonce. Pattaya's full of them. Cops turn a blind eye so when we find one we make sure they know they're not wanted.'

The Moore brothers reached the water's edge. Mark let go of the man's legs, then hit him in the stomach twice, left and right, putting all his weight behind the blows. Slater sagged and Mickey let him fall to the sand. Mark kicked him in the ribs and Slater curled into a foetal ball, whimpering. Mickey kicked his back, swearing with each blow.

Mark beckoned Shepherd. 'Come on, John, give him some.'

Shepherd glanced over his shoulder. Nobody was looking in their direction. He could hear the traffic driving down the beach road and, in the distance, the thud-thud-thud of a stereo system. He turned back to the brothers, who were still kicking Slater and stamping on his limbs. Slater was grunting with each blow but he'd stopped putting up any resistance. His knees were against his chest and his hands covered his face.

Mark knelt down and punched him on the side of the head. 'We don't want your sort here, do you understand?' he shouted. Slater didn't respond so Mark punched him again. 'You get the hell out of Thailand, or we'll kill you.' He pulled the man's hands away from his face. 'You hear me?'

'Okay,' said Slater. 'I get it.' He began to sob. 'I'm sorry.'

'You make me sick,' said Mark, and spat in his face.

Mickey walked around the prostrate man and kicked him in the stomach. 'Bloody paedo,' he said. 'Come on, John. Your turn.'

Tears were running down Slater's cheeks and there was blood on his lips. Mark stamped on his left foot and Shepherd heard something crack. 'He's had enough,' he said quietly.

'He's a bloody nonce,' said Mark. 'You saw him with those kids.' He kicked Slater savagely.

'Go on, John,' said Mickey. 'Give him a kicking.'

Shepherd had no love for paedophiles, but he didn't believe in vigilante justice or in kicking a man when he was down. But Ricky Knight was a villain who'd been inside and, like all villains, he'd have a burning hatred for paedophiles and rapists. He had to stay in character and that meant getting violent. 'Scumbag nonce,' he said, and kicked Slater in the small of the back, grunting loudly to make the blow seem harder than it was. 'Bastard!' Shepherd shouted, and kicked Slater again, making sure he didn't hit the man's kidneys.

Now Mickey was kicking Slater viciously, and Mark stamped on his legs. Slater was crying but, other than curling into a ball, he made no effort to protect himself. Shepherd could see that if they carried on, the man would be crippled for life. He looked towards the beach road. Two Thais were standing by a street-lamp.

'Guys, I think they're cops over there,' said Shepherd.

'Where?' said Mark.

'Over there,' said Shepherd, pointing at the two men. 'One of them just used a radio. We should get the hell out of here.'

'He's right,' said Mickey. 'Let's go.'

Mark knelt beside Slater and grabbed a handful of his hair. 'Get on the next plane out of Thailand or you're dead,' he spat. Slater groaned. Mark pushed his face into the sand, then hurried after Shepherd. Mickey gave Slater a final kick in the stomach and jogged to catch up.

'Does this sort of thing happen a lot?' Shepherd asked Mickey.

'When we find one, we sort him out.'

They ran a couple of hundred yards along the beach, then cut across the sand back to the beach road. The three girls were waiting for them, smoking and talking animatedly. They jumped up and down when they saw the men coming.

'I'll get a baht bus from here,' said Shepherd. He stuck out his hand. 'Thanks for an interesting night,' he said.

Mickey grinned. 'We'll do it again, for sure,' he said.

* * *

Mickey wandered out onto the terrace, sipping his coffee. The espresso was slightly bitter and full-flavoured. He'd had the beans flown in from Colombia and the coffee machine from Italy. It had taken him two weeks to teach his chef to make espresso but now he did it perfectly, day after day. He smacked his lips. 'Lovely,' he said. He heard a bird singing in one of the trees on the other side of the wall and raised his cup to it. 'And a good morning to you, my love,' he said.

Andy Yates was on a sun-lounger by the pool. 'You all right, Mickey?'

'Couldn't be better,' said Mickey. 'Is Chitpong here yet?'

'At the main gate,' said Yates.

The two girls who had come home with Mickey were frolicking in the shallow end of the pool. They waved at him and he waved back. 'Did you bring anyone back last night?' he asked Yates.

'Nah, we didn't fancy them for all night so we went to a short-time hotel off Walking Street,' said Yates. 'Right flea-pit, it was.'

Mickey gestured at the two girls. 'Help yourself to Bee and Boo,' he said. 'Can't for the life of me remember which is which, but they do a great threesome. Very enthusiastic.'

'I might just do that, thanks,' said Yates.

Mickey went inside the main building and over to a large painting of the sun going down in Phuket. It was hinged and he swung it back to reveal a large safe with a numeric keyboard. He tapped in the combination and pulled open the door. Inside there were stacks of banknotes – dollars, pounds, euros and Thai baht. He took out a wad of thousand-baht notes, then closed the safe and replaced the painting. He picked up the phone on the desk by the window and tapped out the number of the main gate. He didn't know the name of the man who answered but he told him to send Chitpong up to the main building. Chitpong was a police sergeant with two elder brothers who were high-ranking police officers in Bangkok. His brother-in-law was a general in the Thai Army. He had his fingers in pies all over Pattaya, from the Turkish baths on Second Street to a golf course and spa on the outskirts of the city. Mickey paid him a retainer of two hundred thousand baht a month to arrange security at the compound. Chitpong hired his own men to work on their days off at the compound and took a cut of the wages Mickey paid them.

Chitpong ambled up the path to the main building. He was wearing his dark brown police uniform trousers, shining black leather boots and a black sweatshirt with the logo of the Royal Thai Police Force across the front. His police-issue Glock was in a nylon holster on his hip. 'Good morning, Khun Mickey,' said Chitpong. He was overweight and like most Thai police officers he favoured a close-fitting uniform so the trousers strained across his groin.

'I need a favour from your friend at Immigration,' said Mickey. 'Landing-card details of a *farang* who arrived last week.' He handed Chitpong a sheet of paper. 'His name's John Westlake. I'm not sure what flight he was on. He's British but he could have flown in from anywhere.' Chitpong took the paper. It was a faxed copy of John Westlake's passport, courtesy of Dominic Windsor. Mickey gave him the wad of banknotes. 'Soon as you can, yeah?' he said.

Chitpong forced the cash into his trouser pocket. 'No problem, Khun Mickey,' he said. 'I'll have a copy sent out before lunch.'

Mickey slapped him on the back. 'You're a star,' he said. He sipped his coffee as Chitpong walked back to the main gate. First he would get as much information as he could about John Westlake or Ricky Knight or whatever his name was. Then he'd decide what to do with him.

Shepherd was getting to the end of a forty-five-minute run on a treadmill set to a five per cent incline when Yates and Black walked in. He raised a hand to them and switched off the treadmill, then joined them in the weights area.

'Last night was a blast,' said Yates. 'I had the mother of all hangovers this morning.'

'You and me both,' said Shepherd. He rubbed his chin. 'Plus I had a sore jaw and bruises all over my body.'

'Yeah, Mark's an animal,' said Black.

'You did all right, though,' said Yates. 'Right up to the moment he kicked you in the head it was fifty-fifty.'

'Yeah, I didn't see that one coming,' lied Shepherd.

When he'd finished his workout, Shepherd picked up his towel and headed for the showers.

'Fancy a swim instead?' asked Yates.

'What? In the sea, you mean?'

'Bloody hell, no,' said Yates. 'You'd be mad to swim in the sea here. They pump raw sewage into it. Nah, back at the ranch. We've got a fair pool. Might get a poker game going later.'

'That's the plan, yeah? Play me for a mug?'

Yates slapped Shepherd on the back. 'We're pussycats, pal. Come on, it'll be a laugh.'

'Okay,' said Shepherd. 'You've talked me into it.'

They walked together out of the gym. 'Where's your Harley?' asked Yates.

Shepherd nodded at his Jeep. 'I'm driving that today. The Harley's misfiring and I've got to get a mechanic to check it over.' In fact the bike was fine but he'd already had several near misses driving the Harley on the Pattaya roads and he felt a lot safer behind the wheel of the Jeep.

Yates climbed onto his Harley and pointed down the road. 'You follow us. We're about ten miles outside town.'

Shepherd got into his Jeep and threw his gym bag into the back. Yates and Black pulled out of the car park on their bikes. Shepherd switched on the engine and followed them. As he drove, he called Sharpe on his mobile and told him where he was going.

'The lion's den, huh?' said Sharpe. 'You want me to take a ride up there to be close by?'

'They live in a compound behind a bloody big wall,' said Shepherd. 'I don't think there's anything you could do. A swim and poker, Moore said. I think I'll be okay.'

'A swim and poker? Won't the cards get wet?'

Shepherd cut the connection. The bikes had accelerated and Shepherd put his foot down. He overtook a family of four crammed onto a 125cc Honda motorcycle, a leathery-skinned father with Buddhist tattoos on his neck, a plump mother with her hair tied back in a bun, a small boy with a Power Rangers backpack clinging to her, and a toddler sitting on the father's lap and holding the handlebars, her hair whipping in the wind. The mother smiled at Shepherd and the small boy waved.

The bikes took a left turn and drove through a village of wooden houses with corrugated iron roofs. They passed a large factory with smoke billowing out of two metal chimneys. There, the road branched into two and the bikes powered to the right, Shepherd behind them.

The compound was about half a mile after the factory. The bikes turned left off the road towards a high concrete wall topped by metal spikes and covered with CCTV cameras. Two well-built Thai men in their late twenties were standing at the entrance. One raised a red and white pole to allow the bikes through. Yates stopped and pointed at Shepherd's Jeep. As Shepherd drove through, the guards saluted him.

The compound had been landscaped with rolling lawns, towering palms and spreading fruit trees. The road curved in front of a Thai-style building, with a sweeping red-tiled roof, and ended in a parking area with spaces for more than two dozen vehicles. There were two black Range Rovers, a red Porsche, a black Humvee, a Bentley convertible, an old MGB sports car and three Toyota saloons. Shepherd reckoned the latter belonged to the staff.

He parked his Jeep next to the Humvee. A flight of steps led to a massive antique carved wooden door that must have been at least twelve feet high. Over to the right, Shepherd glimpsed the roof of a villa, and there was another to the left, shielded by a line of banana trees.

Yates and Black walked over to him. 'How big is this place?' asked Shepherd.

'It's about twelve acres in all,' said Yates. He gestured

at the main building. 'This is where we hang out most of the time, but we've got our own villas for privacy, all state-of-the-art.'

Shepherd heard the buzz of an electric drill and banging from the villa to their right. 'What's going on over there?'

'We're getting Tel's place fitted for his wheelchair,' said Black. 'We're putting in ramps, electric lifts in the bathrooms, lowering the kitchen surfaces, raising electric sockets. We had a disability expert in to tell us what he'll need.'

'He's not going back to the UK?' said Shepherd.

'You've got to be joking,' said Black. 'Have you used the NHS lately? They'd send a home help around a couple of times a week if he was lucky. Here we can get him a couple of sexy nurses living in, pay for any drugs he needs, and if there's anything that has to be done surgically we'll pay for it here. Thai medical care is great, so long as you've got the money. Come on, I'll give you the tour.'

Black and Yates took Shepherd up the steps and through the door into a double-height hallway with a vaulted teak ceiling and a seven-foot-tall golden standing Buddha wreathed in garlands of purple and white flowers. The hallway led to a huge room filled with sofas and teak planters' chairs, a large LCD television on one wall and a library of paperbacks. 'Chill-out area,' said Yates. 'We've got our own satellite dish out back so we can pick up pretty much every channel there is.' He took Shepherd along to a dining room with a table long enough to seat twenty, then opened a door to reveal a private cinema with a dozen La-Z-Boy reclining seats. Shepherd was impressed. He'd thought his own villa was luxurious but it paled in comparison to this.

'The guys are in the bar,' said Black. He and Yates led Shepherd down a corridor that opened into a double-height area, with vaulted teak ceilings and large wooden-bladed fans. It had been fitted out in the style of a hotel bar, with leather sofas and armchairs, a mahogany counter complete with beer taps, a popcorn machine and a full range of spirits. Glass-fronted fridges were filled with wine and soft drinks.

The five-star feel was spoiled somewhat by the three video-game machines, the Wurlitzer jukebox, a massive fruit machine and a pool table.

Mickey and Mark were at the bar, sitting on stools and drinking Singha. They raised their bottles. 'It's Bruce bloody Lee!' Mark laughed.

Shepherd put up his hands. 'Just don't hit me again!'

'Found him in the gym,' said Yates, pouring himself a draught beer. 'He was working on his muscles for a rematch.'

'Bloody wasn't,' said Shepherd.

'He's only breaking your balls,' said Black, as he sat on one of the leather sofas. 'It's what he does for fun.'

'This is one hell of a place, guys,' said Shepherd.

'It's taken a lot to get it this way,' said Mickey. 'We ended up flying in builders from England – the locals just weren't up to it. We let them do the pool and it was a bloody disaster so we had to start again.' He slid off his stool. 'Come and have a look – it's one hell of a pool.'

Mickey wasn't exaggerating. It was Olympic size but designed in the shape of a tropical lagoon, with rocks big enough for sunbathing at one end, two diving-boards at the deep end, and two curved artificial beaches. At the shallow end there was a Jacuzzi big enough for a dozen people, and around the edge, half a dozen teak cabanas, their roofs fringed with palm leaves. A covered area, with a brick-built barbecue the size of a regular kitchen, was positioned to the right, with a circular teak table and a dozen chairs. 'The pool's just over a thousand square metres,' said Mickey. 'One of the biggest free-form pools in the world. We've got two poolboys and three full-time gardeners, plus half a dozen maids and a handyman. Plus two full-time chefs. Plus security. Plus a manager to keep them all in line. Plus an accountant to make sure no one's ripping us off.'

'It must cost you a fortune,' said Shepherd.

Mickey took a swig of his beer. 'It's where we live,' he said. 'It's our home.'

'Even so . . . this is living it large.'

'You only live once, mate. You've gotta seize the day – you've gotta go for it because no one's going to hand it to you on a plate.' He waved at the pool. 'Come on, let's get some use out of it, yeah?'

'I'll get my gear,' said Shepherd. He went back through the bar and outside to his Jeep. When he returned with his gym bag, the rest of the men had joined Mickey at the poolside and were in their trunks.

'Changing rooms over there,' shouted Wilson, pointing at a stone building with a teak roof.

Inside Shepherd found a row of showers and toilets, and ten polished steel lockers. He changed into his shorts and wandered back to the pool. Mickey and Mark were in one of the cabanas, drinking Singha and leaning against triangular Thai pillows. Yates was already in the pool, doing a brisk breast-stroke, his head rising high out of the water each time he brought his hands back to his chest.

'Help yourself to a beer, mate,' said Mickey, jerking a thumb at a small fridge in the back of the cabana. Shepherd bent down and took out a bottle of Heineken. 'Bloody hell, mate, what happened to you?' He was staring at the scar on Shepherd's shoulder. 'That's a gunshot wound, innit?'

Shepherd ran his finger across the scar tissue. 'Yeah.'

'Working?'

'Sort of,' said Shepherd. 'Army.'

'Can I have a look?'

'Knock yourself out.'

Mickey stood up and came over to him. The scar was puckered in a tight circle, darker than the surrounding skin. 'That was one big bullet,' said Mickey.

'Yeah, well, they don't mess around with Kalashnikovs,' said Shepherd.

'No way,' said Mickey.

'In Afghanistan,' said Shepherd. 'Bastard took a pot-shot at me.'

'Let me have a butcher's,' said Mark.

'You were in the army?' asked Mickey.

'No, you soft bastard, I was with the Taliban. Of course I was in the bloody army.'

'You don't look like ex-army, that's all.'

'I'll take that as a compliment.'

'Who were you with?' asked Mickey.

'The Paras,' said Shepherd. It was the first lie he'd told. Everything else had been true, but his Ricky Knight legend didn't include a spell with the SAS.

'So you jumped out of planes and shit?' asked Mark. He took a fresh bottle of Singha out of the fridge and used his teeth to prise off the cap. He spat it over his head and took a swig of the beer.

'That's sort of what paratroopers do,' said Shepherd.

'All paras jump out of planes?'

Shepherd wondered if Mark was joking but it was clear from his earnest expression that he was serious. 'That's right.'

Mark looked at his brother. 'I thought Tel was with the Paras but he never jumped out of a plane.'

'Tel was a squaddie. He just talks big sometimes,' said Mickey.

'When's he coming back?' asked Shepherd.

'Doctors say another week or two.'

'What was the story with the truck?' asked Shepherd.

'The driver was out of his head on booze and amphetamines, hit Tel and went off like a bat out of hell,' said Mickey. 'Cops picked him up an hour or two later but he blamed Tel and they dropped the case.'

'Bastards,' said Shepherd.

'Every time a *farang* and a Thai have a run-in, the cops always side with their own,' said Mickey. 'That's the way it is. We'll have him, though – we know where he lives. We're just biding our time.'

'So, have you fired big guns and shit?' Mark asked Shepherd.

'Again, that's what paras do, Mark,' said Shepherd. 'They jump out of planes and they fire shit.'

'And you did that in Afghanistan?'

'I didn't jump in Afghanistan, but I fired a lot of shit, yeah.'

'Like what?'

'Why the interest?' asked Shepherd.

Mark grinned. 'We fire a lot of shit ourselves,' he said. 'We go over to Cambodia – it's real Wild West over there.

There's an army range where they let you fire pretty much anything you want. Machine-guns, mortars . . . You can even throw grenades.'

'Sounds fun.'

'It's a bloody riot,' said Mark. 'They give you machine-guns and you can shoot at chickens. Shoot them to bits. And if you want they'll let you shoot a cow. You've got to pay for it, and they keep the beef afterwards, but you can kill it.'

'Not sure I'd want to shoot a defenceless cow,' said Shepherd. He sipped his beer and sighed. 'This really is the life, isn't it? You've got yourselves well sorted.'

'We've worked hard for this,' said Mark. 'Bloody hard.' He went back to sit in the cabana. Mickey and Shepherd joined him on the Thai pillows.

'Do you go back to England much?' asked Shepherd.

'Just for business,' said Mickey. 'It's a shit-hole, these days.'

'England's finished,' said Mark. He leaned towards Shepherd. 'You know how many Brits pack up and leave England every year? Two hundred and fifty thousand. A quarter of a million. And when I say Brits, I mean English, the likes of you and me. Real English.'

'Whites, you mean?'

Mark shook his head emphatically. 'It's nothing to do with colour, mate. Tel's as black as the ace of spades but he's as British as you and me. Even served in the army – did two tours in Afghanistan. His parents came over to England in the sixties and he was born in Brixton. He's a West Ham supporter, but apart from that he's a diamond. The point is, Tel's black but he hates the way England's gone down the toilet as much as I do. It's not about colour, it's about culture. I'm English, so are you. You know how many of my relatives died in the First and Second World Wars fighting for our country? Thirty-seven. Thirty-bloody-seven.'

'I'm not sure I get your point,' said Shepherd.

'The point, mate, is that my family shed its blood for our country. Fought and died for it. But now it's not my country any more . . . Our mum died five years ago. Stroke.'

'Sorry to hear that,' said Shepherd.

'By the time she died, her and our dad were the only white people in their street. Every other house it was Asians or bloody Taliban refugees. Me and Mickey got him out, got him a villa in Spain. Happy as Larry he is now, playing poker and sitting by the pool. And you know what? The village he lives in, almost everyone's English. That's how crazy it is. In London he was surrounded by foreigners. He goes abroad and he's with his own kind. The world's gone mad.'

'I'll drink to that,' said Mickey. He clinked his bottle against his brother's, then Shepherd's.

'I wonder how the Spanish feel about it,' said Shepherd.

'What do you mean?' said Mark, frowning.

'It's sort of the same, isn't it? Brits are flooding into Spain and to the Spanish they're foreigners.'

'It's not the same,' said Mark. 'Spain is EU. I've nothing against the Spanish wanting to live in England if that's what floats their boat. The Spanish are okay. What I object to is the fact we give passports to Indians, Pakistanis, Chinese, Serbs, Romanian gypsies, the scum of the earth.'

'Actually, Romania's EU,' said Shepherd. 'They're entitled.'

Mark's eyes hardened. 'What?'

'I'm just saying, Romania's in the EU. They can move to the UK if they want, same as you can live in Romania.'

'Why the fuck would I want to live in Romania? It's a shit-hole.'

Shepherd put up his hands in surrender. 'I'm not arguing with you. Forget I said anything.' He grinned. 'Just don't hit me again, yeah?'

Mark didn't smile and Shepherd could see he wasn't happy. Mark Moore had a short fuse and Shepherd knew it wouldn't take much to ignite it.

'I know what John means,' Mickey said to his brother. 'Guys like us go to live in Spain or Thailand, that makes us the foreigners. They probably don't like it any better than we like Pakis and the rest moving into the UK.'

Shepherd knew he needed to change the subject. The last thing he wanted was a full-blown argument with Mark. Wilson was standing on the springboard over the swimming-pool, bouncing up and down, arms out to the side. He had a line of ornate Thai script running from his left shoulder to his elbow. 'What does that Thai writing on Barry's arm say?' he asked Mickey.

'It says, "I am a twat", that's what it says,' said Mickey.

Shepherd laughed. 'No, seriously, what does it say?'

'It says, "I am a twat", God's honest truth,' said Mickey. 'He's going to get it lasered off once he finds a doctor he can trust.' Mickey took a long pull on his Singha, then wiped his mouth on his arm. 'He had it done not long after we got to Thailand. We were in Bangkok before we came here and he pulled a dancer from the Long Gun Bar in Soi Cowboy. Fit as a butcher's dog she was, hair down to her arse – could suck the chrome off an exhaust pipe. Anyway, Barry there bar fines her for a week and on the second day decides it's a love job.'

'Bar fine?' repeated Shepherd.

'You really are a newbie, aren't you?' said Mickey. 'If you meet a bird in a bar and you want to shag her, you have to pay a fee to the bar. It's usually about a tenner. Once you've paid the bar fine she can go with you.'

Wilson put his hands together and hurled himself inelegantly off the springboard. He hit the water hard, his stomach taking most of the impact. Droplets of water peppered the surface of the pool like rain.

'Anyway, Barry tells this dancer he wants to get her name tattooed on his arm in Thai,' Mickey continued. 'A sign of his love, right? They both get well pissed before they go to see the tattooist and she tells the guy what to write. The next morning Barry wakes up to find she's done a runner with his wallet, his Rolex, his jewellery, his credit cards and his passport. She's cleaned him out. So he toddles along to the tourist police and tells them his tale of woe. They're very sympathetic and ask him if he knows her name. "I can do better than that," says Barry, and he peels off his shirt to show the tattoo to the cops. That's when he finds out that he's got the Thai for "I am a twat" on his arm.'

Wilson pulled himself out of the pool and ran his hands through his hair. He saw Shepherd and Mickey looking at him and scowled. 'What?' he said.

'Just telling him about the love of your life,' said Mickey.

Wilson rubbed the tattoo. 'If I ever catch her . . .'

'What? You'll have "wanker" tattooed on the other, will you?' teased Mickey. 'You soft bugger.' He tapped his bottle against Shepherd's shoulder. 'Word to the wise, mate. Don't ever let a bargirl get close to you. They look like butter wouldn't melt in their mouths but they'll rip your heart out, and your wallet.'

Shepherd raised his bottle in salute. 'I'm not interested in paying for it,' he said.

Mickey chuckled. 'Everyone pays, mate, one way or another.'

Paul Bradshaw continued counting the fifty-pound notes. There were five hundred in all, amounting to twenty-five thousand pounds. The cashier picked up the notes and ran them through an electric counting machine that whirred for a few seconds, then digitally confirmed Bradshaw's total. He took the Western Union form that Bradshaw had carefully filled out and ran it through his computer, then handed him a receipt.

Bradshaw walked out into Edgware Road, past a coffee shop where a dozen men in Arab dress were drinking coffee and smoking aromatic hookahs. He put his hand into his jeans pocket and took out the phone card he had bought from an Arab-run Internet café down the road. There were two phone boxes outside a branch of Woolworths, both covered with lurid postcards advertising the services of local prostitutes. He went into one, lifted the foul-smelling receiver and tapped out the Baghdad number. He knew how easily the authorities could download address books from mobile phones so the phone numbers he needed were committed to memory – he often used mnemonics as an aid.

The number was answered by a timid female voice. 'It's me, Farrah,' said Bradshaw. 'I'm calling from overseas. Please don't say my name.' He knew that the Americans monitored all phone traffic in and out of Iraq and he did not want even his first name to be used on an open line.

'I understand,' she said.

'I've sent you money today.' Her name meant 'Joyful' but he knew there had been no joy in Farrah's life since the death of her husband and unborn child.

'You do not have to do anything for me,' she said.

'It is my duty, and my pleasure,' he said. 'I wish there was more I could to make your pain easier to bear. Money is nothing.'

'You are an angel,' she said.

Bradshaw laughed softly. 'No, I'm not, but I've sent you money today. You can collect it from Western Union, if you show your ID. Do you remember the restaurant we went to, the last time we ate together?'

'I remember,' she said.

'You can collect the money from the bank next to it. They're expecting you.'

'You are my saviour.'

'No, I'm not,' he said. 'I'm sorry – I'm sorry for everything.'

'It wasn't your fault,' she said. 'No one blames you for what happened.'

'I do,' he said. 'Please, collect the money and remember me in your prayers. I will send you more, I promise.'

He put the phone down. Suddenly he felt giddy, as if the blood had drained from his head, and he put his hand against the side of the phone box to steady himself. He did blame himself for what had happened to Yusuf and his family. When Farrah's waters had broken, Yusuf had phoned him and asked if he would take him and his wife to hospital but Bradshaw had been due out on patrol and had refused. If he had gone with Yusuf, if there had been a Westerner in the car, the Americans wouldn't have fired. But Bradshaw had gone out on patrol, and Yusuf and his child had been killed, and Farrah would be in a wheelchair for the rest of her life. Bradshaw did blame himself and would until the day he died. The money he had just sent made him feel a little better, but only a little.

So much had changed since the day Yusuf and the baby had died. Bradshaw had become a Muslim and had come to realise how he'd been misled by his parents, his teachers and his government. He knew now that British soldiers had no right to be killing Muslims in Afghanistan and Iraq, no right to be telling other cultures how to conduct themselves. What had happened in Afghanistan and Iraq had nothing to do with democracy, Bradshaw knew, and everything to do with oil and the subjugation of Muslims. That had to end, once and for all, which was why Bradshaw had become a soldier of *jihad*, determined to right the wrongs of his people. The money he had sent to Farrah was a small fraction of what had been left for him in the safety-deposit box in Knightsbridge. And nobody would be asking him to account for every pound he spent. All his paymasters would be concerned about was whether or not he carried out his mission. And Bradshaw was sure he would succeed and that people would die. A lot of people.

Richard Underwood's mobile phone buzzed. He rolled over and grabbed it before it disturbed his wife. He always had it set to vibrate with the sound off because she was a light sleeper. He checked the screen. He'd been sent a message.

CALL ME. He squinted at the number. It had a 66 prefix, which meant it had come from a mobile on Thailand, but Underwood already knew that. There was only one man who would send him a message as blunt as the one he'd received.

'Work?' mumbled his wife, rolling over and putting her arm around him.

'I'm afraid so,' he lied. 'Sorry.'

'Bastards.' She kissed his neck.

She was half asleep, and Underwood had half a mind to roll on top of her but the other half was too concerned about the message. 'Tell me about it,' he said. He squinted at his alarm clock. It was seven o'clock, only fifteen minutes before his usual waking time. He untangled himself from his wife, showered and put on his work suit, a dark blue pinstripe. His briefcase was downstairs in the hallway and he collected it on the way out, along with the copy of *The Times* on his doormat. He got into his Vauxhall Vectra and started the engine. He had his mobile set on hands-free but he had no intention of calling Mickey Moore on any phone that could be traced back to him. These days, the police and other agencies were capable of listening into and tracing almost every electronic communication anywhere in the world.

He drove to a petrol station four miles from his house and pulled in next to a public phonebox. He got the Thai number from his mobile and tapped it out. As soon as Moore answered, Underwood fed in half a dozen pound coins. 'Mickey, it's me,' he said.

'Dicko, how are they hanging, mate?'

'What do you want, Mickey?'

'You're always tetchy in the morning, aren't you, old lad?'

'Less of the "old", you bugger,' said Underwood. 'Now, come on, I'm in a call box and the meter's running. What do you want?'

'I need someone checked out, mate. Soon as you can.'

Underwood sighed. 'PNC checks are getting bloody risky. Everything's logged, these days, and if there's any come-back, your feet don't touch the ground. And by "your feet", I mean my feet.'

'This one's easy,' said Moore.

'I'm listening.'

'There's a guy out here by the name of John Westlake. Arrived a week ago. I've got his landing card and a copy of his passport and they look kosher, but according to the latest Europol watch list, he's a blagger by the name of Ricky Knight. He's on the run after a big bank job in Birmingham. Tiger kidnapping. Europol are on his case.'

'Sounds like you've got all the info you need, Mickey.'

'I want you to confirm what I know,' said Moore. 'I need you to tell me that Westlake is Knight, but then I need you to do a complete check on Knight. His full CV.'

'It'll be five for the PNC checks,' said Underwood. 'I've a pal in the Border Agency I can run the passport by. That'll be another two. If Knight's done time I'll run him through the Prison Index. That'll be another two. Let's call it a round ten, shall we?'

'Bloody hell, Dicko, you'll be pricing yourself out of the market if you carry on like this.'

Underwood took out a small notebook and a Mont Blanc pen. 'Stop whining and give me the date of birth and passport number,' he said. 'I've got a job to go to, unlike some.'

Stuart Townsend smiled at the girl behind the check-in desk and handed her the small laminated card he always carried. She said something to him but Townsend shook his head and pointed at the card. There was no problem with Townsend's voice but he knew from experience that if he told someone he was deaf they wouldn't believe him.

The girl frowned as she read the card. 'HELLO, MY NAME IS STUART TOWNSEND. FOLLOWING AN ACCIDENT I AM TOTALLY DEAF BUT I CAN SPEAK. I CANNOT SIGN BUT I CAN LIP READ IF YOU SPEAK SLOWLY AND CLEARLY. THANK YOU FOR YOUR UNDERSTANDING.'

The girl handed the card back to him and flashed him a thumbs-up.

He gave her his passport and the email confirming his booking on the Thai Airways flight.

The girl checked his passport and tapped on her keyboard. 'Do you have any bags to check in?' she asked, speaking slowly, her eyes on his.

Townsend held up his small shell suitcase. 'Just this,' he said. 'It fits into the overhead locker.'

'That's fine, sir,' she said. 'You'll have plenty of room in first class anyway. Now, has anyone given you anything to take on board?'

He shook his head. She tapped on her keyboard, then looked up expectantly. He realised she must have asked him a question while she was looking down. Townsend gestured at his ear. 'Can't hear you,' he said. 'I have to see your lips.'

The girl's cheeks flushed. 'I'm sorry,' she said. 'I asked if you knew where the lounge was.' She handed him a boarding-pass and a pass to the Thai Airways lounge.

'I do, yes,' he said.

'Do you need someone to take you through Security?' she asked.

Townsend smiled. 'I'll be fine,' he said. He thanked her and took the escalator up to the departure gates. A man in a fleece jacket watched him go, then made a call on his mobile phone.

Shepherd's phone rang, waking him from a dreamless sleep. It was five o'clock in the morning, which meant it was late at night in England. 'Are you sleeping, Spider?' Charlotte Button asked.

'Not any more,' he said, rubbing his eyes and sitting up.

'Can you talk?'

'Of course I can talk,' he said. 'Exactly what do you think I'm doing out here?'

'Boys will be boys,' she said.

'I can't believe you're saying that,' said Shepherd.

'I'm joking. Where's your sense of humour?'

'It doesn't normally kick in until after breakfast,' he said. 'Which is about three hours away. Believe me, I'd rather be at home than here.'

'Understood,' said Button. 'But at least things are starting to move. Stuart Townsend's on the way to Bangkok. He should be arriving at about four o'clock in the afternoon, your time, with Thai Airways. He's booked into a hotel in Bangkok for one night so expect him in Pattaya some time tomorrow.'

'Any idea what job he's planned?'

'I wish,' said Button. 'It's all on his laptop and it never leaves his side.'

'No clues from where he's been?'

'Have you ever tried following a deaf man, Spider? They're constantly looking around, never off guard. If our guys get too close he spots them. Too far back and they lose him. But he's been on the M25 a few times so we reckon it's somewhere in the south of England.'

'I guess there's no point in me tailing him?'

'No need. He's obviously there to see the Moore brothers,' said Button. 'How are you getting on?'

'I had a spell in the ring with Mark. My teeth are still loose.'

'I thought you SAS types could handle anything that was thrown at them?'

'I had to let him win,' said Shepherd.

'Of course you did,' said Button, sympathetically.

'I'm serious,' said Shepherd.

'And so am I.'

'It's a dominance thing,' said Shepherd. 'I had to show that I could take care of myself, but leave him thinking he's top dog.'

'You don't have to explain anything to me,' said Button.

'Thank you.'

'You fought, you lost, that's all I need to know.'

Shepherd opened his mouth to insist that he'd deliberately lost the fight, but then saw she was only teasing him. 'Ha ha,' he said. 'Anyway, they took me out for a night on the town afterwards and I helped them beat up a paedophile so I think they've accepted me.'

'You did what?'

Shepherd smiled. 'It was part of the initiation,' he said. 'Better you don't know.'

'I think you're right,' said Button.

'They haven't talked about business yet. I didn't see them yesterday and I was waiting for them to call. I don't want to seem too keen.'

'Don't leave it too long,' said Button. 'Someone's just checked you out. A chief superintendent with the Met, guy by the name of Richard Underwood.'

'He's on their payroll?'

'Looks like it, but we've not tracked down a paper trail yet. He's based at Paddington Green, has a clutch of commendations and is only five years away from retirement. But he ran the Westlake name and Ricky Knight through the Police National Computer, and he checked the Westlake passport with the Border Agency.'

'He could only have got that from the Moores,' said Shepherd.

'Exactly,' said Button. 'He was thorough with the Knight legend, I have to say. After the PNC showed up the robbery conviction he ran it through the Prison Index, then made a call to the police liaison officer at Wandsworth.'

'Shit,' said Shepherd.

Button laughed. 'Relax, we had it covered,' she said. 'The officer briefed him on your three-year stint and said you were a hard nut but that you did your time without too many black marks.'

'So, Underwood will give me a clean bill of health?' asked Shepherd.

'Looks like it, if he hasn't done so already. How do you want to handle it?'

'I can't push it too hard,' said Shepherd. 'I'll give it a while, then mention I'm having trouble getting my money out of the UK. Maybe chance my arm and tell them the cops have frozen some of my accounts, crack on that cash might be a problem. But, like I said, it'll have to be casual, these guys are pros. There wasn't even a hint that they suspect me. They were all as nice as pie.'

'You'll be fine,' said Button. 'The fact that they're checking you out and not just cutting you dead means they're interested rather than threatened. Do you need anything?'

'I don't suppose you'd spring for a return flight to the UK so that I can pop back to see my boy?'

'I'd love to, but if the Moores found out it would blow everything,' said Button. 'We can't risk it.'

'I know,' said Shepherd. 'It was just wishful thinking.'

'Soon as this case is closed, you can have all the time off you want, I promise.'

'I'll hold you to that,' said Shepherd.

'How's Razor, by the way? Is he behaving?'

'Good as gold,' said Shepherd.

'Why do I think you're being less than truthful?'

Shepherd laughed. 'Cross my heart,' he said.

'And hope to die?'

Shepherd laughed again. 'I never hope that,' he said. 'Tempting Fate. Something I need to bounce off you. Razor's not happy with his hotel. In fact, it's more of a knocking shop than anything. Is it okay for him to move into a better place?'

'How much better? I don't want him moving into a five-star presidential suite.'

'It'll be within budget,' said Shepherd. 'Certainly a lot less than it'd cost in the UK.'

'I'll leave it up to you,' said Button. 'Sweet dreams.'

Mickey Moore flipped through the *Bangkok Post*. As usual there was little in it to interest him. It was just after ten o'clock. 'Has the paper guy been yet?' he asked Barry Wilson. Each day a man on a motorcycle delivered that day's British tabloid newspapers, sent from England by satellite and printed in Thailand. The two men were sitting on the terrace by the pool. Wilson was eating his regular breakfast of cheese omelette and freshly baked French bread, with sliced mango to follow. Mickey rarely had anything other than black coffee and a cigar for breakfast.

'Nah, he's been late the last couple of days,' said Wilson, through a mouthful of omelette.

'Bastard,' said Moore.

The phone rang in the bar and Davie Black answered it. After a few seconds he appeared at the doorway, holding a bottle of Singha. 'The Professor's just arrived,' he said. 'Taxi's dropped him at the gatehouse.'

Mickey finished his coffee and stood up. 'Where's Chopper?'

'In bed. Where do you think?' said Black. 'He didn't get back until five this morning and the last time I saw him he was going into his villa with two girls.' He grinned. 'At least, I think they were girls. Couldn't tell for sure.' His grin widened. 'Not sure he can half the time.'

'Give him a shout, will you?' said Mickey. 'And if he's got guests, get them off the premises ASAP. Just family in on the briefing, yeah? We'll do it in the chill-out room.'

Black headed over to Yates's villa.

'Any idea what he's got for us?' asked Wilson.

Mickey shrugged. 'The Professor never says a word until he's got all his ducks in a row.' He cupped his hands around his mouth and shouted at Mark, who was lying in the bubbling Jacuzzi. 'Mark, the Professor's here!' Four naked Thai girls were giggling and splashing in the shallow end of the pool. They jumped up and down and waved at Mickey. 'And get those sluts off the premises!' he yelled.

Mark climbed out of the water and wrapped himself in a towel while Mickey went into the hallway to open the front door. He watched as Townsend walked slowly up the driveway, dragging a small wheeled shell suitcase and mopping his forehead with a white handkerchief. Mickey waved and Townsend waved back.

Mickey waited until Townsend was close to him before he spoke. 'Stuart, good to see you,' he said, taking care to pronounce each word carefully. He hugged him. He didn't speak again until Townsend could see his lips. 'Flight okay?'

'Pain in the arse, even in first class,' said Townsend. 'The only movies with English subtitles were the crap Chinese ones.'

There were black bags under Townsend's eyes and the whites were bloodshot. 'You look wrecked, mate,' said Mickey.

Townsend grinned. 'Yeah, I picked up an old favourite from Nana Plaza last night,' he said. 'Had her, a Viagra and a bottle of brandy, then she phoned her sister and after another Viagra a great time was had by all. Now I can barely walk.'

'Why didn't you come straight down to Pattaya?' asked Mickey. 'We'd have fixed you up, no problem. We had a dozen dancers from Living Dolls here last night, all loved-up on ecstasy and ready for anything.'

'Anne's a bit special,' said Townsend. 'I think she really likes me.'

Mickey chuckled and took him along to the chill-out area, where Mark was already sitting on one of the sofas, wrapped in a bathrobe. He waved at Townsend.

Wilson was standing at the bar. He mimed pouring a beer. 'Have you got a Guinness? I could do with the hair of the dog,' Townsend asked.

'Not on tap,' said Wilson. 'Just in cans.'

Townsend frowned: Wilson was too far away for him to read his lips. Mickey touched his arm and repeated what Wilson had said. 'A can will be fine,' said Townsend.

Wilson opened a fridge, took out the Guinness and poured it.

'Where's Terry?' Townsend asked Mickey.

'Bit of an accident. Fell off his bloody bike. Still in hospital.'

'He's going to be all right?' said Townsend.

Mickey grimaced. 'Probably not,' he said. 'Broke his spine.'

'That's a pity,' said Townsend.

'Tell me about it,' said Mickey.

'You're going to be needing his expertise on this one. Not sure it's a goer without him.'

Mickey patted his shoulder. 'Let's see what you've got, Professor,' he said. 'Let me worry about recruitment.'

Townsend took his Panasonic Toughbook from his shell

suitcase and plugged it into the mains. 'Okay if I use the plasma?' he asked Mickey.

'It's an LCD, but knock yourself out,' said Mickey.

Wilson came over with Townsend's Guinness. He took it, knelt down next to the screen and took a connecting lead from his case.

'I don't believe he's deaf,' said Mark, putting his feet up on the coffee-table.

'You always say that,' said Mickey, sitting next to him on the sofa.

'Hey, Professor, your wife gave me a blow-job last night but she wouldn't swallow!' Mark shouted.

'Mark!' protested Mickey.

Mark grinned. 'What?' He gestured at Townsend, who was plugging his lead into the side of the television. 'You said he was deaf. If he's deaf he can't hear me so it doesn't matter.'

'Don't be a tosser,' said Mickey.

'Why the sense-of-humour failure?' asked Mark.

'Because the Professor's a good guy and I don't want you taking the piss,' said Mickey. 'Where the hell would we be without him? Do you want to sit outside a bank for four weeks with a stopwatch?'

Mark held up his hands. 'I apologise.'

'Fine,' said Mickey.

Mark slid off the sofa, went down on his knees and bowed to his brother. 'I am so, so sorry,' he said.

Mickey pointed a warning finger at him. 'Stop taking the piss,' he said. 'Kickboxing or no kickboxing, I can still give you a seeing-to.'

Mark straightened and grinned. Townsend finished connecting his computer to the television and turned. He saw Mark on his knees. 'Something wrong?' he said.

'Just my idiot brother fooling around,' said Mickey.

Yates walked in, unshaven, hair tousled. 'Sorry,' he said. 'Rough night.' He grinned at Black. 'Get me a hair of the dog, Davie. Singha.'

'What's the magic word?' asked Black.

'Now,' said Yates. 'Get me a bloody Singha now! Please.'

Black took a bottle from the fridge and tossed it to him. Yates caught it one-handed and sat next to Mark. He gave the bottle to him, Mark bit off the cap and beer sprayed all over him. He spat the cap over the back of the sofa and gave the bottle to Yates. Mickey stared at them in disgust. 'You two live like pigs,' he said.

'That's what we've got maids for, Mickey,' said Yates, swinging his feet onto the coffee-table and belching.

'Pigs,' repeated Mickey. He nodded at Townsend. 'Ready when you are, Stuart.'

Townsend tapped on his keyboard and a nondescript concrete building filled the screen. There was a sign on a patch of grass in front of it, with the name of the company and the address of its website. 'I've been watching this place for the past two years, on and off,' he said. 'It's one of the biggest cash distributors in the south-east, handles several of the big supermarket chains, collects and delivers to most of the high streets south of the M25.'

He pressed a button on his keyboard. The picture on the screen became a video, hand-held and shot from the front of a car. An armoured van with the company's logo on the side drove up to a set of large metal gates covered by two CCTV cameras. They rattled back and the armoured van drove inside. Its way was blocked by a second security gate. The outside gate rattled shut. 'They use the same

systems prisons use,' said Townsend. 'The main gate opens
into a secure area. The internal gate won't open until the
outer gate has closed. The vehicle is checked by a man on
duty and by CCTV from the control centre. Both have to
give the okay for the van to go any further.'

He tapped on his keyboard. 'The staff entrance is at
the side of the building.' Another picture filled the plasma
screen, of stairs and a ramp leading up to a glass door.
It was covered by two CCTV cameras high on the wall.
'The same double security procedure applies to the
staff. The glass there is armoured and it's opened by
the man inside in the secure area, which is also covered
by CCTV and monitored by the control centre. The
men in the secure area and the control centre both have
to authorise admission. But there's a biometric key, too.
There's an iris scan that has to be approved and has to
agree with the data on a biometric card, which is passed
through a card reader. So there's effectively three checks
to get in – a visual, an iris scan and a company ID card.
If any one of those is off, the secure area can be locked
down.'

'So it's a tiger job?' said Mark. 'We take the family of
one of the managers and he walks us in?' Townsend's eyes
were on the plasma screen so he didn't react.

'Let the Professor tell us what he's got planned,' said
Mickey. 'That's what we pay him for.'

'I hate tiger jobs,' said Mark, 'kidnapping wives and
kids – they're unpredictable.'

Townsend turned in time to catch the last few words.
'Kidnapping isn't going to work,' he said. 'It might get
you in through the main door but it won't get you anywhere
near the main cash depot. Access there is controlled by

biometric passes and two managers act in concert to open the doors.'

'Bloody hell, talk about overkill,' said Black.

'They've learned the hard way what happens if you allow a single manager access to all areas,' said Townsend. 'Their depot in Leeds was done five years ago. The deputy manager's family were taken and he let them in at close of business. Took them for three million quid.' He pointed at the screen. 'This place has ten times that so they're taking no chances. Like I said, access requires duplicate codes and iris scans.'

'So we do a double, right?' asked Mark. 'Take them both.'

Townsend wasn't looking at Mark so he didn't answer. He tapped the keyboard again and a second video started, this showing staff reporting for work at the side entrance. 'The staff have all been issued with phones that have GPS capability so the company knows where its people are twenty-four-seven. And I mean all the staff, not just the drivers. Most of the monitoring is passive – they can go looking for a particular individual if they need to know where he is – but the managers who have the access codes for the high-security areas are actively tracked. If they go to the pub, their bosses know. If there's any deviation at all from their regular schedule, it's picked up and investigated.'

He pressed a key on the laptop and the video was replaced by a Google Earth satellite view of the south-east of England. 'Okay, so here we go,' said Townsend. He tapped on the keyboard and the camera zoomed in until main roads and larger buildings could be seen. 'The depot is on an industrial estate close to a dual carriageway

that's ten minutes from the M25. The location was chosen
for the ease of making deliveries rather than security. The
nearest major cop shop is ten minutes away, and that's
driving flat out. The area is mainly rural so there's bugger-
all chance of running into an armed-response vehicle.
There's another cop shop in the village nearby but it's not
manned all the time. It'll be empty when we go in.'

Wilson laughed harshly. 'We?' he said.

Townsend scowled at Wilson. 'I like to think I'm part
of the team,' he said.

'Yeah, well, you can think that, but at the end of the
day it's me and the guys who go in carrying guns while
you're sat at home watching *Match of the Day*.'

'Leave it, Barry,' said Mickey. 'Go on, Stuart, we're all
ears.' He winced. 'Sorry, no offence,' he added.

Townsend turned back to his laptop and hit another
key. Mark grinned his brother and mimed shooting himself
in the head. Mickey glared at him. On the screen the
depot could clearly be seen, surrounded by a thick wall.
They could see the sterile area, where the vans were
checked, and a car park beyond the second gate where
half a dozen vans were parked in two lines. Three buildings formed a U shape, with the open end facing the main
entrance. Townsend walked up to the plasma screen and
tapped the building on the right. 'This is the admin block,'
he said. 'Every inch of the car park is covered by CCTV,
which is monitored in the control room in the heart of
the admin block. It's always manned by at least three
employees. They monitor the CCTV cameras, the staff
GPS locators and all their vans.'

'How many vans?' asked Mickey, then realised
Townsend wasn't looking at him. He stood up and went

to tap him on the shoulder. 'How many vans?' he repeated, when Townsend was facing him.

'Twenty-six,' said Townsend. 'At any one time four are being serviced and they always have at least four in the car park as back-ups.'

'Three-man teams in the vans?'

'Always,' said Townsend. 'Two in the cab and a guy in the back. He feeds the cash in and out through the hatchway. But you can forget about the vans. The most we'd get knocking one off is a quarter of a mill.' He tapped the admin block again as Mickey returned to the sofa. 'Entrance to the admin block is by biometric scanner again. Only management have access and only then when it's approved by the control room. Again, it's a double-door system so if anything goes awry the sterile area is locked down. Bomb-proof glass, the works.' Townsend tapped the building directly opposite the entrance to the depot. 'This is the main cash-storage area. A steel door pulls back, allowing access to a sterile area. Again, the inner door can only be opened once the outer door has closed. There's another visual check of the van by an operator on the other side of bomb-proof glass and a cross-check by the control centre via CCTV. The van then drives through into the cash-storage area.'

'How much cash is in there at any time?' asked Mark.

Townsend smiled. 'Upwards of ten million,' he said. 'There's a flow in and out. In from the stores, out to the banks. They try to balance it as much as they can but there are still times when there's as much as twenty-five million in there.'

Mickey whistled, impressed.

'Don't get too excited,' said Townsend. 'The cash is at

its peak on Sunday night because they've filled up from shops over the weekend and they don't do the first bank delivery until Monday. But with what I've got planned, time's an issue and there won't be a chance to load twenty-five million into our vehicles. Also, the cash is stored in locked cages and it'll take time to open each one.'

'When are you going to tell us what you've got planned, Stuart?' asked Mickey.

'So you're interested?'

Mickey wagged a finger at him. 'What do you want? You want me to suck your dick, Stuart? Of course I'm interested. Now, spill the bloody beans. That place is a fortress, how the hell do we get in?'

'That's the problem,' said Townsend. 'We really need Terry for this. Or someone with military training.'

'Terry's out of commission,' said Mickey. 'But we might know a guy who could step in for him.'

Shepherd was in the pool swimming slow laps when his mobile phone rang. He pulled himself out of the water and padded over to it, removing the floppy hat he'd been wearing to protect himself from the fierce afternoon sun. It was Yates. 'Hi, Chopper, what's up?' It had been two days since the Professor had arrived in Pattaya and Shepherd hadn't called any of the Moores' gang, not wanting to appear too eager.

'Just wondering what you're doing,' said Yates.

'Swimming. Are you heading out tonight?'

'The guys are having a barbecue at the compound,' said Yates. 'Come on over. We've got a mate here who's got some land for sale – be perfect for you if you still wanna build your own place.'

Shepherd picked up a towel and wiped his face. 'What time?'

'We're starting now. Come over when you're ready.'

Shepherd ended the call and went through the french windows into his bedroom. He rang Sharpe and told him where he was going. Sharpe grunted, as if he was in pain. 'Razor, what are you doing?' asked Shepherd.

'Nothing,' said Sharpe, but Shepherd heard the guilt in his voice.

'Have you got someone there?'

Sharpe grunted again. Then Shepherd heard a muffled voice, as if Sharpe had put his hand over the phone.

'What the hell are you doing, Razor?' asked Shepherd.

'My back was playing up so I ordered a massage,' said Sharpe. 'It's nothing.'

'You're supposed to be watching my back, not arranging to have yours massaged,' said Shepherd.

'I am watching your back, but right now you're in a luxury villa on your way to a barbecue at an even more luxurious villa, while I'm stuck in a hotel room that's barely big enough to swing a cat, listening to God knows what going on in the room above me. So, forgive me if occasionally I pay for something to help me relax.'

'If Charlie finds out you've been having hookers in your room, there'll be hell to pay.'

'First of all, she's a masseuse, not a hooker. And, second, how's Charlie going to find out?'

'I give up,' said Shepherd. 'There's no talking to you sometimes.'

'You know what your problem is?' said Sharpe. A shower kicked into life and the phone was muffled again as Sharpe spoke to whoever was in his bathroom.

'I'm sure you're going to tell me.'

'You need to get laid,' said Sharpe.

'Screw you,' said Shepherd.

'You see, that's where you're going wrong,' said Sharpe. 'You're in a town with more hookers per square foot than anywhere else in the world, but you're the only red-blooded male here who's not partaking of what's on offer.'

'Because I'm here to work, not to screw around.'

'You're not working all the time,' said Sharpe. 'You're entitled to some time for yourself.'

'That's where you're wrong,' said Shepherd. 'I'm under cover twenty-four hours a day. That's how it works.'

'Exactly,' said Sharpe. 'You're under cover as Ricky Knight, a bank robber on the run in the sex capital of the world. Knight would be taking full advantage of what's on offer, so by not dipping your wick you're out of character. You're putting the operation at risk by clinging to your virginity.'

'I'm hardly a virgin.'

'In Pattaya you are, and if the Brothers Grim realise it, they'll smell a rat.'

In the space of less than a minute, Sharpe had managed to spin the conversation around and now he was making it sound as if Shepherd was the one in the wrong. And the hell of it was that his argument was convincing. 'I'm leaving,' he said. 'I'll phone you when I get back.'

'I'll be counting the minutes,' said Sharpe.

Shepherd ended the call. He'd forgotten to tell Sharpe that Charlie had said he could move into a better hotel. He considered calling him back, then thought better of it. It would serve him right to stay where he was for a while.

★   ★   ★

The red and white pole stayed down as Shepherd drove up to the compound entrance in his Jeep. One of the two guards walked over, holding a clipboard, and Shepherd wound down the window. 'ID card,' said the guard. It wasn't one of the men who had been on the gate the first time Shepherd had visited.

Shepherd frowned. 'I don't have one.'

'Passport? Driving licence?' The guard had the world-weary look of policemen everywhere, and a Glock holstered on his hip.

Shepherd took his John Westlake passport from his pocket and showed it to the guard. He checked the name against a list on his clipboard and Shepherd's face against the photograph on the licence, then nodded curtly and handed it back. He spoke to his colleague and the second guard raised the pole. Both men saluted as Shepherd drove through the gate.

Yates was waiting for him at the top of the stairs leading to the main building, wearing an oversized shirt, covered with different-coloured elephants, and baggy shorts. 'We're in the bar,' he said. 'Come on through.'

Shepherd jogged up the stairs. Yates clapped him on the back and ushered him through the hall. 'How many people are coming?' asked Shepherd.

'Lots,' said Yates. They walked by the chill-out room. There was no sound, no buzz of conversation, no clink of glasses, no sign of any sort of party in progress. Shepherd slowed but Yates put a hand in the small of his back, pushing him forward. 'Mickey's going to be doing the cooking and he's a magician with the old char-coal,' said Yates. Shepherd knew that Yates was talking to cover his nerves. Something was wrong, very wrong, and it was too late for Shepherd to do anything about it. 'He had the steaks flown in from Australia, no expense spared,' continued Yates. Shepherd heard the tension in his voice.

They walked into the bar. Mickey and Mark were standing in the middle of the room with their hands on their hips, wearing Nike tracksuits; Mickey's was red and Mark's was blue. Wilson was by the pool table, holding a cue in both hands. Black was sitting on a bar stool but slid off it as Yates closed the door to the bar.

'What's up, guys?' asked Shepherd. He heard the uncertainty in his voice but forced himself to smile as if he didn't have a care in the world.

'Don't give me that, you slag,' said Mickey, walking towards him with his fists bunched. 'We know what you're up to.'

Shepherd stared at him unflinchingly. 'What's wrong?'

'Did you think you'd get away with it?' said Mickey, his face just inches from Shepherd's. 'Did you think you could pull the wool over our eyes like we were born fucking yesterday?'

'Mickey, what the hell is wrong?'

Mickey jabbed his finger at Shepherd's nose. 'Don't you "Mickey" me, you lying slag.'

'Let me sort him out, Mickey,' said Mark. He grabbed the pool cue from Wilson and strode towards Shepherd, swinging it from side to side. 'We know who you are,' said Mark. 'And we don't like slags who take the piss.'

Shepherd's pulse raced but he fought to keep his voice steady. 'What the hell are you talking about?'

Mark pointed the cue at Shepherd's face. 'You slag,' he hissed.

'Don't hit him here,' said Mickey. 'We'll never get the blood out of the floors. Take him outside, do it on the patio.'

'Up,' said Mark, gesturing at Shepherd with the pool cue. Wilson had picked up a second cue and was holding it like a club.

'I don't know what you guys have been taking, but you're making a big mistake.'

'You're the one who's made the mistake,' said Mark. 'Now get up.'

Shepherd's mind whirled. Was Mark telling the truth? Had he made a mistake? Had the bent copper in London kept on digging and turned up his true identity? If that was the case, why hadn't Charlie warned him? 'This is crazy, guys,' said Shepherd. He raised his hands, showing his palms, wanting to appear as non-threatening as possible.

Mark stepped back, keeping the pool cue aimed at Shepherd's face. Mickey picked up his bottle of Singha and took a swig. 'We're going to beat the shit out of you, you lying bastard. Then we're going to bury you out back.'

'Guys, this is madness,' said Shepherd. 'If I've done something to piss you off, just let me know what it is and we'll sort it out.'

'Outside,' said Mark, waving the cue menacingly.

Shepherd glanced around for anything he could use as a weapon but there was nothing within reach other than two crystal ashtrays on the coffee-table.

'Outside,' Mark repeated.

Shepherd did as he was told, stepping through the french windows onto the terrace. A slight breeze ruffled his hair. He heard Mickey and Mark step onto the tiles behind him. Shepherd took a deep breath. He could run for the low wall at the end of the pool, and if he made it that far he could keep low and duck between the palm trees, get to the wall, and if he hit it hard enough he might be able to scramble over the top. He exhaled slowly. Mark was behind him, and there was every chance that as soon as he started to run, the cue would smash down on the back of his head. And even if he made the wall it was topped with razor wire. He forced himself to relax.

'Keep your hands up,' said Mark.

Shepherd slowly raised his arms. Mark was close, maybe close enough to reach if he swung around and lashed out with his foot.

'Anything you want to say?' asked Mickey. 'Anything you want to tell us?'

Mark and Wilson raised their pool cues, hatred in their eyes.

Shepherd wondered what he was getting at. If he knew Shepherd was an undercover SOCA agent he'd have said so already. And he doubted that the Moores would take the risk of killing an undercover officer, even in Thailand. And in the unlikely event that they did decide it was worth killing him, they were hardly likely do it in their own home. He smiled to himself. The brothers were winding him up. He lowered his hands. 'You bastards,' he said. 'You had me going. You know my little secret, yeah?'

Mickey pointed at Shepherd's face. 'We know you're not John bloody Westlake, that's for sure. What did you think, Ricky? Thought we were born yesterday, did you?'

Mark and Wilson lowered their cues, hatred replaced with malicious grins. 'Had you going, didn't we?'

'Having someone threaten to beat my brains out always gets me going,' said Shepherd. He shook his head. 'You bastards.'

Mickey put an arm around his shoulders. 'Come on, let's have a drink,' he said, guiding him back into the villa. 'We've got something we want to run by you.'

Once they were inside Mark went to get cold beers from the fridge.

'Why did you give us all that guff about you being a car thief?' said Mickey as he collapsed onto one of the sofas. 'You ashamed of being a pavement artist?'

Shepherd smiled at that. It wasn't a phrase he'd heard in a long time. 'I'm on the run, Mickey. Probably best that I don't broadcast what I do for a living.'

'The way I see it, Ricky, what we do for a living is nothing to be ashamed of. You've been inside, you've seen the sort of scum that's behind bars in England. Drug-dealers, kiddy-fiddlers, rapists. Compared with them, we're princes.'

'I didn't start robbing banks for the glory, Mickey. I needed the sodding money.'

Mark walked over with bottles of Singha. He handed one to Shepherd and put another in front of Mickey.

'You know what I mean,' said Mickey, picking up his beer. 'You never hurt anyone, right? Not really. You went in with a shooter but it was a tool of the trade. I bet you never pulled the trigger in anger.'

'You pull the trigger, you leave forensics. Everyone knows that,' said Shepherd.

'Exactly,' said Mickey. 'That's what I always tell Mark. If we wanted to shoot at civilians, we'd have joined the police.' He threw back his head and guffawed at his own joke.

Shepherd leaned forward, holding his bottle with both hands. 'What are you saying, Mickey? Are you telling me we're in the same line of business?'

Mickey looked at his brother. 'He doesn't know who we are.'

Mark sat next to Shepherd. 'That's because we've never been caught, Ricky. Unlike you.'

'We're low-profile villains who commit high-profile jobs,' said Mickey. 'Mark's right, we've never been caught. No one's looking for us, our money's in the banking system, we can come and go as we please.'

'Would you have done anything I might have heard about?'

'One of the reasons we've never been caught is because we don't tell tales,' he said. 'We plan everything down to the last detail, we always have an escape route and we only work with people we trust.'

'Yeah, that's what's always let me down,' said Shepherd. 'Other bloody people. Anyway, at least now I can forget about pretending to be someone else.' He raised his bottle in salute. 'To ordinary decent criminals.'

The brothers raised their bottles in unison. 'Ordinary decent criminals,' they echoed.

Shepherd tapped the four-digit code into his burglar-alarm console, then unlocked the french windows to the patio and stood by the waterfall at the end of the swimming-pool as he phoned Charlotte Button.

'I hope you're calling with good news,' she said, as soon as she answered.

'I'm in,' he said. 'Sort of.'

'Sort of?'

'They've told me what they do but they haven't told me what they've got planned. They just told me who they are and we had a barbecue.'

'Very civilised,' said Button. 'Did you get to see the Professor?'

'He wasn't there. And they didn't mention him. They said they'd done some high-profile robberies that were well planned but they wouldn't go into details.'

'We'll keep a watch for him at Heathrow,' said Button. 'So, are you okay?'

'I'm fine,' he said. 'They're not the easiest of guys to hang out with. Mark's got a short fuse so I'm on eggshells.'

'Hopefully it won't be too much longer. In the meantime, any info you can pick up about the job will be gratefully received.'

'I'm on it,' said Shepherd. 'How are you going to play it, Charlie? Are you going to let it run all the way?'

'Let's see what they've got planned,' she said. 'No point in counting chickens. You take care, you hear?'

'Always,' said Shepherd. He ended the call and stood by the pool, listening to the insects chirping. It got louder and louder until he could almost feel the vibrations on his skin. In the far distance he could hear the dull thudding of rock music and the occasional shriek of laughter. There was never a moment of silence in Pattaya. The bars were open day and night, and there were always people in the streets, no matter what the hour. Even in his secluded villa he could hear motorcycles buzzing along the roads, dogs barking and howling in the distance, cars and trucks sounding horns.

He went back inside to his bedroom and put his phone on the bedside table. He didn't feel like sleeping so he switched on the television. He flicked through the channels. There was a large satellite dish on the roof and he had access to more than five hundred, but he couldn't find anything he wanted to watch.

He heard another phone ringing. It was his home mobile, the one he used for personal calls. He'd left it in the bathroom and hurried to get it. It was Liam. 'What's wrong?' asked Shepherd, his heart racing.

'Nothing, really,' said Liam. 'I mean, I'm okay.'

Relief washed over him. His reaction had been irrational, of course. If anything had happened to Liam, he wouldn't have been making the call. 'I'm glad you called,' he said. 'I've been missing you.'

'When are you coming back, Dad?'

It was a good question, he thought. He had been accepted by the Moores but that was only the first step in what promised to be a long operation. It could take weeks, months even, he had no way of knowing. 'I'm not sure,' he said truthfully.

'You sound funny,' said Liam. 'Like you're drunk.'

Shepherd wasn't drunk, but he'd put away half a dozen beers with the Moores and their team. 'I'm just tired,' he lied. 'It's late here.'

'What time is it?'

It was just after two o'clock in the morning. 'Very late,' said Shepherd. 'I was just going to sleep. How's school?'

'School's school,' said Liam.

'Gran and Granddad looking after you?'

'Sure, but it's not the same as being at home. I want you to come back, Dad.'

'I will, as soon as this job's finished, I promise. And I'll take time off. We can have a holiday.'

'I've got school, Dad.'

'Okay, when school's finished. We'll go to Eurodisney or something.'

'You'll have another job by then,' said Liam, reproachfully. 'You always have another job.'

'I'll make the time,' said Shepherd. 'Have you done your homework?'

Liam sighed. 'Yes, I've done my homework. You always change the subject when you know you're in the wrong.'

Shepherd laughed. 'You'd make a good policeman,' he said. 'You've got excellent interrogation skills.'

'I don't want to be a policeman,' said Liam. 'It's a lousy job. You have no life.'

Shepherd knew his son was trying to hurt him, but there was an element of truth in what he was saying. His work as an undercover agent was all-consuming, and it did mean he spent long periods away from home. But Shepherd loved his job; he loved the challenges it presented and the buzz he got from doing it well. But that wasn't something he could explain to an eleven-year-old boy who missed his father. 'What do you want to do?' he asked.

'I want to be a pilot,' said Liam. 'I want to fly jumbo jets.'

'There's a bigger plane now,' said Shepherd. 'The new Airbus.'

'Do you think I could be a pilot?'

'Sure, Liam. You can be anything you want. You just have to study hard and work hard.'

'Or a footballer,' said Liam. 'I want to play for Arsenal.'

'At least I won't have to pay to send you to university,' said Shepherd.

'Or a rock star,' said Liam, warming to the theme.

'It's good to have options,' said Shepherd.

'Can I have a guitar for my birthday?'

There were times when his son could be as transparent as a villain caught red-handed. 'Sure,' Shepherd said, laughing.

'An electric one?'

'We'll go and buy it together when I'm back,' he agreed. 'Liam, is there a reason you phoned me, other than that you want me to buy you a guitar?'

'Oh, yes. Katra called. She wants to talk to you.'

'She's still in Slovenia?'

'Yeah. She sounded upset, Dad.'

'Okay, I'll call her now.'

'She left her number for you.' As Liam dictated, the digits stored themselves automatically in Shepherd's filing cabinet of a memory.

'Dad?'

'Yeah?'

'I miss you.'

'I miss you too, Liam. I'll be back soon. I promise.' Liam cut the connection. Shepherd took a deep breath. He wanted to sleep but Katra wouldn't have phoned Liam unless there was something important she wanted to discuss. He took a deep breath and tapped out her number. He figured that Thailand was probably three or four hours ahead of Slovenia. She answered almost immediately, and when she spoke it was obvious that she'd been crying. 'It's my father, Dan. He died last night.'

'Oh, Katra, I'm so sorry.'

'It was the chemotherapy. It just killed him.'

'I'm sorry.' Shepherd couldn't think of anything else

to say. It had been the same after Sue had died. Friends and colleagues had wanted to find the words to make him feel better, but there were none. When Sue had died she'd left an aching void in his heart that had never been filled, and never would be. And it would be the same for Katra. There was nothing he could say or do that would take away her pain. All he could do was show he cared.

'Dan, it was horrible. He just got weaker and weaker and then he died. I don't know what to do.'

'Honey, I'm sorry. Are your brothers there?'

'They're with me and they're taking care of everything, but I feel so alone even though they're here. Do you know what I mean?' She sniffed and he could hear her blowing her nose.

'I do, Katra. I'm so sorry.' He wanted to stop saying he was sorry, but the words kept tumbling out. He did feel sorry – sorry for her loss and sorry for his inability to help her – but the words meant nothing to her. After Sue's death he had felt completely alone and it had been months before he'd been able to connect with other people again.

'Are you still in Thailand?' she asked.

'Yes, a place called Pattaya.'

'Dan, my father's funeral is in two days. Can you come?'

Shepherd's shoulders sagged and he put his hand over his eyes. His stomach churned. 'Oh, Katra . . .'

'I don't want to be on my own . . .' She sniffed and blew her nose again.

'Katra, I'm sorry, I'm working.'

'It's just one day, Dan. I just need you with me when I say goodbye to him. That's all.'

Shepherd took a deep breath. The combination of beer

and stress was making him queasy. He owed it to Katra to be with her, but the operation was at a crucial phase. Ricky Knight was on the run and he'd only just arrived in Thailand. There was no reason for him to fly back to Europe. If the Moores found out, alarm bells would start to ring and the operation would be at risk. He had to stay in Thailand, no matter how hard-hearted that made him appear. He wanted to be with his son. He wanted to be in Slovenia to support Katra, but he had to stay in Pattaya. He had no choice. 'Katra, I'm really, really sorry. This is just a bad time.'

'It's always a bad time, Dan.' The line went dead.

Shepherd paced around the room. He understood how upset she was over the death of her father, but as much as he felt she was part of his family, he was only her employer. Katra knew little about his job and he couldn't explain to her how important it was that he stayed in Thailand. He walked through the french windows and around the swimming-pool into the kitchen. He took a bottle of Evian water from the fridge and drank it as he went back to the sitting room. He hit redial on his mobile but Katra had switched off her phone. Shepherd groaned. She was right, of course. It was always a bad time. Working under cover meant working twenty-four hours a day, which left no time to be a father, a friend or anything else. Until the operation was over he was Ricky Knight, and Dan Shepherd had to take second place, no matter who got hurt. When the operation was over, when Mickey and Mark Moore and their team were behind bars, he'd do whatever he could to put it right. He just hoped it wouldn't be too late.

★   ★   ★

Bradshaw walked with his shoulders hunched, the hood of his sweatshirt over his head. Kundi was on his right, Chaudhry on his left. They followed the path towards the café in the centre of the park, close to the children's playground. Two West Indians in security uniforms were watching a group of Kosovans playing a coin-tossing game against the wall of the changing rooms.

Talwar and al-Sayed were already at the café, sitting with drinks at an outside table. 'Get me a coffee, and whatever you want,' Bradshaw said to Kundi, handing him a ten-pound note. He went to the table, embraced Talwar and al-Sayed in turn and sat down. Chaudhry pulled up a chair next to him. He opened a pack of Wrigley's chewing-gum and offered it around, but no one took a piece. He unwrapped a stick and slotted it into his mouth.

'How did it feel?' asked Talwar in a hushed voice. 'When you cut the dog's throat, how did you feel?'

'It was just like that,' said Bradshaw. 'Of no more significance than taking the life of a dog. Less than that. It was like stamping on a cockroach. Or an ant.'

'I'll never forget the blood,' said Chaudhry. 'It pumped and pumped, even after the head was off.'

'The body tries to live even when there's no hope,' said Bradshaw. 'It's the nature of the animal.'

'We should do it again,' said al-Sayed. 'Did you see the newspapers today? The whole world is talking about what we did.'

'No,' said Bradshaw. 'It's time to move on.'

'But it was so easy,' said Kundi. 'We should take a policeman next. Or a politician. We could take an MP. They have almost no security when they do their surgeries.'

Chaudhry nodded enthusiastically. 'I'll slit his throat next time, brothers. I'll do the deed.'

The two black security guards walked by, talking in their own language. The men fell quiet until they were out of earshot. Kundi came over to the table with three coffees. He put the cups down and handed the change to Bradshaw.

'Brothers, there are others who will continue what we have started,' said Bradshaw, pocketing the change. 'But we're leaders, not followers, and we're about to take the next step.'

'We're with you, you know that,' said Kundi, sitting down between al-Sayed and Talwar. He lit a cigarette, using his left hand to shield it from the wind blowing across the park.

'We've proved ourselves, haven't we?' said Chaudhry.

Bradshaw put his arm around Chaudhry, his fingers digging into his shoulder. 'Of course you have, brother, of course you have. You all have. You've done everything I've asked of you. No man could ask for better allies in the struggle for *jihad*. I would die for you, brothers, and I would die happily.' He smiled as Chaudhry added his usual five spoonfuls of sugar to his coffee.

'I have a sweet tooth,' said Chaudhry, defensively.

'Brother, it is a small vice,' said Bradshaw. He sipped his coffee and smacked his lips appreciatively. 'You know, brothers, that they used to call coffee the "Muslim Drink"? It was discovered in the ninth century when shepherds in Ethiopia saw their goats dancing after they had eaten coffee beans. From Ethiopia coffee spread to Yemen and Egypt and on to the Middle East and north Africa. From there it was taken by Muslim traders to Italy and then to the rest of Europe.' He raised his cup. 'And now the Muslim Drink is the most popular drink in the United States. Half the infidels killing our brothers in Afghanistan and Iraq start the day with the Muslim Drink. I wonder if they know that.' He sipped his coffee again, then wiped the foam from his upper lip. He looked around to check that they couldn't be overheard, then put down his cup. 'We have the funding, brothers. And I'm confident we can get the equipment we need. Now let us prepare for battle. Let us show the infidels what we can do.'

Shepherd was doing sit-ups by the pool when his mobile rang. 'What are ya doing?' asked Mickey Moore.

'Just killing time until the bars open,' said Shepherd, mopping his face with a towel. 'What's up?'

'Something we wanna show you,' said Mickey. 'We'll be around in ten minutes.'

The line went dead. Shepherd wondered what the brothers wanted. They were obviously already on their way because their compound was a good half-hour's drive from his villa. As he walked around the pool to the french windows that led to the master bedroom, he called Jimmy Sharpe. 'The brothers are on the way over,' he said.

'What's occurring?' asked Sharpe.

'They didn't say. Need to know.'

'Problem, do you think?'

Shepherd pulled a grey polo shirt off a hanger. 'I don't know. Nothing's happened that could have spooked them.'

'Nothing you know about.'

'Thanks for the vote of confidence.'

'Do you want back-up?'

'Just checking in,' said Shepherd. 'If they were going

to do me harm I don't think they'd have called me first. What are you doing?'

'Watching some pirate DVDs I bought on the street.'

'Wouldn't have thought you were a Johnny Depp fan.'

'Pirate as in counterfeit, you idiot, not *Pirates of the Caribbean*.'

'You do know that's against the law, right?'

'Hey, they're all over the place. When in Rome . . .'

'Just make sure Charlie doesn't find out.'

'I won't tell her if you won't. Seriously, if you need me, you know where I am.'

'Yeah, I know. Lying in your room watching counterfeit videos.' Shepherd cut the connection, put on his shirt and a pair of black Levi's and went back to the pool. He heard the horn of Mickey's Range Rover, slipped on his Reeboks and walked quickly down the path to the main gates. He used his remote control and they grated open. Mickey and Mark were both wearing impenetrable Ray-Bans. Mickey was wearing a Singha beer sweatshirt and Mark had a black T-shirt with 'NO MONEY, NO HONEY' written across it in white.

'Get in,' said Mark.

Shepherd climbed into the back and slammed the door. 'What's up, lads?'

'A magical mystery tour,' said Mark. He pressed a button on the stereo and a Rolling Stones song pounded out through the speakers, making further conversation impossible. The brothers bobbed their heads back and forth in time with the music as they drove away from Shepherd's villa. Shepherd settled back in his seat, an uneasy feeling in the pit of his stomach. The road behind was clear but that didn't mean anything because there were two of them and one of him, and if there was a problem they probably had guns.

They drove along a main road and a couple of times Shepherd saw signs for Bangkok but then they turned onto a lane and drove through dusty farmland for about ten minutes. Dogs scratched themselves in the sun, chickens pecked at the ground and old women peered at the car from beneath spreading hats as they swept the areas in front of their wooden houses. They left the paved road and drove along a track. They passed a wooden shack on stilts with a rusty corrugated-iron roof that seemed deserted, then a line of half-completed shop-houses that were little more than concrete and metal skeletons open to the elements. Shepherd took a quick look over his shoulder. There was nothing behind them other than a cloud of dust being kicked up by the Range Rover.

Three Rolling Stones tracks later they pulled up in front of a metal-sided warehouse surrounded by a chain-link fence. A black Cherokee Jeep was already parked by the entrance and behind it Davie Black's Suzuki Intruder and Andy Yates's Harley.

Mickey switched off the engine and twisted around in his seat. 'Someone I want you to meet, Ricky,' he said.

'I'm not really up for a blind date,' said Shepherd.

Mark climbed out and opened the door for him. Shepherd jumped out and stretched, trying to appear casual and unperturbed by what was going on, but his heart was racing.

Mickey headed for the main door. 'Come on, mate,' he said.

Mark was grinning at Shepherd, waiting to see what

he would do. Shepherd smiled back thinly and followed Mickey. He doubted they had brought him to the middle of nowhere to attack him but that didn't make him any less apprehensive.

Mickey pushed open the door and held it for Shepherd. The warehouse was empty, except for three stray dogs sitting in a corner scratching themselves. 'What's going on?' asked Shepherd.

Mickey pointed at an office unit in the far corner of the building. 'Over there,' he said.

The office door opened and Davie Black waved.

'Everything ready?' asked Mickey.

'All sorted.'

Mickey put an arm around Shepherd's shoulders and guided him towards the office. 'Mickey, this cloak-and-dagger is starting to piss me off,' said Shepherd. He felt Mickey's arm tighten around his shoulders.

Black nodded at Shepherd and stepped to the side. Mickey took his arm off Shepherd's shoulders and gave him a push. Shepherd stumbled into the office. Yates was standing in the middle of the room. He was holding a large revolver, pressed close to his leg. He smiled at Shepherd. 'How's it going, Ricky?' he asked.

'Been a funny old day so far,' said Shepherd. Yates didn't have his finger inside the trigger guide but it was the first time Shepherd had seen a gun around the Moores and it was unsettling.

The room had once been an office but now it was bare of furniture. There was a single window, which had been boarded up with pieces of a crate. A faded calendar hung on one wall and overhead a single light-bulb on a frayed flex. Yates moved to the side. Directly under the bulb, a man was sitting on a wooden chair, his head and upper body covered with a burlap sack. His ankles were bound to the legs with duct tape. Barry Wilson was standing behind him, checking that the tape was secure. He straightened up and winked.

'What's going on, guys?' asked Shepherd.

'This is the guy who ran Terry off the road,' said Mark. 'The bastard the police let off.'

The man was shaking and babbling in Thai beneath the sack.

Black closed the door and stood with his back to it, arms folded. Yates went to stand next to him.

'And?' said Shepherd.

'And now we're going to teach him a lesson,' said Mark. He reached under his sweatshirt and pulled out a handgun. A 9mm Beretta 92FS semi-automatic. He chambered a round and handed it to Shepherd.

Shepherd took it. 'Mickey? What's going on?'

'We're going to deal with this piece of shit,' said Mickey.

'So why am I the one holding the shooter?'

'Because you're on our team now,' said Mark. 'All for one and one for all.'

'We're not the three bloody Musketeers.' He held up the gun. 'What the hell am I supposed to do with this?'

Mark pointed at the hooded man. 'Him.'

Shepherd swung round to Mickey. 'This is madness.'

'Look, Ricky, we know you're good at what you do, but we need to be sure you're with us,' he said.

'You want to test me? Is that it? By killing a man I don't know? Didn't I do enough kicking the shit out of that paedo on the beach?'

Mickey grinned. 'You don't have to kill him. Just put

a bullet in each leg. I want him in a wheelchair, same as Terry.'

'And tell me again, I'm to do this because . . .'

'Because we're a team. Because me and the boys want to see you've got what it takes.'

'Think of it as an initiation ceremony,' said Black.

'Like joining the masons,' said Yates. 'But you don't have to roll up your trouser leg.'

The room was stiflingly hot, and sweat was pouring down Shepherd's face. The back of his shirt was soaking and the butt of the Beretta was wet and sticky. He transferred the gun to his left hand and wiped the right on his trousers. 'I thought you'd seen my CV. I thought your tame copper had already spilled the beans on me, and some.'

Mickey's eyes narrowed. 'How did you know I had a tame copper?'

Shepherd groaned. 'Bloody hell, Mickey, I'm not retarded. How else would you get a look-see at my PNC? But that's not the point. The point is that you want me to shoot a guy I don't know just to show willing. How stupid is that?' He transferred the gun back to his right hand.

'You calling my brother stupid?' sneered Mark.

'I said the situation is stupid. I didn't say Mickey was.' Shepherd scowled. 'Maybe you guys are more trouble than you're worth.'

'If you don't want to do it, that's fine,' said Mickey.

Shepherd sighed mournfully. 'No, it's not fine and we both know it's not. It's a matter of trust, and you're saying you don't trust me.'

'You were a soldier, you've been in wars,' said Mark.

Shepherd had fired Berettas before, and the 92FS was a nice weapon. But he'd never shot a man who was bound to a chair and he doubted he ever would. The hooded man had stopped babbling now and was sitting still. Shepherd ran through his options. He either shot the man or he didn't. If he shot the man, he'd be accepted by the Moores. If he didn't, they wouldn't trust him. They'd either let him go and never associate with him again, or they'd do something more final. He looked at Yates, who had the gun over his groin, the barrel still pointing at the ground. He winked at Shepherd and grinned as if he was enjoying watching his predicament. Would they shoot him? thought Shepherd. Would they really shoot him because he wouldn't cripple the guy in the chair? 'I've never shot a man without a good reason,' he said.

'We've got a reason. He put Terry in hospital and the poor bastard will never walk again,' said Black.

Mark pulled the sack off the man's head and tossed it into the corner of the office. 'Come on, Ricky, a bullet in each knee and we're out of here.' The man struggled and the chair rocked from side to side, but the tape held firm.

Shepherd stared at the man. He was in his mid-forties with a squarish face and a large mole under his right eye. There was something familiar about him and Shepherd flicked through the images in his memory, trying frantically to place him.

'Shoot the bastard,' said Mickey. 'Don't piss around.'

Shepherd stared at the man. He hadn't spoken to him, he was sure of that. And he wasn't a face in the background. That meant a photograph. He'd seen the man in a picture, but when? His mind raced.

'What's the problem, Ricky?' asked Mark. 'You lost your bottle?'

'Do you wanna do it?' asked Shepherd, holding the gun out to him. He wiped his forehead with the back of his hand. He was all too aware that he had no backup. Charlotte Button was on a different continent, Jimmy Sharpe was in his hotel room or one of the local massage parlours, and there was no armed-police unit outside waiting to charge in and rescue him. Shepherd's finger tightened on the trigger as he stared at the Thai man's legs. He was a good shot. He could probably miss the knee and put a bullet in the fleshy part of the leg. Providing he didn't hit an artery the wound wouldn't be life-threatening. But shooting an innocent civilian wasn't an option, no matter how the scenario played out.

He looked back at the man's face, and whatever it was that allowed his near-photographic memory to function clicked into place and he remembered where he'd seen him before. It was in one of Bob Oswald's surveillance photographs. He had been standing by the pool holding a bottle of beer, watching Davie Black preparing to dive into the water. His mind raced as he tried to put everything into place. The man wasn't the truck driver who'd run over Norris, he was an associate of the Moores, possibly a friend. That meant it was either a set-up or the man was being punished for something else. Whichever, the equation had changed. If the man was a member of Mickey and Mark's criminal gang, he wasn't a civilian and as such was fair game. He sighted down the gun at the man's right knee and pulled the trigger. The gun jerked in his hand.

The bang was deafening in the enclosed space and the

acrid cordite stung his eyes. For a split second Shepherd thought he'd misread the situation and that he'd actually shot the man. He stared at the knee he'd been aiming at but there was no wound, no blood, no shattered cartilage or bone. He aimed at the other knee and pulled the trigger again, now confident he'd made the right call. The gun kicked in his hand and the man flinched, but there was no scream of pain.

'Steady, mate,' said Mickey. He held out his hand for the gun. 'Blanks, Ricky. You're firing blanks.'

'Why the hell am I firing blanks, Mickey?'

'We just wanted to see how far you'd go, that's all.'

Shepherd's eyes narrowed. 'Like a test, you mean?'

'Don't get all high and mighty,' said Mark. 'You're the new guy. We're entitled to test your limits.'

'You're entitled to get my boot up your arse, that's what you're entitled to,' said Shepherd. He looked back at Mickey. 'Did you put the blanks in the gun, or did he?'

'I did,' said Mark.

'And how many did you put in the clip? Seven? Eight? Nine?'

'Seven or eight.'

Shepherd pointed the gun at Mickey's left leg and pulled the trigger. Mickey jumped back, cursing. 'What do you think, Mickey? Do you trust me now?'

'Yeah, you mad bastard, I trust you. Now put the gun down and let's go have a drink.'

Shepherd fired again, this time at Mickey's groin. Mickey flinched. 'That wasn't funny!' he shouted.

'You trust me, but do you trust Mark? Do you really trust your brother? Because it seems to me that he's not the sharpest knife in the drawer. Are you sure he took out all the live rounds?' He fired again. His ears were ringing now but he could still hear Mickey's ragged breathing. 'Live rounds don't look all that different from blanks, you know. So, are you sure Mark didn't put a live round in the clip by mistake?' He fired again and Mickey jumped back. 'Come on, Mickey, let's talk about trust. Do you trust Mark?' He pulled the trigger again. 'Do you trust him more than me?' Shepherd pointed the gun at Mickey's face. Mickey stared back, breathing through clenched teeth. 'That's seven, Mickey. Mark thinks he put seven or eight in the clip. But what if it was seven blanks and there was a live round? Or two live rounds?'

Shepherd stepped to the side and pointed the gun at Mark's chest. 'What do you think, Mark? Do we trust you? Or is there just the slightest doubt that you might have fucked up?'

'Put the gun down, Ricky,' said Yates. He was holding his gun in both hands, his feet shoulder width apart.

'You can't shoot me, Chopper,' said Shepherd, his eyes still on Mark. 'There's only blanks in my gun, if Mark did what he was supposed to. What do you think, Mickey? Do you trust him enough to let me pull the trigger?'

'You've proved your point, Ricky,' said Mickey. 'You can stop pissing around now.'

'What about you, Mark? Do you trust your judgement?' Shepherd's finger tightened on the trigger.

Mark threw up his hands and turned his head away. 'Get that bloody thing out of my face!' he shouted.

'Tell me to pull the trigger!' shouted Shepherd. 'Prove to me that there's not the slightest chance you fucked up, that you didn't make a mistake.'

Mark backed up against the wall, his hands in front of his face. 'Get him off me, Mickey!'

'Yeah, get me off him, Mickey,' said Shepherd. He grinned at Mark, then ejected the clip, let it clatter to the floor and tossed the gun to Mickey. 'Next time you pricks decide to test me, I'll put live rounds in the gun myself and shoot you both in the knees.' He gestured at the man in the chair. 'Who is this guy anyway?'

'He works for us,' said Mickey. 'We wanted to wind you up. He knew there were blanks in the gun.' Mickey stuck the pistol into the belt of his jeans and pulled the sweatshirt down over it.

'You're out of order, Ricky,' said Mark. 'You shouldn't point a gun at someone unless you plan to shoot them.'

'You wanted me to shoot him,' said Shepherd, gesturing at the man in the chair.

'We were just winding you up,' said Mark. 'There was no need for you to start waving the gun around, blanks or no blanks.'

'You weren't winding me up,' said Shepherd. 'You were testing me and that's what pissed me off. I know who I am. All I know about you guys is what you've told me, and for all I know you're a bunch of wannabes who're starting to believe their own publicity.'

'We're not wannabes,' said Mark.

'Yeah, well, maybe I'll test you and we'll see how you go,' said Shepherd.

'Guys, okay, enough,' said Mickey. He bent down, picked up the clip and ejected the two remaining rounds. He examined them carefully and swore under his breath.

'What?' said Mark.

Mickey tossed one of them to him. 'You were lucky.'

Mark squinted at the bullet. It was a live round, not a blank. 'Shit,' he said.

'Yeah, shit,' said Mickey. 'Next time be more careful.'

'Shit,' repeated Mark, still staring at the round in disbelief.

Yates put his gun into the belt of his trousers and knelt down to untie the man in the chair. 'I did okay?' said the man.

'You did great,' said Mickey. 'Big joke.' He handed the man a wad of banknotes.

'Yeah,' said Shepherd. 'Big, big joke.'

'Come on, don't get all bitter and twisted,' cajoled Mickey. 'It was a bit of fun.'

'Yeah, fun like a heart-attack,' said Shepherd.

'Look, mate, it was a test, sure, but you passed with flying colours. You're on our crew now, and the next job, you're coming with us.'

'When?' asked Shepherd.

'Soon. But, trust me, it'll be worth waiting for. A shed-load of dosh, more money than you can shake a stick at,' he said. 'Now do you want to come see our mate Tel? We said we'd go in today.'

'Do you want me to shoot him, too?' asked Shepherd.

'Good to see you haven't lost your sense of humour,' said Yates. 'You can sit on the back of my bike if you like.'

They went outside, blinking in the hot sun. The Thai got into the Cherokee Jeep with Barry Wilson and they drove off down the track, clouds of dust billowing up behind them. Shepherd and Yates walked over to the Harley.

'I'm guessing you didn't all go through an initiation like that,' said Shepherd.

'There was no need,' said Yates. 'I grew up with Mickey and Mark, lived just down the road from them. We went to school with Davie, played in the same five-a-side footie team as Tel, and Barry used to work in the garage where we took our bikes. We've known each other for years, so we know where we stand.'

'Never been any problems?'

'Hell, we're family, and families are always at each other's throats. But we're tight, Ricky. Tight like you wouldn't believe.'

'You had any run-ins with the cops?'

'A few, over the years. But unless they actually catch us in the act, there's bugger-all they can do.'

'Because you stick together?'

Yates nodded. 'That good-cop-bad-cop crap doesn't work when you're as tight as we are. If they tell me that Mark or Mickey is going to roll over on me, I laugh in their face.'

'Are the cops that stupid?'

'Bloody right,' said Yates, climbing onto his Harley. 'They think they can put the frighteners on anyone but it doesn't work with us. And no one can grass us up because we don't talk to outsiders about business.' He started the engine. Shepherd climbed on to the back. 'That's where you are, mate. You're on the inside. You're one of us now.'

Mickey and Mark came out of the warehouse together. 'Don't blame me if you end up in the bed next to Tel,' Mickey said to Shepherd. 'They're deathtraps, those bikes.'

'He's in safe hands,' said Yates. 'I've never had an accident.' He tapped his head. 'Touch wood.'

Mickey shook his head and climbed into the driver's seat of the Range Rover. Mark made a gun with his hand, pointed it at Shepherd and pretended to fire two shots. Shepherd mimicked the gesture and fired three into Mark's chest, complete with sound effects. Mark laughed and joined his brother in the Range Rover.

Black was the last to leave the warehouse. He climbed onto his Suzuki. Yates gunned the Harley's engine and put the bike in gear. They sped off down the track, closely followed by Black. Shepherd had a sick feeling in the pit of his stomach. Like Yates had said, he was on the inside now. They trusted him, and they'd accepted him. The only thing left to do was to betray them. Betraying people was what he did for a living, but it didn't make him feel any better about it.

The room where Terry Norris was being treated was bigger than Shepherd's hotel suite had been. There was an LCD television with full cable and a DVD player, a small dining-table and a sofa. The hospital was the one that Shepherd had driven by when he'd arrived in Pattaya, the large concrete tower with the red, white and blue sign on the top. Norris was in bed with a cage holding the sheet off his legs, which were still healing. There were several monitoring machines on a table next to his bed but they didn't appear to be connected. A pretty nurse in a tight-fitting white uniform and scarlet nail polish had ushered the men into the room and left now, flashing them a beaming smile.

'She can take my temperature any time,' said Yates, from the sofa. 'Are all the nurses as pretty as her?' he asked Norris.

'Most of them, yeah,' said Norris. 'But they're all good girls. They smile and they flirt but they're either married or virgins.'

'I didn't think there were any virgins left in Pattaya,' said Mark.

'Where's Davie?'

'He had to pick something up,' said Yates, sitting down at the dining-table and beginning to peel an orange.

Norris noticed Shepherd. 'Hey,' he said. 'These guys lack most of the social graces. I'm Tel.' Next to him on a bedside table was a plate with the remains of steak dinner and a glass of what seemed to be beer.

'Ricky,' said Shepherd. Norris held out his hand and Shepherd shook it. The other man's grip was firm. 'How's it going?' asked Shepherd.

'I just want to get out of here,' said Norris.

'We're getting your villa sorted,' said Mickey.

'Did the docs say when you can leave?' asked Yates.

'Next week or the week after, maybe,' said Norris. 'The legs are healing and my blood's back to normal.' He looked across at Shepherd. 'My spleen was ruptured so they had to take it out.'

'Bugger,' said Shepherd.

'Yeah, I broke three ribs, lucky I didn't lose a lung.'

'Ricky here was in Afghanistan,' said Mark.

'Yeah?' said Norris. 'Where were you based?'

'Kabul for a while,' said Shepherd. 'Then Zabul province. The Taliban's backyard. You?'

'Camp Bastion most of the time, but they moved us around Helmand, wherever the Taliban popped up.'

'See much action?'

'Too much,' said Norris. 'But the bastards wouldn't

fight fair. Ambushes, IEDs – they do everything to avoid a fair fight. We should just nuke the lot of them.'

'Ricky got shot,' said Mickey. 'Took a bullet in the shoulder.'

'Friendly fire?' asked Norris, only half joking.

'Nah, it was the Taliban,' said Shepherd. 'But the Yanks did like to shoot at us, didn't they?'

'Worst soldiers in the world, bar none,' said Norris. 'Who were you with?'

'Three Para,' said Shepherd. 'You?'

'First Battalion, the Royal Anglian Regiment. Why did you leave?'

Shepherd rubbed his shoulder. 'After I got shot, I wanted to get the hell out. They couldn't pay me enough to go through that again.'

'You know they pay traffic wardens in London more than our troops out in Iraq and Afghanistan?' said Norris.

'Yeah. Shows you where we stand in the order of things,' said Shepherd.

'Ricky's joining our team,' said Mickey. 'He's going to help us on the new job.'

Norris nodded. 'You done much before?' he asked Shepherd.

'A bit,' Shepherd said. 'It's fair to say I earn more than a traffic warden now.'

'He's on the run after a tiger kidnapping back in the UK,' said Mickey. 'Had a shoot-out with CO19.'

Shepherd grinned. 'A gun went off accidentally. What can I say?'

'Dangerous things, guns,' said Norris. He gestured at his useless legs. 'I was two years in Afghanistan and I didn't get a scratch. I come out here and a drunken prick ruins my life.' He shook his head. 'Life, huh?'

'There's no rhyme or reason to it,' said Shepherd.

'I should have stayed in the army,' said Norris. 'But who knew, yeah?'

'Don't get all morose, you soft bastard,' said Yates. 'We'll get you sorted.'

'Like Christopher Reeve?' said Norris, sourly. 'He died in his chair, remember.'

'Tel, Reeve was paralysed from the neck down. You've got your arms, your body's fine . . .'

'I just can't walk. Or shag. Or ride a bike. Or use the bathroom on my own.'

'That could change,' said Mickey.

'Yeah. And pigs might fly.' He cursed under his breath.

'We'll do whatever it takes, Tel,' Mickey assured him. 'If we find a surgeon who can help, money's no object, you know that.'

Norris put his hand on Mickey's. 'I know,' he said, and added to Shepherd, 'You're on a good team, you know that? Mickey here's a diamond.'

'Yeah, but a rough one,' said Shepherd.

The door opened. It was Black, with a stunning girl in a white mini-skirt. Her hair fell right down her back and she had a tattoo of a butterfly on her left ankle. 'Brought you a visitor, Tel.'

Norris sighed. 'I'm paralysed, you soft bastard.'

'Yeah, but you can still enjoy a lap-dance, can't you?' said Yates. 'Or she can give you a bed bath. With her tongue.'

'Be rude to refuse, mate,' said Mark, 'now that we've gone to all the trouble.'

'It's not the gift, it's the thought that counts,' said Mickey, slipping a large cigar out of its case.

Yates got up off the sofa. 'We'll leave you to it,' he said.

'I've already paid her and given her the money for the taxi home, so throw her out when you're done,' said Black.

'You're all heart, guys,' said Norris. As the men left, the girl was already slipping out of her dress and giggling.

Mickey strode out of the hospital and lit his cigar. A small boy ran over with a water pistol. Mickey pointed his cigar at the boy. 'You shoot me with that and I'll bloody throttle you!' he growled. The boy backed away. 'I mean it!' shouted Mickey. The boy turned tail and ran off down the road. Mickey out held his cigar for Shepherd to admire. 'It's a bloody Cuban, they cost a fortune out here,' he said.

Shepherd laughed. 'You showed him, Mickey.'

'I didn't want it to get wet,' he said.

'Happy new year,' said Shepherd.

Mickey went to his Range Rover. Mark had already climbed in and turned up the volume of the stereo. 'Are you out and about tonight?' asked Mickey. He lit his cigar and blew smoke into the air.

'Why? Someone else you want me to shoot?'

Mickey chuckled and took a long drag on the cigar.

Yates, Wilson and Black walked out of the hospital. Yates was waving his mobile phone. 'That nurse, the cute one,' he said, 'she gave me her phone number.'

'Must be your winning personality,' said Shepherd.

'Nah, he gave her a thousand baht,' said Black.

'You're just jealous,' said Yates.

'Jealous of what?' said Black. 'I'm gay, remember?'

'How can we forget?' said Yates. 'Maybe she's got a brother.'

'You've got too much testosterone,' said Black. 'That's why you're going bald.' Yates's hand went instinctively to his head and Black laughed. 'Got you,' he said.

Black and Wilson got into the back of the Range Rover.

Shepherd gestured at the hotel behind them. 'How's Tel getting on for money?'

'What do you mean?' asked Mickey.

Yates climbed onto his Harley and fired up the engine.

'The hospital bills can't be cheap and it's not as if he's going to be earning any more, is it?'

'Tel's as much a part of this crew as anyone,' said Mickey. 'We pay his bills and he gets a piece of any jobs we do.'

'So what are you saying? It's a seven-way split even though there's only six of us on the job?'

Yates roared off on his bike.

'I'm saying we're a team and that we look after each other,' said Mickey. 'The same thing would happen if it was you in there.'

'Like a mutual-aid society, is that it?'

'Don't take the piss, Ricky. It's the way it is and that's the end of it.'

'Hey, I'm not complaining. I just want to know where I stand.'

'You're on our team now. That's where you stand. You take care of the team and the team takes care of you. And if you've any problems with that, now's the time to say so and be on your merry way.'

Shepherd held up his hands. 'I'm all sweetness and light,' he said.

'I'm serious, mate,' said Mickey. 'We've never been caught, never even come close. We only deal with people we know and trust. Every job we've ever done has been planned down to the last detail. But the main reason we stay one step ahead of the law is that we're a tight group. No one can split us up, Ricky. No one can screw us over, because there's no reason for any of us ever to want out. We split everything, equal shares. We cover each other's backs. No one can come between us. We're family. And families take care of each other, come what may.' He flapped a hand at the hospital behind them. 'Tel's family. So are you now. If, God forbid, anything goes wrong and you end up in there, we'll take care of you. That's how we work.' He puffed on his cigar. 'It's going to be fine,' he said. 'I can feel it in my bones.'

In his shabby office above a charity shop in Brixton, the Malaysian slid a manila envelope across the table to Bradshaw. 'Three passports and three driving licences, just as you required,' he said. He was a lawyer and specialised in immigration cases, but he had a sideline offering fake passports, driving licences and other documents to those who couldn't obtain them legitimately. Bradshaw had been given the lawyer's name by a friend of the imam who had tutored him in the Bradford mosque. The imam had told him that the Malaysian had a cousin who worked for the Passport Agency at their London headquarters, and that he was totally trustworthy.

Bradshaw opened the envelope and tipped out the passports and driving licences. He flicked through them. The passports were dated as having been issued five years previously, but they were brand new. One contained his photograph, the other two were for Talwar and Kundi. The names were fictitious, as were the dates and places of birth.

'And these are perfect?' said Bradshaw.

'They are genuine passports,' said the lawyer. 'They will pass any inspection. They are machine readable but they do not have the chips that the new passports have. And they cannot be renewed. I would not advise using them to enter the United States, where the checks are more stringent.'

'That's okay,' said Bradshaw. 'We'll only be using them in Europe.' The licences had been issued that week using different photographs from the ones in the passports. Again, they looked perfect.

Bradshaw passed him an envelope containing fifteen thousand pounds. 'For ten thousand pounds apiece I can get you completely genuine passports,' said the Malaysian, taking the money out of the envelope. 'The new design with the chip, the details entered into the Passport Agency computer so they can be renewed without any problem in ten years' time.'

'If I need more, I'll be back,' said Bradshaw.

'Recommend me to your friends,' said the lawyer, counting the money. It was all in brand new twenty-pound notes.

Bradshaw stood up, put the passports and licences back into the envelope and stowed it in his jacket pocket. 'I'll do that,' he said.

Shepherd was in a local supermarket putting a carton of eggs into his wire basket when his mobile rang. It was Mickey. 'What are you doing, mate?'

'Shopping,' said Shepherd. 'I've no food in the villa.'

'You should get yourself some staff,' said Mickey, 'a maid and a cook. Cost you a couple of quid a day.'

'Yeah, you're probably right,' said Shepherd. That was a lie. He'd decided against employing any domestic staff because he didn't want anyone overhearing his phone conversations with Button and Sharpe. 'What are you guys up to?'

'Eating,' said Mickey. 'Place called Jameson's. Can you come on over?'

'I've eaten,' said Shepherd.

'We need to talk,' said Mickey. 'It's time to get things moving.'

'The next job?'

'Exactly.'

'Where's Jameson's?'

'Side-street off Second Road. You can't miss it, it's signposted.'

'I'll drive over now,' said Shepherd.

It took him twenty minutes to find the place: an Irish pub with a black and white façade. He left his Jeep in the car park next to Mickey's black Range Rover and walked inside. Shepherd saw Mickey and Mark sitting at a corner table with massive fry-ups. He sat down and a waitress brought a menu. 'Just beer,' said Shepherd. The Moore brothers both had bottles of Singha by their plates.

Mark waved a fork at a television on the wall. 'Did you see that, mate?' he asked, through a mouthful of egg and bacon. 'The bloody Muslims have killed a judge back in England.'

The television was tuned to Sky News and a blonde woman with an impossibly smooth forehead was talking earnestly to camera. In a box to the left of the screen there was a grainy colour picture of a middle-aged man in an orange jumpsuit with panic-stricken eyes. 'I saw the video on the Internet. They slit his throat.'

'Where?' asked Shepherd.

'London,' said Mickey. 'Happened last week but they only put the video up yesterday.'

'They won't show it on Sky,' said Mark, 'but you can watch the whole thing on the Internet. Blood goes everywhere, mate. Everywhere. Horrible way to die.'

'Did anyone claim responsibility?'

'Well, it wouldn't be the Catholics, would it?' said Mark. 'Bloody Muslims, who else?'

'There are lots of different groups,' said Shepherd. 'Factions.'

'Don't think they said,' muttered Mark. 'Probably Pakis. Makes me sick. If they hate Britain so much they should push off back to Pakistan.'

'They're British, Mark,' said Shepherd. His beer arrived.

'Nah, mate. You're British, I'm British, most of the guys drinking in this pub are British. But some nutter whose parents came over on the boat from Pakiland and who starts chopping the heads off judges, he ain't British. He might have a British passport, but if I had my way I'd take it off him and send him packing back to Pakiland.' He punched his brother's shoulder again. 'Get it? Pack 'em off to Pakiland.'

'You hit my arm once more and I'll shove that fork up your arse,' said Mickey. 'You sure you don't want to eat, Ricky? Kim does a great breakfast.'

'It's eight o'clock in the evening,' said Shepherd.

'It's an all-day breakfast,' said Mark.

'It's a one-way ticket to intensive care,' said Shepherd. He was amazed at the amount of cholesterol the brothers were putting into their bodies. Fried eggs, bacon, mushrooms, onions, chips, and thickly buttered toast. While there was no doubting their fitness, they both had thickening waistlines and Shepherd was all too well aware that once you hit middle age it was a lot easier to put weight on than lose it. But the breakfast did smell good and the bacon was just the way he liked it, well done but not too crisp. He sighed. 'Okay, you've talked me into it. I'll have the same.'

Mark waved the waitress over and ordered for him.

The newsreader was replaced by a serious-looking man in a trench coat standing in front of JFK airport in the United States. A news headline flashed across the bottom of the screen. 'American Passenger Jet Crashes Into the Sea.' The reporter said that the plane had been bound for France and that the Coast Guard were looking for survivors. The authorities hadn't said which flight it was but the airport was operating normally and there was nothing to suggest it had been a terrorist incident.

Shepherd leaned forward. 'When are you going to tell me what you've got planned?' he asked, his voice low.

'After we've finished here,' said Mickey. 'We'll take you to our office.'

'Where's that?'

Mark tapped the side of his nose and winked. 'Need to know, mate,' he said. 'But you'll be wishing you'd worn something warmer.'

'What do you mean?' said Shepherd. 'It's in the nineties outside.'

Mark and Mickey laughed. 'You'll find out,' said Mickey.

'Davie, Barry and Chopper are on the way. We'll wait for them and then get started.'

Shepherd shivered and stamped his feet on the metal floor. 'I'm freezing,' he said. His breath feathered in the icy air. 'How long are we going to be in here?'

'Bracing, innit?' said Mickey. He raised his shot glass to Shepherd. It was made of ice, and the vodka it contained was just below zero. 'Cheers.'

Shepherd touched his own ice glass to Mickey's and knocked back the vodka. The alcohol warmed his chest as it went down, but it didn't make his fingers or toes feel any better. A small Thai girl wrapped in a padded coat with a fur-lined hood was jiggling up and down, her arms wrapped around herself. Mickey pointed at their empty glasses. 'Come on, love, top us up. And let's try the raspberry one this time.'

Yates, Black and Wilson put their shot glasses on the bar and the girl poured raspberry vodka into them, then bounced up and down again.

They were in the Minus 5 Ice Bar, a short walk from Jameson's, on the ground floor of a hotel building. Two slim girls had flirted with them at the entrance before leading them through an all-white bar to a corridor with rows of padded coats and a box of gloves. Mickey had sneered disdainfully at the warm clothing and ushered them to what appeared to be the door to a meat locker. One of the girls pulled it open and they entered a bar where the temperature was just below freezing. The furniture had been carved from ice and draped with fur and the space was dotted with ornate ice sculptures.

'Down the hatch, lads!' shouted Mickey, and all five

men sank their vodka, then slammed the empty glasses on the bar.

Black's glass shattered into ice shards. 'Don't know my own strength.' He laughed.

'Mickey, what the hell are we doing here?' asked Shepherd. 'I'm freezing my balls off.'

Mickey hugged him. 'Don't be such a softie,' he said, and waved at the girl. 'More vodka, darling, the pepper one this time.' He pointed at one of the large speakers near the ceiling. 'And turn up the volume, will you?' The girl did so and Mickey pointed at an ice sofa. Shepherd sat down, Mickey next to him. 'The reason we talk business in here, old lad, is that it's just about the most secure place in Pattaya. The manager lets us have the place to ourselves when we're here, the girl speaks hardly any English, and as we're in a metal box lined with ice there's no chance that the place can be bugged.'

'I get that, but why can't we wear the coats?'

'Because we're English and we're used to the cold.' He banged his shot glass against Shepherd's. 'Down the hatch!' They both drank, then Mickey put his mouth so close to Shepherd's ear that he could smell the alcohol on his breath. 'Okay, here's the story,' he said. 'There's a money depot we like, state-of-the-art security but we've found a way in.'

'Here in Thailand?'

Mickey laughed. 'There's no point in robbing baht, mate,' he said. 'No – good old British pounds and lots of them.'

'I'm wanted back in England – have you forgotten that?'

Mark squatted down next to Shepherd. 'Ricky Knight

is wanted, but you can go back under any name you want,' he said. 'We can get you a new passport, easy as pie.'

'Not if they've posted my picture and red-flagged me.'

'That red-flag nonsense is bollocks,' said Mickey. 'We can fly into Dublin and from there to Heathrow. There's no immigration checks on flights from Dublin. But if you're nervous you can take the train to Belfast and fly from there.'

'Or the ferry,' said Mark. 'Getting back to the UK is the easy bit.'

'So what's the hard bit?' asked Shepherd.

'It's all relative,' said Mickey. 'What we do is never easy, but with the right planning and preparation, anything is possible.'

'Yeah, I had an uncle who told me that once. Nothing is ever impossible, only improbable. Mind you, he died without a penny to his name.'

'Trust me, we can all get into the UK,' said Mickey, 'and out. We've done it before. Now, the place we're looking at is just outside London. Like I said, state-of-the-art security but the take is worth the trouble. We're talking millions, Ricky. Millions.'

'Sounds tasty. But how do you know so much about a depot in England if you're based here?'

'We've got a guy who does the research, and he's done us proud with this one,' said Mickey. 'In and out in six minutes – we'll be long gone before the cops arrive.'

'In and out of a high-security depot in six minutes? How?'

Mickey tapped the side of his nose. 'That's need to know, mate. And, at the moment, you don't need to know.'

'I thought I was part of the family.'

'You are, mate. But you're like a cousin, the one who always gets drunk at weddings and throws up over the bride. We have to learn to trust you.'

It was after three o'clock in the morning when Shepherd got back to his villa. He'd left his Jeep in town, knowing he had drunk far too much to be at the wheel of a car. The local police didn't seem interested in enforcing the drink-driving laws, but Shepherd knew his limitations as a driver. He used his remote control to open the electronic gates, then tapped in the code to deactivate the burglar alarm. He did a quick walk-through of the villa because he knew from experience that security systems were not infallible, and once he was satisfied that the place was secure he went down the corridor to the master bedroom and took one of the pay-as-you-go phones from the safe. He lay on the bed and called Charlotte Button. She answered on the third ring. 'It's on,' said Shepherd. 'It's on and it's big. Millions, Mickey said. Somewhere outside London.'

'Cash?'

'A money depot.'

'And what's the plan?'

'They won't tell me yet. They're being all Secret Squirrel but they can't stay like that for long. Soon as I know, you'll know.'

Bradshaw, Kundi and Talwar went to Sarajevo on separate flights. Bradshaw flew British Airways from Heathrow, Talwar also departed from Heathrow but on an Austrian Airlines flight, and Kundi went Lufthansa from City airport. Each carried a holdall, and at the bottom of each holdall were paperback books. Five-hundred-euro notes had been carefully inserted between the pages so that they wouldn't be picked up by the airport scanners. Together they took six hundred thousand euros out of the country.

They met up in the coffee shop at Sarajevo airport and Bradshaw rented a car, using one of the licences he'd bought from the Malaysian lawyer in Brixton. He drove while Kundi sat in the front passenger seat with a street map on his lap. They drove to the Holiday Inn and parked behind the hotel.

Bradshaw twisted around to face Talwar in the back seat. He pointed at the three holdalls on the seat next to him. 'You guard them with your life,' he said.

'I will,' said Talwar.

'If anything goes wrong, the men who gave me that money will track us down and kill us as a warning to others,' said Bradshaw.

'I understand. Don't worry,' said Talwar. He took off his glasses and polished them with his handkerchief. It was a nervous habit, Bradshaw knew. Like Chaudhry's gum-chewing, Kundi's cigarette-smoking and al-Sayed's rash. They were all signs of the pressure the men were under.

'We'll talk to this guy, and if he comes through, I'll call you and you bring the money,' said Bradshaw.

'And if you don't call?'

'I will call,' said Bradshaw. 'Just be ready.' He had bought Vodafone pay-as-you-go mobiles for them all in London and had set them up for international roaming.

He and Kundi got out of the car. Bradshaw held the door open for Talwar so that he could get into the driver's seat, then he and Kundi walked into the hotel's reception area. 'What does he look like?' asked Kundi.

'He's Dutch,' said Bradshaw. 'Mid-thirties. Crew-cut. He used to be in the French Foreign Legion so he's one tough son-of-a-bitch. I haven't actually met him but we've spoken on the phone.' His mobile rang and he took it out of his pocket. 'Yeah?' he said, but there was no one on the line. A big man in a black coat was watching them, holding a mobile phone. He put it away as he walked towards them.

'Is that him?' asked Kundi.

'No,' said Bradshaw. 'That'll be one of his heavies.'

The man came up to them, his hands deep in his coat pockets. 'You are Bradshaw?' he asked, with a heavy Slavic accent.

Bradshaw nodded.

'You have ID?'

'I have a passport, but not in that name.'

The man cocked his head to the side. 'I do not understand.'

'I'm Paul Bradshaw, but I'm travelling under another name.'

'So you have nothing to confirm that you are Paul Bradshaw?'

'You just called my phone. Isn't that proof enough?'

The man frowned. He took his right hand out of his pocket and scratched his ear. 'Show me your passport,' he said eventually. Bradshaw did as he was told. The man looked down his nose at Kundi. 'You too.' Kundi gave the man his passport. The man studied both documents, then handed them back. 'Come with me,' he said.

He took them out of the hotel to where a black stretch

Mercedes was waiting, its engine running. He opened the rear door and spoke to whoever was inside, then nodded for Bradshaw and Kundi to get in. He slammed the door behind them and got into the front passenger seat. Alex Kleintank was sitting in the back. He was in his early thirties, clean-cut and wearing a black suit with a grey shirt. He offered his hand to Bradshaw. 'You're Paul?' he said, with only a trace of a Dutch accent.

'Alex?' said Bradshaw. 'Good to meet you.' They shook hands. He made no attempt to introduce Kundi but Kleintank nodded at him.

'So, you were in the army with Chris?'

Chris Thomas had been Bradshaw's conduit to Kleintank. After leaving the army, Thomas had set up a private security company with a fistful of contracts in Iraq and had sourced most of his equipment from Kleintank. He had contacted Kleintank and vouched for Bradshaw, though he had no idea what Bradshaw wanted to buy. Bradshaw had said he was acting as middle-man for an African dictator who wanted arms, and Thomas had taken him at his word.

The limousine moved away from the kerb. 'I'll take you to our warehouse,' said Kleintank. 'I'll think you'll be happy with what I've got to show you.'

They drove through the city. Even though the conflict that had ripped apart the former Yugoslavia had ended years earlier, reminders were etched into the buildings in the form of bullet holes and shell damage that had yet to be repaired. As a child, Bradshaw had watched the news bulletins about the Yugoslavian ethnic cleansing and the mass graves filled with butchered civilians but he hadn't understood what the fighting was about. It was only years

later, after he had become a Muslim, that he had finally
seen it for what it was – an attack on Muslim brothers by
Christian Serbs. The West had stood by and watched as
the Serbs butchered Muslim men, women and children.
For years they had refused to intervene. Bradshaw knew
why that was: it was because, at its core, the Christian
West hated Muslims, all Muslims. In the same way that
the West had stood by and watched as Hitler had sent the
Jews to the gas chambers, the Serbs had been given free
rein to slaughter the Muslims of Yugoslavia.

'You've been to Sarajevo before?' asked Kleintank,
disturbing Bradshaw's reverie.

Bradshaw shook his head. 'Why do you base yourself
here?'

'Because it's Europe but not Europe,' said Kleintank.
'There are always advantages to be found in the grey
areas. And the police are more malleable than elsewhere.'
He grinned. 'Money talks louder here than in the European
Union.'

'Are you okay if I smoke?' asked Kundi.

The Dutchman smiled. 'Not in the car, I'm afraid,' he
said. 'My wife and I are ex-smokers and she hits the roof
if she smells smoke in the car. She always assumes the
worst.' He grinned. 'Wives, huh? What can you do with
them? Are you two married?'

Both men shook their heads.

Kleintank's grin widened. 'Enjoy your freedom,' he said.
'Trust me, it goes out of the window when you put a ring
on their finger.'

The Mercedes pulled up in front of a weathered stone
building with a tiled roof. The upper floors were pockmarked with bullet holes but the tiled roof had been

patchily repaired. A man in a sheepskin jerkin pulled open a big wooden door and the car drove inside. The warehouse was piled high with wooden and metal boxes, and a yellow fork-lift truck was parked at the far end of the building. Kleintank got out, Bradshaw and Kundi following him. Three men in leather jackets were sitting at a table playing cards. There were handguns in front of them, and stacks of new banknotes. They stared impassively at Bradshaw and Kundi, then returned to their game.

'Over here,' said Kleintank, from beside a stack of wooden boxes. Some had Chinese characters stencilled on the side, others cyrillic lettering. One of the boxes was already open, revealing half a dozen gleaming Kalashnikov assault rifles.

Kleintank pulled back the lids of two boxes standing side by side on the concrete floor. Nestling in straw were two missile-launcher units and two missiles. 'The Holy Grail,' said Kleintank. 'The SA-7, built under licence in Slovakia.'

'SA-7b, to be precise,' said Kundi.

'You know your missile-launchers,' said Kleintank. 'You said you wanted two. I can sell you the pair for sixty thousand euros.'

'They are blue,' said Kundi.

'Blue, red, green, the colour doesn't matter. What matters is that they go bang when you pull the trigger and, believe me, these will go bang.'

Bradshaw put a hand on Kundi's shoulder. 'What's wrong, brother?' he said.

'They're practice weapons,' said Kundi. 'That's what they do in the West – they paint their practice weapons blue.'

Bradshaw's jaw tightened. 'What's going on, Alex? Are these the real thing or not?'

Kleintank held up his hands. 'They're not fakes,' he said. 'They're the real McCoy. Those are live one-point-eight-kilogram high-explosive fragmentation warheads with impact fuses.'

'They're practice weapons,' Kundi repeated. 'I fired one in Pakistan. They are not guided – there is no infra-red guidance unit.'

'But they can be fired,' insisted Kleintank. 'They will bring down a bridge or a building.'

'We're not interested in shooting at bridges or buildings,' said Bradshaw.

'I had two Stingers, but I had a cash buyer,' said Kleintank. He nodded at the weapons. 'I could sell them to you for fifty thousand euros the pair. That's a good price.'

'They're not what we want,' Kundi said.

'I need to talk to my friend,' said Bradshaw. He walked with Kundi to the far end of the warehouse.

'He's trying to cheat us,' said Kundi. 'He knows exactly what he's selling us.'

'But they will fire, right?'

Kundi nodded. 'They will fire. But they are used for training purposes. He is right, you can point one at a building and you'll hit it, but they're useless against a moving target. Two were fired at an Israeli passenger jet taking off from Mombasa in 2002 but both missed. The Kenyans found the abandoned launch units near the airport and they were both blue.'

Bradshaw rubbed his chin thoughtfully.

'What are you thinking?' asked Kundi.

'That a bird in the hand is worth two in the bush,' said Bradshaw. They went back to the Dutchman.

Kleintank was talking on his mobile phone but snapped it shut as the two men walked up. 'So, do we have a deal?' he asked.

'They're not what we want,' said Bradshaw. 'Do you know anyone else who might have one with a guidance system? Either a Grail or a Stinger?'

'You want me to put you in touch with my competition?' said Kleintank.

'I just want a missile with a guidance system,' said Bradshaw, 'but if you point me in the right direction, I'll take one of them off your hands.'

'One is thirty thousand euros,' said Kleintank.

'You said fifty thousand for two.'

'But you don't want two,' said Kleintank. 'If you only take one I have to find another buyer. That takes time, and with every buyer I meet, there are risks.' He patted one of the wooden crates. 'These are in demand, but the Americans don't want them being sold, which means there's a lot of undercover agents trying to take them off the market. If I show these to the wrong people, I could end up in the Ukraine with a cattle prod up my arse.'

'I'm not sure how much demand there is for practice weapons,' said Bradshaw. 'I only need one like this. I will pay you thirty thousand euros, in cash, if you put me in touch with someone who can sell me one with a guidance system.'

'You have the money with you?' asked Kleintank.

'It's close by,' said Bradshaw.

Kleintank wrinkled his nose as if he was considering

the offer, but Bradshaw knew he had already made up his mind.

Kleintank nodded. 'Let me talk to my friend,' he said. He walked away from them, tapping a number into his mobile phone. As he talked he paced around the card table, occasionally looking at Bradshaw and Kundi. After a few minutes he came back, his phone still in his hand. 'I have a friend in Nice who can help you,' he said.

'Friend or competitor?' asked Bradshaw.

Kleintank smiled. 'We're in the same business – sometimes we compete, sometimes we help each other. Marcel and I were in the Legion together, so I trust him with my life. He does a lot of business with South American nations.'

'And he has a Grail with a guidance system?'

'He has a Stinger. Fully operational. Sixty thousand euros.'

'Tell him we'll take it,' Bradshaw said, 'subject to it being as described.' He gestured at the practice Grail missiles. 'Is there any easy way of getting one to Nice so that I can combine the shipments?'

Kleintank grinned. 'Everything is easy if you have the money,' he said.

Shepherd was in Tony's Gym at ten o'clock. He ran on a treadmill for forty-five minutes, then spent half an hour lifting weights, working on tone and fitness rather than building bulk. There was no sign of the Moore brothers or any of their crew. After he'd showered, he left his Jeep in the gym's car park and took a motorcycle taxi to the beach road where he bought two cappuccinos from Starbucks and walked to Sharpe's hotel.

Sharpe was wearing nothing but boxer shorts and looked as if he'd had even less sleep than Shepherd. He took the coffee and sat on his bed, running a hand through his unkempt hair.

'Hangover?' asked Shepherd.

'I think there's something in the beer here,' said Sharpe.

'Yeah, it's called alcohol.' Shepherd sat down on the chair by the window. 'Things are moving,' he said. 'They're setting up a big score and it's going to be soon.'

'Can't be soon enough for me,' said Sharpe. 'Every time I go outside someone offers me cheap sex or throws a bucket of water over me. It's too bloody hot and my stomach's playing up.' He looked over at Shepherd. 'Have you noticed that no one chucks water over the cops? The Thais don't and neither do the Westerners. You see anyone dealing with the cops here, it's "Yes, sir, no, sir, three bags full, sir," from the Thais and the Westerners. I saw a big Brit guy on a scooter pulled in for not wearing a helmet and he was as meek as milk. Promised not to do it again, said he was sorry, handed over a couple of hundred baht. Even did that thing they do, putting his hands together like he was praying.'

'It's called a *wai*.'

'Yeah, well, he did that too. There was no cheek, no answering back, no bad language. I'm sure if the same guy had been pulled in back in the UK, he'd have been giving the cop all sorts of abuse. And you know why that is?'

'I guess a combination of their tight brown uniforms and the big guns on their hips.'

'Because here they're scared of the cops, that's why.'

'I was right, then.' Shepherd swung his feet up onto Sharpe's bed.

'It's not the guns,' said Sharpe. 'It's respect for the uniform. We've lost that back in England. No one respects the police any more. Here, it's the way it used to be in England fifty years ago.'

Shepherd grinned. 'You're an old fart, Razor, but you're not old enough to remember when the police commanded respect.'

'I'm third-generation police, you know. My dad and his father before him were cops in Glasgow. My granddad's long gone but I can still remember him and my dad swapping stories. They had real stories, too, not like the cops these days where the most exciting thing they do is to fill out a crime report or appear on *Crimewatch*. Guys like the Moores, they'd have been nipped in the bud with a few clips around the ear when they were kids, and if that hadn't worked they'd have been nicked on their first or second job. My dad and granddad knew every bad apple on their beat, their names and where they lived, what car they drove and when they were up to no good.'

'Yeah, things have changed.'

'You never walked a beat, Spider. I know the SAS is no picnic but you went from abseiling down buildings with a machine-gun to working under cover. You were never throwing drunks into a van on a Saturday night or trying to take a knife off a guy high on crack.'

'I meant society's changed,' said Shepherd. 'And the police have changed along with it.'

'Damn right things have changed. Intelligence back then was in the head of the local bobby. Now it's guys like Kenny Mansfield sitting in their offices and staring at their screens. They might understand the statistics and how to use databases but they don't understand people. Cops like my dad and his dad, they understood people.'

'So what's the solution?'

Sharpe chuckled and sipped his cappuccino. 'There is no solution, Spider. We just have to accept the way things are and deal with it. But I know one thing for a fact. Before the days of the Police and Criminal Evidence Act, and before everything a cop did was subject to public scrutiny, the police did a pretty good job of maintaining law and order, even in a tough city like Glasgow.'

'Because they could get away with breaking the rules, you mean?'

'They broke them and they bent them, sure,' said Sharpe, 'but my dad and granddad both said the same thing – they never put away someone who didn't deserve it.'

'Now you're starting to sound like a vigilante, Razor,' said Sharpe.

'My dad told me about a drug-dealer on his patch, a guy by the name of Willie Mackenzie. Mackenzie was a mid-ranking dealer but he was heading for the big-time. Heroin was his drug of choice, but he'd deal in anything. The Drugs Squad finally got Mackenzie on a GBH charge after he took a razor to one of his competitors. Blinded the guy, scarred him for life. For some reason the judge gave him bail, and over the next two months every witness told the police they'd had a memory lapse. One had his lapse in intensive care, the other forgot everything after someone poured petrol through his letterbox. Mackenzie never stood trial for the GBH.' Sharpe took another sip of coffee. 'A couple of months later my dad was on the team that busted a gang bringing in a consignment of heroin from the Continent. The drugs were in a ware-house near the docks. The gang had already started distributing the gear and guess what? Five kilos turned up in the boot of Mackenzie's car. That, and a statement from one of my dad's informants that he'd seen Mackenzie at the warehouse, was enough to have him sent down for ten years.' He waved his paper cup at Shepherd. 'You're a great one for fairness, Spider. Now you tell me that what happened isn't fair.'

'It's fair, but it's not right,' said Shepherd. 'There's a difference.'

'Mackenzie got what was coming to him and the police made sure it happened.'

'He must have known your dad set him up.'

Sharpe shrugged. 'My dad was a hard bastard and he wasn't scared of a piece of shit like Mackenzie. Not that it made any difference. Mackenzie died in prison, knifed by a lifer.'

'You're not thinking about framing the Moore brothers, are you, Razor?' asked Shepherd, only half joking.

'Chance'd be a fine thing,' said Sharpe. 'Those days are long gone. You know, the only time my dad ever got hurt in the job, he was hit by a car and spent a month in hospital. During that month more than five hundred people came to pay their respects. And the guy who did it, he handed himself into the cops after a week. You know why?'

'I'm assuming because someone threatened to break his legs.'

Sharpe grinned. 'And you'd assume right. There was respect back then. Respect for the uniform and respect for the man. They've still got it here in Thailand, but we've lost it in England.'

'Maybe you should move here,' said Shepherd.

'It's too hot for me, and that water-throwing thing is a bloody nuisance.'

'It's only once a year,' said Shepherd.

His phone rang. He motioned for Sharpe to stay quiet and took the call.

'Where are you?' asked Mickey.

'On my way to Starbucks for a coffee. What's up?'

'Got your passport with you?'

'Why? Do I need it to buy coffee?'

'Don't piss me about, mate. We're on our way to Phnom Penh – Cambodia.'

'I know where Phnom Penh is, Mickey. Do you want to tell me why or is it still need-to-know?'

'We're booked on a flight this afternoon so you get the hell back to your place and pack. We'll pick you up.' Mickey ended the call abruptly.

Shepherd held up the phone, a quizzical look on his face.

'What's wrong?' said Sharpe.

'I'm going to Cambodia.'

'What the hell for?'

'I don't know.'

'Do you want me to come with you?'

'Too risky,' said Shepherd. 'You'd have to scramble to get a ticket. And if they were going to do me harm, they could do it here as easily as in Cambodia.' He stood up and dropped his Starbucks cup into the overflowing bin. 'I've got to go. Can you tell Charlie what's happening?'

The Bangkok Airways jet landed smoothly and taxied to the runway. Shepherd was at the front of the plane with

Mickey and Mark while Wilson, Yates and Black were by
the emergency exit in the middle. When they got off, a
Cambodian soldier in creased fatigues was waiting for
them. He shook hands with Mickey, who introduced him
to Shepherd. 'This is Wilbur,' said Mickey. 'We can never
pronounce his name, so that's what we call him.'

The soldier saluted, then offered his hand. Shepherd
shook it. Wilbur was in his late forties, his skin so dark
that it was almost black, and both cheeks covered with
old acne scars. He wore a thick gold chain around his
right wrist and several gold rings.

'Wilbur's brother is the aide to one of the generals here
so he makes sure we're well looked after,' said Mickey.
'Anything we need, we just ask him.' Wilbur grinned,
showing a gold canine tooth.

They waited for Wilson, Yates and Black to get off the
plane, then Wilbur walked them through the diplomatic
channel and outside the terminal to where two white
Toyota Landcruisers with military drivers were waiting
for them. 'You come with me and Mark,' Mickey said to
Shepherd. Wilson, Yates and Black climbed into the second
vehicle. 'We'll check into the hotel later.'

'Where are we going?' asked Shepherd.

'It's a surprise,' said Mark.

Wilbur got into the front passenger seat of the second
vehicle, which pulled away from the terminal first.

'I don't have to shoot anyone, do I?' asked Shepherd.
Mickey and Mark burst out laughing, but they wouldn't
tell him what was so funny.

Mickey opened a window and lit a cigar. Their driver
put the car in gear and they left the airport. There were
far fewer vehicles on the roads than there had been in

Thailand, and those that Shepherd did see were older and less cared-for than their Thai counterparts. The houses they passed were of poorer quality too, mainly wooden shacks with corrugated-iron roofs. Even the animals in the fields seemed undernourished compared to their Thai cousins.

They powered past a rusting bus, its roof piled high with boxes and suitcases, every seat taken and a dozen people standing. There was a school on their right, and most of the children in the dusty playground were barefoot. Several waved at the Landcruisers and Shepherd waved back.

After driving for just under half an hour they turned off the main road on to a potholed track that led to a wire-fenced compound where two Cambodian soldiers with assault rifles on shoulder slings saluted and pulled back a wheeled barrier. The Cambodian flag fluttered from a pole by a guardhouse where another soldier stood, idly picking his teeth. In the distance, Shepherd heard the distinctive crack-crack-crack-crack of Kalashnikovs set on automatic.

Mickey twisted in his seat. 'Don't get jumpy, they're on our side,' he said.

'I'll bear that in mind,' said Shepherd. 'What is this place?'

'It's a firing range run by the army. They let tourists play with guns. We've been over a few times and we've asked Wilbur to fix up something special for us.'

'Specifically?'

'Need-to-know, mate.'

'You do love your secrets, don't you?'

'You'll know soon enough,' said Mark.

Shepherd saw some wooden buildings to the left and a line of human-shaped metal targets in a row in front of a stack of sandbags. The two Landcruisers left the track and drove across the grass towards a clump of coconut palms. A couple of minutes later they came to a wall made of concrete blocks. It was about thirty feet long and ten tall. The Landcruisers pulled up beside an open Jeep in military camouflage colours with two soldiers in green fatigues smoking cigarettes, which they threw away when they saw Wilbur.

'Right, come on,' said Mickey, opening his door. He strode to the Jeep and stuck an arm around Wilbur. 'Nice one, mate.'

'Two thousand dollars each,' said Wilbur. 'Like we agreed.'

'Cheap at half the price,' said Mickey. He beckoned to Shepherd. 'Come and look at these, Ricky.'

Shepherd peered into the back of the Jeep. Two Chinese-made rocket-propelled grenade launchers lay on a piece of sacking. Next to them were four backpacks, which Shepherd assumed contained the grenades and launch charges.

'This isn't a team-building exercise, is it?' Shepherd pointed at the wall. 'This is a dress rehearsal, right?'

Mickey chortled. 'No flies on you, are there?'

Wilson, Yates and Black were coming over to the Jeep. 'What's the plan, Mickey?' said Shepherd. 'We're going to be shooting armoured cars? If so, you can count me out.' He picked up one of the RPGs and hefted it onto his shoulder. 'This would blow an armoured car into a million pieces, kill everyone in it and destroy all the cash.'

'Give me some credit.'

'So what's it about? What are we doing here?'

Mickey took his cigar case out and lit a cigar. 'Okay. You remember the building we talked about? The money depository?'

'I've not got Alzheimer's, Mickey.'

'We're not going in through the front. We're going in through the back. And we're using RPGs.'

'No way,' said Shepherd.

'That's the plan,' said Mickey.

'I might be stupid, but why don't we just blow the wall with explosives? A shaped charge would do the job a treat. And we'd have more control over the shape of the hole we make. RPGs are all well and good but they can be a bit hit-and-miss.'

'Yeah, well, if you're the pro you say you are, you won't bloody well miss,' said Mickey. 'That's why we're here – to check you can fire one of those things.'

'I didn't mean miss literally,' said Shepherd. 'I meant that with an RPG there's an element of chance in the type of damage it'll do. A controlled explosion would give you more control . . .' He smiled thinly. 'That's why they call it a controlled explosion.'

'Yeah, but using explosives means we'll lose the element of surprise,' said Mickey. 'The wall is covered by CCTV and all sorts of sensors so they'd see us as soon as we got anywhere near the wall. Let's say we rush to the wall, fix the charge, retreat to a safe distance, detonate the charge and then rush back to the hole. How long's that going to take? Two minutes?'

'Give or take,' admitted Shepherd.

'So that's two minutes we lose,' said Mickey. 'And we reckon that from the moment they know we're there to the cops turning up is a minimum of six minutes. So, if we use a shaped charge we lose a third of our time. But if we let fly with an RPG from two hundred metres, the first they'll know we're there is when the wall's in bits.'

'Okay, I get it,' said Shepherd. 'We're in and out in six minutes.'

'Five,' said Mickey. 'One minute before the cops get there, we're off, back across the fields. They'll turn up at the front of the building while we're roaring away in SUVs.'

Mark lit a cigarette. 'What do you think?' he asked.

'RPGs through the back wall,' said Shepherd. 'Whose idea was that?'

'The Professor,' said Mark.

'And who the hell is The Professor?'

Mark shrugged. 'He's a guy we use to plan our jobs.'

'He knows what he's doing,' said Mickey. 'Plans everything down to the last detail. If he says an RPG will take down the wall, then it will. So, the million-dollar question, Ricky, is can you fire that thing?'

'I can fire it,' said Shepherd. He glanced at the concrete wall. 'This is a test, right?'

'A test of the equipment, and a test that you know what you're doing.' Mickey bowed theatrically. 'So, let's see you do your stuff.'

Shepherd lifted up the launcher and presented it to the brothers side on. 'Right, for those of you who haven't been paying attention, this is a shoulder-fired, single-shot, smooth-bore recoilless launcher. At the front is the muzzle, just behind that is the front iron sight, behind that is the trigger assembly and behind that is the optical sight.' He pointed at the section in the middle. 'This is a wooden heat shield, and behind it is the breech.'

He replaced the launcher on the sacking and picked up one of the backpacks. 'The grenade that the launcher fires is carried in two parts, the warhead, which is attached to a sustainer motor, and the booster charge.' He took a cone-shaped warhead unit from one backpack, and a cylindrical booster charge from another, then screwed them together to form one unit. 'The booster charge kicks the warhead out of the launcher. It's basically a small strip powder charge. Once the warhead is about eleven metres away from the launcher, the sustainer rocket kicks in. As soon as the warhead has left the launcher, small fins spring out that help keep it on target. There's no internal guidance system so you have to make sure you're aiming at what you want to hit. Any questions?

'Just fire the bloody thing,' said Mark. 'No one likes a smart arse.'

Shepherd slid the warhead into the launcher and rested it on his shoulder. He grinned at Mark. 'Okay, you go and stand in front of the wall. See if I can shoot that cigarette out of your mouth.'

'Yeah, and why don't you go screw yourself?' said Mark. 'Go on, let's see what it does.'

Shepherd chuckled and turned to aim at the wall, checking first that no one was standing behind him. The backblast could be fatal. There was little in the way of wind so he centred the sight on the middle of the wall, braced himself, and gently squeezed the trigger. There was a loud whooshing sound and the warhead burst out of the launcher. A second later the sustainer rocket burst into life with a puff of white smoke and a second explosion. The warhead slammed into the wall.

Shepherd lowered the launcher. Several bricks had been destroyed but the wall was still standing.

'Do another,' said Mickey.

Shepherd prepared another warhead and slotted it into the launcher. He glanced over his shoulder and saw Mark behind him, lighting another cigarette. 'Mark, mate, the backblast from this thing will fry you alive,' he warned.

Mark waved an apology and jogged to the Jeep. 'Fire in the hole!' shouted Shepherd, taking aim at the hole he'd already made in the wall. He pulled the trigger and the second warhead shot through the air.

The second explosion did much more damage and left a hole big enough for a man to walk through. Shepherd put down the launcher and went to inspect it with Mark and Mickey. Yates, Black and Wilson followed. Close up, Shepherd could see that the wall was actually two walls, separated by thick steel mesh. The warheads had gone right through. Half a dozen concrete bricks had been reduced to dust and another dozen had been blown to gravel. The metal mesh had been torn apart. 'That'll do it,' Mickey said. 'We're in business.'

'Okay?' Wilbur called.

Mickey gave him a thumbs-up. 'Big okay!' he shouted. 'Come on, let's get a drink.'

'They serve booze here?' said Shepherd, incredulously. Alcohol and guns were a dangerous mix.

'It's Cambodia, mate,' said Mickey. 'Anything goes.'

They piled back into the Landcruisers and drove across the firing range to a cluster of wooden buildings, one of which served as an office. The Cambodian flag fluttered from the roof and off to the side a camouflage awning shaded a large table and half a dozen teak planter's chairs.

The Moores and Shepherd got out of their Landcruiser, which they had parked at the side of a long concrete block with a wooden door at one end. From inside they heard the crack of small-arms fire. Outside seven men in their thirties were standing around a Cambodian soldier who was showing them a selection of handguns. The men were all wearing T-shirts and cargo pants and had the look of former servicemen. As he walked past them, Shepherd heard two talking in Russian. 'Who are those guys, Mickey?' he asked.

'Probably tourists. Anyone can come here and fire gear, providing they've got the cash.'

Wilbur walked over to them. 'Do you want to fire an M60?' he asked.

'What's that?' said Mickey.

'Machine-gun,' said Shepherd. 'Seven point six two calibre. Big boys' toy.'

'Let's go for it,' said Mickey.

Wilbur took them away from where the Russians were being briefed to a firing range where three water-filled oil barrels had been placed in front of a pile of sandbags, behind which was a sloping bank of earth, twice the height of a man. A hundred feet away a trestle table held three green ammunition boxes and half a dozen orange ear-protectors. On the ground next to it was an M60 with a metal stand attached to its barrel. Shepherd picked it up. It had been cleaned and oiled and appeared serviceable.

'How much?' asked Mickey.

'A dollar a round,' said Wilbur, lifting a belt loaded with rounds out of one of the boxes.

'How many does it fire?' asked Mickey.

'Five hundred and fifty rounds a minute,' said Shepherd.

'Bloody hell,' said Mickey.

'You can fire single shots – you just release the trigger,' said Shepherd. 'Keep pressing it to fire a burst.'

'You've fired one, yeah?'

'Sure,' said Shepherd, 'but only in training. You could cut a man in half with a burst. It's a hell of a weapon.'

'You want to shoot a cow?' asked Wilbur. 'For a cow, one hundred dollars.' He grinned, showing his gold canine. 'But farmer keeps the meat, okay?'

'There's no way I'm shooting a cow,' said Shepherd.

'Up to you,' said Wilbur. 'We have turkeys. Ten dollars each.'

'The barrels will be just fine,' said Shepherd.

'Spoilsport,' said Mark.

The men put on ear-protectors. Wilbur fed in the belt, then showed Mickey how to hold it, with his left hand gripping the carrying handle and his right hand holding the trigger mechanism. Shepherd adjusted the nylon sling to take some of the weight of the gun. 'Just do single shots until you get the feel of it,' said Shepherd. 'If at any time you feel it getting away from you, just let go of the trigger. Ready?'

'Oh, yes,' said Mickey.

Shepherd pushed the safety lever forward and up so that it was in the fire position and cocked the weapon. 'Let her rip,' he said.

Mickey took a deep breath and pulled the trigger. Even through the ear-protectors the noise was deafening, and they could feel the thud-thud-thud of the shots vibrating through their stomachs. 'Bloody hell!' yelled Mickey. He squinted at the barrels. 'Did I hit anything?'

'Sand,' said Shepherd. 'You were ten feet to the left.'

Mickey corrected his aim and let loose another short burst. The first three shots hit the barrel on the right and water spurted out, but the rest ripped into the sandbags. The recoil of the M60 took some handling, Shepherd knew, but it was fun watching Mickey trying to cope with it. 'Die, you motherfucker!' screamed Mickey, as he pulled the trigger and sent a dozen rounds into the earth bank behind the sandbags. He grinned at Shepherd. 'Wanna go?'

'Sure,' said Shepherd. He took the M60 from Mickey, and slipped the sling over his shoulder. He put his feet shoulder-width apart, left foot slightly forward, and gently pulled the trigger. The first couple of rounds went to the right but he edged the front sight to the left and the rounds began to thud into the middle of the three oil barrels. Water spurted from the holes punched in the metal and Shepherd let a dozen rounds hit home.

He could feel his heart pounding and the adrenaline kicking in as it always did when he fired heavy weaponry, even when he was only shooting at targets. Guns for Shepherd had always been tools of the trade, a means to an end, but that didn't mean he didn't enjoy letting rip with a big chunk of artillery. He let loose another burst, gripping the handle tightly to absorb the recoil. The acrid cordite made his eyes water and tickled his throat, but he grinned when the middle barrel sprouted another half-dozen streams of water.

Mickey slapped him on the back. 'Great shooting,' he

shouted. Shepherd put the M60 back on the ground and took off the ear-protectors.

'You handle the gun well,' said a voice behind him. Shepherd turned. One of the Russians had been watching them. He was a big man, well over six feet, his head shaved to disguise a rapidly retreating hairline. He had a square jaw, a large diamond in his right earlobe and a geometric tattoo running around his left forearm, just above the elbow.

Shepherd shrugged. 'Fires itself, pretty much,' he said.

The Russian nodded. 'It is a nice gun. But we have a better one in Russia.'

'The PKS?' said Shepherd.

A look of surprise flashed across the Russian's face. 'You know of the PKS?' he said.

'Pulemet Kalashnikova Stankovy. Sure. One of the Kalashnikov family. Same calibre as the M60.'

'You have fired one?'

'No,' lied Shepherd. 'Only read about it.' In fact, as part of his SAS training, he had been taught to strip and fire every type of NATO and Soviet-bloc hand-held weapon there was.

'May I?' asked the Russian.

Shepherd indicated Mickey. 'You'd better ask him, he's paying for the rounds.'

Mickey lit a cigar. 'Help yourself.'

Shepherd put on his ear-protectors again and the Russian picked up the heavy M60 as if it was made of balsawood. Shepherd tapped his ear-protectors but the other man shook his head. He turned the gun towards the barrels and let off a short burst. The oil barrel to the left bucked and wobbled as the shells tore into it.

The Russian fired a second burst into the middle barrel. The gun barely moved in his shovel-like hands. A third burst hit the final barrel, smack in the middle. Shepherd was impressed. 'You've fired one before,' he said.

The Russian laughed. 'I've fired more than one,' he said. He gave the weapon to Wilbur one-handed. Wilbur grunted as he took the weight. 'You are English?' said the Russian.

'Yeah,' said Shepherd. 'You're Russian?'

The man extended a vast hand. 'Sergei,' he said.

'Ricky.'

'You've come all the way from England to shoot guns?'

'We live in Pattaya now,' said Shepherd.

'Me too,' said the Russian. 'You go to Walking Street?'

'It has been known.'

'My partner and I have a bar there,' said Sergei. 'Absolute A-go-go. Have you been in?'

'I don't think so.'

'You should come by. We have the prettiest girls in Pattaya. Where are you staying in Phnom Penh?'

'I don't know – we haven't checked in yet,' said Shepherd.

Mickey took his cigar out of his mouth. 'The Raffles.'

Sergei slapped his chest. 'That's where we're staying,' he said. 'It's the best hotel in the whole town.'

'That's what they say,' said Mickey.

'Let me buy you Englishmen a beer, and you can explain why you are so keen to sell your football teams to my countrymen.'

They walked over to the main building. Under the camouflage awning a battered and rusting fridge was connected to a frayed wire that ran from an open window. A young soldier was standing by it and the Russian waved at him. 'Beers for all my friends.' The soldier opened the fridge, took out cans of Heineken and handed them around. Yates and Black opened theirs and went to look at an old military motorcycle that was leaning against a coconut palm. Wilson was talking to Wilbur, who was holding a Kalashnikov assault rifle.

Shepherd popped the tab on his can and sipped.

'So, you were in the army, yes?' asked the Russian.

'How did you know?' asked Shepherd.

'A soldier can always tell another soldier,' said Sergei. 'It's in the eyes, it's in the walk.' He punched Shepherd on the shoulder. 'And you, my friend, were in the army, I'd stake my life on it.' He gesticulated at Mickey and Mark, who were looking at a poster of a cutaway diagram of a Kalashnikov assault rifle that had been pinned on the wall by the window. 'Those two, they're hard and they can handle guns, but they've never been in a battle, never ducked as bullets flew over their heads so close you can feel the heat.'

'You might be surprised,' said Shepherd.

Sergei sat down in one of the planter's chairs. 'There's a difference between being fired at and being in battle,' he said. 'It changes your outlook on life.'

'That's for sure,' agreed Shepherd.

'You were in Afghanistan?'

'Yeah, I was in Afghanistan a few times.'

'Special Forces? Were you SAS, Ricky?'

'Bloody hell, no,' said Shepherd. 'I was a paratrooper. I never wanted to be one of the boys in black. Too much like hard work.'

Sergei raised his can in salute. 'Bloody right,' he said. 'Special Forces are psychos, all the ones I've met. Give me a regular soldier every time. You know where you are with a soldier. What is it the Americans call them?'

'Grunts,' said Shepherd. Wilson called to Black and Yates and the three men went into the indoor firing range with Wilbur.

'Yes, grunts. I like that,' said Sergei. 'Grunt. It's real. Down to earth. I was a grunt and proud of it. I did three tours of Afghanistan,' he said. 'I was there in 'eighty-five and again in 'eighty-seven, and I was there when we pulled out in 'eighty-nine. You know, you will never win in Afghanistan, my friend. If the Russian army couldn't beat the bastards, you and the Americans won't stand a chance.'

'I won't argue with you on that score,' said Shepherd. 'When did you leave the army?'

'Three years ago,' said Sergei. 'We'd had enough, all the men in my unit. We'd done four bloody tours in Chechnya. Four. And they were going to send us back. And you'd laugh if I told you what they paid us. We were sick of it. While the Mafia were bleeding the country dry and the oligarchs were buying mansions in London, and football teams and private jets, we were being bombed and shot at for less than you pay the men who take away your garbage. So when I told my men I was off, they came with me.'

'To Thailand?'

'There are big opportunities in Asia, my friend. Big money to be made. The police are easy to handle, the local Mafia are bone idle and they back down if you show you mean business, so everyone leaves us alone.'

'And what is it you do, Sergei?'

Sergei looked at him suspiciously. 'You are not a policeman, are you, Ricky?'

Shepherd laughed. 'If you knew anything about me, that's the last question you'd ask,' he said. 'I'm just interested. I'm looking for business opportunities myself, that's all.'

Sergei studied him for a few seconds, then nodded. 'You are a good guy, Ricky,' he said. 'I like you.' He punched Shepherd's arm, just hard enough to hurt. 'The business I do, I will not lie to you, my friend, it's illegal.'

'All the best businesses are,' said Shepherd.

'Maybe I will tell you some time,' said the Russian. 'When we are drunk. But now I want to shoot some chickens.' He drained his can, crushed it with his hand, and tossed it into a waste bin. He pointed a finger at Shepherd. 'Tonight we can do some serious drinking,' he said.

Mickey was sitting at a corner table in the Elephant Bar when Shepherd walked in. He already had a cigar going, and took a long pull as Shepherd sat down. A waiter asked what he wanted and he ordered a Jameson's and soda with ice. He was pleasantly surprised when the waiter said, 'Certainly, sir.'

'You off the beer, mate?' asked Mickey.

'Just felt like a whisky.' Shepherd sat back in his chair and sighed.

'What's wrong?' said Mickey.

'If I tell you, you'll just tap your nose and tell me it's need-to-know and that I don't need to know.'

Mickey blew a tight plume of smoke at a wooden-bladed ceiling fan above their heads. 'Try me,' he said.

Shepherd interlinked his fingers. 'Okay, here's the thing,' he said. 'This guy who plans your jobs, the Professor. He wants to use RPGs to blow through a reinforced-concrete wall.'

'Right.'

'But you've got to understand that an RPG isn't a wall-buster, not in the way you want. It's designed to shoot through heavy armour, say a foot-thick sheet of steel. It might make a small hole in a wall, but that's all.'

'So we use more than one,' said Mickey.

'Then timing becomes a problem. Even a skilled oper-ator takes about fifteen seconds to reload. Then time to aim. So if it takes four warheads to blow a big enough hole, that's going to take you a full minute and a half, at least.'

'So we go in with four RPGs. Each ready to fire. You pick one up, you fire, you put it down, you pick up the next one. Bang. Bang. Bang. Bang.'

The waiter returned with Shepherd's drink on a stainless-steel tray. He put the glass, a napkin and a bowl of salted peanuts on the table and backed away. Shepherd was just about to ask Mickey about the RPGs he intended to buy when Sergei appeared at the doorway. 'The Russians are coming,' he said.

Three other men appeared, all big guys, well muscled and, like Sergei, with diamond earrings and geometric tattoos on their forearms. They walked over to where Shepherd and Mickey were sitting. 'We're going out to a bar we know,' said Sergei. 'You should come.'

'What's it called?' asked Mickey.

'The Red Rose.'

'The one with the upstairs rooms and the circular beds?'

The Russian grinned. 'That's the one.'

'We'll see you there,' said Mickey.

Sergei clapped Shepherd on the shoulder with his huge hand. 'You come, Ricky. We'll get drunk and talk, okay?' The Russians headed off.

When they'd gone Shepherd said, 'Okay, I accept that three or four or maybe five RPGs might well blast a big enough hole in a wall for us to get out the money, but then what? You start using ordnance like that and every armed cop in the country will be after you. Plus the SAS, plus the spooks, plus anyone else with a gun.'

'We'll be long gone by the time anyone gets near the place.' He blew another tight plume of smoke at the fan. 'We'll be driving over farmland in four-by-fours. The armed cops will be in ARVs, which look great and go fast but they're bugger-all use over ditches.'

'And what about helicopters? What about the eye in the sky?'

Mickey grinned. 'The nearest police helicopter is a ten-minute flight away and that's assuming it's in the air, which it almost certainly won't be. There've been cutbacks and they're refusing to pay the pilots overtime so by the end of the month they're pretty much grounded unless it's a missing kid or something.'

'The Professor told you that?'

'He's thorough,' said Mickey. 'He covers all the bases.'

'And what about inside the building? What sort of manpower will we be facing?'

'We'll go in at dawn and there'll be no one in the money-handling area,' said Mickey. 'Any personnel on site will be in the admin block. It'll take them two minutes at least to get through to where we are, and once they see our firepower they'll sit tight and wait for the cavalry.' He winked at Shepherd. 'You worry too much, mate,' he said. 'All this has been planned down to the last detail. All you've got to do is handle the firepower. It'll be like taking candy from a baby.'

'Not sure you'd want to point an RPG at a baby, but I get your drift,' said Shepherd. 'So is that the plan? Get an RPG from your army mates here and blow our way into the depot?'

'Not Cambodia,' said Mickey. 'We could get one here, no trouble, but then we'd have to get it from Cambodia to the UK and that would be a problem and a half. No, we're going to pick one up in Europe.'

'Pop into Arms R Us you mean? Mickey, you can't just drop into a store and buy an RPG.'

'If you know the right people you can. And our Professor knows the right people.' Mark and Yates walked in, followed by Black and Wilson, and came over to them. 'Fancy the Red Rose?'

Yates grinned. 'Didn't Mark hit someone there last time?'

'He hits someone wherever we go,' said Wilson.

'I'm sorted,' said Black. 'I might catch up with you guys later.' He headed out of the hotel. 'Where's he going?' asked Shepherd.

'He's got a boyfriend who works for one of the NGOs here,' said Mickey. He stood up. 'Come on, we'll show you the delights of the Red Rose.'

They went out to Reception. The two Landcruisers were parked in front of the hotel. Wilbur was sitting in the front passenger seat of one vehicle and climbed out to shake hands with Mickey. 'Wilbur takes care of us on our evenings out,' Mickey explained to Shepherd. 'Phnom Penh's not the same as Bangkok – it can get a bit dicey after dark. It helps to have a few guys with guns around.' There was a large revolver in a leather holster high on Wilbur's hip.

Mickey and Shepherd got into the Landcruiser with Wilbur and the rest of the men climbed into the second vehicle. They drove along the Mekong river, past dozens of outdoor cafés and bars, then turned away from it, the four-wheel drives lurching over potholes and cracks in the road. There were few street-lights and most weren't working.

The Red Rose bar was down a small road filled with parked motorcycles. A group of men sharing bottles of brandy watched them walk in. One muttered something and Wilbur turned to give them a hard look before he followed Mickey inside.

Sergei was sitting at the bar, a bottle of Black Label whisky in front of him. When he saw Shepherd, he held up his bottle and beckoned him over. A dozen Cambodian girls, all wearing pink evening gowns with sequins at the neck, rushed over and swarmed around the new arrivals, grabbing for their hands and trying to pull them to the booths that ran around the bar. Shepherd held his up, dropped the right to make sure his wallet stayed in his pocket.

'You'll love it here, Ricky,' said Yates. 'Costs you a lot less than it does in Pattaya, and the girls are up for anything. And there's none of that "My mother's in hospital" or "The water buffalo's sick, please help me" crap.' He pointed at a stairway at the far end of the bar. 'And you can take the birds upstairs to give them a seeing-to.' He picked up a girl, who laughed and wrapped her legs around his waist, then walked over to one of the booths with her to order a drink from a waitress. Wilson followed him with two girls in tow.

Two more clutched Mark and led him to the bar. 'Sisters!' he shouted to Shepherd. 'I've got sisters here!'

Shepherd sat on the stool next to the Russian and nodded when Sergei offered him a shot of his whisky. 'Soda water and ice,' he told one of the two barmen.

'You ruin a good whisky with water?' said the Russian.

'I won't tell you how to drink vodka if you don't lecture me about whisky,' said Shepherd. 'Where are your friends?'

'Upstairs with hookers.'

'Oi, Ricky!' Wilson was going up with three girls. 'See you up there, yeah?'

'Definitely,' said Shepherd, though he had no such intention.

Sergei shook his head sadly. 'The women here, they are so small,' he said, 'and ugly.'

The Russian had a point: most of them were barely five feet tall and had bad skin and lank hair. 'Why do you Englishmen like such ugly women?' asked Sergei.

'Don't go tarring us all with the same brush,' said Shepherd.

Sergei frowned. 'What do you mean – what brush?'

'I mean we're not all the same.'

'What does that have to do with brushes?'

'It's a nautical expression, from the days when English ships ruled the oceans. They were made waterproof with tar but I'm not sure why it wasn't a good idea to use the same brush. The point I was making is that not everyone is here for the girls. I came over with Mickey to shoot a few guns. And your mates are upstairs, too, remember? So they're not fussy either.'

Mickey had joined Mark in his booth and they were sitting with their arms around giggling bargirls.

'Now, Russian girls, they are the best in the world,' said Sergei. 'They are fit and they are fiery. They have spirit. These Asian girls are like dolls. They tell you what you want to hear, they do what you want to do. A Russian girl is like a wild horse. You can ride them but you can never tame them.'

'Nice analogy,' said Shepherd.

'Analogy?'

'You describe them perfectly,' said Shepherd. He wasn't exactly sure of the dictionary definition of analogy. 'But I have to say, most of the Russian women I've seen aren't especially pretty. And no offence, but a lot seem overweight.'

Sergei bellowed with laughter and slapped Shepherd on the back hard enough to rattle his teeth. 'No offence, my friend.' He gripped Shepherd's neck with his huge hand and squeezed. 'I like that. You say, "no offence," but then you say something very offensive. But I am not offended. I am talking about Russian girls, not Russian women. That is one of the sad facts of life, that many of the fit wild horses grow up to be fat pigs. That is why I shall never marry, just trade horses.' Sergei picked up his glass and clinked it against Shepherd's. 'To fit women,' he said.

'To fit women,' said Shepherd.

They both drank, then Sergei banged his glass down on the bar and refilled it with neat whisky. 'What about you, Ricky? Did you ever marry?'

'I'm like you, a horse-trader,' he said. Sergei slapped him on the back again. Shepherd hated having to deny that he had once been married. Every time he did so, it was as if he was betraying Sue and Liam. But his family had no place in his undercover work. He was Ricky Knight, and Ricky Knight wasn't a family man.

'You should come visit my bar in Pattaya,' said Sergei. 'We have Russian girls dancing. Fit Russian girls. And you can screw them for the same price as the Thai hookers. Think you can handle a Russian ride, my friend?'

'I'll give it a go,' said Shepherd. He sipped his beer. 'So, you said you'd tell me what you do in Pattaya. Other than running a go-go bar.'

'Because you want to move in on my businesses? You want to steal the bread from my mouth?'

'As I told you before, I'm just interested,' Shepherd assured him. 'It doesn't look like an easy place to make money – the Thais seem to have it all sewn up in their favour. Foreigners can't own land, they have to have Thai partners in any company they set up, and everyone I've spoken to says that if a foreigner takes a Thai to court the court will always rule in favour of the Thai.'

'The businesses I'm in, we don't go to court.' He made a gun with his hand and pointed it at Shepherd's temple. 'We have other ways of resolving disputes.' He drank another shot of neat whisky. It was his fifth since Shepherd had entered the bar, and he'd already worked his way through half the bottle. Sergei was a big man, though, and clearly used to drinking, and Shepherd could see that he was a long way from being intoxicated. Shepherd could handle his drink but he knew he'd be no match for the Russian and was trying to pace himself.

'So what do you do?' asked Sergei. 'Where does your money come from?'

'This and that,' said Shepherd.

The Russian chuckled. 'This and that? I like that. This and that. That means you do not want to tell me.'

Shepherd put his head close to the Russian's. 'Can you keep a secret, Sergei?'

The Russian nodded seriously. 'Sure.'

'Me too,' said Shepherd. He slapped the Russian on the back.

For a few seconds the Russian didn't get the joke and stared at Shepherd with deep furrows in his brow. Then realisation dawned and he spluttered whisky across the bar and burst into laughter. 'You are a very funny man, Ricky,' he said.

'A lot of people say that,' said Shepherd. 'Seriously, you want to know what I do?'

The Russian nodded.

'I sell cars,' said Shepherd.

'You don't look like a car salesman,' said Sergei.

'That's what I do,' said Shepherd. 'I was a soldier and I got fed up with the crap money and the crap officers so I started selling cars and I'm good at it.'

Sergei gestured at the Moore brothers, who were now deep-kissing the girls they were with. 'Your friends, too?'

'They're property developers.'

'They don't look like property developers and you don't look like a car salesman.'

'What do we look like?'

The Russian chuckled. 'You look like trouble.'

'That's my middle name,' said Shepherd.

Mickey and Mark stood up and swayed unsteadily.

Mickey waved at Shepherd, bleary-eyed, and pointed upstairs. 'Going for a shag!' he shouted.

'Have one for me,' Shepherd called back. The brothers walked unsteadily towards the stairs, a bar girl on either arm. A waitress hurried to their table and cleared away the empty glasses.

'What is shag?' asked Sergei.

'Sex,' said Shepherd.

'You do not want a girl, Ricky?' asked Sergei.

'I'll wait for the Russian ride you promised me,' said Shepherd. 'Is that your business, bringing in Russian girls?'

Sergei's eyes narrowed, but then he smiled. 'It's part of what we do.'

'You bring girls into Thailand?'

'We do everything,' he said. 'We recruit them in Russia and the Ukraine, we get them passports and pay for their tickets. Then we put them to work.'

'And the police don't stop you?'

The Russian rubbed his thumb and fingers together. 'We take care of the police and they take care of us.'

'And you can make decent money? I'd have thought there'd be too much competition from the Thais.'

Sergei grinned. 'Men don't want to eat burgers every day, sometimes they want a steak. The Thai women, they're all the same. Black hair, brown eyes, brown skin. Our women offer variety. And the Thai men can't get enough of them. Our girls work three, four times a day at two thousand baht a time. That means a girl can earn around a hundred and fifty thousand baht a month, which she splits with me fifty-fifty. That's more than two thousand dollars a month from each girl, and I've got more than twenty here. Another ten in Phuket.' The grin widened. 'Yes, it's good money, my friend.'

Shepherd raised his eyebrows. If the Russian was telling the truth, he was bringing in three-quarters of a million dollars a year from prostitution alone.

'But we make more money from them than just by selling their bodies,' Sergei continued. 'We use them to carry drugs too. We load their suitcases with heroin when they fly home and we pay off Customs in Russia.'

'Nice,' said Shepherd.

'Very nice,' said Sergei. 'The money we make from the girls and the drugs we put into property. Condominiums, villas, shopping malls. Then we rent them out. Thailand is a gold mine, Ricky, if you know what to do. We sell arms. Plenty of countries out here want to buy weapons, and the Soviet bloc is full of them. Drugs, arms, girls, we have our fingers in many cakes.'

'Pies,' said Shepherd. 'You have fingers in pies, not cakes.'

'Pies, cakes, it's all the same,' said Sergei. 'Better than being a grunt,' he said. 'And better than selling cars, too.'

Marcel Calvert pointed at the metal case with the claw he used instead of a right hand. 'It is what you want, no?' he said.

Kundi looked up from the missile assembly. 'It's fine,' he said to Bradshaw.

'Alex said sixty thousand euros,' said Bradshaw.

'It's a fair price,' said Calvert. He tapped the case with his claw. He was a good-looking man with a shock of black hair that he kept flicking away from his eyes. He was wearing a long-sleeved white cotton shirt with brown cargo trousers, and had a Bluetooth unit in his left ear.

'You only have the one?' asked Bradshaw.

'You need more?'

'I would prefer two. Or three.'

Calvert rubbed his chin with his claw. 'I sold two last month,' he said. 'They're hard to get. The Americans are taking as many as they can off the market and there are always buyers.' He gestured at the metal case. 'You're lucky I have that one.'

The wooden crate from Sarajevo, containing the Grail missile Bradshaw had brought from the Dutchman, was next to the Stinger. Kleintank had arranged it to be flown to Nice on a private plane while Bradshaw, Talwar and Kundi had travelled by train.

'Did you need anything else?' asked Calvert, turning towards the stacks of crates and boxes in the metal shelving that ran the full length of the warehouse. 'I have assault rifles, small arms, grenades . . .'

Bradshaw patted the Stinger. 'This is all I need,' he said.

He went outside to the Citroën van with Kundi and took a bulky envelope from Talwar. He left Kundi outside and went back to Calvert with the money. Calvert held the envelope in his claw and used his hand to take out the notes. He fed them into an electric banknote counter and pressed a button. It whirred and he looked at the display. 'Perfect,' he said.

Bradshaw's eyes were on Calvert's claw. 'That happened in the Legion?' he asked.

'Algeria,' said Calvert. 'Booby-trapped door.' He shrugged. 'Shit happens. Alex said you were a soldier, too.'

'Iraq,' said Bradshaw.

'Another messy war,' said Calvert. 'It's the Muslims, they don't fight like men. If an enemy stands up and shoots at you, you can shoot back. But the Muslims fight like cowards. They plant bombs and use children and women as shields.'

Bradshaw said nothing.

'What can you do against an enemy who thinks killing yourself in the name of Allah means an eternity in Heaven being attended to by seventy-two black-eyed virgins?' Calvert continued. 'How stupid is that? But the pigs are too stupid to see how ridiculous their religion is so they continue to queue up to die. And when they do fight, they fight like cowards. You know what they did? They attached a hand grenade to the front door of a house, and they had two snipers upstairs. They fired at our convoy, killing two of our men, then escaped down a drainpipe. I was first through the door. That's how they fight, with snipers and booby traps. The West can never win against an enemy that fights like that.'

'You sell grenades,' said Bradshaw. 'Isn't there something ironic in that?'

'It's business.'

'Would you sell to the Algerians?'

Calvert laughed drily. 'A good question,' he said. 'It's never arisen, but I think not.' He turned back to the Stinger. 'What about delivery? For another five thousand euros I can deliver them anywhere in Europe. Ten thousand if you want them in Britain.'

'No need,' said Bradshaw. 'We have our own transport.'

★   ★   ★

Mickey Moore slammed on the brakes of the Range Rover and skidded to a halt just inches from the gates to Shepherd's villa.

'You break them, you pay for them,' warned Shepherd.

'What do you care? It's a rental.' Mickey laughed. 'So, when are you going to get a place of your own?'

'I figured the job we've got coming up will pay for it, so I'm going to leave my money offshore. I assume you've no problem getting it here, right?'

'A guy in London does it for us. He's an Indian, but he's okay. No matter what the currency, he can wash it and get it into the banking system.'

'That's what I'll do, then,' said Shepherd. 'Any idea what my share's going to be?'

'It'll be big,' said Moore.

'Ballpark?'

'More than enough to buy yourself any place in Pattaya. And have change. But we won't know for sure until the day.'

'But it's money we're after, right? It's not another Brink's-Mat?' Robbers who had targeted Heathrow airport in 1983 had got away with ten tons of gold worth more than twenty-six million pounds but most of them had been caught and sent down. 'Gold leaves a trail, Mickey. Diamonds too. I'm happier if it's cash in hand.'

'Don't worry, Ricky. It's cash.'

Shepherd took out his remote control and opened the gates. 'You want to come in for a beer?'

'Rain check,' said Mickey. 'We'll be out on the town tomorrow.'

Shepherd grabbed his holdall and climbed out of the Range Rover. He waved as Mickey drove off, then walked along the path to the front door. He let himself in, deactivated his burglar alarm, then showered and changed before he phoned Charlotte Button. 'How was Cambodia?' she asked.

'Like the Wild West,' he said. 'You will not believe what they're planning. RPGs. Rocket-propelled grenades. Whatever the job is, they plan to blow their way in.'

'Any idea when or where?'

'They won't tell me,' said Shepherd. 'But they wanted to check I was familiar with RPGs.'

'Which, of course, you are.'

'Which, of course, I am. So, now it's a question of getting the gear into the country.'

'Any thoughts on how they're going to do that?'

'I get the impression that Townsend has given them a contact somewhere in Europe.'

'We'll have a look at his Internet traffic, see if there's a clue there,' said Button. 'Any hints you can get would be much appreciated, Spider. I don't need to tell you that RPGs are serious weaponry.'

'It's a step up from sawn-off shotguns, that's for sure. They won't tell me what the score's going to be, other than that it's big. And they're going for cash.'

'I'll get our analysts on the case right away, pulling up lists of possible targets,' said Button.

'You might see if they've any Indian contacts, too,' said Shepherd. 'Mickey says they use an Indian guy to do their laundry. That's all I have. I didn't want to press.'

'How much access do you have to their place?'

'I come and go. Why? What are you thinking?'

'If there's any way you could have a look around, check their computers, see if Townsend left anything with them . . .'

'It'd be pushing my luck, Charlie,' he said. 'They're in

and out of each other's villas and there's a big staff that always wandering around.'

'What about getting a bug in there?'

Shepherd exhaled through his teeth. 'I don't want to sound negative, but if they found it and suspected me, it would be thank you and goodnight.'

'Give it some thought,' said Button. 'The more intel we have, the better.'

'What's the story about the judge who was killed?' asked Shepherd.

'Nasty business,' said Button. 'Whoever did it was below MI5's radar, but that's par for the course, these days. The video was on the Internet within hours of his body being found. Now we're on a high alert for copycats. But what do you do? Issue police protection for every possible fundamentalist target? There aren't enough police in the country for that.'

'And the plane that crashed leaving New York? Are they still saying mechanical failure?'

'Early days, but Homeland Security says there's no suggestion of terrorism and no flights have been grounded.'

'I guess accidents happen. It's just that now every time something goes wrong you think the worst.'

'The way of the world, I'm afraid,' agreed Button.

'There's something I want to run by you,' said Shepherd. 'I met a Russian in Cambodia, a nasty piece of work. He's into human trafficking and drugs and I don't know what else.'

'Any UK involvement?'

'Not that I know of,' he said. 'But I was wondering if we could get Europol on to it.'

'He's Russian, you said?'

'Yeah, but the Thais aren't going to do anything about him and he's using trafficked girls as drugs mules. Like I said, a nasty piece of work.'

'The world's full of his sort. We can't get them all,' said Button. 'You know our brief – drugs, organised crime and trafficking in the UK.'

'Serious and organised,' said Shepherd.

'What?'

Shepherd smiled. 'Just something Razor was talking about.'

'And how is the lovely Mr Sharpe?'

'He's fine. Watching my back.'

'Not offending the Thais too much, I hope.'

'Actually, he seems to like the locals.'

'And you're okay with just him as your back-up? Now things are moving along, I could send reinforcements.'

'There'd be nothing to do,' said Shepherd. 'It's just a matter of waiting for the off. What about you?'

'Me?'

'The time we met at the safe-house, it looked as if you were sleeping there.'

Button didn't say anything for a few seconds. 'Why, Spider, are you concerned about my welfare?'

'I just thought . . .' He tailed off. He wasn't sure exactly what he thought.

'I had a late-night meeting and a morning meeting and I couldn't face the drive home,' she said. 'But thank you for worrying.'

'I wasn't worried . . .' began Shepherd, but again words failed him.

'Everything's fine,' she said. 'But even if it wasn't, it's not a conversation to have over the phone.'

'Got it,' said Shepherd.

'But thank you,' she said. 'Seriously.'

'No problem.' Shepherd cut the connection. He could feel his cheeks reddening and felt embarrassed at the way the conversation had ended. Button was right: her sleeping arrangements were none of his business. He glanced out of the window. The sky was darkening. Another night in paradise.

Bradshaw, Kundi and Talwar sat in their van, watching Calvert climb out of a Renault Mégane limousine and walk to the front door of his house. They waited until he had gone inside before they drove off.

'Are you sure you want to do this, brother?' asked Kundi.

'He insulted Allah,' said Bradshaw. 'The Koran is clear, he must die.'

'Then we'll all do it,' said Talwar. 'We'll do it together.'

'I'll do it alone,' Bradshaw said. 'It was me he was talking to when he insulted Allah. It's up to me to right the wrong.'

'You're putting what we're doing at risk,' said Kundi, quietly.

Bradshaw faced him, his eyes burning. 'If we do not stand up for Allah when He is defamed and abused, then what are we fighting for? Why bother with *jihad* if we stand by and allow the infidel to defile our God?' He took a deep breath and forced himself to be calm. He smiled slowly. 'This has to be done, brother,' he said. 'It is the will of Allah.'

'Then you should kill the infidel,' said Kundi softly. '*Allahu akbar.*'

'*Allahu akbar*,' echoed Bradshaw and Talwar.

Bradshaw got out of the van and walked to the wall around Calvert's house. They were in an upmarket area of the city, well away from the tourist areas by the sea. The houses were expensive, built within the last ten years, each with a high wall and a metal gate to maintain privacy. No CCTV cameras covered the wall, and there was no razor wire to deter intruders, but Bradshaw assumed that, as an arms dealer, Calvert must have security measures in place so he put on a baseball cap and pulled the brim low over his face as he walked over to the gate. There was a bellpush and a brass grille. He pulled on a pair of tight-fitting leather gloves and pressed the bell. After a few seconds Calvert asked in French who it was.

'It's me. There's a problem with the consignment,' said Bradshaw.

There was a few seconds' silence. When Calvert spoke again his voice was clipped and impatient. 'You shouldn't have come here,' he said. The gate buzzed and opened. Bradshaw strode towards the house, head down in case there were cameras he hadn't seen. Calvert had the front door open for him. 'Come in, come in,' he said. 'How did you know where I live?'

'I followed you,' said Bradshaw.

Calvert frowned as he shut the door behind them. 'What do you mean?' he said.

Bradshaw slapped him across the face, and Calvert staggered backwards into a side table. 'When you insult all Muslims, you insult me. But, worse, you insult Allah.'

'Fuck you,' said Calvert, wiping his bloody mouth with his sleeve.

'So I've come back to show you that all Muslims are not cowards.'

'By ambushing me? By sneaking up on me in the dark? That proves that you're a man, does it?'

'By fighting you.'

'Bullshit,' said the Frenchman. 'If you'd wanted to fight me you'd have done it in the warehouse. But you didn't because my men were with me. So you sneak back at night like a coward.'

'I'm no coward,' said Bradshaw. He slid a carving knife, its blade wrapped in newspaper, from his pocket.

Calvert held up his steel claw. 'You want to fight a man with one hand,' he said. 'You call this a fair fight?' He spat on the floor in front of Bradshaw. 'You Muslim pig.'

'You will burn in Hell for all eternity,' said Bradshaw, tightening his grip on the handle of the knife.

Calvert lurched to the left and, with his hand, he groped for a drawer in the table behind him. Bradshaw glimpsed a semi-automatic pistol. He stepped forward and thrust the knife into the Frenchman's chest. He drove it between the two bottom ribs, twisted it up and in, ripping through the right lung and puncturing the heart. Blood trickled from between Calvert's lips as he stared fixedly at Bradshaw.

'You can beg Allah the Most Merciful for His forgiveness,' said Bradshaw. 'Tell Him that you were killed by a true warrior of the *jihad*. Tell Him that.' He gave the knife a final push and Calvert's eyes clouded. He slumped to the marble floor.

Bradshaw rewrapped the blade and slid it back inside his jacket. He listened but the only sound in the house was the ticking of an ornate grandfather clock at the far

end of the hallway. Blood was pooling around Calvert's
chest and Bradshaw stepped carefully over the body. There
was an intercom unit to the left of the door. One button
bore the insignia of a key and Bradshaw pressed it, then
let himself out of the front door. The gate was opening
and he jogged towards the waiting van. Kundi already had
the engine running.

Shepherd walked into the Penthouse Hotel and went up
to Sharpe's floor. He knocked on the door and, after a
few seconds, heard footsteps. 'Who is it?'

'Immigration police,' said Shepherd. 'Open the door,
you daft sod, I come bearing gifts.'

He heard the lock click and Jimmy Sharpe was blinking
at him. He had a towel wrapped around his waist and was
holding an icepack against his forehead.

'Don't you wear pyjamas?' asked Shepherd.

'Not when I'm sleeping alone,' said Sharpe. 'It's two
o'clock in the morning, what do you want?'

Shepherd held out the carrier-bag he was holding.
'A drink,' he said. Sharpe took it and pulled out a bottle
of Johnnie Walker Black Label and six bottles of soda
water. 'They'd never heard of Jameson's,' Shepherd
added.

'I've no ice left,' said Sharpe, opening the bottle and
retrieving two glasses from the bathroom. 'Used the last
of it in the icepack.'

For the first time Shepherd noticed the bruising around
Sharpe's left eye. 'That's not from where I slammed you
into the wall, is it?' he asked.

'Nah, I had a bit of an incident,' said Sharpe.

'Razor . . .'

'Wasn't my fault,' said Sharpe, opening the whisky. 'I ran into Jason Reece, the burglar I helped put away. The one we saw at the Scotland Yard briefing.'

'He recognised you?'

'Yeah. I was leaving a massage place off Walking Street just as he was going in. He started giving me all sorts of abuse. I had to shut him up.'

'How exactly?'

Sharpe pulled a face. 'I didn't have time for anything fancy,' he said.

'You head-butted him?'

'It was a spur-of-the-moment thing,' said Sharpe. 'I just hit him and legged it. Spider, he was effing and blinding and causing a right scene. I just wanted out of there but he grabbed me. It wasn't my fault.' He poured whisky into the glasses and added soda water.

'Anyone see you?'

'The girls in the massage place and a couple of tourists in the street, but I wasn't followed. I'm in the clear.'

'Yeah, but you're confined to barracks for the duration, you know that? Hell's bells, Razor, what were you thinking?'

'It was instinctive. He grabbed me, I gave him the Glasgow kiss.'

'I meant what were you thinking about, going to a massage parlour?'

'I was bored,' said Sharpe. He handed Shepherd a whisky and soda. 'So, what's up?' he asked, sitting down on the bed.

Shepherd sipped his whisky. 'You ever wonder why we do what we do?'

'A shade under forty grand a year,' said Sharpe.

'But you're on a higher pay scale than me and will be for the foreseeable future.'

'That's the answer? Money?'

'We do a job, Spider. We catch bad guys and the state pays us to do that. What's eating you?' He held the icepack against his forehead and winced.

Shepherd took a gulp of his whisky and soda and sighed. 'When I was in Cambodia I met this Russian. He's based here in Pattaya. Right son-of-a-bitch. Traffics hookers and uses them to take drugs back to Russia. Former army and all his guys are former army, too.'

'And?'

'And I told Charlie about him and she doesn't want to know.'

'Because he's Russian?'

'Because he's Russian and because he's not committing crimes in England.'

'She's got a point,' said Sharpe.

'He's a far worse criminal than the Moore brothers, Razor. Drugs and prostitution, and I bet there's a fair bit of other stuff too. Mickey was telling me that the Russians are behind protection rackets out here and they've started house robberies where they go in and beat the shit out of everyone there.'

'Yeah, they've been doing that in Spain for years,' said Sharpe. 'Not just the Russians, the Serbs, the Bosnians, most of the Central European mobs.'

'Right, so I have this guy almost on a plate, right? If Europol or whoever were to target him, they'd have him in weeks. Surveillance would link him to the girls with the drugs and it'd be conspiracy to export class A drugs and that'd be that.'

'Except he's Russian.'

'Right. Which means it's none of our business.'

'And, like I said, Button's got a point. Even if we were to make a case against him, what then? Last I heard neither the Thai courts nor the Russian judicial system pay any attention to the Crown Prosecution Service.'

'But SOCA is prepared to spend a small fortune to put the Moore brothers away. They had Oswald taking snaps for weeks, they've had Townsend under surveillance in the UK for months, they've got you and me out here – my villa alone is costing more than eight grand a month.'

Sharpe's jaw dropped. 'You didn't tell me that before,' he said.

'It's none of your business.'

'Eight grand a month? This place costs about twenty quid a night.'

'It's part of my cover, Razor. Neither of us is here on holiday.' He drained his glass and held it out for a refill. Sharpe obliged, and topped up his own glass. 'The thing is, Mark and Mickey Moore are villains, no question of that. But they don't traffic women and they don't deal in drugs. They rob banks. They steal money that, in most cases, is insured.'

'Don't tell me they're victimless crimes,' said Sharpe, wagging a warning finger at Shepherd. 'They wave shotguns around and they kick the shit out of anyone who gets in their way.'

'They're villains, sure, and we'll put them away for their villainy. But, Razor, they're not evil. They're not trafficking in human misery, be it prostitution or hard drugs. I'm not saying they're Robin Hoods because they're not, but they're not bad people. Not in the grand scheme of things.'

'They're breaking the law, and we're paid to uphold it.'

'Well, maybe we could be doing better things, that's all I'm saying.' He sighed. 'I'm starting to think maybe Moira was right.'

'Moira?'

'My mother-in-law. She wanted to know why I was being sent to Thailand when there was so much shit going on in England.'

'She said "shit" did she?' Sharpe guffawed.

'No, but that's what she meant. And, let's face it, she's right. We've got disaffected Muslims planning God knows what, we've got kids being knifed on our streets, a murder rate in London higher than New York, and drugs everywhere. And what are we doing? We're on the trail of a group of guys who steal from financial institutions. The City is full of guys with fewer morals than the Moore brothers, but because they wear suits and have the right accents, they get away with murder.' He smiled. 'I don't mean that literally.'

'You're forgetting the guns, Spider. Merchant bankers only wave shotguns around if they're shooting pheasants.'

'Right, and when they get caught taking chances with other people's cash, the Government bails them out with taxpayers' money.'

Sharpe sipped his drink. 'When was the last time you saw Caroline Stockmann?' he asked quietly.

'Why do I need to see the office shrink?' asked Shepherd, quickly. Too quickly, he realised. He took a deep breath and held the glass to his forehead. 'Why's it so hot in here?' he asked.

'Because the aircon's seized up, and don't change the subject.' He raised his glass and grinned mischievously. 'Don't forget I've been on the same interrogation courses as you.'

'How is a chinwag with a psychiatrist going to help me?' asked Shepherd.

'Because what you're going through is textbook Stockholm syndrome.'

'Bullshit,' said Shepherd.

'You're a long way from home, Spider. Away from your friends and family in an unfamiliar environment. The people you're closest to right now are the Moore brothers, and you've always been good at empathising. That's why you're such a good undercover agent. But, if you ask me, this time you've gone a bit too far.'

'Screw you, Razor. I didn't come here for a character reading.'

'Subconsciously you did. And I'm saying that to you as a friend. A real friend.'

'You're saying I've crossed the line,' said Shepherd. He smiled ruefully. 'You think I've gone over to the dark side.'

'Aye, Luke Skywalker, and if you do that the force will no longer be with you.' He grinned. 'Look, you'll be fine. You just need to take a step back and re-evaluate your situation. And stay focused. We're out here to get the Moore brothers and their crew. Everything else is a distraction.'

Shepherd rested his head against the back of the chair and gazed up at the ceiling. 'You're right,' he said.

'You sound surprised,' said Sharpe. 'You know what you need?'

'A few weeks' holiday with my son,' said Shepherd.

'A massage,' said Sharpe. 'A nice soapy massage. It'll relieve all that tension.'

Shepherd chuckled. 'You are bloody incorrigible.'

Bradshaw studied the map as Kundi drove the rented Citroën van slowly down the dual carriageway on the outskirts of Nice. 'I don't like left-hand drives,' said Kundi.

'You're doing fine,' said Bradshaw.

Talwar was in the back of the van with the boxes containing the Grail and the Stinger missiles. They had stopped at a supermarket and bought two dozen cases of beer and wine, which they'd stacked around the weaponry.

Bradshaw glanced at his Casio wristwatch. The Motorail train for Calais wasn't due to leave for another hour. Everything was on schedule. He took out his mobile phone and switched it on. He didn't trust mobiles: the Government's intelligence agencies could listen in to every conversation made and read every text sent, and they could locate any user within minutes, but he was on the move and he had to stay in touch with Chaudhry so he had no choice. He didn't store any numbers in it and he kept it switched off when he wasn't using it. He waited until the phone had powered up and tapped out Chaudhry's number. He answered on the third ring, and didn't identify himself. 'We're on our way,' said Bradshaw.

'Did everything go okay?' asked Chaudhry.

'Everything is on schedule. We'll see you in Calais.' Bradshaw cut the connection and switched off the phone.

Shepherd was in Tony's Gym, running hard on a tread-mill, when his mobile rang. He'd left it on the console of his running machine and squinted at the display. It was Mickey. He pressed the green button to take the call, and slowed the treadmill to four kilometres an hour. 'Hi, Mickey, what's up?'

'Are you on the job, mate?' asked Mickey.

'I'm running,' said Shepherd.

'Who's after you?'

'I'm in the gym,' said Shepherd.

'You need to get home and pack your toothbrush,' said Mickey. 'We're off to Arms 'R Us.'

'Where exactly are we going?' asked Shepherd.

'We'll tell you at the airport. Mark's driving around to pick you up.'

'I need my passport, right?'

Mickey chuckled. 'Don't worry, Mark's got it. Just pack for a day or two, hand luggage only so we don't have to piss around checking in bags.'

As soon as Mickey ended the call, Shepherd stepped off the treadmill and phoned Sharpe. 'So we don't know what name you're flying under or where you're going?' said Sharpe.

'That's right, so I need you at the airport to report back to Charlie because I might not be able to call. Tell her the flight I'm on and leave it up to her to arrange surveillance if she wants it.'

'Do you want me to get on the flight?'

'No need,' said Shepherd. 'I think they trust me, I'll be back here in two days. They're going to pick me up at the villa so I'm thinking we'll be at the airport in about three hours. You'd better head off there now.'

'On my way,' said Sharpe.

Shepherd cut the connection and went straight to his

Jeep without changing. He drove quickly back to his villa. There was no sign of Mark so he took a quick shower and changed into a clean polo shirt and jeans. As he was about to pack his holdall, a car horn sounded outside the villa, three long blasts. Shepherd hurried down the driveway to the gates, used his remote control and they creaked open. 'Give me a couple of minutes to get my shit together,' he called.

Mark wound down the window. 'We've got time for a beer,' he said. He switched off the engine and followed Shepherd into the villa. 'Not a bad place,' he said, looking around. 'But you're paying too much.'

'Mickey said you had my passport.'

Mark reached into the back pocket of his jeans and pulled it out. He handed it over. The picture was Shepherd's but the name was Graham Moreton. Shepherd examined the passport. It looked genuine and had been issued by the British Embassy in Bangkok.

'It's real and it's in the system,' said Mark. 'We've got a guy in the embassy. He isn't cheap but he's sound.'

'A Brit?'

'Thai.'

Shepherd slipped it into his shirt pocket. 'So, where are we off to?'

Mark tapped the side of his nose. 'Need to know.'

'Give me a clue so I know what to pack,' said Shepherd. 'Hot, cold, raining, snow?'

'Germany,' said Mark. 'Where's the kitchen?'

'Over there,' said Shepherd, pointing. 'Beer's in the fridge.'

Shepherd went to the master bedroom and threw two clean shirts, underwear and two pairs of socks into his

holdall with his washbag. He decided against taking his
UK mobile phone with him, locked it in the wardrobe
safe and grabbed a sports jacket off its hanger. Then he
went to join Mark by the pool. 'Nice enough gaff, this,'
said Mark. 'Pool's a bit small but the view's all right.'

'I'm not much of a swimmer,' said Shepherd. 'So, who
else is on this trip?'

'Just you, me and Mickey,' said Mark. He finished his
beer and tossed the bottle into the pool. 'What?' he said,
when he saw the disgust on Shepherd's face. 'You said
you weren't much of a swimmer. Anyway, you've got a
poolboy, haven't you? Come on, let's go.'

Mark drove at his usual breakneck pace and ninety
minutes later they were pulling up in the long-stay car
park at the airport. He locked the Range Rover and they
walked together to Departures. Mickey was already there
and took them to the Lufthansa check-in desk. Shepherd
didn't see Jimmy Sharpe, which meant one of two things
– he was watching from a discreet hiding-place or he
hadn't made it to the airport in time. Mickey had booked
them into business class on the direct flight to Munich
and they went through Immigration to sit in the lounge
before the flight boarded. They talked about football, the
bars and the weather. The one thing they didn't talk about
was the reason for the trip.

Kundi edged the Citroën van down the rails to the ground.
'Easy does it,' said Bradshaw. Ahead, two little blonde girls
were waving at them from the back of a Mercedes estate
car. Bradshaw waved back. Immediately the two little girls
put their fingers in their mouths and pulled faces at him,
waggling their tongues and staring at him cross-eyed.

Bradshaw laughed. 'Kids,' he said. The Mercedes accelerated, the little girls continuing to pull faces until they were out of sight.

Bradshaw took his mobile phone from his pocket, switched it on and tapped out Chaudhry's number. The call went straight to voicemail. Bradshaw switched off his phone and put it away. He had a map on his lap and traced the route from the Motorail depot to the ferry terminal. He glanced at his watch. 'Are you hungry, brothers?' he asked.

'I could eat,' Kundi said.

'Me too,' said Talwar. He nodded so enthusiastically that his glasses slid down his nose. He pushed them back up again.

'We'll stop on the way,' said Bradshaw.

They had spent the night in a four-berth couchette on the train from Nice. It was the most efficient way of getting the van and its contents across the country. There had been no security checks getting on or off the train, and the service had operated with an efficiency that put British train operators to shame.

They stopped at a small roadside café and ordered steak and chips, freshly baked bread and orange juice. While they were waiting for their meal, Bradshaw took out his phone and switched it on again. This time Chaudhry answered. 'Where are you, brother?' asked Bradshaw.

'Just driving away from the Eurotunnel terminal,' said Chaudhry. He was bringing one of his father's delivery vans from England. 'Shouldn't be long before I'm there.'

Bradshaw scanned the car park from the café window. There were only half a dozen vehicles in it and there was an area behind a rubbish skip that wasn't overlooked by the road. He gave Chaudhry directions to the café, then ordered three cappuccinos from the grey-haired waiter. They were just finishing their coffee when Chaudhry arrived. Bradshaw went out and showed him where to park, then brought him inside.

'Is everything okay?' whispered Chaudhry, as they sat down.

'Everything is going as planned,' said Bradshaw. 'We have an hour before we're due at the ferry terminal, so you have time to eat and then we'll transfer the equipment to your van.'

'I don't see why we have to fly back while you and Samil go on the ferry,' said Talwar.

'Because two men in a delivery van will arouse no suspicion,' said Bradshaw. 'Four men, especially when three are Asian, will attract attention.'

'That's racist,' said Kundi.

'Of course it's racist,' said Bradshaw, 'so we fly below their racist radar. Samil and I are just two delivery drivers heading home. Samil will be using his family's van and his licence and insurance are in order. You and Talwar return the rented van and fly back to England. The infidels are none the wiser.'

'You are right, brother. I'm sorry.' Kundi took out a packet of cigarettes but Talwar pointed at a French no-smoking sign. He sighed and put it away.

'There's nothing to be sorry about,' Bradshaw said. 'You are a true warrior for Islam. And soon we will show the world what true warriors can achieve.'

Shepherd followed the Moore brothers off the plane. 'Now what?' he said. A sign pointed to Immigration but the brothers seemed in no hurry to leave the airport.

Mickey grinned. 'We can grab a bite to eat here,' he said. 'That food on the plane, couldn't touch it.'

The brothers had flown together at the front of the business-class section and Shepherd had been in the middle with an empty seat next to him. He'd watched a movie and slept a little but he was still dog tired. 'Where are we going, Mickey?' asked Shepherd, 'And don't give me any of that need-to-know crap.'

'Sarajevo,' said Mickey. 'There's an arms dealer who can get us RPGs.'

'And you need me because . . .?'

'Because you'll be able to tell us if the gear is kosher,' said Mickey. He pointed at a coffee shop. 'Come on – I need caffeine. How much do you think they fine you if you light up in a German airport?'

Chaudhry drove off the ferry in first gear. 'What if they stop us?' he asked. Ahead, half a dozen Customs officers, in yellow fluorescent jackets, were looking carefully at the vehicles as they moved slowly down the ramp onto the Dover quayside.

'They won't,' said Bradshaw.

'How can you be so sure?' said Chaudhry. 'We have weapons in the back, and if they find them they'll throw away the key.'

Bradshaw could hear the rising panic in the other man's voice, and his forehead was bathed in sweat. 'They're not looking for weapons,' he said coldly. 'They're looking for drugs, and we don't fit the profile for drug smugglers.'

'How can you possibly know that?'

'Because you're Asian and I'm not – it's not a mix

that's normally associated with drug smugglers. Because we're in a totally legitimate van with the name of your father's company on the side. Because we're both clean-shaven and dressed casually. Because we're both looking totally relaxed. Smile, brother. Think calm thoughts and smile.'

'If they stop us we're dead.' Chaudhry licked his lips nervously. He took out a packet of gum and his hands shook as he unwrapped a stick and slipped it between his lips.

'Keep your hands on the wheel,' said Bradshaw, calmly. Chaudhry did as he was told.

One of the Customs officers, a woman in her forties with dyed blonde hair, was holding a chocolate and white spaniel on a long leash.

'See the dog?' said Bradshaw. 'It's a drugs dog. That's all they're interested in. But if they do stop us, they'll ask us questions first. And, providing we answer their questions, they won't search us.'

'What sort of questions?'

'Chit-chat,' said Bradshaw. 'Where have we been, what do we have in the van, where are we going – the questions don't matter. What they're looking for are signs of nervousness, signs that something isn't right. Only then will they search. And even if they do open the back, all they will see is cases of wine and beer. And we fit the profile of booze runners. There's no way they're going to start pulling all those boxes out.' He patted Chaudhry's knee. 'Relax and think happy thoughts.'

Chaudhry forced a smile. They drew level with the Customs officers. A grey-haired man with bored eyes waved them on. Bradshaw nodded at the man but was ignored. 'See? Allah is smiling on us.'

'*Allahu akbar,*' said Chaudhry.

'*Allahu akbar,*' agreed Bradshaw.

Mickey had booked them into suites at the Radon Plaza Hotel, just five minutes from Sarajevo's international airport. There was no one to meet them, but the immigration queues were short, and less than half an hour after the wheels of the plane had touched the runway they were checking in at Reception.

Mickey told Mark and Shepherd that they had an hour before they were due to meet the man who would supply them with RPGs. 'Now we're here, do you think you could tell me who the hell we're going to be dealing with?' said Shepherd. Mickey opened his mouth to reply but Shepherd held up a hand to silence him. 'I'm not doing business with the IRA or the Libyans or any other terrorists. The way the Yanks rule the world, we could all end up in Guantánamo Bay if things go wrong.'

'You worry too much,' said Mickey. 'The guy's Dutch, and he's as legit as an arms dealer can ever be. He deals with a lot of governments and most of the major arms manufacturers. He's a middleman, sells to countries that are a bit on the less-than-democratic side.'

'You mean dictators,' said Shepherd.

'Dictators, not terrorists,' stressed Mickey. 'But the politics mean sod all to me. All I care about is that the Professor says he can supply us with RPGs.'

Shepherd wasn't interested in picking a fight with Mickey, but he wanted to get as much information about the arms dealer as he could. 'And how do we get the RPGs into the UK?'

Mickey grinned and tapped the side of his nose.

'Don't tell me,' said Shepherd. 'Need to know.'

'And you don't,' said Mark.

Mickey punched Shepherd's shoulder. 'Shower and shave and we'll meet down here in an hour.'

The three men went up to their rooms. Shepherd showered and changed into a clean polo shirt, then watched BBC 24 news. Nurses in England were threatening to strike, two Members of Parliament had resigned after being caught fiddling their expenses, and a youth had been stabbed in a London street. There was a report on the plane that had crashed into the sea after leaving JFK airport. A journalist standing on a boat said that the Coast Guard were pulling bodies from the sea, that there were no survivors, and that the authorities were suggesting catastrophic engine failure was to blame.

His bedside phone rang. 'We're heading down now,' said Mickey. 'Don't bring your mobile with you. He's paranoid about bugs and tracking devices.'

'Understood,' said Shepherd. He left his phone in the room safe, picked up his jacket and went down to Reception. Mickey and Mark were already there, sitting on a sofa by the entrance. Shepherd joined them. 'What does he look like?'

'He's Dutch, probably wearing clogs and carrying tulips,' said Mark. 'With his finger in a dike.'

Shepherd shook his head sadly. 'What are you? Twelve?'

Mark lit a cigarette as a big man walked in through the revolving doors, looked around the reception area and came towards them. The three men stood up. 'You are the Englishmen?' he asked. His accent was Slavic and he had the build of a man who worked out but used steroids to add bulk to his muscles. He wore a long black coat over a charcoal grey suit, and a grey shirt buttoned to the neck.

'As English as chicken tikka massala,' said Mickey.

The heavy didn't understand and frowned. 'You have ID?' he asked.

Mickey handed him his passport and the man squinted at it. 'You can read, yeah?' asked Mickey.

The man gave it back to him and stared at him with cold grey eyes. 'Yes, I can read,' he said. 'I need to pat you down.'

'What?' said Mark.

'I need to check that you are not carrying weapons.'

'And do we get to pat you down?' asked Mark.

The man pulled open his coat and jacket just enough for them to glimpse a semi-automatic in a nylon holster.

'So, let's get this straight,' said Mark. 'You've got a gun but you want to make sure we don't have weapons? How fair is that?'

'I need to check,' said the man, flatly. 'Mr Kleintank insists.'

Mark seemed bewildered, but raised his arms and allowed the man to pat him down. 'Satisfied?' he said.

Mickey held up his hands. 'Go on, knock yourself out. But be careful around the groin area. I wouldn't want you giving me a hard-on.'

The man remained stony-faced as he patted Mickey down, then did the same with Shepherd. 'All three of you are coming?' he asked.

'That's the plan,' said Mickey.

The heavy nodded, took them outside and opened the rear door of a stretch Mercedes. Mickey looked inside. There was a driver in the front seat but the rear of the car was empty. 'Where is he?'

'Mr Kleintank is at the warehouse.' He waited until Mickey, Mark and Shepherd were seated before closing the door and getting into the front passenger seat.

Shepherd looked out of the window as the limousine drove through the city. He had been in Sarajevo once before, spending two months in the city soon after he'd joined the SAS. That had been in 1995, during the last few months of the siege, when Serbian forces had been launching sniper and mortar attacks daily from the surrounding mountains. More than twelve thousand men, women and children had been killed during the four-year siege, and fifty thousand were injured, the vast majority of casualties being civilians. Shepherd had been one of an eight-man SAS team tasked with taking out a particularly vicious sniper, who had made a point of shooting his victims in the legs to disable them, then killing anyone who went to their aid. The Serb and his Dragunov sniper rifle had been responsible for a dozen such killings. The SAS had spent a month watching him work, and a further three weeks in hides up in the hills, waiting. Shepherd hadn't been the one to kill him, but he had been close enough to see a colleague's bullet take a big chunk out of the man's skull. Shepherd had felt no remorse for the way in which they had tracked and killed him. He had no respect for snipers because they killed at a distance. It wasn't how real men fought. Real men fought face to face, man to man, and put their own lives on the line. Snipers hid in the shadows, and the Serbian snipers who had set siege to Sarajevo were the worst of the worst because they had targeted civilians.

The city had changed a lot since Shepherd had left. The streets were full of shoppers, students sat at outdoor cafés and there were a lot of new buildings. There were still reminders of the siege, though: the crosses on the graves in the city-centre park, masonry chipped by gunfire, and indentations in the roads showing where mortars had once wreaked death and destruction.

The limousine drove to an area of the city he wasn't familiar with, but his near-photographic memory kicked in and he was constantly aware of where he was in relation to his hotel. They drove down a narrow road lined with apartment blocks, and then through an industrial area. Shepherd realised that the driver wasn't taking a direct route to the warehouse, probably hoping to keep them in the dark as to its location.

Eventually they pulled up in front of a metal-sided warehouse. Across the street Shepherd saw a man with a broken nose sitting in a nondescript Toyota who, he thought, was a lookout. The man put his mobile to his ear and began to talk.

The heavy took them in through a side door to where Kleintank was pacing up and down and barking in Dutch into a phone. He was in his early thirties with a crew-cut and sharp features, about five feet eight inches tall. He was wearing a black cashmere overcoat and gleaming patent leather shoes.

He snapped his mobile shut and put it away. 'I'm sorry about the formalities,' he said, 'but Sarajevo is a dangerous city.'

'Yeah, well, south London's no bed of roses, mate,' said Mickey.

Kleintank smiled. 'I'm sure that's so,' he said. 'So, to business. I'm afraid I've got good news and bad news.'

'I don't want bad news,' said Mickey. 'I just want to buy a couple of RPGs.'

Kleintank grimaced. 'That's the bad news,' he said. 'I sold the last ones two days ago. A cash buyer turned up and I never turn down cash.'

Mickey scowled at the Dutchman. 'You told my man you had RPGs for sale.'

'And when I talked to him that was the case. But things change. Some guys from the Tamils needed them at short notice and they paid over the odds.' He held up his hands, palms out. 'What can I say?'

Mark pointed a finger at him. 'We've flown all the way over to this shit-hole and now you're telling us you don't even have an RPG?'

Kleintank was unabashed. 'It's a fluid business. Stock comes and stock goes. I've got more coming from China. As soon as they arrive I'll let you know.'

'Screw that,' said Mark. 'You said you had RPGs and now you haven't.' He turned to his brother. 'Can you believe this shit? Townsend's fucked us over.'

'What's the good news?' Mickey asked the Dutchman.

'I've got a Grail missile and launcher. Better than an RPG.' He folded his arms 'Much better,' he said.

Mickey turned to Shepherd. 'What do you think?'

Shepherd shrugged. 'The Grail's a ground-to-air missile. More for shooting planes than anything else.'

'A missile is a missile,' said Kleintank.

Shepherd didn't reply. He doubted that Kleintank was

too stupid to know the difference between an RPG and a Grail. He was just a salesman who wanted to offload the product he had.

'Okay, let's see it,' Mickey snapped.

Kleintank went to a wooden crate and pulled open the lid. 'It is in perfect condition,' he said.

Shepherd looked at it. 'It's a practice model,' he said.

'Of course,' said Kleintank. 'That's why it's blue.'

'What does that mean, practice model?' asked Mickey.

'There's no infrared guidance,' said Shepherd. 'You just point and fire, and hopefully the missile goes in a straight line.'

'That's fine, then,' said Mickey. 'We don't need it to jump through hoops, do we?'

'How many do you have?' Shepherd asked Kleintank.

'Just the one,' said the Dutchman. 'I did have two but I sold the other to some English guys last month. I can let you have that one for forty thousand euros.'

Mickey put a hand on Shepherd's shoulder and whispered, 'This one'll do, Ricky. Let's not look a gift horse.'

'The practice models aren't built to the same standard as the ones meant for the field,' said Shepherd. 'If a practice launcher fails, you just get another. If it fails to launch in the field your operation's blown.'

'This will fire,' said Kleintank.

'You can't know that for sure,' said Shepherd. 'I'd be a lot happier with a back-up, or a field model.' He turned to Kleintank. 'This English guy, what was he planning to shoot at? The practice models are no good against moving targets.'

'They didn't say. They just said they wanted one with an IR guidance system,' said Kleintank, 'but they took one of mine anyway.'

'They? There was more than one?'

'Ricky, this is what we need,' said Mickey. 'We need to take out a wall, that's all.'

'I get that, but what's going to happen if on the day I pull the trigger and nothing happens?'

'It will fire,' said Kleintank, but Shepherd ignored him.

'We need more than one,' he told Mickey. 'Three or four to be on the safe side.' He turned to the Dutchman. 'The guys you sold the other to, have they taken delivery already? Maybe we could buy theirs.'

'I flew it to Nice for them.'

'But they're English, you said.'

'One was as English as you, but his friends were Asians. Pakistanis, I think.'

'What did they say they wanted it for?'

'I didn't ask, same as I'm not asking you what you're planning to do with RPGs.'

'But they're still looking to buy one with a guidance system?'

'I managed to get them a Stinger,' said Kleintank, 'but it was a lot more expensive than this.'

'The guy that sold them the Stinger, does he have RPGs?'

Kleintank shook his head. 'The Tamils have been buying everything,' he said, 'and there's a lot going into Iraq at the moment. Iranian money, but the weapons get shipped direct to Iraq.'

'Who is this guy, the other dealer?'

Kleintank's eyes hardened. 'You're asking a lot of questions.'

'Just pursuing all our options.'

'Well, the only option you have is in this crate, and it's going to cost you forty thousand euros.'

'Thirty.'

'Mickey . . .' said Shepherd.

Mickey held up a hand to silence him. 'I'm making an executive decision, Ricky.'

'Then we need to talk now,' said Shepherd. 'You want me on the team for my expertise, and right now you're not listening to a bloody thing I'm saying. We either have a quiet word now or I'm out of here.'

'Ricky—'

'I'm serious.'

'Relax, mate,' Mickey said. 'If you want a chinwag, you've got it.' He led him to the far corner of the warehouse, away from Kleintank and Mark. When they were out of earshot, his face darkened. 'Don't you fucking make me lose face like that again, Ricky, you hear? This is my crew, right, and you're just a hired hand.' His fingers dug deep into the muscles of Shepherd's shoulder. 'Do you get my drift?'

'It's not about face, Mickey,' said Shepherd. 'It's about getting the right tools for the job. Kleintank just wants to offload what he's got in stock – he doesn't care whether it'll work or not.'

'It's a missile and we need a missile.'

'There's missiles and there's missiles, Mickey. And stop squeezing my shoulder, will you? You're nowhere near the nerve.'

Mickey took away his hand. 'If you weren't interested then why the Q and A?'

'I wanted to see how much he knows,' said Shepherd. 'He said he sold a practice Grail to British Asians who want to shoot down a moving target. He's talking about terrorists, Mickey. Why else would Asians want a surface-to-air missile? They want to shoot a plane, but you can't hit a plane without infrared capability or some sort of tracking facility.'

Mickey frowned. 'Speak English, will you?'

'Even when it's taking off or landing, a plane is moving too fast to shoot down without some way of moving the missile in flight,' said Shepherd, patiently. 'You have to fire the missile, then tell it which way to go once it's launched. It can chase the heat of the plane's engines or it can be radar-guided, but what you can't do is fire the thing and forget about it, which is all you can do with a practice model.'

'And?'

'And I think he sold it to them knowing it wouldn't do the job and now he's trying to do the same thing to us. That's why I'm quizzing him, to see if he's just stupid or if he's deliberately trying to pull the wool over our eyes.'

'But we don't need IR whatsit because we're not chasing anything,' said Mickey.

'No, but we need a decent explosive charge. The Grail has a warhead weighing just over a kilo. An RPG has a two-kilo warhead. If you're shooting at a plane or a heli-copter then a kilo of high explosive is fine, but we want to blast through a high-security wall and I don't think a single one-kilo warhead is going to do it.' He cocked his head at Kleintank. 'He's trying to sell us a pig in a poke, Mickey, and even if it pisses you off to hear that I still have to tell you.'

Mickey nodded slowly. 'All right, mate. So, it's an RPG or nothing?'

'Mickey, I think we're going to need at least three. You saw how it went in Cambodia. We might be lucky and the first one does the job, but we might need more. RPGs are tank killers – that's what they were designed to do – but metal and concrete are totally different materials. They can blast walls apart, but if we're talking about a high-security wall it might take two or three goes. I'd be happier with four, to be honest.'

'The Professor said one should do it.'

'And he's probably right. But what if the RPG is a dud? Or what if we fire it and the hole's only a couple of feet across? We're going to look pretty stupid either way.'

'Okay, Ricky, you've talked me into it.' He slapped Shepherd on the back. 'You did the right thing.'

He and Shepherd went back to where the Dutchman was standing. 'We're going to pass, Alex,' said Mickey. 'Sorry to have wasted your time.'

'What?' said Mark. 'We've come all this way for nothing?'

'We need RPGs, and that's the end of it,' said Mickey. 'Let's go.'

Chaudhry backed the van into the storage area – Bradshaw had rented the space for a year, paying in cash and showing his fake driving licence as identification. It had a yellow metal pull-down door and a bare concrete floor. The company that ran the facility offered twenty-four-hour access and was used to people coming and going at all hours. There was a large building containing small units, but Bradshaw had rented one of the largest, double height with space enough to park a dozen cars. It was in a line of units behind the main building, and while there was

CCTV coverage of the entrance and the fence around the facility, there was none of individual units. It was a ten-minute drive to Heathrow airport.

Bradshaw was standing behind the van, guiding Chaudhry in, then banged on the side to tell him to stop. He applied the handbrake and killed the engine. Bradshaw switched on the lights and pulled down the door. Chaudhry climbed out of the van. 'I can't believe it was that easy,' he said.

'What do you mean?' asked Bradshaw.

'We drove missiles into the country and no one looked twice at us.'

'There's just too much traffic between England and the Continent,' said Bradshaw. 'They don't have the time or the resources to check even one per cent of what comes in.' He began to pull out the cases of wine and lager and piled them on the concrete floor. Chaudhry helped him. Once they had removed a dozen, they were able to take out the two missiles. They placed the two large crates carefully on the floor, then put the wine and beer back into the van.

'Now what do we do?' asked Chaudhry.

'We get the vehicle we need,' said Bradshaw. 'Something like an old furniture van, something where we can remove a section of the roof so that we can fire the missile, and big enough to allow the backblast out. I know of a car auction where they sell commercial vehicles. I'll see what they have.'

'And then we're ready?'

'The van will have to be modified but, yes, then we'll be ready.'

Chaudhry's eyes blazed with enthusiasm. 'It's going to be bigger than anything anyone's ever done here, isn't it?'

'Far bigger,' said Bradshaw. 'It'll change this country for ever. It'll change the world. Once we show what we can do, we'll have the power to make changes. They'll have to listen to us.'

Chaudhry grabbed Bradshaw impulsively and hugged him so hard that the air was squeezed from his lungs. 'We will be heroes, brother. Our names will be remembered for all time.'

Bradshaw released himself gently from Chaudhry's grasp. 'For all time,' he repeated.

Shepherd rubbed his belly as he got into the lift with Mickey and Mark. 'My guts are playing me up,' he said. 'I feel like shit.' He winced and leaned against the lift's mirrored wall.

'Come on, Ricky, we're heading out later,' said Mickey. 'There's a brothel on the outskirts of the city that's got great Latvian hookers.'

'How the hell would you know that?' asked Shepherd. 'You said it was your first time here.'

'The power of Google,' said Mark.

'I can't go,' said Shepherd. 'I'm gonna have the runs real bad – I can feel it.'

Mickey grimaced. 'More information than we need,' he said. 'You stay in bed, sleep it off.'

The lift stopped at Shepherd's floor and he got out. 'Sorry to be a wet blanket,' he said. As soon as the lift doors closed behind him, he straightened and went to his room. He opened the door and hung the 'Do Not Disturb' sign on the outside, then went back along the corridor and waited for the next lift down. He walked through Reception and headed outside to the nearby taxi rank.

The first driver was a man in his fifties with a sweeping handlebar moustache. 'I hope you speak English,' said Shepherd.

'I speak Canadian,' said the man, 'which is almost the same.'

Shepherd laughed and climbed into the front passenger seat. He explained to the driver that he didn't know the name of the road he wanted to go to, but he did know how to get there. The driver switched on the meter and followed Shepherd's directions while he told him his life story. He and his wife had fled the city six months after the siege began, paying a Serbian people-trafficker twenty thousand dollars to get them out of Sarajevo and into Canada, where they claimed asylum. They were given residency and eventually citizenship, but had returned to Sarajevo. After fifteen minutes the driver pointed out that they had doubled back but Shepherd told him not to worry and just to keep the meter running. The driver tossed him a street map but it was no help, and Shepherd had no choice other than to retrace the circuitous route that Kleintank's driver had taken.

He had the taxi driver drop him a couple of hundred yards from Kleintank's warehouse, paid him and walked the rest of the way, keeping an eye out for any surveillance. The Toyota that had been parked outside had gone, and so had the stretch Mercedes. A coach drove by and Shepherd lowered his head so that no one could see his face. Once it was out of sight, he walked up to the warehouse and along to the side entrance. The Toyota was there, parked next to a black Porsche Cayenne SUV with Croatian plates. Shepherd heard voices inside. He hesitated, wondering if he was doing the sensible thing.

He wanted to talk to Kleintank, to find out what else, if anything, the Dutchman knew about the three Brits who had bought the Grail missile, and he wanted to do it without arousing his suspicions. It was going to be a difficult line to tread but Shepherd knew he had to try. In an ideal world he'd be going in with a gun but he wasn't armed. He smiled at the thought that there were thousands of weapons just a few yards from where he was standing.

His best chance of getting information from Kleintank was to ask him about the arms dealer in France. He would spin Kleintank a line that it would be easier for them to take delivery in France and offer him a commission on any arms he bought from the second dealer. He'd just have to hope that word didn't get back to the Moores, but if it did he could claim he had been trying to help by coming up with an alternative supplier. He took a deep breath, knowing he was over-thinking the situation. He was always at his best when he thought on his feet, when he allowed his natural instincts to kick in. He eased open the door and walked inside.

A man was standing by the crates at the left of the door. He was in his late forties with grey hair cut short and thin, unsmiling lips. He was wearing a weathered leather bomber jacket, beige trousers and dark brown loafers with tassels. He heard Shepherd's footsteps, and as he turned, he pulled a Glock semi-automatic from a shoulder holster. Shepherd froze and his jaw dropped. It was Richard Yokely, an American who had once worked for the CIA but who was now employed by a black-ops group called Grey Fox, which Shepherd knew was nothing less than a presidential assassination squad. They had met in London, Iraq and Northern Ireland. Yokely was a government-sanctioned killer and one of the most dangerous men he had ever met, the last person he'd expected to see in an arms warehouse in Sarajevo.

Yokely grinned but he kept the gun aimed at Shepherd's chest. 'Spider Shepherd, as I live and breathe,' he said.

At the far end of the warehouse two men were standing over Kleintank. They were both in their mid-thirties with hard eyes, close-cropped haircuts, denim shirts, jeans and heavy workboots. One had a broken nose, the other a scarred lip. They were in the process of stripping Kleintank of his clothes but they had stopped when they heard Shepherd walk in. Broken Nose straightened up and took a silenced semi-automatic from a shoulder holster. Shepherd realised it was the man he'd seen sitting outside in the Toyota during his first visit to the warehouse, the man he'd assumed was Kleintank's lookout. Broken Nose and Scarred Lip both gazed at Yokely, waiting to find out what he wanted them to do. 'It's okay, I know him,' said Yokely. The two men relaxed and Broken Nose put away his gun. They went back to stripping off Kleintan's clothing. Shepherd couldn't see if the Dutchman was dead or unconscious.

Yokely walked towards Shepherd with an amused smile. 'You do turn up at the most inconvenient times, don't you?' he asked.

'What the hell are you doing here, Richard?'

'Tidying up some loose ends,' said the American. 'I'm going to have to ask you to go now, Spider.'

'I can't do that,' said Shepherd.

'Yes, you can. You turn around, you walk away and you don't look back.'

'Is he dead?'

'Not yet,' said Yokely.

'You're going to kill him, right?'

'Not your business, old friend.'

'We're not friends, Richard. We're just guys whose paths cross from time to time.'

'You owe me.' Yokely's finger was still on the trigger of his Glock but the barrel was now pointing at the floor.

'I owe you a favour. I don't owe you a man's life.'

'Not just any man,' said Yokely. 'But that's not the point. You owe me. You owe me big-time. So turn around and walk away. You're right, we don't have to be friends but I'm going to do what I have to do, no matter what.'

'You did me a big favour, I'm not denying it. But there's a hell of a gap between a debt of honour and being an accomplice to a cold-blooded murder.'

'I don't need your complicity,' said Yokely. 'I just need you to go.'

'Why?'

'Because I don't want you here.'

'I mean, why do you want to kill him? What's he done?'

The gun moved. Now it was pointing at Shepherd's knee and the American's finger was still on the trigger. 'You're making this very difficult for me, Spider.'

'You think murder is easy?'

Yokely snorted. 'If it was anyone else but you . . .'

'What, Richard? What would you do? Would you shoot me, is that what you're saying?'

The gun didn't move but the finger tightened on the trigger. Yokely shook his head slowly. 'I've got a job to do. And you're in my way.'

'This is Sarajevo, way out of your jurisdiction.'

Yokely grinned savagely. 'I represent the United States of America, which means the whole Goddamned world is my jurisdiction. And it's like George W said – you're either with us or you're against us.' He gestured at Kleintank with the gun. 'Him, he's against us. What about you, Spider? Which side are you on?'

'There's no sides in this,' said Shepherd. 'There's just you and me and the guy you're threatening to kill.'

Yokely took a deep breath, then exhaled slowly. He stared at Shepherd, his lips a tight line. The barrel of the gun moved slowly until it was aimed at Shepherd's stomach. 'You heard about the plane that crashed leaving JFK?'

Shepherd nodded. 'Engine failure, they're saying. It crashed into the sea.'

'Yeah, well, they're saying what they've been told to say,' said Yokely. 'The real scenario is being kept under wraps. Islamic fundamentalists shot it out of the sky. And they shot it out of the sky with a missile supplied by that piece of shit. So he made his choice and now it's time for him to pay the piper.'

'What sort of missile?' asked Shepherd.

'A Stinger.'

'Evidence?'

'This isn't a court, Spider. And you're not judging me.'

'You're sure it was a Stinger? Because if it was a Stinger, it wasn't Kleintank that supplied it.'

'It was a Stinger, of that there's no doubt. And my sources tell me it came from the Dutchman.'

'Then I'd check your sources,' said Shepherd. 'I've just bought a training Grail from him and that was the best he had. Stingers didn't even enter the equation. He said he had a contact in Nice with Stingers. Maybe someone's got their lines crossed.'

'He could have sold it weeks ago,' said Yokely. 'Just because he didn't have one for you doesn't mean he didn't have them last week. Or last month.'

'And you'd kill him without checking, would you? Because if it wasn't him, it must have been somebody else. And you're going to let them get off scot-free.'

Yokely didn't say anything but his jaw tightened a fraction.

'Richard, you need to check your source on this.' He nodded at Kleintank. 'You wouldn't want collateral damage, would you?'

Yokely smiled sardonically. 'We're not in a position to check the source,' he said.

'Aggressive information retrieval?' asked Shepherd.

'We're operating under considerable time pressure,' said Yokely.

'And your source is dead?'

Yokely sighed and lowered his gun. 'You wouldn't be lying to me, would you? To save his skin?'

'First of all, I'm not stupid. I know that if I lie you'll find out down the line and you're one man I wouldn't want mad at me. Second of all, you're right, of course, I do owe you a favour.'

Yokely slid his gun into a nylon shoulder holster and adjusted his shirtsleeves. 'Don't you just hate it when people lie to you, Spider?'

'Everybody lies,' said Shepherd, 'one way or another. Can we go somewhere and talk? I'm getting nervous hanging around here.'

Yokely glanced at Broken Nose, who was pulling off Kleintank's underwear now. 'Keep him on ice,' he said.

'Like he was in a fridge,' Broken Nose said.

Yokely flashed Shepherd an apologetic look. 'He watches a lot of Tarantino movies,' he said.

'Don't we all?' said Shepherd.

The young man with a well-tended goatee beard placed the two cups of coffee on the table in front of Shepherd and Yokely. They sat in silence until he was out of earshot. Yokely stirred in two spoonfuls of brown sugar.

'What's going on, Richard? What the hell are you doing in Sarajevo?'

'Retribution,' said Yokely. 'Pure and simple. The people I work for want everyone involved in the bringing down of that jet taken care of in a timely fashion.' He sipped his coffee and smacked his lips appreciatively.

Three pretty girls in short dresses and high heels sat down at a neighbouring table, all lip-gloss and painted nails, designer sunglasses perched on their heads, expensive mobile phones in front of them. That was one of the big differences between modern Sarajevo and the city Shepherd had visited previously – back then there had been no pretty girls. Pretty girls were always the first to leave a war zone.

'I thought revenge was a dish best served cold.'

'Not in this case,' Yokely said.

'We're talking about government-sanctioned murder?'

'You might be, Spider, I'm just having a coffee with an old friend while we chew the fat.' He took another sip. 'This is good,' he said. He looked around the market square they were sitting in. 'Won't be long before Starbucks sets up here.'

'Is that a good thing or a bad thing, Richard? I would have thought you'd be in favour of American expansionism in all its forms.'

'I don't like their coffee,' said Yokely. 'Best coffee in the world is in Italy. Followed by France.' He raised his cup. 'I'd put this a close third.'

'What about London?'

Yokely chuckled. 'Let's just say that I can see why you're a nation of tea-drinkers.' He put down his cup. 'So, why are you buying a Grail missile?'

Shepherd looked pained. 'I'd rather not say.'

'You said it was a training model so that means no guidance system.'

'Which is why your guys couldn't have used it to shoot down the plane at JFK. One thing Kleintank did tell me was that three Brits were looking to buy a Stinger a few weeks ago. A white guy and two Asians. Don't suppose your guys in New York were Brits?'

Yokely shook his head. 'Saudis.'

'Why am I not surprised?' said Shepherd. 'You know, considering that most of the guys behind the nine-eleven attacks were Saudis, I never quite understood why George W decided to invade Afghanistan and Iraq. Wouldn't it have made more sense to go into Saudi Arabia?'

'Only one of the pilots was a Saudi,' said Yokely. 'There was an Egyptian, a guy from the United Arab Emirates and a Lebanese. But I know what you mean. No one involved was from Iraq or Afghanistan. But that wasn't the point.'

'Yeah, well, maybe one day you could explain it to me, but I don't think this is the time or the place. This job you're on, it's revenge, pure and simple, you said.'

'The analogy I was given is that no one fucks with Jews since what they did after Munich. They hit everyone involved, and by making it personal they made sure that the whole world got the message.'

'I think that was an Israeli thing rather than a Jewish thing,' said Shepherd.

'Semantics,' said Yokely. 'But as a strategy there's no question that it worked.'

'So you're flying around the world like some sort of government-backed vigilante killing everyone involved?'

'I'm subject to total deniability,' said Yokely, 'but I'd say that pretty much sums it up.'

'Sometimes I just don't understand the world you live in,' Shepherd said sadly.

'It's called the real world,' said Yokely. 'They murdered three hundred and twelve people. Men, women and children. Christians, Jews, Muslims and probably atheists too. Blew them out of the sky. A totally random attack, lashing out at innocents to cause death and destruction with no thought as to who they were killing. What I'm doing is the total opposite. I'm taking out specific targets, every one of whom deserves exactly what they get. I can justify what I'm doing, Spider, to myself and to others. Do you think the terrorists can do the same?'

Shepherd didn't reply. He decided that Yokely's question was rhetorical but even if it wasn't, he didn't have an answer. He had been a soldier for almost ten years, and had killed in the line of duty, but he had always known the nature of the enemy he was up against and, more often than not, that the enemy was trying to kill him. The terrorists killing in the name of Islam chose their targets at random and, more often than not, their victims included women and children. Shepherd had no respect for men who targeted innocents, but that didn't mean he could condone killing them without trial. There was a world of a difference between despising an enemy and summarily executing them.

'For whatever reason our worlds have collided on this one and we should be sharing what we know instead of guarding our turf,' said the American. 'I've been a lot more open with you than I should have been and I think I deserve a *quid pro quo*.'

'I would have thought a dollar *pro quo* would be more appropriate,' said Shepherd.

'Wow, the Brit makes Latin jokes,' said Yokely. 'And he tries to change the subject again. Spill the beans, Spider.'

Shepherd stared at Yokely, then nodded slowly. 'Okay,' he said. 'I've infiltrated a group of armed robbers who need a missile for the job they've got planned. The guy who put the job together gave us Kleintank's name for the ordnance.'

'And the plan is to point a Grail at the tellers and demand they hand over their takings? Sounds a bit like overkill.'

'There's a wall involved,' said Shepherd. 'We were in the market for a few RPGs but all Kleintank had was the training Grail. I told Kleintank we weren't interested so we're going to have a rethink about where to get the RPGs from. But while I was chatting with Kleintank he let slip about the Brits who wanted a Stinger and I came back here for a chat.'

'A chat?' said Yokely. He grinned malevolently. 'We're not too different, you and I, are we?'

'Chalk and cheese,' said Shepherd. 'I was just going to talk to him.'

'About what?'

'About the Brits he sold the Grail to. They've now got a Grail and a Stinger and that can only mean one thing.'

'You think they're home-grown fundamentalists who want to bring down a plane? Nasty.'

'I was going to pass on any info to our anti-terrorism people,' said Shepherd. 'But that's a non-starter after what you've done to Kleintank.'

'Don't expect me to apologise for doing my job,' said Yokely. 'First I knew you were involved was when you came barging in with a bad attitude.' He sipped some coffee. 'Okay, here's the scoop. You might be right that Kleintank didn't sell the Saudis the Stinger directly, but we've traced it to him. His fingerprints are on the smoking gun, metaphorically speaking. He operates in a small world so he sure as hell will know something. I'll put him through the wringer and share any intel with you.'

'You could blow my case, Richard. If Kleintank talks to my guys, alarm bells might start ringing.'

'Give me some credit, Spider. We'll take him well away from here.'

'Rendition?'

Yokely grinned. 'Haven't you heard? We don't do that any more. We'll find a place here, somewhere secluded. You let me know when you're in the clear. Deal?'

'Okay.'

'You've got that look again,' said the American.

'What look's that?'

'The look that says you're not sure if you can trust me.'

'That'd be right,' said Shepherd.

'We're on the same side, Spider,' said Yokely. 'Our methods might be different, but we're the good guys in this fight.'

'I hope so,' said Shepherd.

'What do you mean, you hope so?'

'I just feel that sometimes what we do in the fight against terrorism turns us into the sort of people we shouldn't be, that maybe the way we react sort of justifies what the terrorists are doing.'

Yokely frowned. 'I don't get your drift.'

Shepherd shrugged. 'Not sure if I can even explain it to myself. But I don't like the way the world's changing, especially my country. We regard everyone, no matter who they are, with suspicion.'

'You're starting to sound like a regular liberal, Spider. You're not having second thoughts about your career, are you?'

'I do what I do because I enjoy it, and because I feel I'm doing something worthwhile. I make a difference, I really do. I put bad guys behind bars where they can't hurt people. This case I'm working on now, they're armed robbers. They point loaded guns at people and scare the shit out of them. I've put drug-dealers away, I've investigated murders and arms dealers, and I've stopped terrorists, and I know that the world is a better place because of the work I've done. Not much better, maybe, but better nonetheless.'

'But the times they are a-changing?'

'I'm part of the system, and I'm not sure that the system is acting in the best interests of its people. Now the system treats us all as if we're guilty until we prove otherwise.

We've made even thinking about terrorism a crime now. We're putting people in prison because they're visiting the wrong websites or having the wrong files on their computers, and that can't be right. They say it's a War Against Terror but it feels to me like we're becoming the sort of totalitarian society that—' Shepherd stopped and put up his hands. 'Don't get me started on politics.' He laughed. 'I'm just a humble civil servant.'

'Yours not to reason why,' said Yokely.

'When I was a soldier, I followed orders, but I was never given an order I disagreed with. If I was told to put my life on the line, I always knew the reason why. And as a cop I knew that I was risking my life to put the bad guys behind bars. But what's happening now . . .' He was unable to finish the line of thought.

'You know you have a standing offer to come and work with me,' said Yokely.

'With you, or for you?'

'In this line of work, Spider, you're your own boss most of the time.'

'You were going to kill Kleintank, weren't you? If I hadn't been there, you'd have killed him in cold blood.'

'That's what I do,' said Yokely.

'It's what you do, but I don't think I could be as callous about the taking of human life.'

Yokely chuckled. 'Callous? Is that how I appear to you?' He lowered his voice. 'Don't think for one moment I don't care about what I do. Don't think that I don't have second thoughts. But, like you, I do what I do for the greater good. And I know for a fact that the world is a safer place – and, yes, a better place – because of my actions.' He sat back and finished his coffee, then put the cup back on its saucer. 'You're always a great one for fairness, aren't you? It's a word I've heard you use a lot over the years. You think life should be fair even though you know it rarely is.'

Shepherd grinned. 'I can't argue with that.'

'Then consider this. What I do is fair, Spider. The people I . . . I don't like to use the K-word,' he said. 'It sounds like I'm doing something immoral. I prefer a word like "remove" or "eliminate" because all I'm doing is taking them out of a society they want to destroy. The people I remove are dangerous. They're the true stone-cold killers. They're the ones who will kill women and children without a thought, who plan and scheme to cause death and destruction without once considering the grief and pain they cause. Putting them on trial and then behind bars serves no purpose, but removing them does. Removing them makes the world a better place so I'm happy to be part of a system that does just that. Do I worry about what I do? Damn right I do, and that's what makes me better than them. I don't enjoy doing what I do, don't ever think that. I do it because somebody has to, and I'm qualified. And, frankly, Spider, so are you. Well qualified.'

'I wish I had your confidence,' said Shepherd.

'Confidence?'

'Self-belief. You know what you're doing is right. There's not one iota of self-doubt in you.'

'Is that your problem? You're doubting yourself?'

Shepherd shook his head. 'I'm fine about myself,' he said. 'It's the system I work for that I'm having second thoughts about. I'm a small cog in a large machine but it's a machine that wants to incarcerate its citizens for three months without trial and send them to prison for just thinking about being a terrorist. It's a machine that wants to take fingerprints and DNA samples from all its citizens on the off-chance that one day in the future they might break the law.'

Yokely tapped his class ring on the table top. 'What I can't work out is whether you're trying to talk yourself into working with me, or out of it.'

'I'm ambivalent,' said Shepherd.

'Then jump ship,' said Yokely. 'You'll get a bigger pay cheque and you'll be doing a worthwhile job.'

'Maybe,' said Shepherd.

Yokely looked at his wristwatch, a Rolex Submariner with a green bezel. 'I've got to go,' he said. 'I'm on a deadline.'

'So, how do we leave this?' asked Shepherd.

'You call me when you're ready to work with me.'

'I meant the Dutchman,' said Shepherd.

'I knew that,' said Yokely. He flashed Shepherd a smile. 'As I said, I'll talk to Kleintank, then keep him under wraps. If I get any intel about your British terrorists, I'll pass it on to you.'

'Thanks, Richard,' said Shepherd.

'Yet another favour you owe me,' said the American. He stood up and held out his hand. 'You take care of yourself,' he said.

Shepherd shook it. 'You, too.'

Yokely squeezed Shepherd's hand. 'I mean it, Spider. It's a rough world out there and I'd hate it if anything happened to you because your mind wasn't on the job.'

* * *

Bradshaw scrutinised the approaching plane through his binoculars. It was a Boeing 747 belonging to British Airways, the perfect target. The plane's flaps were up and its wheels were down as it headed for the runway. The aircraft was about eight hundred feet up and still five miles from the airfield. Bradshaw was sitting in a two-year-old blue Ford Mondeo that he'd found through the classified adverts in the *Evening Standard*. It was the perfect car for surveillance and nobody had given him a second look as he parked close to the river Brent, a small tributary that flowed into the nearby Thames. From where he was sitting he had a perfect view of the planes on the easterly approach to the airport. That was the favoured route for Heathrow in the morning. It would also be the perfect place to fire a missile as a short drive through Brentford would take him to junction two of the M4. He had an *A–Z* street directory on his lap and marked his location with a cross. He turned on the engine and put the car into gear. He wanted to find another three or four possible sites before it got dark.

Shepherd pressed the button to call the lift. It was just after eight o'clock. As the doors opened, he saw two figures standing inside and stepped out of their path. He did a double-take when he realised it was Mickey and Mark. They were laughing at something and Mickey was waving an unlit cigar. Their jaws dropped when they saw Shepherd. 'What are you up to, mate?' asked Mickey.

Shepherd's mind raced as he tried to come up with a convincing explanation for being out of his room. 'I feel like shit,' he said, keeping his voice to just above a whisper.

'Like a knife in my guts. I've asked Reception if they can get me something from a pharmacist.'

'You should have called room service,' said Mickey.

'Well, they said they'd get me sorted. Are you guys heading out?'

'Yeah, don't wait up,' said Mark. 'Do you want us to bring you a hooker back?'

Shepherd forced a smile and rubbed his belly. 'Do I look like I want a hooker?' he said.

'Leave him alone, Mark,' said Mickey. 'You can see he's hurting. Probably that airline food,' he said sympathetically. 'You should be okay by tomorrow.'

'Could be a burst appendix,' said Mark, and Mickey glared at him. 'All right, all right,' he said. 'Come on, let's get the hell out of here.'

'Our flight's at midday,' Mickey said to Shepherd, 'so we'll be checking out at nine.'

Shepherd walked into the lift and pressed the button for his floor. As the doors closed, he watched the brothers stride through Reception. He closed his eyes and exhaled. It had been a close one, but he was fairly sure they'd believed his story.

Alex Kleintank opened his eyes. His head was pounding and it was hard to breathe. His ears were blocked and he tried swallowing to clear them but that didn't help. He was moving from side to side and he couldn't work out why. Then his vision cleared and he saw he was upside down. The ceiling above him was swaying from side to side and then, with absolute terror, he realised he was naked. He was hanging from the ceiling by his feet. He tried to move his arms but his wrists were bound.

A figure appeared in front of him. He saw brown shoes with tassels and light brown trousers. Kleintank was trying to speak but his mouth was so dry he could only croak. The man bent down to look at him, then straightened and said something. Hands grabbed Kleintank's shoulders and lifted him up. The neck of a plastic bottle was forced between his lips. It was water and he drank greedily, then the hands let go of him, he dropped down and began to swing again. 'Who are you?' he asked. 'What do you want?'

The man with the tassels on his shoes was holding what looked like a black metal stick. 'We need to talk, Alex,' he said.

'About what?'

'Your customers.'

Kleintank coughed and tasted blood at the back of his mouth. 'What do you want to know?'

Blue sparks crackled across the top of the black stick that the man was holding. It was a cattle prod. Kleintank's heart pounded and he felt his bladder muscles weaken. 'Everything,' said the man. The cattle prod crackled again.

It was early in the afternoon when Shepherd's Lufthansa flight arrived in Bangkok. This time they were met off the plane by a man in a safari suit with a clipboard, who welcomed Mickey and carried his bag for him. He took them to the diplomatic channel where a bored immigration officer took their photographs and stamped their passports.

Mickey offered to drop Shepherd at his villa. Both men were tired. They had flown overnight from Germany and there had been two babies in the business-class compartment who had cried from the moment that the aircraft's wheels had left the runway.

'What happens now?' asked Shepherd, as Mickey drove down the motorway to Pattaya.

'About the RPGs?' Mickey asked. 'I'll talk to the Professor, see what other contacts he's got. What about you? Do you know anyone?'

'Let me think about it,' said Shepherd. 'A lot of the guys I served with have left and there's a few working in hotspots where they might be able to get their hands on RPGs.'

Mickey fumbled for his cigar case as he drove one-handed.

'Let me,' said Shepherd, as the Range Rover sheered across the road. He took out a cigar and handed it to Mickey, who bit off the end and spat it through the window, then pressed in the cigarette lighter.

Shepherd laughed. 'You're just about the only person I know who uses his cigarette lighter socket to smoke,' he said. 'Everyone else uses them for their phones or MP3s.'

Mickey grinned. 'I've smoked since I was a kid. My dad's been a smoker for forty-odd years and his lungs are fine.' He blew smoke through the window.

'This Professor guy, what's his story?'

'He plans jobs down to the last detail. Works for a few crews like ours and we pay him a percentage. We've used him for the last three jobs and they went without a hitch.'

'How would he know about Kleintank?'

'That's his business,' Mickey said. 'Part of the job is about planning, but the beauty of the Professor is that he puts all your ducks in a row. He tells you what equipment you need and where you can source it. He's made our lives a lot easier.'

'Wish I'd had him for our last job. It all went tits up when we changed vehicles.'

'What happened?'

Shepherd sighed. 'You know, I'm still not sure,' he said. 'It was a tiger job. We had the manager's family and we did a great job conning the staff so we hardly had to use any force.'

'Big score?'

'Massive. We got about a hundred grand cash but it wasn't about the money. We had someone on the inside who'd tipped us off about some bearer bonds in one of the safety deposit boxes. Two million.'

'Sweet,' said Mickey.

'Yeah, well, it would've been if we'd got away with it. We were switching vehicles and armed cops turned up waving their Hecklers. I managed to leg it but everyone else was nabbed.'

'I heard you shot a cop.'

Shepherd looked at him.

'What? I had to have you checked out, didn't I?'

'I shot *at* a cop,' said Shepherd. 'That's not the same as shooting a cop. I fired a warning. I'm not stupid, Mickey.'

Mickey patted his leg. 'You're too sensitive, mate,' he said.

Mickey dropped Shepherd in front of his villa. Shepherd offered him a beer but he said he wanted to get home. Shepherd waited until the Range Rover was out of sight before he let himself into his villa and deactivated the burglar alarm. He went through to the sitting room, turned on the television and phoned Charlotte Button. 'Please tell me Razor got to you in time,' he said.

'O ye of little faith,' laughed Button. 'We had a man waiting for you in Munich and he watched you board the flight to Sarajevo. He got on the flight with you and followed you to your hotel.'

'He was good,' said Shepherd, 'because I didn't see anyone.'

'He's one of SOCA's best. Snag is, he was solo so, other than keeping tabs on you at the hotel, there wasn't much he could do. How did it go down?'

Shepherd frowned. Had Button's watcher seen him leave the hotel and get the taxi back to Kleintank's warehouse? He had looked for a tail and was sure no one had followed him in the taxi, so maybe he'd been lucky. One-man surveillance was difficult in perfect conditions, and Button's man had been working in unfamiliar territory.

Shepherd explained what had happened when the Moore brothers had met Kleintank. Button waited until he had finished before she said, 'So you're telling me you told Mickey Moore not to buy the missile? What the hell were you thinking?'

'What do you mean?' asked Shepherd. His heart began to pound. Charlotte Button was nobody's fool.

'You had him right where we wanted him,' said Button. 'We both know that the Grail wouldn't do much more than dent a high-security wall, though he obviously doesn't. So all you had to do was to keep quiet and let them get on with it. That they're doomed to fail doesn't make it less of a bust. We'd still have caught them in the act.'

'First, Terry Norris is in a wheelchair, not in a coma,' said Shepherd. 'He's a weapons expert, and he'd know right away that we didn't have the right tools for the job.

If he told Mickey that, it would cast doubt on my credibility.'

Button was silent while she considered what he had said. 'Fair point,' she said eventually. 'And second of all? I assume there is a second of all?'

'Kleintank said he'd sold another Grail missile to some Brits.'

'Anything in the way of a description?'

'One's white, the other two are Asian. From what Kleintank said, I think they've already acquired a Stinger from an arms dealer in Nice.'

'I'll pass it on,' said Button. 'Is there a third of all?'

'A third of all?'

'Did anything else happen that I should be aware of?'

'Like what?'

'I don't know,' said Button, 'it's just that my Spider sense is tingling. Anything I should know about?'

Shepherd gritted his teeth. Button had an uncanny knack of knowing when something was on his mind. It was one of the qualities that made her such a good manager of undercover agents. But he couldn't tell her that Richard Yokely had been in Sarajevo, or what he had been doing there. 'Nope,' he said. 'I'll just keep tabs on the brothers, and as soon as they nail down the RPGs we'll be sorted.'

'What are their options?'

'They've got contacts, I'm sure. They know army people in Cambodia but there's a shipping problem from Asia. Kleintank did say he had more RPGs coming in from China, but I'm guessing that once the Professor hears Kleintank let them down he'll come up with other options.'

'He's back in the UK so we'll keep an eye on him,' said Button. 'This Kleintank, any idea where he's based?'

'He's Dutch but all I've got is his name,' said Shepherd. 'I did have a thought, though.'

'I'm listening.'

'What if we did a set-up? Put him onto one of our people posing as an arms dealer. We've done it before. We get them on video buying the weapons and bust them before they go in.'

'Wouldn't they think that a bit convenient?'

'I could spin them a line about a former army buddy who's now in the weapons business. See if they bite.'

Button considered his suggestion for a few seconds. 'I'd prefer to see who they come up with,' she said. 'But if it drags on we'll maybe start being a bit more proactive. Let's see how it goes. In the meantime you take care.'

'Always,' he said, and cut the connection. He felt guilty at having lied to Button, but he had no choice.

Almost immediately his phone rang. The display was blank. He knew before he answered that it was Richard Yokely. 'How's the lovely Charlotte?' asked the American.

'I knew it was a mistake giving you my phone number,' said Shepherd. 'Were you listening in?'

'No, sir, I wasn't. A gentleman never eavesdrops on a lady.'

'But you could if you wanted to, right?'

Yokely chuckled. 'A gentleman never tells,' he said.

'Where are you, Richard?'

'In a land far, far away,' said Yokely. 'I have something for you.'

'I'm all ears.'

'And there's the rub, as the Bard might have said,' said Yokely. 'Anything I tell you is for your ears only. You can never say where the information came from.'

'That's a given,' said Shepherd.

'I'm serious,' said the American. 'You can do what you want with the information, but no one must know who gave it to you.'

'Do you want me to swear on a stack of Bibles?' said Shepherd.

'I just want you to understand what you're agreeing to,' said Yokely. 'If you renege on our agreement, it won't be your mortal soul that's in danger.'

Shepherd feigned shock. 'Why, Richard, are you threatening me?'

'Do you want me to end the call now?'

Shepherd could tell from the American's tone that he was serious. 'I already said. I'm all ears.'

'The Dutchman sold a Grail missile to two Brits. One of the Brits was white, the other was Asian. There was a second Asian who brought the cash. Might have been a Brit, too. They bought a single Grail, a practice model, but the white Brit was adamant that he wanted a missile with a guidance system. Kleintank put him in touch with a Frenchman, a guy called Marcel Calvert. He's a former Legionnaire, lives in Nice. Kleintank confirmed that Calvert had a Stinger for sale and sent the three Brits on their merry way.'

'Did they say what they wanted the missiles for?'

'I love your naïveté, sometimes.'

'I'll take that as a no,' said Shepherd.

'What I have got is the name of the white guy. Paul Bradshaw. Former soldier, served in Iraq. And I have the number of a pay-as-you-go cell phone that he's using. He was introduced to Kleintank through a mutual friend, another former soldier called Chris Thomas. Thomas runs a security company in Iraq now.'

'Kleintank told you all this?'

'I can be very persuasive. Do you want the cell number or not?'

'Please.' Yokely told him and it filed itself away in his infallible memory. 'You can spread the word, but you can't identify your source,' said Yokely. 'You have a good day now.' The line went dead.

Shepherd put down the phone. He stared at the television with unseeing eyes. He had some serious thinking to do before he phoned Button again. But there was someone he could call immediately. He stood up and paced around the room as he tapped out the mobile number of Major Allan Gannon. The Major answered promptly. 'Long time no hear, Spider,' he said. 'How are the forces of law and order, these days?'

'Same old,' said Shepherd. He could hear automatic gunfire in the background. 'Are you in the middle of something?'

'Just running a few VIP guests through a Killing House exercise,' said the Major. 'We've got the shadow Home Secretary and a couple of his minions on a fact-finding tour so we're using them as hostages in a live-fire rescue scenario.' He guffawed. 'A couple of the guys are wondering if they'd get away with an accidental shooting but I've laid down the law.'

'Look, boss, I need your help.'

'I assume you mean in a professional capacity,' said the Major, drily. 'Or do you just need a few quid?'

Shepherd had known the Major for more than ten years and had served with him in most of the world's hot spots, including Northern Ireland, Sierra Leone and Afghanistan, and had trained with him everywhere, from the jungles of Brunei to the Arctic wastelands of northern Norway. 'I need information on an ex-military guy who might be up to mischief,' he said. 'His name's Paul Bradshaw. He's bought two surface-to-air missiles on the black market and I need some background.'

'I assume there's a reason for you not doing this through unofficial channels.'

'I'm sorry, boss, I can't say.'

'The circles you move in, Spider,' said the Major. 'Things were so much easier when you were in the Regiment.'

'Tell me about it,' said Shepherd.

'Six six came up as the dialling code. You're in Thailand?'

'Pattaya,' said Shepherd. 'Infiltrating a group of bank robbers.'

'When are you going to get a real job? You know the Regiment would have you back in a heartbeat. And if they didn't, there's always a place for you on the Increment.' The Major was head of the Increment, the Government's best-kept secret, a group of highly trained Special Forces soldiers who were used on operations considered too dangerous for Britain's security services, MI5 and MI6. The Major reported directly to the Prime Minister's office and he was able to draw on all the resources of the Special Air Service and the Special Boat Service, plus any other experts he required.

'I'm thinking about it,' said Shepherd, 'but at the moment, I'm mid-operation.'

'And this guy Bradshaw is out there in Pattaya?'

'Negative,' said Shepherd. 'He was in Sarajevo, then Nice. Now I don't know where he is. He spent time in

Iraq.' Shepherd gave the Major the pay-as-you-go mobile number that Yokely had given him. 'He's tight with a guy called Chris Thomas who runs a security outfit with contracts in Iraq. So far as I know, it was Thomas who put Bradshaw in touch with the arms dealer. The dealer is a Dutchman by the name of Alex Kleintank. Kleintank sold Bradshaw a practice Grail missile.'

The Major chuckled. 'Kleintank? Little tank? Perfect name for an arms dealer. Do you need Thomas checking out, too?'

'Just Bradshaw,' said Shepherd. 'He went to Nice to see a French arms dealer, name of Marcel Calvert, and he bought a Stinger missile from him. Now he's off the radar.'

'I'll check and get back to you,' said the Major. 'You be careful out there. They call it the Land of Smiles but more Brits die in Thailand than in Iraq and Afghanistan combined.'

'Yeah, I heard that,' said Shepherd. He ended the call and flopped down on the sofa. He tried not to think about the damage he was doing to his relationship with Charlotte Button. If she ever found out he was going behind her back, there would be hell to pay.

Mickey and Mark Moore stood at either side of Shepherd, holding an arm each tightly. 'Guys, I don't want to look at ladyboys, I really don't,' Shepherd protested.

'It's fun,' said Mark.

'It's sick,' said Shepherd. He tried to get away from them, but they wouldn't release him.

'Do you want me to kill them for you, Ricky?' said a deep, guttural voice behind Shepherd. The three men turned to see Sergei standing in the middle of Walking Street, his hands on his hips.

Shepherd grinned. 'That'd be great – go for it.'

'Where are they taking you?' asked the Russian.

'To look at ladyboys.'

Sergei threw back his head and roared. 'If that's what they want, let them. You can come and see some real women with me,' he said. 'Russian women.'

'It's a laugh,' said Mark.

'Being gay is nothing to be ashamed of,' Sergei said solemnly.

Mark flushed. 'I'm not bloody gay!'

Sergei's face broke into a grin. 'I'm joking,' he said. 'I saw you in the Red Rose, remember? I know you like girls. Lots of girls.'

'Exactly,' said Mark.

'But one of the girls was complaining that she couldn't sit down after what you did to her.' Sergei mimed rubbing his backside. Shepherd and Mickey laughed.

'Where's your place?' asked Mickey.

The Russian pointed down Walking Street towards a red sign in the shape of a vodka bottle with Absolute-a-go-go in the middle. Below the sign was a window and in it a lithe blonde in a white thong bikini was dancing around a chrome pole. In the street below, a group of Korean tourists was filming her with video cameras. 'The drinks are on me,' said Sergei.

'You've talked us into it,' said Mickey. He raised his cigar. 'Okay to smoke?'

'It's my bar, you can do what the hell you want,' said Sergei.

They walked along to Absolute-a-go-go. It was on an

upper floor so they went up a flight of red-carpeted stairs past a sign that promised a happy hour from six o'clock until seven. A Thai man with the look of an off-duty cop saluted Sergei and pulled back a red curtain.

Mickey, Mark and Shepherd followed him inside. It was a big bar with rows of blue fake-leather seating and two dancing podiums with chrome poles. The bases of the podiums were white translucent tiles through which shone fluorescent lights, which gave the place a clinical feel.

Pretty Thai waitresses in white shirts, short black skirts and pencil-thin black neckties hurried around, but the dancing girls were Caucasian. There were two pneumatic blondes dancing topless and a stunning redhead in a red thong and high heels doing a solo show on the second podium. Around the bar other pretty girls in silk robes were sitting with customers, bottles of champagne in front of them. 'We're more upmarket than the other bars,' said Sergei. He snapped his fingers at a passing waitress and ordered champagne with four glasses. 'The bar fine is a thousand baht, and the girls have to ask for at least two thousand.'

'How many have you got here?' asked Mark.

'About thirty, but we've got more coming,' said Sergei. 'Belarussians. All virgins.'

'Really?' said Mark.

Sergei banged his fist on the table. 'Virgins? You think there is such thing as a Belarussian virgin?' he bellowed.

Two more girls joined the redhead. One was a blonde with wavy hair, green eyes and milk-white flawless skin, the other a brunette with a pageboy hair-cut and dark brown eyes. She was like Charlotte Button, Shepherd thought, disconcerted. She saw him staring at her and dropped him a little curtsy.

'You like her?' asked Sergei.

Shepherd reddened like a schoolboy who'd been caught looking at a pornographic magazine. 'She's fit,' he said, getting back into character.

'I'll get her over,' said Sergei, standing up.

Shepherd pulled him back down. 'I was just looking,' he said.

'Don't you want to fuck her?'

'She reminds me of someone, that's all.'

'Someone you want to fuck?'

Shepherd groaned. 'Leave me alone, Sergei. If I want to get laid, I'm more than capable of taking care of it myself.'

Sergei's champagne arrived. He opened it and poured for them, then stood up and raised his glass. 'To the best country in the world,' he said. They all raised their glasses. 'Russia!' shouted Sergei and drank.

Mickey, Mark and Shepherd stood up, too, and drank to his toast.

'So, what else do you do, other than run this bar and shoot chickens in Cambodia?' asked Mickey, as he sat down.

'You didn't tell them?' Sergei asked Shepherd.

Shepherd shrugged. 'I figured it was between you and me,' he said.

Sergei nodded approvingly. 'You are a good man, Ricky,' he said. 'You don't talk too much.' He poured more champagne into Shepherd's glass. 'We run a few bars, we bring in girls, we have our fingers in many pies,' he said to Mickey. 'We sell arms from the Soviet bloc, we offer protection for companies that need it, we do a nice line in exporting various commodities to Europe. We do anything that makes money.' He raised his glass. 'To Thailand, the Land of Opportunity!'

Mickey, Mark and Shepherd raised their glasses, downed the champagne and banged their glasses on the table. Sergei refilled them, then waved at a waitress to bring another bottle.

'You're serious about the arms dealing?' asked Mickey.

'Serious as a bullet in the face,' said Sergei. 'Why, Mickey, do you want a gun?'

Mickey looked at Mark, who nodded.

'We need some special gear, Sergei,' said Mickey.

'Special, how?'

Shepherd felt a soft touch on his leg and turned. The brunette was sitting next to him. She brushed his cheek with her lips. 'Buy me a drink?' she whispered into his ear. Her hand crept up his thigh and she smiled. She had the same amused look in her eyes that Charlotte Button often had. His cheeks reddened and his mouth dried. 'You're very cute,' she said. She waved at a waitress, made a drinking motion with her hand, then pointed at Shepherd. The girl went over to the bar.

Shepherd smiled at her as he strained to hear what Mickey was saying to Sergei. 'RPGs,' said Mickey. 'We need three at least. Four would be better.'

Sergei patted the pockets of his jeans. 'I am afraid I do not have any on me,' he said.

'But you can get them, right?'

'No problem,' said Sergei. 'Do you know what RPG stands for?'

Mickey frowned. 'I'm not retarded. Rocket-propelled grenade.'

Sergei shook his head emphatically. 'That's what the

Americans would like you to think, but it's a Russian thing.'

'Russian?' repeated Mickey.

'He's right,' said Shepherd. 'Ruchnoy Protivotankovyy Granatomyot. Hand-held anti-tank grenade launcher. The Russians came up with it first but RPG fits rocket-propelled grenade so that's what the Yanks called them. Strictly speaking, the grenades aren't powered by rockets.' He tried to ignore the girl's hand on his thigh – it was becoming increasingly persistent.

'You are a smart man,' said the Russian.

'That's what they say,' said Shepherd. 'But can you get us RPGs?' He put his hand on top of the girl's to stop her attempts at arousal.

'I can get you anything you want, my friend,' said Sergei, 'providing you have the money.'

Mickey held up a hand to silence him. 'Before you say anything else, let's adjourn to our office.'

The Russian frowned. 'You have an office?'

Sergei downed his vodka, dropped the ice glass onto the metal floor and stamped on it. Shards ricocheted around the bar. 'Call this cold?' he shouted. He stripped off his shirt and tossed it onto one of the sofas. 'This is summer in Siberia. This isn't cold.'

Mickey, Mark and Shepherd were shivering by the main bar, holding ice shot glasses filled with raspberry vodka. They swallowed their drinks and threw their glasses against the wall.

House music pounded through the powerful speakers and Mickey waved the Russian over to the bar. 'So, you can get us RPGs?'

'No problem,' said Sergei. 'Anything military is for sale in the former USSR, from tanks to nuclear weapons.'

'Bullshit,' said Mark. 'You can't get hold of nuclear weapons.'

The Russian snorted. 'Of course I can't. But they are around if you know the right people. And you have to have enough money.'

'We don't want nuclear bloody missiles,' said Mickey. 'We just want RPGs.'

'RPGs are easy,' said Sergei. 'I have a friend who sells them by the truckload to the Tamil Tigers.'

'How much?'

'Depends on what sort of warheads you want. And he gives a discount for big orders.'

'We don't want a big order,' said Mickey.

The Russian rubbed his chin. 'Maybe five hundred dollars each.'

'That's all?' said Mark. 'Five hundred dollars for an RPG?'

'That is for the firing unit,' said the Russian. 'The warheads are extra.'

'How much extra?' asked Mickey.

'It depends on the type of warhead you want. For instance, he can sell you thermobaric warheads. Chinese-made, great quality.'

'Thermo-what?' said Mickey. He waved at the shivering waitress to bring over another bottle of vodka.

'Thermobaric,' repeated Sergei. 'WPF 2004s. Major warhead.'

'Not what we want,' said Shepherd.

'Why not?' asked Mark.

'I can get you them for a good price,' said Sergei. 'A thousand dollars each. A discount if you buy a lot.'

'They're not what we need, Sergei,' said Shepherd again. He blew on his hands but it didn't make them feel any warmer. 'Thermobaric warheads are full of an inflammable liquid that disperses on impact and then ignites,' he explained to the Moores. 'They kill people but don't do much damage to buildings. Say you've got a sniper in an upstairs room. You fire one through the window and the guy fries. The building might burn but structurally it'll be okay.'

'So it's the exact opposite of what we want,' said Mickey.

'You got it in one,' said Shepherd.

The waitress brought over the vodka with more ice shot glasses. Mickey twisted off the cap and poured slugs. 'Cheers!' he said.

'Sergei, ideally what we want is a PG-7VR.'

Sergei nodded. 'I think we can get some,' he said.

'Can we speak English here?' said Mark, shouting to make himself heard over the music.

'PG-7VR,' said Shepherd. 'It's a tandem warhead. It was designed to penetrate modern tanks and can blast through two feet of armour. Effectively it has two warheads, a smaller one followed by a larger one. The whole thing weighs about four and half kilos and can travel about two hundred metres. I reckon two will do the job, three to be on the safe side.'

'We'll go with four. Four warheads and four launchers. That way we won't have to waste time reloading.' Mickey looked at the Russian. 'And you can get them?'

'Does the pope shit in the woods, Mickey?' said Sergei. 'Does he?'

'Okay, here's the problem, Sergei,' said Mickey. 'We don't want them in Moscow or Kiev, or anywhere else in the former Soviet bloc. We want them in Europe, the closer to England the better.'

Sergei pulled a face as if he had an unpleasant taste in his mouth. 'That's not so easy, my friend,' he said.

'They're no good to me in Russia, mate,' said Mickey. 'We can get them in Cambodia if we need to, but they'll send them by ship and it'll take for ever. We need them going overland and we need them as soon as possible.'

Sergei leaned across to Mickey and put his mouth close to his ear. 'I will try,' he said, 'but first I want you to suck my dick.'

Mickey punched the Russian's arm. 'Sergei, you sad bastard, if you can get us what we need, I might just do that.'

The Russian slapped Mickey's thigh. 'You are a good man, Mickey, for one who was named after a mouse.'

The two men laughed. 'Seriously,' said Mickey, 'we need them in Europe. The further west the better.'

The Russian nodded thoughtfully. 'It can be done, but the further from Russia, the higher the price.'

'Money isn't a problem,' said Mickey. 'I can pay you here in cash, any currency you want.'

'I will talk to my friend,' said Sergei.

'Tell him Holland's favourite,' said Mickey. 'If he can get the RPGs that far, I can get them into the UK.'

Sergei grabbed the vodka and filled fresh ice glasses. He raised his in the air. 'To crime!' he said.

'To crime!' they echoed, and drank. Mickey winked as Shepherd put his empty glass back on the table.

Shepherd winked back.

'Nice one,' said Mickey. 'Looks like we're on, Ricky.'

Shepherd's stomach tightened. Mickey regarded Ricky Knight as a friend, someone he could trust, but Ricky Knight didn't exist. Ricky Knight was really Dan Shepherd, and Dan Shepherd was working to put Mickey in a twelve-by-eight-foot concrete box for the next twenty years or so. He reached for the vodka. He needed to be doing something, even if it was just pouring drinks, because the more Mickey smiled at him, the guiltier he felt. It was one of the dangers of working under cover, Shepherd knew. To get close to the target he had to empathise, and through empathy came closeness and eventually friendship. But, like everything else in his under-cover life, the friendship was false, based on lies. Every move Shepherd made worked to one aim: to betray Mickey and his team. It was what Shepherd did for a living and it was something he was good at, but the fact that he was working on the side of law and order and Mickey's crew were villains who happily broke the law didn't make him feel any better about what he was doing.

Shepherd paid a baht bus to drive him back to his villa. The driver wanted three hundred baht and Shepherd was too tired to argue. He let himself into the villa and phoned Charlotte Button. 'We've got the RPGs sorted,' said Shepherd.

'So it's on?'

'It's on, but I'm worried about the way it's falling into place.'

'What's wrong?'

'My involvement,' said Shepherd. 'Their contact in Sarajevo couldn't come up with the goods. But the Russian

I met out in Cambodia, the guy based in Pattaya I told you about, has said he can supply us and that he can get the gear to the UK.'

'So what's the problem?' asked Button.

'I was the first point of contact with Sergei,' said Shepherd. 'I started talking to him and it was me who introduced him to the Moores. Without me, they might never have met him.'

'You're worried about entrapment? Didn't you suggest that we use one of our own people to pose as an arms dealer?'

'This is different. Sergei is the real thing. And I talked to him about weapons before the Moores did. Then I introduced him to the Moores.'

'But they were the ones who asked Sergei to supply them with RPGs?'

Shepherd grimaced. 'It's a grey area,' he said. 'We were all there when it came up.'

'But it was the Moores who asked the Russian to supply them with RPGs?' insisted Button.

'Yes, I guess so.'

'You guess so?'

'Mickey was the one who actually asked for the gear, but we were all there.'

'So it's not a problem,' said Button. 'That hardly counts as entrapment. But it's not going to be an issue anyway. We'll be catching them red-handed with the money, and you won't be giving evidence against them so no one is going to try shifting the blame on to you.'

'I just wanted you to know.'

'It's noted,' said Button. 'Do you know when you'll be leaving?'

'Everything's on a need-to-know basis with me,' said Shepherd. 'I've got my bag packed ready for the call.'

His intercom buzzed. 'What's that?' asked Button.

'I've got a visitor. As soon as I know when we're leaving, I'll call you.'

Shepherd disconnected and went to the intercom. 'Who is it?'

'It's Olga.'

'Olga?'

'From the bar.'

'Which bar?'

'Did you forget me already?'

Shepherd frowned, then remembered the pretty brunette in Absolute-a-go-go. The one who had been stroking his thigh until he had left to go to the ice bar. 'Olga, it's late,' he said.

'Sergei told me to come,' she said. 'Please let me in. My taxi has gone already.'

Shepherd didn't want her in the villa, but he didn't want to leave her alone in the darkened street either. He pressed the button to open the gate and went to the front door.

Olga had changed into a blue denim miniskirt and a yellow top that showed off a perfect midriff. She was wearing long silver earrings, strappy high heels, and carrying a shiny gold handbag with a fringe on the bottom. She waved as she walked up the path to the front door. 'Hi!' she said.

Shepherd folded his arms. 'Olga, how did you know where I lived?'

'Sergei asked your friend. The one who smokes cigars all the time.'

'Mickey,' said Shepherd. 'Terrific.'

She stopped and stood with her weight on one hip. 'Don't you like me?' she said, pouting.

'It's not that,' he said.

'Good,' she said. She smiled brightly and walked past him into the hallway. 'Can I have a drink?' she asked.

'Kitchen's that way,' said Shepherd, gesturing to her left. He closed the front door and followed her. She dropped her handbag on the table.

'I saw the way you watched me when I was dancing.' She opened the fridge. 'And how you reacted when I touched you.'

'You're pretty. And . . .'

She took out a bottle of white wine and showed it to him. 'Can I have this?' she said.

'Sure,' said Shepherd. He took it from her and fished a corkscrew out of one of the drawers.

'And?' she said. 'You said I was pretty, and . . .'

'And you reminded me of someone.'

'Your wife?'

'I don't have a wife,' he said.

'Girlfriend?'

Shepherd opened the bottle and poured her some wine. 'Not a girlfriend,' he said. 'Someone I worked with, but she's older than you.'

She sipped her wine and then licked her upper lip. 'You want to have sex with her, yes?'

Shepherd's stomach lurched. 'No,' he said.

She stepped towards him and ran her finger down his chest. 'I think you do,' she said. 'You can, you know. You can make love to me and pretend I'm her.' She kissed his cheek. 'You can do to me anything that you want to do to her.'

He could feel her warm breath on his skin and took a step back. 'Olga, I can't.'

She took another sip of wine and peeped at him over the top of her glass. She had a knowing glint in her eyes that reminded him of the way Charlotte Button looked at him sometimes.

'How old are you?' he asked.

'Old enough,' she said.

He poured himself some wine. 'Seriously, how old are you?'

'Twenty-two,' she said.

Just about half Charlie's age. Young enough to be her daughter. But she had the same soft dark chestnut hair, the same high cheekbones, the same brown eyes, so brown they were almost black, the same slim figure and shapely legs. Her voice was different, of course, but she had the same confidence as Charlie, the same way of walking, with her shoulders back and her head held high, as if nothing in the world scared her.

Shepherd took out his wallet and gave her five thousand baht.

'You don't have to pay me,' she said. 'Sergei said I was a present.'

'That's just to say thank you for coming,' he said. 'You have to go now. You can tell Sergei that I was an animal in bed, if you like.'

'I want to stay with you,' she said earnestly. 'It's not because of Sergei, it's because I like you.' She sounded like a schoolgirl talking to her first love.

'I like you, too, but you can't stay.'

'Why not?'

'Because it wouldn't be fair. It wouldn't be fair to you,

and it wouldn't be fair to . . .' He tailed off, not wanting to finish the sentence.

'To the woman you want to screw?' She laughed, and he knew she was teasing him. She put down her glass and tried to put her arms around his neck, but he took a step back.

'I can't,' he said.

'I'm clean,' she said. 'I saw the doctor for a check last week.'

'It's not that, Olga,' he said. 'Really. But you have to go. I'm sorry.'

'Are you sure?' she said. She started to undo her top but he held up his hand to stop her.

'No,' said Shepherd. 'I'm not. But you have to go.'

'You're a nice man, Ricky,' she said. She picked up her handbag and put away the money he'd given her.

'I'm not,' he said. 'But thank you.'

She kissed his cheek. 'Whoever she is, she's a very lucky woman,' she whispered. Then she turned and walked away.

The bidding went up to six thousand pounds quickly but within two minutes only one other bidder was interested in the ten-year-old removal van. He was an elderly man in a sheepskin jacket and a flat cap. Once the bidding went above four thousand his lips had formed a tight line and deep lines creased his forehead. Bradshaw had an easy smile on his face each time he raised a hand to increase his bid. He would pay whatever it took to win the auction and he and Kundi had twelve thousand pounds in cash between them, which was far more than the van was worth.

Under the rules of the auction they hadn't been allowed

to test-drive it but they had been able to run the engine and, according to Kundi, it was worn but serviceable. He had crawled under it to check the brakes and the suspension and pronounced it suitable for their needs. The name of the removals company that had previously owned it had been painted over but it was still just about visible, along with the company's website address and telephone number. It was perfect, so Bradshaw continued to smile and bid.

The middle-aged man dropped out at six thousand eight hundred pounds and the auctioneer banged down his gavel. Half an hour later, having paid in cash, Kundi was driving down the M25 with Bradshaw in the passenger seat.

Shepherd woke to the sound of his mobile phone ringing. It was seven o'clock in the morning, which meant it was midnight in England.

'Sorry about the time but I figured you'd want the Paul Bradshaw intel ASAP,' said the Major. 'It took me longer than I thought to get it – the guy I needed to speak to is out in Iraq.'

'Not a problem, boss,' said Shepherd, sitting up and running a hand through his hair. He reached for a bottle of Evian water on his bedside table and took a swig from it as the Major carried on talking.

'Bradshaw joined the King's Royal Hussars straight out of school and was a Challenger tank gunner. His career was satisfactory, rather than exemplary, tried hard but wasn't especially good at anything. He did two tours in Iraq, handled himself well. During his last tour he was based in Al Amara in Maysan province. A lot of Brits died there. It was a testing ground for IEDs from Iran, but he was lucky, had a few near misses but returned without a scratch. He left a year ago and enrolled on an engineering degree course.'

'Why did he leave?'

'No reason given,' said the Major. 'Obviously he was interviewed and given a dozen reasons why he should stay but he wanted to go back to Civvy Street so that was that.'

'No emotional problems, no post-traumatic stress disorder?'

'He was fine,' said the Major. 'At least, as fine as someone who has done two tours in Iraq can ever be. There was one black mark on his record. An Iraqi interpreter he worked with was killed at an American roadblock and Bradshaw wanted the guys who shot up the man's car to be charged, but of course it didn't happen. Bradshaw seemed to take it personally. He wanted the Americans punished and the interpreter's family compensated.'

'How did it play out?'

'Bradshaw was given the usual American run-around, told that the men had been cleared by an internal inquiry, all the usual bullshit. He wouldn't take no for an answer and he confronted one of the American soldiers and threatened to blow his head off. His squad pulled him away and it was kept quiet, but from what I've been told he was only seconds away from pulling the trigger.'

'You think that might have set him off?'

'Who knows?' said the Major. 'By the time he was back in England he was hunky-dory and the Hussars were sorry to lose him. His mate Chris Thomas left at the same time. He's back in Iraq now, running his own security company and making a small fortune. Quite a few former Regiment guys are working for him and he's a straight arrow, by all accounts.'

'Any idea what Bradshaw's doing?'

'We're not geared up for that,' said the Major. 'Once they leave the military we don't keep tabs on them. We'd have to run a check through the cops or other agencies, and you wouldn't want me to do that because it'll start raising red flags.'

'Thanks' said Shepherd.

'There's more,' said the Major. 'That other arms dealer you wanted checking out. Marcel Calvert. He's dead.'

Shepherd closed his eyes. Richard Yokely knew about Calvert. Had the American gone to Nice and killed him? 'What happened?'

'He was knifed in his house. Nothing was stolen so the local cops don't think it was a robbery, but a knife killing doesn't sound like a professional hit.'

Shepherd opened his eyes. He doubted Yokely would kill with a knife. But if not Yokely, then who? 'A knife is personal,' said Shepherd. 'But Bradshaw didn't know Calvert. It was Kleintank who put him in touch with him.'

'Might be just one of those things,' said the Major. 'If Bradshaw is a Muslim convert preparing to wreak havoc on the West, he'd hardly be likely to stop to knife an arms dealer, would he?'

'Who knows?' said Shepherd.

'Now, do you want some really bad news? The phone number you gave me was last used in Calais.'

'Shit,' said Shepherd.

'It was used to call another UK pay-as-you-go number,'

said the Major. 'That was in France, too. Since then they've remained switched off. You don't have to be a detective to work out that he was either coming over on the ferry or through the Eurotunnel. Presumably with his missiles.'

'When was this?'

'Two days ago.'

'Shit,' repeated Shepherd.

'You must have suspected as much,' said the Major.

'Yeah, but having it confirmed brings it home,' said Shepherd. 'And it sure as hell cuts down on my options. Can you find out where he is?'

'That's not easy, Spider,' said the Major. 'If it was me, I'd talk to the spooks but the lovely Charlotte is still very tight with Five and I'm sure they'd be straight on to her. And I'm guessing you wouldn't want that.'

'She won't be happy if she knows I went behind her back,' admitted Shepherd.

'And is there a reason why you can't be up front with her?'

'It's complicated,' said Shepherd.

'I'm not sure what else I can do,' said the Major. 'I can keep a watching brief on the phone he used. And the number he called. I have a contact at GCHQ who'll do it as a favour. And I suppose I can have some of our military intelligence people have a sniff around if I make it clear that it's to be kept away from other agencies. But, hand on heart, that's all that's within my gift right now.'

'Thanks, Major.'

'I wish I could do more, Spider.'

Shepherd's Ricky Knight phone began to ring and it

Mickey Moore was calling. 'I've got to go, boss. Sorry.' Shepherd cut the connection and answered Mickey.

'Where are you?' said Mickey, with no preamble.

'My villa.'

'We're on,' said Mickey.

'When?'

'The clock's ticking,' said Mickey. 'Get around to our office at three o'clock this afternoon and have your bag packed. Just hand luggage. We'll be back in three days.' The line went dead.

Shepherd walked outside and paced around the swimming-pool, considering his options. He didn't have many, and most of those involved Charlotte Button getting very, very angry. Button demanded complete loyalty from her agents, and there would be hell to pay if she ever discovered that he had done a deal with Richard Yokely behind her back.

The girl poured lemon vodka into three ice glasses then shoved her gloved hands into her padded jacket and jogged up and down, her breath feathering in the freezing air. Shepherd carried the drinks to where Mickey and Mark were sitting. The three men downed them and hurled the ice glasses at the walls of the bar.

'It's all sorted,' said Mickey. 'Your mate Sergei can get the RPGs to Holland and I've got mates there who use fast boats to bring wacky-baccy into the UK so they'll get them over for me.'

'First, Sergei isn't my mate – I don't want any flak if he lets us down. I met him for the first time on your shooting trip to Cambodia.'

'Relax, mate,' said Mickey. 'Sergei is sound.'

'And, second, I hope you can trust your wacky-baccy mates. They'll be screwed if they get caught bringing RPGs into the country.'

'They never get caught,' said Mickey. 'They've been doing it for years. They use rib boats with massive engines and they can outrun anything that Customs have. They'll bring our gear over to the Northumbrian coast and we'll pick it up there. Chopper and Davie are already in the UK, and Barry's in Ireland, fixing up our transport there. The Russian assures me that the RPGs will be in France tomorrow. You're flying to Dublin today with me and Mark, and we'll drive over on the ferry to Holyhead.'

'There's no direct flights between Bangkok and Dublin,' said Shepherd.

'We'll go via Amsterdam,' said Mickey.

'Where do we stay in Ireland?'

'We'll be straight on to the ferry. If all goes to plan we'll be back in three days.'

'Are you still treating me like a mushroom or can I ask a question?' said Shepherd.

'Depends on the question,' said Mickey.

'The take is going to be what?'

'We won't know for sure,' said Mickey. 'Money moves in and out every day. Could be anywhere between ten and twenty million.'

'Well, my question is, what do we do with the money? I don't think we're going to be flying out with suitcases full of cash.'

Mark laughed. 'We give it to the laundryman,' he said.

'So when do I get my share?'

'When we all do,' said Mickey. 'The guy we use, he's solid. We've used him before.'

'So basically we hand between ten and twenty million quid to this guy in the UK and we get on a plane to Thailand?'

'That's the plan,' said Mickey.

'And what's his cut?'

'Fifteen per cent,' said Mickey.

'Bloody hell,' said Shepherd. 'That's almost as bad as the taxman.'

'He's worth every penny,' said Mickey. 'Once he's got the money, it's as good as in the bank.'

'I'm assuming you won't tell me who he is so I can check his references?'

Mickey chuckled and waved at the waitress for more vodka.

'The thing is, Mickey, you're asking me to hand over my share of twenty million quid to a guy I don't know. I'm not thrilled about that. What if he does a runner?'

Mickey leaned closer to Shepherd and grinned wolfishly. 'We know where he lives and where his kids go to school, and he knows that we know.'

'I'm not complaining,' said Shepherd. 'But I'm putting a lot of faith in you. And him.'

The waitress carried a tray of vodka shots over and placed it on the table. 'We know what we're doing, Ricky,' said Mickey. 'We've got a winning formula, and so long as we stick to it, we'll do just fine.'

'I'll drink to that,' said Shepherd, and picked up his ice shot glass. They all drank their vodkas down in one and then smashed the glasses against the wall.

Bradshaw rested the ladder against the side of the removal van and held it as Kundi climbed up and onto the roof. 'What do you think?' asked Bradshaw.

Kundi knelt down and tapped it. 'It'll cut like butter,' he said.

'And can you weld something in there to hold the piece until we need to remove it?'

'I think I can run a metal rim around the bit I cut out and then it'll sit back in place. I can't guarantee it'll be waterproof.'

'That's not a problem. We won't be taking it out in the rain.' He held the ladder steady as Kundi climbed down.

The two men walked to the back of the van and pulled down the tailgate. Talwar, Chaudhry and al-Sayed were waiting by the oxyacetylene equipment they would use to cut the hole.

Bradshaw pulled himself up onto the tailgate, then helped Kundi climb inside. They peered up at the inside of the roof. Bradshaw mimed holding the missile launcher on his shoulder and showed Kundi where he should stand, close to the back of the van. 'This is how we do it,' said Bradshaw. 'Jamal will be in the back, sighting through the hole in the roof. Samil will be with him, in case a problem arises. They'll have limited vision, so I'll be nearby, watching the approaching planes from a vantage-point. As soon as I've selected a target, Rafee and Kafele are to lower the tailgate, allowing the backblast to escape. Jamal will fire the weapon, and I will video it. Once the missile is fired, Jamal is to drop the remains of the launcher, rush with Samil to my car and we drive off. Rafee and Kafele torch the van, then run to the second car and drive in the opposite direction.'

'Why does Jamal fire the weapon?' asked Chaudhry.

'It doesn't matter who fires it. We're doing this together,' said Bradshaw. 'We're a team.'

'If it doesn't matter, why can't I be the one to fire it?'

'Jamal is older,' said Bradshaw. 'That's the only reason.' Chaudhry's enthusiasm was admirable, but had to be tempered with deliberation. 'This will be the first of many attacks, brother,' he said. 'We are not *shahid*, not killing ourselves, we'll live to fight again and again. There will be other occasions when you will pull the trigger.'

Chaudhry nodded. 'I'm sorry, brother,' he said. 'You are right.'

Bradshaw smiled. 'Allah is right, brother. I am just His servant.'

As soon as he got back to his villa, Shepherd phoned Charlotte Button. 'It's on,' he said. 'We leave tomorrow. I'll be told then what flight, but we're going through Amsterdam so I don't think there'll be too many options.'

'The target?'

'They're still playing Secret Squirrel.'

'Do you think there's a trust issue?'

'I think it's the way they are, that's all.'

'I don't want you doing this without any back-up,' she said. 'I want some form of electronic surveillance if nothing else. I need to get a GPS locator to you.'

Shepherd knew she was right. 'The Dublin to Holyhead ferry would be the best bet,' he said. 'We're flying from Bangkok to Amsterdam, Amsterdam to Dublin, and taking vehicles over on the ferry. You could slip me the locator there and get the cars tagged.'

'I'm on it,' she said.

'How far do you want me to run?' asked Shepherd.

'There are no lives at risk, the way I understand it.'

'Straight in through the wall, grab the cash and off

over the fields. They'll be armed but they're not expecting trouble. Yates and Black are already in the UK – I assume they're travelling under different names. They'll be picking up the RPGs. Wilson is in Dublin, arranging transport.'

'And have they said what they're doing with the money? One assumes they don't take it with them back to Thailand.'

'They're giving it to the Indian laundryman to put into the banking system.'

'Any idea who this financial wizard is?'

'Need-to-know,' said Shepherd. 'And I don't need to know. All I know is that he's Indian and they've used him before. They haven't let slip with a name and I haven't been able to push it.'

'Let it run all the way then,' said Button. 'We can't afford to let them get back to Thailand but I would like to pick up whoever it is that's doing their laundry. Are you okay with that?'

'Makes my life easier,' said Shepherd. 'When will you pull them in?'

'Are they leaving the same way they arrive? On the ferry?'

'I assume so,' said Shepherd.

'Then we'll take them as they're about to leave the country. I'll have people at Holyhead and we'll have the airports covered too, just in case.'

'What shall I tell Razor?' asked Shepherd.

'As soon as you leave, he can pull out,' said Button. 'Tell him I look forward to seeing his expenses claim.' Shepherd laughed. 'Yours too,' said Button.

'Don't worry,' said Shepherd. 'I've been keeping receipts.'

'Is there anything else?'

Shepherd screwed up his face. He hated lying to his boss but if he told her what he'd learned from Richard Yokely she'd never forgive him. And neither would Yokely. 'Sort of,' he said. 'But it's off the case.'

'I'm listening.'

Shepherd gritted his teeth. Then he took a deep breath. 'Remember I mentioned the Brits who'd been buying the Grail from Kleintank?'

'Vividly.'

'I was talking to Mark tonight and apparently he'd been chatting to Kleintank while Mickey and I were giving the Grail the once-over. He'd got a name from Kleintank. Paul Bradshaw. Former army.'

'Why would Kleintank open up to Mark Moore?'

'They were just chatting,' said Shepherd, cringing because he knew how weak his story was. 'Kleintank also said Bradshaw had been to see an arms dealer in Nice by the name of Marcel Calvert. I only found out tonight.'

'Okay, I'll get Bradshaw checked out. And this Calvert. Did Moore tell you anything else?'

Shepherd wanted Button to check the phone Bradshaw was using, but there was no good reason for him to have the number. 'That's all, pretty much. Mark likes to talk when he's had a few, and we did a lot of drinking tonight.'

'All right, Spider, you take care of yourself. Call me as soon as you know what flight you're on and I'll have surveillance ready.'

Shepherd ended the call. Guilt formed a hard knot in his stomach and he knew his relationship with Button would never be the same again.

*   *   *

Bradshaw sounded the horn of the Ford Mondeo he was driving. Three short blasts followed by a slightly longer one. The metal door rattled up and al-Sayed stepped to the side to give him room to drive in. He eased the Mondeo past the removal van and parked behind it, followed by Kundi in a Volvo. They had bought the Volvo for cash at a south London auction. Like the Mondeo it was less than two years old and he had pronounced it in good condition. They had filled the tank at a petrol station on the way back to the self-storage depot, and Kundi had checked the engine oil and tyre pressures. Al-Sayed brought the door down while Talwar and Chaudhry walked over to the Volvo.

'It's nothing special,' said Chaudhry. He unwrapped a stick of gum, folded it in half and popped it into his mouth.

'They don't need to be special,' said Bradshaw. 'They need to be nondescript. They need to blend. Once we've carried out our task, we won't be driving away at high speed. We'll be driving at a regular speed obeying all the rules of the road, and we'll hide among the thousands of other cars that'll be on the road.'

Chaudhry pulled a face. 'Volvos are boxy,' he said. 'They're a housewife's car.'

Bradshaw laughed. 'Then you can be in the Mondeo with me, Samil.'

Mark and Mickey picked Shepherd up in their Range Rover and drove him to the airport. They spent ninety minutes in the KLM business lounge before boarding their flight to Holland. Mickey and Mark drank two bottles of champagne between them but Shepherd stayed with mineral water. He told them he didn't want to risk an upset stomach. After the food service, the brothers slept but Shepherd stayed awake. It wasn't the robbery that was preying on his mind, it was Paul Bradshaw and the Asians, and what they planned to do with their surface-to-air missiles. If they launched a terrorist attack at one of the country's airports and brought down a plane, the responsibility would lie at Shepherd's door. In a perfect world he'd simply tell Charlotte Button everything he knew and let her pass the information to the relevant agencies. With luck, the police and the security services would be able to track them down and neutralise the terrorist cell before they were able to launch an attack. But it wasn't a perfect world. Richard Yokely had made it clear that Shepherd was not to divulge the source of his information and the American was not a man to be crossed. Shepherd had told Button about the missiles, Bradshaw's involvement and the arms dealer in Nice, and just hoped that would be enough for her to put the rest of the puzzle together. If she didn't Shepherd would have no choice but to tell her everything, and if he did that his job would be on the line and Richard Yokely on his case. Neither option would have a pleasant outcome.

Shepherd felt as if he'd been backed into a corner with no way out. And while his mind went around in circles, trying to come up with a solution, he knew that the clock was well and truly ticking. Having got his missiles into England, Bradshaw wouldn't wait long to use them – the longer he waited, the more likely it was he'd be caught. There could only be one possible target, and that was a passenger jet. But without knowing where he intended to strike, preventive measures were out of the question – there were simply too many airports, too many planes and too many passengers.

Andy Yates scanned the horizon with his binoculars. 'There's a dozen boats out there,' he said. 'How the hell are we supposed to know which one we're looking for?'

'Just keep an eye out for a fast boat heading this way,' said Davie Black. They were sitting in a black Jeep Cherokee on a beach on the Northumbrian coast. He tapped the TomTom GPS unit sitting on the dashboard. 'They'll come right to us.'

'I don't understand why they're doing this in broad daylight.'

'Because it's a busy stretch of water, and even with night-vision goggles it's dangerous at the speed they travel at,' said Black. 'Stop worrying.' He studied the sudoko puzzle in the newspaper in front of him.

'What is it with you and those puzzles?' said Yates.

'Exercise for the brain,' said Black. 'Same as you like to exercise your mouth.'

Yates lowered the binoculars. 'You're turning into a grumpy old poofter.'

'And you're a boring old fart,' said Black.

'But you love me, really.'

Black shook his head in disgust and looked at his watch. 'They're late,' he said.

'If they don't come, we're screwed.'

'If they don't come we find someone else to come up with the RPGs and we do the job somewhen else.'

'Somewhen?' said Yates, grinning.

'What?'

'There's no such word.'

'You know what I mean, and that's all that matters,' said Black.

Yates put the binoculars back to his eyes and gazed out over the sea again. 'Here we go,' he said. He handed them to Black and pointed to the right. Black saw a needle-shaped boat heading their way, carving through the water like a knife. 'Bloody move those things, don't they?'

'Mickey says even the navy doesn't have anything that can keep up with them on the water,' said Yates. 'Only thing that can match them is a helicopter.'

Black climbed out of the Jeep and checked the beach. It was just after dawn and no one was around. The wind coming off the North Sea was bracing even in the summer months, and other than the occasional insomniac dog-walker the beaches were usually empty at this hour. If there had been anyone to pay any attention to the Jeep, the plates were false and both men were armed.

The boat streaked towards them, and Yates joined Black. They were both wearing fleece jackets, wellington boots and leather gloves, with woollen hats that could be pulled down as ski masks if necessary. They walked across the firm sand to the water's edge.

The hard bottom of the rib boat meant it could come right up onto the beach, providing the rotor was swung out of the water. It slowed as it got nearer the shore, but its onboard GPS kept it heading directly for them. As it came closer Yates could see two men in dark blue weather-proof jackets standing behind the windshield. The figure on the right waved and Yates waved back. There was a third figure in the back of the boat, and as it roared into the shallows he swung the outboard motor towards the front so that the rotor lifted out of the waves. The boat's momentum carried it forward and it scraped along the sand.

'Quickly! Quickly!' shouted the man holding the motor.

Yates and Black waded into the surf. One of the men at the front of the boat moved back and helped Yates to drag one of four wooden boxes over the side. He and Black carried it to the sand and put it down carefully, then hurried back. In less than five minutes they had unloaded all four and the boat was speeding towards Holland.

Shepherd managed a few hours' sleep but he didn't feel rested when the lights came on in the cabin and the crew began serving breakfast. He didn't want to eat but he drank three cups of coffee. They landed on time and spent two hours at Schiphol airport in Amsterdam before catching an Aer Lingus flight to Dublin. Mickey, Mark and Shepherd travelled separately on the Irish plane and didn't meet up until they had passed through Immigration, where overweight plainclothes Garda Síochána officers barely glanced at their British passports.

Barry Wilson was waiting for them outside the terminal in a long-wheelbase Land Rover Defender with Irish plates. Mickey climbed into the front, Shepherd and Mark into the back. 'Everything sorted?' asked Mickey.

'No worries,' said Wilson. 'Chopper called to say they'd got the gear from Holland and were driving down to the meet.'

'I love it when a plan comes together.' Mickey took out a cigar and lit it.

Wilson drove them to the long-stay car park where there was a second Land Rover Defender. Wilson gave a

set of keys to Mickey. 'Do you know where the ferry
terminal is?'

'Near the sea, right?' said Mickey. He blew a cloud of
smoke out of the window. 'I'll follow you.' Wilson reached
under the dashboard and pulled out a print-out of an
Internet booking for an afternoon ferry sailing and a
parking ticket. Mickey took it and climbed out of the car.
'Come on, Ricky, you can ride shotgun,' he said.

Shepherd took his holdall with him and walked over
to the second Land Rover. Mickey got into the driving
seat and Shepherd sat next to him. Wilson headed out of
the car park and Mickey followed. He grinned when he
saw a GPS unit mounted on the dashboard. 'Cheeky
bugger – do I know where the ferry terminal is!' He patted
the GPS. 'If I don't, this gizmo sure as hell does.'

The journey took forty-five minutes. Men in fluorescent jackets pointed the way to the waiting area where
they joined queues of cars, horseboxes, trucks and cara-
vans preparing to board. After a half-hour wait, the two
Land Rovers drove separately onto the ferry and parked
on different levels. The four men met up in the spacious
lounge close to the restaurant. A member of staff with a
heavy Polish accent issued what were probably safety
instructions, but as her voice was barely intelligible none
of the passengers paid her any attention.

'Wanna eat?' asked Mickey. He took his cigar case out
of his pocket, then saw a sign that said smoking was
permitted only outside on deck so he scowled and put it
away.

'Just coffee,' said Shepherd.

Mickey and Mark went over to the cafeteria while
Wilson and Shepherd sat at a table by a large picture

window. Shepherd flicked through his copy of the *Irish Times*. As he looked up he saw a young Asian man in a brown leather jacket and Armani jeans walking away from the cafeteria with a bottle of water. It was Amar Singh, one of SOCA's technical experts. Shepherd had worked with him for more than five years, initially on a police undercover team and latterly with SOCA. Singh studiously avoided eye contact as he went towards the men's toilets in the middle of the ship.

Shepherd put down his paper. 'I need a leak,' he said.

'Have one for me,' said Wilson.

He found Singh checking that the two stalls were empty. When he had satisfied himself, he took a Nokia mobile from his pocket and handed it to Shepherd. 'Long time no see,' he said.

'Been busy?' asked Shepherd, taking his own phone from his jacket pocket. He had already removed the Sim card. He gave the phone to Singh and took the replacement.

'Same old,' said Singh. He indicated the phone in Shepherd's hand. 'The GPS locator will give us your position around the clock. It still functions whether or not it's switched on and it looks the same as the regular phone so only an expert will be able to tell that it's been modified.'

'What if the battery loses its charge?' asked Shepherd.

'Then you're screwed, so keep it charged,' said Singh, slipping Shepherd's phone into his jacket. 'Have you got the details of the transport?'

'Two Land Rover Defenders, Irish plates,' said Shepherd. Singh took out a small notebook and Shepherd gave him the registration numbers.

'Passengers aren't allowed on the car decks while the ship's at sea, but I need you to keep an eye on the guys in case they decide to go walkabout,' said Singh.

'No problem,' said Shepherd.

'Message from Charlie about that army guy you mentioned. He almost certainly killed the arms dealer in Nice – he had hi-tech micro cameras all around the house and there's video of an IC One male sticking a knife into him in the hallway. Could well be Bradshaw. Charlie wants to know if you've any other info because he's gone off the radar.'

'Not much more I can tell her,' said Shepherd. 'What's she found out?'

'He was a tank gunner based at Abu Naji camp during his last tour. If he did convert to Islam he kept it a secret from his army buddies. Got an honourable discharge and enrolled on an engineering course at South Bank University. Was a model student during his first year but no one's seen him for the past two weeks. Charlie fears the worst.'

'Yeah, understandably,' said Shepherd. 'If he's gone AWOL with surface-to-air missiles, it can't be good news.'

'That's why she's asking for more intel on him,' said Singh. 'She's had him red-flagged but there's no record of him entering the country from France so she's assuming he's got fake ID.'

'Not sure I can help,' said Shepherd. 'I don't suppose she's going to go public?'

'Can't do that without causing a panic,' said Singh. 'You can imagine what it'd do to the aviation business if we start telling people a crazed fundamentalist's about to shoot down passenger jets.'

Singh was right. And if Button did go public with Bradshaw's details, it would drive him further underground. 'Tell Charlie if I get anything, I'll call or text,' he said.

'Be lucky,' said Singh, and left the toilet. Shepherd went into one of the stalls, sat down and installed his Sim card. He switched on the phone and went back to join Wilson.

Bradshaw stood at the rear of the removals van and examined Kundi's handiwork. 'What do you think, brother?' asked Kundi.

'You've done a good job,' he said. Kundi had used the oxyacetylene torch to cut out a large section of the roof, then hinged the piece so that it could be lowered, with the hinges above the cab. It reached almost halfway down the length of the van meaning that the missile would have to be fired at the back, but that wasn't a problem. There would still be enough room to keep the tailgate up until Kundi was ready to pull the trigger.

'I'll run a seal around the edges, then fit locking bolts at either side to hold it in place,' said Kundi.

'They need to be quick-release,' said Bradshaw. 'And Chaudhry has to be able to release them standing on the floor. We won't have time for him to be messing around with stepladders.'

'I'll have a pole with a hook on the end that'll release the bolts.'

'Just make sure it doesn't slam down on his head,' said Bradshaw. 'Once it's done we'll start practising, I want him to be able to do it blindfolded.' He dropped off the tailgate onto the concrete floor. Talwar and al-Sayed were on either side of the van, wearing white overalls and

carefully repainting the furniture-removal company's name
and logo. Bradshaw grinned at Talwar's attempts to re-
instate the phone number. 'Is that a three or an eight,
Rafee?' he asked.

'A three,' said Talwar, wiping his forehead with the arm
of his overalls. 'Shall I redo it?'

'It has to look perfect,' said Bradshaw. 'Anything out
of the ordinary might attract attention.'

'Is mine okay?' asked al-Sayed, scratching his neck. The
skin below his right ear was red raw and a thin rivulet of
blood trickled down his neck. He wiped his fingers on his
overalls.

'It's fine,' said Bradshaw, encouragingly, and al-Sayed
beamed.

Bradshaw moved to the corner of the storage area to get
a better view of the van. Once the painting was finished, it
would look like any of the company's other vehicles. The
alterations made to the roof wouldn't be seen by anyone
passing, and the van still had its original licence plates. The
tax disc was out of date but Chaudhry was arranging to get
a fake one made that would pass all but the closest inspection. Not that Bradshaw was over-worried about the van
being stopped and checked. It would remain in the storage
area until the day it was going to be used, and it was only
a short drive to Heathrow, the busiest airport in the world.

The two Land Rovers drove off the ferry shortly after
two o'clock in the afternoon. They were among the last
vehicles to leave and for the next hour they powered down
the outside lane of the A5 overtaking the trucks and cars
that had disembarked before them. By the time they
reached the bridge linking Anglesey to the mainland the

traffic was lighter. It began to rain and the windscreen wipers struggled against the downpour.

Mickey's mobile rang. 'Yeah, Chopper, how's it going?' His face creased into a broad smile. 'Excellent, mate. See you there, yeah?' He put the phone away. 'They're in London now, on the way to the warehouse. Your mate Sergei came through with flying colours.'

'He's not my mate, Mickey,' said Shepherd. 'When do I get to check the gear? I hope he doesn't try to shaft us with dummies.'

'Why would he do that?' said Mickey. 'If he wanted to rip us off, he could have just taken our money and run.'

'Fair point. But I'll need to check them before we get into position. We'll look pretty silly if I pull the trigger and nothing happens.'

'We're meeting them at the warehouse,' said Mickey.

'And when do we do the job?'

'Dawn,' said Mickey. 'First thing tomorrow. Forty-eight hours from now we'll be back in Pattaya.' He beat his hands on the steering-wheel. 'I love this job,' he said.

'It's not so much a job as a vocation,' said Shepherd. 'Do you want me to share the driving?'

'I'm okay. Give Mark a call and tell him to stop at the next service station. I could do with a coffee and we've got to change the plates.'

Shepherd took out his mobile. He weighed it in the palm of his hand, knowing it was relaying their position to Charlotte Button and her SOCA team. He phoned Mark and passed on Mickey's instructions.

Ten miles down the road, they pulled into the service-station car park and stopped in a far corner. Mark and Wilson pulled up behind them.

Mickey took two sets of UK plates from under his seat and climbed out. He gave one set to his brother and the two men quickly took off the Irish plates and replaced them with British ones, then all four went inside. Mickey, Mark and Wilson sat down at a table while Shepherd went over to the Costa Coffee counter. 'Hey, Ricky, bring some sandwiches, yeah?' called Mark.

'What did your last slave die of?' asked Shepherd.

'Self-abuse,' said Mark. 'He was a right wanker.' He sniggered at his own joke.

Shepherd paid for the coffees and a selection of sandwiches and carried them to the table. 'I still can't get my head around the fact that we're on our way to rob a place we've never seen,' he said as he sat down. 'Normally I'd spend weeks or months casing a joint.'

'The Professor does all that for us,' said Mickey, reaching for a sandwich. 'That's what we pay him for.'

'And you trust him? What if he decided to set you up?'

'He gets ten per cent of the take,' said Mickey. 'He makes his money when we make ours. There's no benefit to him in stitching us up.'

'Who else does he work for?' He sipped his coffee.

'He never says. He doesn't say a dicky-bird unless it's need-to-know,' said Mickey. 'That's why I trust him. He's never told me anything about his other clients and I'm pretty sure he never tells them one word about me.' Mickey took a bite of his sandwich. 'You're not getting nervous, are you, mate?' he said, through a mouthful of bread, egg and cress.

'Wary rather than nervous,' said Shepherd. 'I'm the new guy on the block, remember? I'm on a job with faces I've not worked with before, on a way to rob a place I've never seen, using rocket-propelled grenades to break in, then handing over the money to someone I've never met. And on top of that, two guys I don't know are taking a quarter of the money between them.'

Mickey laughed. 'Yeah, I can see your point,' he said. 'You'll just have to trust us, mate. Same as we have to trust you.'

Shepherd smiled, but the knot of guilt tightened in his stomach.

Mickey finished his sandwich and belched. 'Final stretch, lads,' he said.

Shepherd and Mickey reached London in the middle of rush-hour and spent the best part of an hour and a half crawling through traffic. The warehouse was on an industrial estate to the south-west of the city. Mickey phoned Yates as they drove onto the estate and he had the delivery door open for them as they approached.

Mickey drove in first, then Wilson, and the door rattled down behind them.

Davie Black was standing by a table, pouring water from a kettle into coffee mugs.

Shepherd climbed out and walked to the four wooden crates that were sitting on the ground next to a black Jeep Cherokee. 'Hasn't anybody opened them?' he said.

Yates shrugged. 'What's the point? We wouldn't know if they were the real thing or not.' He pointed at the Chinese characters stencilled on the side. 'Besides, they've got Chinky writing on them, so that's got to be a good sign.'

'Where's the Jeep's tool-kit?' asked Shepherd.

Black got it for him and he used a screwdriver to lift

off the lid of one of the crates. He pulled away the poly-styrene packing material to reveal the launcher unit, which he lifted out. 'It's the real McCoy,' he said. He checked the other three launchers, then went through the packs containing the warhead units and booster charges.

'Okay?' asked Mickey.

'Perfect,' said Shepherd. 'What about the rest of the gear? The shooters? We are going in with shooters, right?'

'Mark and I'll pick them up later,' he said. 'We've got a lock-up in Bromley with everything we need.'

'And what do we do until the off?'

'We hang around here until six thirty, then head out.'

Black pointed at five camp beds against one wall. 'We've got all mod cons,' he said.

'And I've got a pack of cards if anyone fancies losing some of their share in advance,' said Yates.

Bradshaw walked around the removals van, nodding. 'You've done well, brothers,' he said. The van had been painted white with the logo and company details in dark green. There was no indication of the modi-fication that had been made to the roof. It was just before ten o'clock at night. 'We shall do it tomorrow morning,' he said.

'So soon?' said al-Sayed, scratching his neck.

'We're ready,' said Bradshaw.

'We need to practise,' said Kundi, taking out his packet of cigarettes.

'We have time,' said Bradshaw. 'We have plenty of time to go through it. Then we sleep, then we pray, and then we go to the airport.' He grinned and put his arms around

Al-Sayed and Kundi. 'Tomorrow, my brothers.' Talwar and Chaudhry were stripping off their overalls. 'Are you hungry?' asked Bradshaw. The men nodded. 'Okay, first we practise, then we eat. Tonight we will eat like kings, because tomorrow we will be warriors.'

'Wakey, wakey, rise and shine,' said Mark, kicking Shepherd's camp bed. He held out a mug of coffee. 'Breakfast's ready and I want mine.'

Shepherd blinked to clear the sleep from his eyes, sat up and took the mug. 'Cheers, mate.' He looked at his watch. It was half past five. Mickey and Yates were standing by a Sony laptop computer, peering at the screen. Shepherd took a gulp of coffee and grimaced as he discovered there was sugar in it.

'Come and have a look at this, Ricky,' shouted Mickey. 'You're always complaining we don't keep you in the loop.'

Shepherd stood up and carried his mug to the computer. Mickey had inserted a thumb-drive into it and was scrolling through a series of photographs on the disk. 'The depository is twelve miles away,' said Mickey. He stopped at a Google Earth picture of an industrial estate. 'This is where we're going,' he said. He pulled back so that they could see a dual carriageway about a mile from the estate. 'We'll come down this road. At this time in the morning there won't be much traffic around. And we turn off here.' He tapped the screen at a road that curved away from the dual carriageway. Then he ran his finger along the road to farmland. 'This runs between two farms,' he said. 'There are plenty of Land Rovers around so no one will pay us any attention. We drive down to these gates.

They're padlocked but we cut the lock and drive across the fields.'

'What sort of crops?' asked Shepherd.

'Potatoes,' said Mickey, 'and grass. It'll be rough but the four-wheel drives can handle it. We have to cross two ditches but we've got the metal bridges that'll get us across.' He gestured at four metal trusses leaning against the wall. They were about twelve feet long and two wide, made of ridged steel. 'They'll take the weight, no problem.'

Mickey went in closer on the Google Earth picture so that they could see the wall of the depository and the field beyond. 'We stop here, two hundred yards from the wall. We're out of coverage of the CCTV cameras so we've all the time in the world. You and me will be with the RPGs. Mark, Davie, Barry and Chopper will be in the other Land Rover and the Jeep. As soon as we let fly with the first RPG, they'll head for the wall. You let fly with the second RPG and we'll see what the damage is. If we need a third or fourth, it's your call. Then we pile into the Land Rovers and it's full steam ahead.' He jabbed a finger at a large white dot on the screen. 'We stop the vans here. The CCTV cameras are fixed and they're covering the wall, not the field. Providing we don't get any closer to the wall than this, no one will know what we're driving. Once we're out of the area, we're free and clear.'

'I was wondering about that, because the Land Rovers are pretty distinctive,' said Shepherd.

'The Professor spent weeks casing the place and he's got every base covered,' said Mickey. 'We let Davie and Chopper attack the hole with pickaxes to widen it if necessary, then Mark and Barry will go through with wire-cutters to get into the money trolleys. Then we follow and it's just a matter of logistics – how much money we can get into the vehicles in six minutes.'

'Sort of *Supermarket Sweep*, but without Dale Winton,' said Mark.

'Then we go. We head back across the fields, over the metal ramps, and onto the dual carriageway.'

'Back here?' said Shepherd.

'Nope, we've another changeover area fixed up where we swap vehicles.'

'Where's that?' asked Shepherd.

Mickey grinned.

'Don't tell me – need-to-know.'

'It's where we give the cash to the laundryman and switch to clean vehicles,' said Mickey. 'Then we're straight to the airport.'

'Airport? I thought we were taking the ferry back to Dublin.'

'No need, mate,' said Mickey. 'No one's going to be looking for us on the way out. We'll fly to Amsterdam and get the EVA flight there.'

The previous evening Mark had taken the Land Rover out and had returned two hours later with three large aluminium suitcases. Now Mickey pulled out one of the cases and flicked the locks open. Inside three sawn-off shotguns nestled in foam rubber with three boxes of cartridges.

'Choose your weapons, guys,' he said. He opened the second case, which held another three shotguns and ammunition.

Shepherd picked one up and pretended to examine it while his mind raced. Button was expecting the gang to head to Holyhead and Dublin. He had to get word to her that they were flying out of the country.

Yates twirled a shotgun and pointed it the wall. 'You looking at me?' he snarled, in a reasonable imitation of Robert De Niro. 'Because I don't see anyone else here.'

Mark was slotting cartridges into one of the guns. Mickey opened the third aluminium case to reveal dark blue boiler-suits, black ski masks, black leather gloves and nylon slings to hold the guns. 'Everything the best-dressed man needs to carry out the perfect robbery,' he said.

The five men finished praying and stood up. 'Soon it will be time, my brothers,' Bradshaw said. 'Are you ready?' Talwar, al-Sayed, Chaudhry and Kundi nodded enthusiastically. 'We shall practise again. When we do it for real there must be no hesitation.'

Kundi climbed up onto the tailgate, then held out his hand to help Chaudhry up. Bradshaw joined them. They moved into the middle of the van while al-Sayed and Talwar raised the tailgate and locked it. Kundi switched on a small electric lantern hanging from the wall. It gave just enough light for them to see what they were doing.

Bradshaw stood in the corner, close to the tailgate and next to the crated Stinger missile. He clicked the digital stopwatch on his Casio. 'Begin,' he said.

Chaudhry picked up two metal poles and handed one to Kundi. At the end of each pole there was a curved hook, and the two men used them to unlatch the bolts in the roof of the van. The panel dropped and they used the poles to steady it and lower it to the floor. Light flooded in from the fluorescent lights in the ceiling.

Chaudhry opened the crate and Kundi took out the

Stinger, then manoeuvred it carefully onto his shoulder. He stood with his left foot on the roof panel and sighted up through the hole. The blowout disc at the end of the launch tube was about a foot away from the tailgate. Kundi checked that the battery coolant unit was in place, then unfolded the antenna and removed the cap from the front end of the weapon. 'Ready to fire,' he said.

'Right. I'll be on the mobile as I check the incoming planes,' said Bradshaw. He took his phone out of his pocket and pretended to talk into it. 'Target sighted, two minutes from you,' said Bradshaw.

'Target sighted, two minutes,' repeated Chaudhry.

Kundi kept the launch tube pointing up through the roof.

'Ninety seconds,' said Bradshaw.

'Ninety seconds,' repeated Chaudhry. He chewed his gum mechanically, eyes staring fixedly ahead. There was no need for him to look up through the roof. His role was solely to pass on Bradshaw's instructions.

The seconds ticked by, the only sound the breathing of the three men in the enclosed space, and Chaudhry's chewing.

'Sixty seconds,' said Bradshaw.

'Sixty seconds,' repeated Chaudhry. 'Lower the tailgate!' he shouted.

Outside the van, Talwar and al-Sayed unlocked the tailgate and swung it down, then moved quickly to the front of the van, away from the potential backblast.

'Thirty seconds,' said Bradshaw.

'Thirty seconds,' repeated Chaudhry.

Kundi flicked his thumb across the safety switch but didn't activate it. 'Safety off,' he said.

'Twenty seconds,' said Bradshaw.

'Twenty seconds,' repeated Chaudhry.

The seconds ticked slowly by. Bradshaw's mouth was dry and he swallowed. 'Ten seconds,' he said.

'Ten seconds,' repeated Chaudhry.

Chaudhry and Kundi began to count down from ten, their voices blending into one. 'Nine, eight, seven, six, five, four, three, two, one . . .'

'Acquisition tone on,' said Kundi. 'Listening for the steady tone. Steady tone achieved.' He mimed pressing the uncaging switch with his left hand, 'Reconfirm steady tone,' then pulling the trigger with his right index finger. 'Missile launched,' he said. '*Allahu akbar.*'

'*Allahu akbar,*' repeated Chaudhry. He grinned at Bradshaw. 'Perfect, yeah?'

'Perfect,' agreed Bradshaw, glancing at his stopwatch. Kundi put the Stinger down, then jumped to the ground. 'Right, you'd now head for my car,' said Bradshaw. 'Remember, you walk, you don't run.' He pointed at Talwar and al-Sayed in turn. 'Then it's up to you,' he said.

Talwar hurried to the van's cab and retrieved a red plastic petrol can. He walked quickly back to the tailgate and mimed slopping petrol inside. Then al-Sayed pretended to strike a match and throw it in. 'Whoof!' he said.

'And that's it,' said Bradshaw, stopping his timer. 'Rafee and Kafele go back to their car, and we're away. From firing the missile to getting everyone into the cars shouldn't be more than sixty seconds. The fire will destroy all the physical evidence. We drive slowly, we obey the rules of the road. No one will be any the wiser.'

He switched on his mobile phone. 'I'll tell you what each plane is before they pass over. I should be able to give you at least two minutes' warning of a suitable target, possibly four minutes, depending on the cloud cover.' He turned to Chaudhry. 'What is your mobile number, brother?' Bradshaw had bought a new pay-as-you-go Sim card and had told Chaudhry to do the same.

Chaudhry grimaced, embarrassed. When Bradshaw saw his face fall, he knew what had happened. 'I told you to change it,' he said.

'I'm sorry, brother. I switched it off in France and forgot about it.'

Bradshaw frowned. 'You haven't used it since?'

'Definitely not,' said Chaudhry.

Bradshaw sighed. 'You should never use a Sim card more than once, brother. If they know you have a phone they can track you and listen in to your calls.'

'I'm sorry,' said Chaudhry.

'It's probably okay,' said Bradshaw. 'Switch it on and I'll call you so you have this number.' Chaudhry did as he was told. Bradshaw rang him and Chaudhry stored the number. 'If anything happens on the road, call me,' said Bradshaw. 'But no chit-chat.'

'I understand,' said Chaudhry, still crestfallen.

'Right,' said Bradshaw. 'Let's go through it one more time. Then we can do it for real.'

Shepherd was just stepping into his boiler-suit when he felt his phone vibrate in his jeans pocket. He had set his mobile to ring silently but the vibration was insistent until the caller went to voicemail. 'Mickey, I'm going to use the loo,' he said.

'Not your bloody stomach again?' Mickey was checking the action of his sawn-off shotgun.

'I'll be fine,' said Shepherd. He went into the gents', made sure the door was closed and took out his phone. The Major had called and left a message. Shepherd didn't bother to listen to it. He rang the Major straight away.

'It's good news, bad news, I'm afraid,' said the Major.

'I'm listening,' said Shepherd.

'The good news is that one of those mobile numbers was switched on for a few minutes this morning. The bad news is that it was located ten miles from Heathrow airport.'

'Which phone was it?' asked Shepherd.

'It wasn't the one Bradshaw was using,' said the Major. 'It was the one he called in Calais. It was switched on at seven this morning. Then it received a call from another pay-as-you-go phone then both were switched off. They were at the same location.'

'Ten miles from the airport?'

'Exactly,' said the Major.

'How close were the phones?'

'No way of telling, I'm afraid,' said the Major. 'Neither phone has GPS capability so all we can do is track them to the closest transmitters and triangulate. But I'd guess they were at the same location and were running a test. Spider, if they have a Stinger at Heathrow . . .'

'I know, I know. Is there any way the Increment can get involved?'

'We don't have the resources to put a full protective screen around Heathrow,' said the Major. 'A Stinger has a ceiling of – what? Two thousand feet? That means in theory it could be fired anywhere within a twelve-to fifteen-mile radius of the airfield. The only way we could get that sort of saturation is by using the police and the army. And even then you couldn't guarantee total coverage.'

'And if they see that sort of reaction they'd know they'd be rumbled so they'd pull back,' said Shepherd. 'They'd just have to wait until the security was downgraded and then launch an attack.'

'So, what are you saying, Spider? We do nothing?'

'I say we wait, see if the phones go on again and see where they are. Then react. Are you okay with that, boss?'

'You're asking a lot,' said the Major. 'If they bring down a plane and it gets out that we had the intel we're screwed.'

Shepherd heard footsteps outside the toilet and ended the call. He shoved the phone into the back pocket of his jeans, adjusted his boiler-suit, then leaned over the sink and drank from the tap as the door opened behind him. It was Yates. 'You okay, mate?'

Shepherd straightened up and wiped his mouth on the back of his hand. 'Yeah, my stomach again.'

'Soon be over,' said Yates. 'Don't worry, everyone gets pre-show nerves. Even Mickey. He's all laughing and joking on the outside but I know his stomach's churning along with ours. He just hides it better.'

'Cheers.'

'I'm serious,' said Yates. 'You're a pro, Ricky, you'll be fine.'

'Yeah, it's gonna be a blast, literally,' said Shepherd, trying to sound enthusiastic.

As Yates went to the urinal, Shepherd returned to the warehouse. Mark had already climbed into the driving seat of one of the Land Rovers. Wilson got in beside him. Two of the steel mesh girders had been fixed to its roof rack, the others to the second Defender's.

Mickey stored his gun under the driving seat and waved Shepherd over. 'You ride with me, Ricky,' he said. He was already wearing his gloves and Shepherd put his own on as he got in. The four RPGs were in the back, hidden under a tarpaulin.

Black got into the Jeep Cherokee and fired the engine.

'Rock and roll!' shouted Mickey. 'Chopper, where the hell are you?'

Yates came running out of the toilets, zipping up his boiler-suit. He picked up his gun, slotted it into the nylon sling and ran over to the Jeep. Black pointed to the door and mimed opening it. Yates jogged over to the control unit and pressed the button. Mickey drove out first, followed by Mark. Yates pressed the button to close the door as Black drove through, then climbed in next to him.

Shepherd bent down and slid his sawn-off shotgun under his seat. He felt his mobile phone in the pocket of his jeans under the boiler-suit. Satellites high above the earth would be fixing his position to a few feet enabling Charlotte Button to keep track of him, but that didn't mean he was any less alone.

As they drove, Mickey chatted away. About football. About Pattaya. About the weather. It was his way of covering his nerves, Shepherd knew, so he just listened. Everyone reacted differently to stress. Some people external-ised it with conversation or physical tics, others went quiet, sweated or froze. Mickey was a talker, and Shepherd was a thinker. Shepherd's way of dealing with a stressful situ-ation was to consider his options, calculating the best and worst possible scenarios, and always having his escape route mapped out. All that was going through his mind as he smiled and listened to Mickey babble.

'Here's our exit,' said Mickey, eventually. He indicated left and checked in his rear-view mirror that Mark was doing the same. The three vehicles came off the motorway. All around them were fields, with well-kept hedgerows and copses of spreading trees. Now that they were off the dual carriageway there was little traffic. Mickey pointed at the GPS unit on his dashboard. 'The Professor even gave us the co-ordinates of the field,' he said.

They passed a farmhouse to their right and a dog barked, but Shepherd didn't see anyone around. Half a mile further on there was another farmhouse, this one well back from the road. A middle-aged man in a donkey jacket was using a hosepipe to wash down the wheels of his tractor but he didn't even look up as they drove by. Mickey kept the Land Rover at just below forty miles an hour and a close eye on his GPS unit.

'We're coming up to the field,' he said. He wound down the window and waved for Black to overtake in the Jeep, then pulled in to the side as he drove by. Yates flashed them a thumbs-up. A hundred yards ahead a five-barred metal gate was locked with a length of heavy chain. Yates climbed out with a pair of industrial wire-cutters and severed the hasp of the padlock. He unhooked the chain and pulled open the gate. The three vehicles drove through and Yates pulled the gate shut behind them, then threaded the chain through to make it look as if it was locked.

The Land Rover bucked over the rutted furrows and Shepherd put his hand to the roof to steady himself. The field was bare soil that looked as if it had been ploughed prior to planting. The steering-wheel kept trying to tear itself out of Mickey's grasp and he cursed. Shepherd glanced over his shoulder. The other Land Rover and the Jeep were close behind.

Mickey turned to the right and tried to focus on the GPS unit. 'We'll do the first ditch, Ricky,' he said. 'It's coming up. Take down the two trusses and put them over it. Then watch as we cross.' He grinned. 'Don't screw this up, mate, or the game's over before we've even started.' He slammed on the brakes and Shepherd climbed out. Twenty feet ahead a six-foot-wide ditch separated the ploughed field from pasture. Two chestnut horses stood stock–still, watching Shepherd, their heads up and ears back.

Yates got out of the Jeep and ran to help. Shepherd untied the first truss and pulled it off the roof rack. Yates grabbed the other end and they carried it over the field to the ditch and carefully laid it across. Then they ran back for the second and placed it parallel to the first. Shepherd ran over one of the trusses to the pasture and helped Yates reposition them so that they matched the vehicle's wheelbase.

Shepherd motioned for Mickey to drive across. Mickey edged the Land Rover forward and Shepherd guided him on to the trusses. Mickey accelerated and surged over.

Yates ran back to the Jeep and climbed in as Wilson drove the second Land Rover across the makeshift bridge under Shepherd's guidance.

The wheelbase of the Jeep was slightly narrower but the metal trusses were wide enough to take account of the difference and Black drove over confidently. Shepherd climbed back into Mickey's Land Rover and all three vehicles powered across the field. The horses watched them go, then went back to chewing the grass.

'Just hope no one moves them,' said Shepherd. 'Then we'd look bloody stupid.'

'We'll be back in fifteen minutes,' said Mickey. 'And, according to the Professor, the farmer's daughter doesn't come to see the horses until she's finished school.'

The field sloped to the right and Mickey had to steer left to compensate. The ground got rougher and the Land Rover bounced up and down on its suspension. 'See what I mean? The cops would never be able to follow us across this,' said Mickey. 'Even if they could drive around the facility, which they can't. They're gonna arrive at the front door and sit there like a right load of plonkers. By the time they work out what's happened, we'll be miles down the motorway.' He slowed and drove around a copse of sycamores. 'Second ditch coming up,' he said.

As soon as Mickey braked, Shepherd had the door open. He ran to the other Land Rover. Mark was already getting out and the two men unfastened the second set of metal trusses and laid them one at a time over to the ditch. This time Mark crossed, adjusted the position of the trusses and beckoned them over. Shepherd got back into the Land Rover and slammed the door.

As they drove slowly over the ditch, Shepherd saw the wall of the money-storage depot for the first time. It ran the full length of the field and was close to twenty feet high. Beyond it he could see a pitched tiled roof with a clump of radio transmitters and a satellite dish in the centre. He took a deep breath, and tried to relax.

There were CCTVs at the corners of the building but they were aimed along the wall and not across the field.

'Here we go,' said Mickey, halting about two hundred

feet from the wall. The other Land Rover and the Jeep pulled up behind him. Mickey and Shepherd climbed out and went to the rear of the vehicle. Mickey pulled open the door and threw back the green tarpaulin that covered the four RPG launchers, the warheads and the booster packs.

The launchers were wrapped in sacking. Shepherd opened the warhead packs and took the four warheads out, laying them carefully on the floor of the vehicle. He took four booster charges and screwed them one by one into the sustainer charges on the warheads.

Mark was walking towards them, pulling on his ski mask. 'Everything okay?' he asked.

Shepherd inserted the first warhead unit into the launcher and handed it to Mickey. 'Hang on to that for me,' he said. He inserted the rest of the warheads into the three remaining launchers. He held one and left the other two on the floor of the Land Rover. 'Ready when you are,' he said to Mickey.

'Let's do it.'

Shepherd went down on one knee and looked through the sight, centring on the section of wall directly in front of him.

Mickey looked at his watch, noting the time. He glanced at Mark, who was adjusting the stopwatch on his wristwatch. As he turned back, Shepherd pulled the trigger. The booster charge fired and the warhead shot out of the launcher, leaving a plume of smoke behind it. A second later the sustainer charge kicked in. 'Six minutes from now!' shouted Mark.

Shepherd held out his hand for the launcher Mickey was holding as he watched the warhead smash into the wall and detonate. The noise was deafening and he felt the shock waves in his stomach. Three large concrete blocks disappeared and those above it were cracked. Shepherd put the second launcher on his shoulder, then took a quick look behind him to make sure no one was there. Satisfied that the area was clear, he squinted through the sight, aiming just below the hole made by the first warhead. He braced himself and pulled the trigger. He watched the warhead streak through the air and hit the wall. This time masonry flew into the air and there was a cloud of concrete dust. As the wind whipped the dust away he could see a gaping hole in the wall.

'One more for luck?' said Mickey, handing him a third launcher.

Shepherd took it. He checked over his shoulder that all was clear, sighted just above the hole he'd already made, and pulled the trigger.

As the third warhead streaked away, Black stamped on the accelerator and the Jeep surged forward across the field. Mark got back into the second Land Rover and he and Wilson followed Black.

The warhead slammed into the wall just above the hole and a dozen concrete blocks spilled to the ground in a cloud of dust. Shepherd stood up and pulled down his ski mask. The hole was now more than large enough for them to get through into the depository.

'Well done, mate,' said Mickey. 'Now let's not hang about. The cops will be here in just over five minutes.' He picked up the two discarded launchers, took them to the Land Rover and tossed them into the back. Shepherd did the same with the third launcher and slammed the door.

Black brought his Jeep to a halt at the edge of the

blind spot of the CCTVs covering the wall. He and
Yates jumped out holding their pickaxes and raced
towards the hole. The second Land Rover pulled up
alongside the Jeep. Mark and Wilson jumped out holding
wirecutters.

Shepherd and Mickey climbed into their vehicle and
Mickey switched on the engine. 'Yee-haa!' he shouted, and
put it in gear. Shepherd pulled the gun from under his
seat as the Land Rover lurched forward, wheels spinning
on the damp grass, and fitted it into his nylon sling so
that it nestled under his left armpit.

Black and Yates attacked the hole with their pickaxes.
What blocks remained in place had been loosened by the
three explosions and within seconds there was a space
almost big enough to drive a car through.

Mark and Wilson ran towards the hole. Black and Yates
stepped to the side to let them through, then dropped
their pickaxes, pulled out their guns and followed them
inside. It had been less than a minute since Shepherd had
fired the first warhead.

Mickey stopped next to Mark's vehicle and threw open
his door. From the other side of the wall they heard a
shotgun blast and Mickey cursed. 'What the hell?' he said.
He ran towards the hole and stepped over the broken
masonry. Shepherd followed him, pulling his weapon from
its sling.

They emerged through the hole into a storage area
the size of a basketball court, filled with mesh-sided trolleys full of cash. At the far end there was a wall of metal
bars with a door set into it. On the other side of the bars
two men in overalls were lying face down. Mark was
standing with his gun pointed through the bars and

screaming at them to stay on the floor. One had wet himself and urine was pooling at his groin. The other's hands were clasped behind his neck and was muttering what sounded like the Lord's Prayer. 'What the hell's going on?' shouted Mickey.

'Cleaners,' said Mark.

'Don't tell me you've killed them,' said Mickey.

'They're okay,' said Mark. 'They're as good as gold now, but I've told them what'll happen if they so much as look at us wrong.'

'But the cleaners only come in on Friday,' said Mickey.

'That's not the bloody point, is it?' shouted Mark. 'They're bloody well here now.'

'You sure they're not cops?'

Mark laughed. 'Do they look like bloody cops? One's pissed himself. They're just cleaners. The Professor screwed up.'

'Keep them covered,' said Mickey, putting away his gun. 'If they move, shoot them in the legs.'

Shepherd knew Mickey was bluffing. The cleaners were no threat – they had no weapons and wouldn't be able to identify them because they were all wearing masks.

Wilson had already cut the chains on four of the trolleys and pulled the doors open. He was reaching into one and pulling out plastic-wrapped parcels of twenty-pound notes, which he was handing to Yates. 'Come on,' said Mickey. 'We've got four and a half minutes to go.'

Shepherd put his gun in its sling, went to one of the opened trolleys and grabbed at packages of money. Each was the size of a briefcase. He took half a dozen and sprinted for the hole. Yates was already ahead of him. They ran to Mark's Land Rover, stacked the packages in the boot area and raced back to the hole. They passed Mickey who had eight packs in his arms. Wilson appeared at the hole with an armful. He gave it to Shepherd, who ran back to the vehicles. His arms were hurting and his chest was burning. He was used to running in boots with a rucksack full of bricks, but the weight in his arms was straining a whole new set of muscles. Sweat was pouring down his face under the ski mask, but he ignored the discomfort. He passed Mickey again and the two men grunted at each other.

Shepherd dropped the packages on top of the previous batch, then sprinted back to the hole. Black and Wilson ran out carrying money and Shepherd ducked through the wall as Mickey was coming out. Mark was still covering the two cleaners with his gun.

As Shepherd ran to one of the trolleys he looked up to see a battery of CCTV cameras covering the whole money-storage area. 'The cleaners can't do anything, mate!' he shouted to Mark. 'And they already know we're in. You might as well leave them and help us with the cash.' He grabbed at packages containing ten pound notes.

Mark looked over his shoulder, then up at the CCTV cameras. 'Yeah, you're right,' he said. He ran to one of the trolleys, put his shotgun in its sling and picked up some packages. The two cleaners stayed where they were, faces down, too terrified to move.

Shepherd clutched seven packages to his chest and ran to the hole. Yates was about to come through but he stepped to the side to allow Shepherd through first.

He clapped Shepherd on the back as he went by. 'Well done, mate.'

'Three minutes to go!' shouted Mickey, as he passed Shepherd.

Shepherd ran to Mickey's car and put the money on top of the unfired RPG. His lungs were burning and his clothes were soaked with sweat beneath the boiler-suit.

Mark appeared at the hole with a bundle and ran towards the vehicles, while Black and Wilson followed Shepherd back into the storage area. One of the cleaners was getting up. Wilson swung up his gun and screamed at the man to stay down.

Shepherd grabbed more packages and ran for the hole, closely followed by Black.

They passed Mickey who was tearing back to the building, panting. 'Bloody hell, we're earning our money today,' he gasped.

The back of Mickey's Land Rover was packed with cash and he had pulled the tarpaulin over it. Shepherd took his load to the Jeep and stacked it in the back. As he jogged across the field, Mickey yelled they had two minutes to go. Time for two more trips, so long as they kept up the pace.

Shepherd collected another pile of packages, then raced neck and neck with Black to the Jeep. They threw in the money and dashed back to the depot. Mark thrust five packages of cash into Shepherd's hands, all fifty-pound notes. Shepherd ran back to the Jeep, threw his burden into the back and stepped aside for Black to do the same. He pulled the tarpaulin over the money as Black climbed into the driving seat, than ran to Mickey's Land Rover. Mickey was loading cash into the rear of Mark's. 'Everyone out?' Mickey shouted at Shepherd. He glanced at his wristwatch. 'Time's up.'

Shepherd did a quick headcount. Black and Yates were in the Jeep, Mark was running towards Mickey with an armful of money, Wilson just behind him. 'All clear,' shouted Shepherd.

Mickey and Shepherd ran to their vehicle and climbed in. Mickey started the engine a fraction of a second after Mark, and the two Land Rovers pulled tight turns and raced back towards the ditch. The Jeep followed, blue smoke belching from its exhaust. As they reached the middle of the field the horses centered away, heads tossing, tails down.

Mickey pulled off his ski mask and grinned. 'See?' he said. 'Perfect.' He beat on the steering-wheel with his gloved hands.

Shepherd took off his ski mask and wiped the sweat from his forehead with the sleeve of his boiler-suit. He felt his mobile phone in his pocket and tried to quell the guilt in the pit of his stomach.

Chaudhry was driving the removal van and Kundi was in the passenger seat. A hundred yards ahead Bradshaw was in the Ford Mondeo, and fifty yards behind Talwar and al-Sayed were in the Volvo. The three vehicles were driving in the inside lane at just under the speed limit. Chaudhry was used to driving delivery vans but this one was far bigger than anything he'd had before. It was nothing more than a large rectangular box on wheels but it was difficult to turn, requiring constant touches on the wheel to keep it in a straight line when there was even the merest hint of a cross-wind.

'Are you okay?' asked Kundi.

'I'm fine, brother,' said Chaudhry.

'Scared?'

Chaudhry flashed him a tight smile. 'Nervous,' he said, 'but not scared. What we are doing we do for Allah, so He will protect us.'

Ahead, in the sky, an airliner was descending towards Heathrow.

Mickey slowed the Land Rover to just over thirty miles an hour and squinted at the GPS. 'Give Mark a call and tell him to catch up. We're almost there,' said Mickey.

Shepherd fished out his mobile, tapped in Mark's number and relayed the message. Two minutes later the Land Rover appeared behind them, with the Jeep a hundred yards or so back.

Mickey indicated left and the three vehicles turned into the industrial estate. 'That's the one,' said Mickey, pointing at a unit with a sign on it saying, 'Advanced Electrical Suppliers'. Parked outside was a Series Seven BMW and a white Transit van in which two young Asian men were sitting. 'And there's Pinky's motor.'

'Pinky?' said Shepherd.

'Pinky Patel, our laundryman.'

Shepherd filed the name. It was the first time Mickey had identified the man who would be cleaning their money and putting it into the banking system.

Mickey brought the Land Rover to a halt. 'Bang on the door, mate, let him know we're here.'

Shepherd climbed out and jogged to the main entrance. There was an intercom and he pressed the button. After a few seconds the electric door rattled open. Mickey drove in, followed by Mark. As Shepherd followed, Yates and Black arrived in their Jeep. The gate closed behind them.

Pinky Patel was a big man in a grey suit that flapped around his legs as he walked. His head was almost perfectly round and his mahogany-brown skin was baby-smooth, but his hair was thinning and he had a comb-over, held in place with lashings of hair gel. His moustache, though, was luxuriant. He grinned as Mickey climbed out of his vehicle and walked over to him with his arms outstretched. 'Mickey, Mickey, Mickey,' he said. 'My favourite customer.'

'Pinky, you sweet-talking sod,' said Mickey, 'I bet you say that to all the blaggers.'

The two men hugged. 'Everything went well, I assume,' said Pinky.

'As always,' said Mickey. He released Pinky and introduced Shepherd. 'This is Ricky, our new recruit.'

Pinky shook hands with him. He had a large opal ring on his little finger, which bit into Shepherd's hand. 'You have joined a very successful operation, Ricky,' he said.

'Just take good care of my share and I'll be happy,' Shepherd replied.

Mickey grinned at Pinky. 'He's a bit suspicious,' he said.

'It's a lot of money,' Shepherd said to Pinky, 'and I don't know you.'

Pinky grinned good-naturedly. 'I would not risk betraying your trust or Mickey's,' he said. He gestured at his enormous waistline. 'I am a big target, if ever anyone should decide to shoot me.'

Mark slapped the Indian on the back. 'We'd never shoot

you, Pinky,' he said. 'Not with a gun, anyway. A harpoon's the only thing that'd bring you down.'

Pinky roared with laughter.

Yates and Black were unloading the money from the back of their Jeep and piling it on the table. 'These are all twenties,' said Yates. 'Each pack is a hundred grand.' He dropped ten of the plastic-wrapped packages on the table. A million pounds. Black put a similar pile next to it.

'We've got tens and fives,' said Mark. 'Plus a few packs of fifties.'

Wilson held up a plastic pack of fifty-pound notes. 'Got to love the fifties,' he said.

'Sooner we join the euro, the better,' said Mark. 'That five-hundred-euro note has got to be a robber's dream. You'll be able to shove enough in your back pocket to buy a Ferrari.'

Patel went to the table to inspect the money. 'Mickey, what happens to the stuff we leave behind?' asked Shepherd. 'The stuff in the warehouse we stayed in last night, the Land Rovers, the gear we were wearing?'

'All part of the Professor's package,' said Mickey. 'As soon as we're out of the country, he sends in a clean-up crew.' He took a cigar out of his case and lit it. 'They don't know us. All they know is that they're cleaning up. Even if they talk, they know nothing.'

Shepherd's phone vibrated. He took it out and looked at the screen. It was the Major. Shepherd walked away and pressed the green button to take the call. 'Both phones are on, and they're close to Heathrow,' said the Major. 'They're to the east of the airfield, which is where landing traffic approaches from. Near Boston Manor, close to the M4.'

'They're active,' said Shepherd, flatly.

'I've asked for a chopper from 27 Squadron at RAF Odiham and they're ten minutes from the Knightsbridge barracks,' said the Major. 'As soon as it gets here I'll send a troop out.'

'Have you told the locals?'

'I don't want to muddy the waters,' said the Major. 'Where are you?'

'Not far from Heathrow,' said Shepherd.

'Can you get there?'

'Looks like I'll have to,' said Shepherd. He ended the call and walked over to the Land Rover he'd been riding in. He reached under the passenger seat and pulled out his sawn-off shotgun.

Mickey and Mark were talking to Patel and didn't look around as Shepherd walked up. He cocked the shotgun and pointed it at Mickey's head. 'Sorry, mate,' he said. 'Change of plan.'

Bradshaw adjusted the binoculars to focus on the third plane in the queue to land. It had the livery of BMI and it was a small airliner, probably a commuter plane coming in from Manchester or Glasgow. Bradshaw spoke into his mobile. 'No targets on approach yet,' he said. He knew exactly what he wanted. He wanted a British Airways plane and he wanted it to be a Boeing 747. That would be worth waiting for. From where he was sitting he could see the removals van parked in the lay-by, underneath the flight path. He could see al-Sayed in the passenger seat, staring fixedly ahead. The vehicle didn't look out of place. The hole in the roof couldn't be seen from the road and there were no houses nearby overlooking it. Anyone driving past would assume that the men inside were taking a break. Only at the last moment would the tailgate come down and the missile be fired.

Mickey stared in disbelief at the shotgun in Shepherd's hands. 'Don't piss around, Ricky. Didn't your mum never tell you not to point guns at people?'

'I need the keys to the Land Rover, Mickey,' said Shepherd, keeping the shotgun levelled at Mickey's face.

Mickey's frown deepened. 'What the hell's going on?'

'Give me the keys!' bellowed Shepherd.

Pinky Patel backed away, his hands in front of his face, muttering to himself. Yates and Black looked over from the table where they had been counting the money. 'What's going on, Mickey?' shouted Yates.

'I don't have the time for this,' said Shepherd. 'Give me the keys.'

He heard the click of a gun being cocked behind him. 'Put down the gun, Ricky,' said Mark.

Shepherd moved quickly, stepping to the side. Mark was about twenty feet away, standing next to the Jeep. 'Stay where you are, Mark,' said Shepherd. 'Just let me get out of here and no one gets hurt.'

'Put down your gun or I'll shoot you,' said Mark.

'Yeah – well, from where you're standing you'll hurt me, but I'm so close to your brother that there'll be nothing left of his head. So you're the one who's going to have to drop his gun.'

'Ricky, what the hell's going on?' said Mickey. 'Are you ripping us off?' He sounded more irritated than afraid.

'I need the Land Rover, that's all.'

Mickey reached slowly into his pocket and took out the ignition keys. He held them out. When Shepherd tried to take them, he snatched them away and held them tight in his fist. 'You're not going to shoot me, Ricky. It's not in your nature.'

Shepherd pointed the shotgun at the ceiling and pulled the trigger. Bits of tile crashed to the floor and a fluorescent light fitting shattered. Glass and metal tinkled around them. Shepherd pumped the gun to reload and pointed it at Mickey again. 'Give me the keys,' he said. He turned to Mark. 'You take one step closer to me and I'll do your legs.'

'Why do you want the Land Rover?' asked Mickey.

'Give me the keys!' shouted Shepherd. He jammed the barrel of the shotgun under Mickey's chin.

Mickey smiled tightly and tossed the keys to his brother. Mark caught them with his left hand, keeping the shotgun steady with the right.

Shepherd kept the shotgun barrel pressed against Mickey's throat. He looked at Mark. 'Give me the keys or I'll pull the trigger, I swear.'

'He won't, Mark,' said Mickey. 'He's not going to do a damn thing.'

Shepherd's finger tightened on the trigger.

Yates walked up to Mark and stood behind him. 'Come on, Ricky, relax. Just tell us what's wrong.'

'I want the Land Rover. Now, give me the keys!' Mark grinned and put them in his pocket. Shepherd's heart was pounding, but he knew that screaming at the men wasn't going to do any good. They were armed robbers, they were used to loaded weapons and violence and the only way he could prove he was serious was by pulling the trigger.

'There's five of us here, mate, six if you include Pinky,' said Black.

The Indian threw up his hands. 'Don't involve me in this!' he protested. 'This is nothing to do with me.' He backed away and crouched behind the Jeep.

'Will you all calm down?' said Mickey. 'Nothing's going to happen.'

'Give me the keys!' Shepherd hissed at Mark.

'There's five of us, and how many shells in the shotgun?' said Yates.

'You can't shoot us all, mate,' said Wilson, lining up next to Yates. He was also holding a shotgun levelled at Shepherd's chest.

'He's not going to shoot anybody,' said Mickey, quietly. 'If he was going to shoot me he'd already have done it. He's talking tough but he knows he can't do it.' He grinned at Shepherd. 'Ain't that right, mate?'

'Mickey . . .' said Shepherd.

'Prove me wrong,' said Mickey. 'Pull the trigger, because if you don't Mark's going to walk over, take that gun off you and shove it up your arse.'

'Don't do this, Mickey,' said Shepherd.

'Take the gun off him, Mark,' said Mickey, as he stared intently at Shepherd. Mark walked slowly towards him, keeping his gun trained on Shepherd's face. Shepherd in turn kept his shotgun pressed to Mickey's throat. Mickey continued to grin as Mark got closer. 'You can't do it, can you?' said Mickey.

Shepherd gritted his teeth. Mickey was right. No matter what the provocation, no matter how high the stakes, he couldn't shoot an unarmed man.

'It's over, mate,' said Mickey. Mark placed the barrel

of his shotgun against the side of Shepherd's head. His finger whitened as it tightened on the trigger. 'Put your gun down,' said Mickey. 'Because my brother isn't as soft as you. You can trust me on that.'

Shepherd cursed and took the shotgun away from Mickey's throat.

'You slag!' shouted Mark, and he slammed the butt of his shotgun against Shepherd's jaw.

Bradshaw focused on the third plane in the landing sequence. It was a Boeing 747 but sporting the livery of one of the American airlines. As much as he hated the Americans, he wanted to bring down a British jet. He wanted to hurt his country. There would be time enough later to turn his hatred on American targets. Two miles behind the 747 a fourth plane was just a small black dot against the blue of the sky. And behind that, not yet visible even through his binoculars, was a fifth, and a sixth. Heathrow was one of the busiest airports in the world. It was only a matter of time before the perfect target came into view.

Mark kicked away Shepherd's shotgun and it spun as it clattered across the concrete. 'You slag, pull a gun on my brother, would you?' he said, aiming his gun at Shepherd's legs.

Shepherd rolled onto his back and sat up. The blow had stunned him but nothing was broken. He stared up at Mark. 'Like Mickey said, I couldn't pull the trigger.'

'Yeah, and like he said, I bloody well can.'

'Hold your horses,' said Mickey, taking control. 'Pinky, get the bloody hell up off the ground, will you?'

The Indian appeared from behind the Jeep, wiping dust from the knees of his suit.

'Chopper, Davie, have a quick look outside,' said Mickey. 'Anything untoward and we might have to go out guns blazing.'

Yates and Black jogged to the entrance and disappeared outside.

'I'm going to blow his bloody legs off,' said Mark. 'Trying to steal from us, the thieving slag.'

'I wasn't after your money,' said Shepherd, getting unsteadily to his feet.

'One thing at a time,' Mickey said to his brother. 'Let's get the money sorted first.'

Yates and Black came back inside. 'Looks kosher,' said Black.

'Right, change of plan. Pinky, can we move the cash to your office now?'

Patel pulled a large red handkerchief from his trouser pocket. 'It's not a problem, Mickey. My boys were going to collect it here but I can tell them to meet me at the office.'

'I want the cash out of here now. We'll put what we can into your Beamer. Get your motor in here. As soon as the cash is loaded, off you go.'

Patel hurried outside, wiping his forehead with his handkerchief.

'Barry, you help Chopper and Davie.'

'It won't all fit in the Beamer,' said Yates.

'What's left over you leave in the Jeep and take to Pinky's place. Then you get the hell out of Dodge. We don't know how secure we are here. It could all go tits up at any moment.'

'Mickey, we've got to talk,' said Shepherd.

'We've got nothing to say to you, slag!' shouted Mark.

'Leave it, Mark,' said Mickey. 'We safeguard the cash, then find out what the hell's going on.'

They heard Pinky start up the BMW. A few seconds later the car edged inside the industrial unit and parked next to the Land Rover. Pinky opened the boot and Yates, Black and Wilson piled in the cash.

Shepherd took a deep breath. 'Listen to me, Mickey. This is just about the most important conversation you're ever going to have in your whole life and you have to believe that everything I'm about to tell you is the truth.'

Mark stepped forward and raised the butt of his shotgun. Shepherd flinched and raised his arm to block the blow. Mark swung the gun down and tightened his finger on the trigger. 'Shut the fuck up, slag!'

'Just let me talk,' said Shepherd.

Mark handed the gun to his brother. 'I don't need that to sort this slag out,' he said.

'Leave it, Mark. There'll be time for that later,' said Mickey, but Mark ignored him.

'I'll talk to you,' Mark said to Shepherd. 'I'll talk you into the middle of next week.' He threw a punch that Shepherd just managed to block, pushing Mark's arm to the side with the flat of his hand. Mark's knee came up and slammed into his gut. Shepherd staggered back, winded.

Mark pressed forward, punching with both fists. Shepherd threw up his hands, trying to ward off the blows, but Mark hit him twice in the chest. Shepherd lashed out with his foot but Mark hooked the leg with his left hand and twisted it so that Shepherd fell to the ground. Mark kicked him in the ribs and Shepherd rolled to the side, then struggled to his feet.

'Mark, just listen to me, will you?'

Mark shuffled on the spot and kicked out with his right leg, twisting into a roundhouse kick at the last minute that caught Shepherd on the side of the head and sent him crashing to the ground again.

Yates, Wilson and Black finished loading the money into the BMW and slammed the boot. Patel beeped his horn and drove out of the building as the three men put the rest of the cash into the back of the Jeep.

Shepherd got to his feet and wiped his mouth with the back of his hand – his lip was bleeding. Mark bounced up and down on the balls of his feet, grinning triumphantly.

'We're done, Mickey,' said Yates.

'Off you go,' said Mickey. 'Drop the cash at Pinky's. I'll call you, let you know what's happening.'

Yates gestured at Shepherd. 'What about him?'

'We'll take care of him,' said Mark.

Yates, Black and Wilson piled into the Jeep and drove off. Mickey cradled the shotgun as he faced Shepherd.

'Mickey, we need to talk,' said Shepherd.

Mark scowled, then moved towards Shepherd, throwing two punches to his face before kicking him in the chest. Shepherd was already moving backwards, which lessened the damage but the blows still hurt.

Shepherd glared at him and wiped his mouth again. Mark was grinning as he wove from side to side, faking punches and making snorting sounds. 'All right, big man,' said Shepherd. He straightened up, flexing his fingers.

Mark had his hands held high in front of his face, Muay

Thai-style, and shuffled forward on the balls of his feet. Shepherd knew that Mark was the better kickboxer, no question of that, but they weren't in the ring now and Shepherd was no longer constrained by the rules of the martial art.

'Come on, big man,' said Shepherd, calmly. 'Give it your best shot.'

Mark moved forward, fists flailing. Shepherd kept his hands at chest level, fingers slightly curved, then his left arm went up to block a punch and he hit the inside of Mark's arm hard. With his right hand he grabbed Mark's wrist, then dropped down, pulling the arm with him. He slammed his left hand down on Mark's elbow, locking the arm in place, and as Mark lost his balance, he crouched low, keeping the arm locked. Mark fell to the ground cursing and Shepherd released his grip. Mark rolled onto his back but Shepherd was quicker and dropped on top of him, trapping Mark's arms with his legs. Shepherd's right hand flashed up, his fingers curled into talons, and he raked them down towards Mark's eyes. Mark saw the blow coming and screamed in panic, knowing he was defenceless and that the fingers were going to gouge into his eye sockets. Shepherd pulled the attack, freezing his hand just inches from Mark's face. Mark had gone white, and Shepherd could feel him trembling. 'Are you happy now?' he snarled.

Mark was gasping for breath as he stared up at Shepherd.

'I could have blinded you, Mark. Or just as easily killed you.'

'But you didn't,' said Mickey, pressing the barrel of his shotgun against the side of Shepherd's head.

Shepherd reacted instinctively, his right arm shot up,

knocking the shotgun away. Then he jumped to his feet and grabbed for Mickey's throat with his left hand. He twisted the shotgun from Mickey's grasp and kicked him in the stomach, sending him hurtling back against the bonnet of the Land Rover. Then he stepped to the side so that he could cover both brothers with the shotgun. 'Will you two just listen to me?' he said. 'I need the Land Rover. That's all.'

'What are you playing at, Ricky?' said Mickey, rubbing his throat. Mark got to his feet, still shaken by Shepherd's attack.

'A group of terrorists is about to shoot down a plane at Heathrow. At the moment I'm probably the only person who can stop them.' He gestured at Mark with the shotgun. 'Now give me the keys.'

'How do you know?' asked Mickey.

'We don't have time for this,' said Shepherd. 'Just give me the bloody keys and I'm out of here.'

'Why aren't the cops after these terrorists?' asked Mickey.

'There isn't time,' said Shepherd. 'And the cops aren't geared up for dealing with terrorists with surface-to-air missiles.'

'This is connected with Kleintank, isn't it?' said Mickey. 'The Dutchman and his bloody missiles.'

'I don't have time to explain,' said Shepherd. 'People are going to die if I don't do something. A lot of people.'

'Give me the keys, Mark,' said Mickey.

'You don't believe this shit, do you?' said Mark.

'Just give me the keys.'

Mark fished them from his pocket and tossed them to his brother. Mickey caught them one-handed.

'Mickey, we don't have time for this.'

'What are you going do, mate? Shoot me? We've already established that ain't gonna happen.'

'You've got your money, your lads are away. All I want is the bloody vehicle.'

'And with that you're gonna stop the terrorists?'

'I'm going to try.'

'And you're not bullshitting? They're planning to shoot down a plane?'

'God's honest truth, Mickey.'

Mickey nodded slowly. 'I believe you,' he said. He looked at his brother. 'I'm going with him. You check that the guys are okay, make sure Pinky gets the cash sorted.' He headed for the Land Rover.

'You're bloody mad,' Mark shouted after him.

'Maybe,' said Mickey. 'But he could have killed you then, with his bare hands. I saw it in his eyes. But he didn't. He's one of the good guys, Mark, and if there are bastards about to shoot down a plane, I'm up for stopping them.'

'Mickey, you don't have to,' said Shepherd.

'Get in the bloody car before I change my mind,' said Mickey. He climbed into the Land Rover and slammed the door. Mark shook his head, bewildered, as he watched Shepherd walk to the vehicle and climb into the front passenger seat where he cradled the shotgun on his lap.

Mickey switched on the engine. 'Where to?' he asked Shepherd.

'Just head for the airport,' said Shepherd. 'And put your foot down.'

★   ★   ★

Bradshaw looked through the binoculars at the third plane on the approach to the runway. His heart raced as he saw the bulbous nose and four massive engines of a Boeing 747 with the red, white and blue British Airways livery on the tail. 'Potential target sighted,' he said into his mobile. 'Just over five minutes away. Get ready.'

'Affirmative,' said Chaudhry, at the other end of the line.

'It's a jumbo jet,' said Bradshaw. 'Just what we need.' He put down the phone and picked up the video camera that had been lying on the front passenger seat. He switched it on and focused on the removals van, then pressed pause and put the camera back on the seat. The video of the downing of the British Airways jet would become one of the most-watched terrorist incidents of all time, he would make sure of that.

The Land Rover hurtled down the outside lane of the M4. The vehicle was built for crossing rough terrain, not for speeding along at ninety miles an hour, and Mickey had to keep a tight grip on the steering-wheel. A white Saab was blocking his way and Mickey pounded on the horn until it moved over.

Shepherd called the Major. 'I'm on my way,' he said.

'The helicopter's not here yet,' said the Major. 'Soon as it leaves, I'll tell you.'

'Where do I go?' asked Shepherd.

'Near as the GCHQ guy can tell, it's Boston Manor, near to Boston Manor Park. You'll have to take junction two off the M4. They're somewhere near the junction between Boston Manor Road and the Great Western Road.'

Shepherd scrolled through the GPS unit on the dashboard with his left hand.

'And, Spider, he's tapped into the phone. One of the guys is calling in the planes as he sees them. He's got a British Airways 747 in his sights.'

'I'll call you back, boss,' said Shepherd, ending the call. He patted Mickey's shoulder. 'We've got to go faster,' he said.

Bradshaw lost sight of the commuter plane as it descended below the terminal buildings. The jumbo jet was now second in line for landing. 'Target is four minutes from you,' he said into the phone. He heard Chaudhry repeat the time, his voice slightly muffled by the chewing-gum in his mouth. Bradshaw felt light-headed and fought to keep his breathing steady. His adrenal glands were in overdrive and his heartbeat pounded in his ears. Four more minutes. Two hundred and forty seconds. No time at all. But for the people in the plane coming in to land, it was all the time they had left to live.

Shepherd's mobile rang. 'The helicopter's just left with a counter-terrorist troop on board,' the Major said. 'At full speed they're ten minutes away. Spider, they might be too late. Where are you?'

'Coming up to junction two now,' said Shepherd. 'I don't know how long it's going to take to drive through Brentford.'

'The spotter just called four minutes, Spider. That's all the time you have.'

'Roger that,' said Shepherd, and cut the connection.

★   ★   ★

Kundi kept the launch tube pointing at the sky. The Stinger was heavy but he barely felt the weight on his shoulder. He swallowed and blinked. In the sky overhead he saw a bird of prey, a kestrel, hovering. The bird flapped its wings, looking downward, waiting to kill. Kundi felt he was like the kestrel, poised to attack. But unlike the bird he wasn't killing by instinct or for food. He was killing for Allah, and there was no nobler cause.

He heard the phone buzz in Chaudhry's ear.

'Target sighted, two minutes,' said Chaudhry. He turned to Kundi. 'Are you okay, brother?'

Kundi didn't reply. His whole being was focused on the patch of clear blue sky directly above his head.

'They're going to shoot down a 747 in less than four minutes,' said Shepherd. 'Can we get there by then?'

'Not if we leave the motorway,' said Mickey. 'We'll slow to a crawl once we're driving through Brentford.'

Shepherd leaned forward to get a closer look at the GPS. 'We're coming up to junction two now,' said Mickey. 'What do you want to do?'

'Stay on the motorway,' said Shepherd. 'Can we go any faster?'

'My foot's on the floor, mate,' said Mickey.

The jumbo jet was so close now that Bradshaw felt as if he could reach out and touch it. Its flaps were down and its nose had gone up as it prepared for its final approach. He put the mobile phone to his mouth. 'Ninety seconds,' he said.

The motorway curved to the right. Shepherd looked to the left, but he didn't know what he was looking for. Were they on a hill? Were they in a field? Or had they sought cover in a wood or a building? He opened the window and stuck his head out. The wind made his eyes water as he twisted his head to squint up at the sky. Behind them there was a 747 in the livery of British Airways, the red, white and blue wavy lines across its tail. It was to the left of the motorway, on its final approach.

'Is that it?' asked Mickey, shouting to make himself heard over the noise of the slipstream. 'Is that the plane?'

'I think so,' said Shepherd.

Time had slowed to a crawl. Kundi couldn't remember the last time he had taken a breath. The kestrel had gone. The sky overhead was clear except for a few wispy clouds high overhead. It was as if all his senses had gone into overdrive. He could smell Chaudhry's sandalwood aftershave. He could hear the engines of the approaching plane and he could feel the vibrations through the floor of the van. He felt as if he was one with the Stinger missile on his shoulder, as if it had somehow become an extension of himself. He heard Bradshaw on the phone. 'Sixty seconds.'

'Sixty seconds,' repeated Chaudhry. He twisted around and shouted to Talwar and al-Sayed, 'Lower the tailgate!'

Kundi stared fixedly at the sky. Outside he heard Talwar and al-Sayed fumble with the bolts.

'Mickey, pull over,' shouted Shepherd. 'Get onto the hard shoulder.'

Mickey flipped the turn indicator and swerved across the three lanes of the motorway.

Shepherd pulled his head back and looked at the

GPS unit. They were directly opposite the park. 'Stop here – they're around here somewhere,' he said.

Mickey pulled up and switched on his hazard indicators. Shepherd threw open the door and rushed over to the grass verge. In the distance he could see a furniture van parked in a lay-by. He shaded his eyes against the sun with a hand and scanned the area, still not sure what he was looking for. Mickey was at his shoulder. 'This had better not be a wild-goose chase, mate,' he said.

Shepherd looked at the fast-approaching airliner. He tried to work out its route in relation to the ground. He pointed at the furniture van. 'That's got to be it,' he said.

Kundi heard the tailgate rattle down behind him. 'Thirty seconds,' said Chaudhry. He moved to the side, and Kundi flicked his thumb across the safety switch. 'Safety off,' he said.

'Twenty seconds,' said Chaudhry.

Time had virtually stopped. Kundi could hear the roar of the approaching jet and the vibrations rattled the sides of the van.

'Ten seconds,' said Chaudhry.

Kundi began to count on autopilot, barely aware that Chaudhry was counting with him. 'Nine, eight, seven, six, five, four, three, two, one . . .'

'Acquisition tone on,' said Kundi. 'Listening for the steady tone. Steady tone achieved.' He pressed the uncaging switch with his left hand. The beeping was replaced by a steady tone, the signal that the IR targeting system had locked onto the plane. 'Confirm steady tone,' he said, as his finger tightened on the trigger. '*Allahu akbar.*'

★　　★　　★

Mickey's jaw dropped as the two Asians pulled down the tailgate to reveal what was inside the furniture van. 'Would you look at that?' he shouted. 'What the hell is it?'

'A Stinger missile,' said Shepherd, calmly. They were just over two hundred yards from the removals van but could clearly see the Asian man holding the missile launcher and pointing it up at the roof.

Shepherd dashed to the back of the Land Rover, pulled open the rear door and grabbed the last remaining RPG launcher from under the tarpaulin. Mickey was talking again, asking questions, but Shepherd ignored him. His heart was pounding – he had only seconds to act. He seized the warhead, slotted it into the launcher, then turned and dropped onto one knee in a smooth motion. He focused on the van, levelled the launcher, took a breath and pulled the trigger. The warhead streaked away and the sustainer motor kicked in, leaving a white trail behind. It seemed to cut through the air in slow motion and Shepherd felt his world collapse to the point at which his whole being was concentrated on the warhead and its target.

The 747's engines were screaming and Mickey was shouting something. Then the warhead slammed into the back of the removals van and it erupted in a ball of flame.

The video camera in Bradshaw's hand continued to record but he was no longer looking through the viewfinder. He stared at the 747 as it continued on its approach to the runway. He had no idea what had happened. He had been concentrating on the roof of the van, not wanting to miss the moment when the missile streaked towards the plane, but the vehicle had exploded. It was as if the jumbo jet had caused it to blow up, but Bradshaw knew that was impossible. A cloud of black smoke curled up from the wreckage and was whipped away by the turbulence in the wake of the descending jet. Bradshaw sat in the car, trying to collect his thoughts. His hands were shaking. He forced himself to breathe. He had no idea what had happened but he knew he had to get away from the area. He put the video camera on the passenger seat, turned on the engine and drove off.

Shepherd stood up and dropped the launch unit. The base of the removals van was still burning, though the rest of the vehicle was in a thousand pieces, scattered across the road. There were body parts among the wreckage: a head had rolled against the pavement, an arm was lying in the gutter, the hand clenched into a fist.

'What the hell just happened?' asked Mickey.

'We saved four hundred lives, give or take,' said Shepherd, 'and now you've got to get out of here. There's an SAS helicopter on the way.'

'Who are you?'

'You don't want to know,' said Shepherd. 'You have to go.'

'Are you a cop?'

'No.' That much was true. He worked for SOCA and that meant he was a civil servant, not a police officer.

'Then who the hell are you? James Bond?'

Shepherd laughed. 'No, I'm not James Bond.'

'But you're not Ricky Knight. And you're not John Westlake.'

'It doesn't matter who I am or who I work for. Mickey, you have to go.'

'What's your real name? You can tell me that much.'

'Dan,' said Shepherd.

'Well, fuck you, Dan. Are we screwed?'

'Define screwed.'

'Are CO19 cops gonna be coming around the corner in the next few minutes?'

'If they are, it's not down to me. But the SAS are on their way.'

'The money? The money's dodgy?'

'It's fine, so far as I know. They were letting you run to see where you took it.'

'They know about Pinky?'

'Not yet.'

'No tracking, no bugs?'

Shepherd shook his head. 'They're tracking my phone. That's all.'

'They?'

'You have to go, Mickey.'

'How long have we got?'

'I don't know,' Shepherd said. 'But after what just happened I think all flights into and out of the UK are going to be grounded for a while. They're expecting you to go to Holyhead for the ferry so if I were you I'd get to St Pancras and onto the first Eurostar to Paris.'

'And if we get back to Thailand?'

'Nothing's changed,' said Shepherd. 'You're as safe there now as you were before.'

Mickey nodded. 'You're a bastard,' he said, but there was no venom in his voice.

'I know,' said Shepherd. 'It's what I do.'

Mickey stuck out his hand. Shepherd shook it. Mickey's

grip was firm and dry and he looked Shepherd in the eye. 'Thanks,' he said.

Shepherd didn't know what to say. He wasn't even sure what Mickey was thanking him for.

'What do you want doing with your share?' Mickey asked.

For a moment Shepherd thought he was serious, but then Mickey released his hand, made a gun with it, pointed it at Shepherd's face and mimicked the popping sound of a silenced automatic. 'Got you,' he said. He winked and got back into the Land Rover.

As it sped off, Shepherd gazed at the still-burning debris, which was all that remained of the van. 'That went well, all things considered,' he muttered to himself.

In the distance he heard the whoop-whoop of a helicopter's rotor. He stood where he was, his hands outstretched to the side to show that he wasn't a threat, and waited for the SAS to arrive.

'You did what?' There was disbelief on Charlotte Button's face. They were sitting in the office where it had all begun less than two weeks earlier. Shepherd had brought a cup of Starbucks tea with him but it sat untouched on her desk.

Shepherd knew the question was rhetorical, so he didn't reply.

'Where are they?'

'I don't know.'

'You just let them drive away?'

'What do you want me to say, Charlie? That I was outmanned? That I was outgunned? That I closed my eyes and counted to ten and when I opened them they'd gone?'

'What I want, Spider, is the truth.'

'Mickey Moore helped me take out a terrorist cell. That's the truth.'

'His gang stole twelve million pounds,' said Button, flatly.

'Exactly. Money. They stole money. Pieces of paper. We saved four hundred lives, Charlie. Four hundred souls.'

'That's no reason to give five hardened criminals a get-out-of-jail-free card. And you let them get away with the money.'

'There'll be other chances to catch them.'

'Like hell there will. We've got enough now. Your evidence alone will put them away.'

Shepherd folded his arms. 'They helped me, Charlie. Because of what they did, and what they didn't do, four hundred people are alive this morning who should have died.'

'The company they raided won't see it that way. And I don't think my bosses will, either.'

'Then screw them,' said Shepherd. 'Four hundred lives against twelve million quid. That equates to thirty thousand pounds a life, Charlie. Thirty lousy thousand.'

Button's eyes hardened. 'This isn't about money.' She threw up her hands. 'What the hell am I going to do with you?'

'If sacking me helps, then sack me. But I'm not going to give evidence against the Moores after what Mickey did yesterday. Hell, we should be giving him a medal.'

'And the terrorist cell. How did you know about them?'

'I can't say.'

'You mean you won't say.'

'I mean I can't. I gave my word.'

'I sense the hand of Richard Yokely in this.' She stared at him with unblinking eyes.

Shepherd sat back in his chair. 'You know, if you play your cards right on this it could make us all look good. We took out a group who were going to blow up a jumbo jet. We saved the day. Spin it the right way and all the agencies come out covered in glory.'

'How, exactly?'

'You say that the intel came from an MI5 informer. I was nearby on another case. You made the decision for me to intervene and thank God you did. I'm sure your friends in Five will back you up. Because if they don't, they're going to have to explain how a group of home-grown terrorists got hold of a surface-to-air missile and came within seconds of using it. If that gets out, nobody looks good.'

'The media won't buy it.'

'The media doesn't have to. I assume there'll be a blackout on what happened anyway. No one's going to want to admit what really happened so your masters are going to be spinning it. Car accident, maybe, or a freak fuel-tank explosion. No one saw the RPG hit them and, so far as I could see, all that was left was debris. Come on, Charlie, there was nothing about it in this morning's papers or on TV. The whole thing's already been tidied away, right?'

'That's not the point.'

'It's absolutely the point. The Government can't afford to admit what happened so there'll be a whitewash. All I'm saying is that a little bit of that whitewash needs to spread the way of the Moore brothers. There'll be another time to get them, down the line. I don't see them retiring in the near future.'

'So now you're setting yourself up as judge and jury? Is that it?'

'I'm not judging them. I know they're villains and they deserve to go down for their villainy. But what Mickey did yesterday has to count for something. The system is now so flawed that it can't cut them any slack, but I can. That's all I'm doing, Charlie. I'm cutting them some slack.'

'And what do I tell the company they stole from?'

Shepherd smiled. 'Tell them to build a bigger wall.' He picked up his coffee and took a sip. 'Are we done?'

'You seem to be treating this like some sort of a joke,' she said. 'You could go to prison for what you're doing.'

'I doubt it,' he said.

'You could lose your job.'

'You mean you could sack me?'

She nodded slowly. 'Yes, I could.'

Shepherd sipped his coffee again, then put it on the desk. 'But you won't.'

'You're very sure of yourself.'

'Because I know you, Charlie. And I know that you know I'm right. We live in a world of shit and occasionally, just occasionally, we get the chance to do the right thing.'

'And letting Mickey and Mark Moore go is the right thing?'

'In this case, yes.'

'I wish I had your confidence,' she said.

'You know I'm right,' said Shepherd.

She looked at him, then smiled slowly. 'Yes,' she said. 'You are. Damn you, but you are.'

would have been on the trail as soon as they had identified the men in the wreckage of the removal van. Checks would be made, photographs would be shown around the local mosques, phone records would be checked and eventually they would identify him. Bradshaw had no wish to rot in prison, to grow old and infirm surrounded by infidels. It was time to go, and to go in a blaze of glory. It was time to join the ranks of the *shahid*.

He had been on the London Eye twice, using it as a vantage-point from which to select the perfect target. In a perfect world he would have loved to fire the missile at 10 Downing Street, the home of the prime minister, but nowhere in the vicinity afforded him a clean shot. He had considered firing at the Houses of Parliament or Big Ben but he doubted that even a direct hit would do much more than superficial damage to the massive building. At best he would smash a few windows and damage the stonework, but casualties would be limited. He considered Buckingham Palace as a symbolic target but had decided that he should be attacking the Government of Britain and the people, not its queen. As he rode around in the glass and metal body, he finally realised that the London Eye itself was the perfect target.

There were plenty of offices on the north side of the Thames and it didn't take Bradshaw long to take a lease on a high floor with windows overlooking the Wheel. The block was air-conditioned and the windows were sealed, double-glazed, but he had used a glass-cutter to make a large hole in the middle window to shoot through.

All his preparations were now complete. Bradshaw had changed his appearance since he'd driven off in the Mondeo. He'd abandoned his car in a supermarket car park, then gone inside and bought a pair of scissors, some black hair dye and a pair of reading glasses. Later he had booked into a cheap hotel in Bayswater and cut and dyed his hair. He had found a manual for the Grail missile on the Internet, downloaded and printed it out, but basically all he had to do was to point it at the target and pull the trigger and that would be the end of it. The missile would streak across the river and hit the Wheel in the centre, destroying the mechanism that held it up and provided the power to turn it. It would smash down into the river, the pods would break and the people inside would either be crushed or drown. The image of the broken Wheel would travel around the world, Bradshaw knew. As would the video he had already prepared, in which he swore his devotion to Islam, his love of Allah and his hatred of the West. He had left the video on a thumb-drive in the care of a trusted friend, who would post it on several fundamentalist websites within minutes of the explosion.

Bradshaw had sent what remained of the money he had been given to Yusuf's widow in Baghdad. It did nothing to lessen the guilt he felt, but at least it would make Farrah's life a little more bearable. He looked over his shoulder at the piles of Calor gas canisters surrounded by cans of petrol. It had taken two dozen trips to bring them into the office, hidden inside a wheeled suitcase. The back-blast from the Grail missile would ignite the petrol and the heat would explode the gas cylinders, blowing out a big chunk of the front of the building. It probably wouldn't be enough to bring the building down, but that didn't matter. Bradshaw simply wanted to die in a blaze of glory, literally, so that he could take his place in Heaven.

He was ready. He had made his peace with God and

STEPHEN LEATHER

Hot Blood

Dan 'Spider' Shepherd is used to putting his life on the line. It goes with the turf when you're an undercover cop.

Now working for the Serious Organised Crime Agency, Shepherd is pitting his wits against the toughest criminals in the country. But then a man who once saved his life is kidnapped in the badlands of Iraq, forced to take part in a ransom video, and the Government doesn't want to know.

With the execution deadline only days away, Shepherd and his former SAS colleagues know that the only way to stop his friend being murdered is to put themselves in the firing line in the most dangerous city in the world – Baghdad.

'A brilliant read that stands out of the morass of so-so military thrillers around nowadays' *News of the World*

Out now

HODDER

STEPHEN LEATHER

Dead Men

Former SAS trooper turned undercover cop Dan 'Spider' Shepherd knows there are no easy solutions in the war against terrorism.

But when a killer starts to target pardoned IRA terrorists, Shepherd has to put his life on the line to protect his former enemies. Whilst he is undercover in Belfast, a grief-stricken Saudi whose two sons died under torture in the name of the War On Terror is planning to avenge their deaths by striking out at two people close to Shepherd.

As the Muslim assassin closes in on his prey, Shepherd realises that the only way to save lives is to become a killer himself.

'He explores complex contemporary issues while keeping the action fast and bloody' *Economist*

Out now

HODDER